PRAISE FOR STINA LINDENBLATT

Decidedly with Baby

"Oh my goodness this book was so much fun!!!"—For the Love of Books

"So many laugh out loud moments that you do not want to be reading it in public or be ready for some weird looks. I speak from experience here."—The Subclub Books

"There are steamy moments but you are just left with feel good melty moments more."—Books Are Love

Other Books By Stina Lindenblatt

"...I was captivated by the shenanigans of this duo. Not to mention laughing out loud and blushing. Boy do these two turn up the heat."—The Subclub Books (*Decidedly off Limits*)

"A feel good, sensual, intoxicating and sexy love story; if you love contemporary romance you do not want to miss Decidedly Off Limits."—Slick, Guilty Pleasures (*Decidedly off Limits*)

Sweet, sexy and invigorating, Decidedly off Limits is a friends to lovers story that is truly a breath of fresh air!—Read & Share Book Reviews (*Decidedly off Limits*)

"...a truly unique and utterly swoon-worthy romance." —Mary Dubé at Frolic/USA Today's HEA (*Decidedly by Chance*)

"Stina Lindenblatt writes an emotional, heartfelt story about single parenthood, friendship, and love. Add to that great chemistry and tons of feels and this is a great book for anyone who enjoys this trope."—Ari at Red Hatter Book Blog (*Decidedly by Chance*)

"...it's an opposites-attract romance that will evoke all the feels." —Mary at USA Today HEA/Frolic (*Fix Me Up, Cowboy*)

"I just love this book!...add in some tense situations and five (YES FIVE!) hot, sexy, alpha, ex-navy SEALS and you got me!" —A Book Lover's Emporium Book Blog (*While You Were Spying*)

"While You Were Spying is a heart pumping sexy read! You've got action, intrigue and suspense and then on the other hand you have sexual tension, swoony romance, and sassy banter."— Julia Red Hatter Book Blog (*While You Were Spying*)

"It's light, it's fun, great characters and a little dash of conflict for spice."—Red Hot Blue Reads (*Fix Me Up, Cowboy*)

"Everything – the plot, the characters and the dialogue – made this story captivating."—Harlequin Junkie (5 star Top Pick review for *My Song For You*)

"I love that Stina Lindenblatt was able to layer this book with so much depth, mystery, hurt, friendship, and of course love."— Four Chicks Flipping Pages (*This One Moment*)

"Heartfelt, evocative, mesmerizing, and riveting, you absolutely won't want to miss this masterful romantic suspense!"— Book Addict (One More Secret)

ALSO BY STINA LINDENBLATT

CONTEMPORARY ROMANCES

Carson Brothers Series

One More Chance

One More Secret

One More Betrayal

One More Truth

SPICY ROMANTIC COMEDY NOVELS

By The Bay Series

Decidedly Off Limits

Decidedly with Baby

Decidedly with Love

Decidedly with Mistletoe

Decidedly by Chance

Decidedly with Luck

Decidedly with Wishes

Copper Creek Series

Cowboy Most Wanted

Once Upon a Cowboy

Fix Me Up Cowboy

Visit stinalindenblattauthor.com for more books

DECIDEDLY WITH BABY

SPECIAL EDITION

STINA LINDENBLATT

*To everyone who understands
the power and beauty of love...*

DECIDEDLY WITH BABY

PART I

DECIDEDLY WITH BABY

A BY THE BAY NOVEL

1

HOLLY

Sex—it was a life-altering event. From the time your hormones came to life and encouraged you to get laid, you were pretty much screwed.

It was a bargaining chip.

A stress reliever.

Some girls needed to love the guy in order to do the deed. Others were only in it for a good time; commitment wasn't in the books.

Sometimes it rocked one's world.

Other times you wondered why you had even bothered—the guy had no idea how to make a woman come. Unfortunately, they didn't wear a warning label.

They *really* should.

And sometimes sex came with consequences. The kind of consequences that started with you in the bathroom, the peed-on pregnancy test doing its thing next to you on the counter.

There it was, by the sink as I finished washing my hands. My life? Now at the mercy of a frigging piece of plastic.

If there was ever a time to fail at something, this would be it. Except, when had I ever failed at anything I did?

Never. That was when.

I dried my hands and escaped the bathroom as though it contained a ticking bomb. Kelsey and Erin, my closest friends, were standing in the hallway of my apartment with expectant looks on their faces. I shrugged. "I don't know yet." I indicated over my shoulder to the bathroom. "It's in there...but I can't look."

"Do you want me to tell you?" Kelsey asked. Her tone had enough sympathy to overflow an Olympic-sized swimming pool. Sympathy with a splash of excitement. Kelsey loved babies.

Normally, I was a brave woman. I had moved thousands of kilometers from my home in Australia to do my MBA in the U.S., even though there were plenty of great schools back home. After that, I'd landed a brilliant job here in San Francisco. Every day, I lived, breathed, survived in the testosterone-dominated world of finance which required me to be a brave and confident woman.

But normally brave and confident me couldn't find even a millimeter of courage to check my fate when it came to the pregnancy test.

I nodded in response to Kelsey's question.

"Okay," she said softly, possibly to avoid freaking me out more than I already was. *Good luck with that.*

She entered the bathroom with Erin and I trailing after her as though she were a brave warrior princess getting ready to slay the evil dragon.

I would have gladly taken an evil fire-breathing dragon any day over what was really waiting for us. Behold Holly—destroyer of all things not so pleasant. For that, I could be kick-ass confident.

My bathroom wasn't large by any stretch of the imagination, but it had never felt so small until that moment. And it had nothing to do with the three of us crammed into the space. Of course, Erin being eight-months pregnant didn't help either. And right now? She was the poster woman of what the plastic stick possibly held for me—a future involving multiple trips a day to the loo.

She glanced longingly at the toilet. I guess that was my hint to get this over with ASAP.

Kelsey picked up the stick and studied it.

"What does it say?" *Bonus points to me for not squeaking when I asked the question.*

She didn't say anything at first, her expression not giving any indication of what she was thinking—or what answer stared back at her.

"Did it work?" I asked. There was always a chance I had done it wrong. Peeing on a stick wasn't as easy as it sounded. Or maybe the test was faulty. There was always that too.

She nodded slowly, still staring at the stick. Then her gaze slid to mine, and without her saying anything, I knew the answer. Sympathy and awe and happiness all shone back at me. "You're going to have a baby."

She handed me the test and the answer was there for the world to see.

But it was the wrong answer.

I wasn't pregnant. I was sure of it.

Pregnancy tests weren't a hundred percent accurate. They were ninety-nine percent accurate. It said so on the box. Which meant one out of a hundred times they were incorrect.

And this test was that magical one—the test that got the answer wrong.

Right?

2

JOSH

Two months earlier

Quiz time. What makes an NHL hockey player both excited and fearful at the same time? That's right. The final minutes of game seven during the Stanley Cup playoffs. More so when the two teams are tied and the game could go either way.

Too bad for the Rock—it hadn't gone our way.

Anaheim was advancing to the finals.

And we were now on an early vacation.

But first...we had to pull up our extra large, big-girl panties and congratulate the other team.

Like little boys who lost their favorite toy truck, we skated in a single line and congratulated each member of their team, including the support staff. Some of the congratulations were spoken half-heartedly; I didn't know those guys and they didn't know me.

I gave Sutter, my former teammate, a one-armed hug. Until he was traded a few years ago, he used to play for the Rock. "Congratulations. You deserve this, man." Sutter had been my mentor the first year I played for the team. He was the guy who kept me from becoming a much bigger cocky ass than I was now. Now I was one-eighth cocky ass—maybe a little more during a full moon.

Although compared to Grant—the pain-in-the-ass Ducks defenseman—I was fucking Snow White.

No, I didn't mean literally fucking her, not that I would complain if I did get to. But if we were talking about getting to fuck a Disney princess, it would totally be that red-haired mermaid—what was her name?

"Now I have to hope Jenny doesn't go into labor until after the playoffs," Sutter said.

I stared at him for a heartbeat, letting his words sink in. "I didn't realize you guys were expecting."

His face beamed with pride. You would've thought his team had won the Stanley Cup instead of the Campbell Bowl. Not that the Campbell Bowl was anything to sneeze at.

But we weren't talking about the much-coveted trophy here. We were talking about a small human who did nothing but shit, cry, and generally take over your life.

I shuddered at the thought. There weren't any babies in my future. I'd learned the hard way that the NHL and kids weren't a good mix.

Just ask my old man.

If you could find him.

Sutter and I didn't get a chance to talk further. The guys behind us were waiting for us to get moving. The Ducks were eager to get their trophy and we were eager to leave.

Once we were finished with the congratulations, we returned to the locker room.

"Are you heading out tonight?" Mark asked Travis and me. You couldn't miss the wistful expression that passed briefly on his face. Even his scraggly playoff beard couldn't hide it.

"I'm meeting up with some friends," I told him, knowing that the only thing he was doing tonight was diaper duty.

"You're still joining me and the guys later at The Unicorn, right?" Travis asked me.

"I will if I can," I replied, spying Coach Woodcroft heading our way with the look he always wore whenever he had to deliver bad news...the type of bad news involving a media request.

"Hoffer," he said, "they're asking for you."

Mark and Travis snickered and started to turn away.

"Not so fast, gentlemen," Woodcroft said. "They asked for all three of you."

I did my own share of snickering. *Fair is fair.*

One of the assistant coaches led us from the safety of our locker room to the awaiting media in the dressing room. They separated into flocks, each pecking at their own victim with their questions.

"How did you feel tonight's game went?"

"The Rock's defense was on fire for this game. In what way do you think it could have gone better?"

"What are your expectations for next year?"

The questions seemed never ending, and only delayed me from getting together with Trent and his girlfriend, Kelsey. And let's not forget Holly, the redhead he worked with who could easily be mistaken for that mermaid Disney princess—only a lot hotter.

And with a sexy Aussie accent.

No, I haven't fucked her.

But don't think for a moment that she hasn't starred in a few of my fantasies, when it was just me, my hand, and the shower.

How did I meet her? She was at a dinner party Trent and Kelsey had thrown a few months ago. After getting together with them a few more times, Holly and I eventually became friends. But our friendship didn't mean fantasizing about her was off limits—even if I didn't want to date her.

Nothing against Holly. I didn't date. Period.

But it was cool having Holly for a friend. She was that female you could call when you needed advice and knew your male buddies wouldn't know the answer. Or rather, they would have an answer—but it was always a bullshit one. She was that friend who teased you about your manwhore ways but without any judgmental crap.

And the added bonus? She liked movies, but she didn't feel the need to drag me to lame chick flicks.

Mark was scooting toward the locker room doors, doing his best to escape.

"I need to go now," I said, attempting my own great escape.

I had barely stepped through the doorway when Travis practically rammed into me from behind. I chuckled. "What, you didn't want to stick around for more questions?"

"Christ, no. Besides, the sooner I'm out of here, the sooner I can get laid."

Guess I wasn't the only one with that post-game mission in mind.

3

HOLLY

Quick, name the one person you'd rather not talk to on a Friday night...while you're still at the office?

First question—what was I doing at the office on a Friday night? Easy. Where else would you expect a workaholic to be?

Okay, I wasn't planning to spend the entire night here. I did have a life after all.

I also wasn't planning to talk to my mother on the phone while at the office on a Friday night—yet here I was doing exactly that.

"I tried calling your apartment." Her tone for the last word was like battery acid with a dash of honey. My mother didn't do apartments. And definitely not apartments the size of—as she had put it—my parents' swimming pool.

She was exaggerating. *Mostly.*

Did I feel that my apartment was too small? Not at all. What did I need a large apartment for anyway? With two bedrooms, mine had plenty of space for me, especially since I spent more time at work than I did there. Besides, it was a nice apartment located in a Victorian house not far from the bay. I loved it, even if my mother didn't.

I didn't bother to point out she'd been calling my cell phone earlier, but I had let her go to voicemail. I hadn't expected her to then phone my work number, which was why I'd answered it.

Although I had no idea, in retrospect, who else would've called me at 9 p.m. at work on a Friday night, which was Saturday afternoon in Sydney.

"I was just about to leave," I said. "What can I help you with?" Even though she and Dad had a financial planner, it didn't stop her from asking my advice.

Not that she necessarily listened to it, but it was one of the few things we could talk about that didn't leave me feeling as though she was judging me in the worst possible way.

"First," she said, "while it's commendable that your career is important to you, you shouldn't be working at the office so late. Especially not on a Friday night."

Said the woman who spent my childhood doing the same thing. Only difference was, she had three kids and I was completely kid-free.

I didn't even have a pet.

"I'm meeting up with friends in a few minutes," I pointed out. *I do have a social life, Mum.* A social life that wasn't all about being seen by the right people in the right places—something Mum had specialized in my entire life.

"Good. The reason I'm calling is to inform you that my mother died." A small amount of emotion snuck into her otherwise cool voice.

"Nanna's dead?" The words barely squeezed past shock and despair. I coughed to clear my throat. "What happened?" She had been fine the last time I talked to her.

"Heart attack. The funeral is on Thursday."

I bit my lip to hold back the building sob. "I'll be there."

"Good." Her voice wavered slightly. "Send me your travel information, and I'll have Simon pick you up at the airport."

I smiled a little at the thought of seeing my thirty-year-old brother. "Okay." I had no idea if she'd heard my reply. She'd ended the call the moment the word had left my mouth.

My gaze fell to the small, framed photo on my desk. The woman crouched on the ground with an adorable baby wallaby cuddling a teddy bear? That was Nanna. She had found him injured and nursed him back to health.

The photo had been taken at Christmas, when she was full of life, her cheeks glowing, her eyes holding the mischievous light that was all Nanna. Both of us were wearing ratty denim shorts and had dirt smudged on our makeup-free faces. Surprised? I know—the complete opposite of how people in San Francisco normally saw me.

I examined my perfectly manicured French tips, then brushed my fingers along the light-gray pencil skirt and the cream-colored cashmere cardigan hugging my breasts. Nanna wouldn't have recognized me like this.

In San Francisco, I was more like my mother.

I shuddered at the thought—then turned off the computer, straightened my desk, and switched off the office light. Even workaholic Trent had left several hours ago, something that was new for him ever since he started dating Kelsey. I sent her a text that I was on my way.

The bar they'd picked was the furthest thing from a sports bar they could have found. The upbeat jazz music playing in the background? If I didn't know better, I could've sworn Nanna had requested it especially for me. It was one of her favorites.

I grinned at the memory of her humming it while trying to give Marcus, the baby wallaby, a bath. By the end of it, Nanna and I were soaked—Marcus, not so much.

Kelsey and Trent were deep in conversation when I approached the table. Josh wasn't there yet—and wouldn't be for another few hours—but they already had drinks in front of them, and a strawberry daiquiri was sitting at one of the two empty spots. *Gimme, gimme.*

Kelsey glanced up and grinned. "Hey, you actually made it."

I laughed and the people at the next table visibly cringed. That's right. I won the gene pool jackpot. I had beautiful, long auburn hair that looked like fire when the sunlight hit it just right. My skin was creamy and perfect—other than a splattering of freckles on my nose—and I had a great body (which I did work hard at, so there was that).

What I hadn't been blessed with was a beautiful laugh like Kelsey. When she laughed, angels sang. When *I* laughed, they burrowed their heads in the ground and prayed their agony would end quickly—or at least that the world would end soon.

Oh, well. No one was perfect.

But it was that one imperfect trait that turned guys off. I knew it. They knew it. So all was good.

It didn't cause me to stop laughing, though. Life was too short not to laugh. Nanna had taught me that.

"Of course I made it," I said, taking my seat. "I stayed late at the office to watch some of Josh's game." I took a sip of my drink. "Wow, that's good." *Now let's keep them coming.*

How did I meet Josh? Kelsey and Trent had hosted a dinner party a few months ago and he was invited. The two of us had hung out together as friends since then—as in, seeing-a-movie-together, Josh-helping-me-move-furniture, and I-need-a-woman's-opinion kind of friends. Was it possible to be friends with a guy and sex not be involved? Absolutely. And unlike with some couples who invited their single friends out like a matched pair, neither Kelsey nor Trent entertained expectations that Josh and I would become a couple.

Which was a good thing because I couldn't see it happening. Even if he was hot and my body got all tingly whenever I saw him. Josh didn't come off as the settling-down type. Not that he needed to settle down when women were more than happy just to have sex with him—no commitment required.

How did I know? I'd seen him being hit on a few times; I swear the guy was a magnet for horny women. Did it ever bother me? Not at all. It was always fun giving him a hard time about it afterward. And yes—he did occasionally leave with a few of them.

Was *I* the settling down type? Well, I wasn't looking to get married and I wasn't looking to start a family. My career? That was my baby.

Maybe this was why Josh and I had become friends over the past few months. We were perfect for each other—strictly as friends.

And hopefully my body would eventually be fully onboard with that.

Kelsey, Trent, and I chatted until Josh eventually showed up, looking like he had just finished playing triple overtime. Not once did I mention Nanna. Not once did I let on that something was wrong. I just happily worshiped my drink.

And once I'd finished worshiping it, I started on round two.

"Enjoy life, Holly," Nanna's laughing voice said in the back of my head. "You need to seize life by the horns and all that clichéd crap, and enjoy it while you can. You don't want to be like your parents—miserable all the time."

I raised my glass as if to say cheers to her.

"Did I miss anything?" Josh asked as he sat in the empty chair next to me—and a happy heat that had nothing to do with the alcohol made a mad dash to my girlie parts.

All right, ten percent had to do with the alcohol. But the rest was unmistakable lust.

Down girls. This was Josh—Trent's friend—we were talking about. We were totally not going there.

Somehow the "down" and "going" part got twisted in my

head, and an image flashed across my mind of him actually going down on me.

And that was like tossing gasoline on a fire. *Kaboom!*

I squirmed in my seat, hoping no one noticed how aroused I was.

The waitress picked that moment to check if we needed another round of drinks. I ordered a third daiquiri. "I'm taking a cab home," I announced at Kelsey's worried expression.

"Are you okay?" she asked.

"Yes. My mother phoned before I came here to tell me my grandmother died." Did that sound I-don't-want-to-ruin-your-fun casual? Somewhat close to that maybe?

"Oh, God. I'm so sorry, Holly." Kelsey looked ready to fling herself across the table and hug me. Did I mention how much I loved her? I could guarantee Mum wouldn't be hugging me when I showed up for the funeral. More like running around like an emu with its arse feathers on fire while she spoke to the caterer about the event.

"It's okay," I said brightly, thanks to the brilliant invention known as a strawberry daiquiri. "She wouldn't want you to feel sad or sorry about it. She's probably watching from Heaven, wondering when I'm going to toast her with tequila shots."

Josh chuckled. The god of laughter had definitely been more generous with him. It was a sexy, full-bodied laugh that made delicious places I didn't know existed on my body ache with desire.

Hmm. Maybe that wasn't such a good thing. Now I was even hornier than before. As in, I'm-ready-to-jump-him-at-the-table horny.

Josh waved the waitress over and ordered a round of shooters for him and me.

"You really don't want one?" he asked Kelsey. Trent was driving them back to her home afterward.

"I'm positive," she said. "Tequila and I had a bad run-in at a party once and I haven't been able to touch the drink since."

"Looks like it's just you and me then, Hot Stuff," he said to me.

The corner of my mouth slid up. "Okay, Cool Stuff."

The space between Kelsey's eyes crinkled in confusion. "Hot Stuff? Cool Stuff? Am I missing something here?"

"He's referring to my hair color," I explained, "and I'm referring to his occupation."

She laughed. "Got it!"

The waitress returned a few minutes later with lemon wedges, salt, and shooter glasses filled with tequila, all of which she set in front of Josh and me.

I dipped my finger into my tequila, smeared the liquid on the back of my hand, and sprinkled salt on it. Josh did the same, only instead of using his finger, he used his tongue...and my mind instantly imagined where else he could use that tongue—preferably on the ache between my legs.

The ache wholeheartedly agreed with that, and I came within a centimeter of groaning out loud. Not the rolling-your-eyes kind of groan. More like the *Oh-God-oh-God-oh-God-do-me-now* groan.

I mentally sent the image of Josh's tongue on my body packing to a deserted island, never to be seen again.

He lifted his glass and I did the same. "To your grandmother."

"To hockey."

He gave a small nod, almost as if thanking me for not bringing up what had happened earlier. We then licked, shot, and sucked our way to happiness—or at least close enough to it for now. Josh's gaze dropped to my mouth and the lemon wedge there, and his eyes darkened.

I removed the lemon from my mouth and glanced over at Kelsey and Trent, checking if they too had noticed Josh's reaction. That would be a no. They were busy being cozy with each other, Trent caressing her knee.

I pushed aside the momentary pang of sadness that Trent had fallen in love with Kelsey instead of with me. Until two months ago, I had been falling for Trent, only to discover he was in love with my friend.

But anyone could tell they were perfect together. Plus he wanted to have kids one day, as did Kelsey. Me? Not so much.

For me, my career was my one-and-only goal in life. Was I against kids? Not at all. I was just against the idea of being like my own parents. They weren't the ones who had raised my brothers and me. That honor had gone to Nanna and our nannies.

All thirty of them.

That's right, thirty.

Now, before you envision my brothers and me as the modern-day von Trapp family, let me point out—the problem wasn't us. That award went to Mum.

"Lydia, why does Holly have that tiny speck of dirt on her? That's completely unacceptable."

"Julia, Holly's B+ in English lit is unacceptable. You are expected to ensure she gets only straight As. If you can't remember that, you might want to reread the employment contract."

"Bertha, why is Holly climbing a tree? Didn't we agree that was unacceptable behavior for a young lady?"

Point taken? I thought so.

With some of the nannies, we had rejoiced when they'd quit after the first month or two. They could've easily been close cousins of Hitler—minus the German accent. I still shuddered at the memory. If my parents hadn't driven them away, my brothers and I might've considered going von-Trapp-kids on them.

There had been a few nice nannies in the mix, but they weren't around long enough to become the surrogate parents we needed—the loving and supportive parents our friends had. The nicer the nanny, the shorter their stay with us. My brothers and I had it down to a science when it came to predicting how long a nanny would last.

That skill came in handy with my current career. I was great at predicting things and creating the ultimate algorithm for the situation at hand.

But if there was one thing my parents had taught me (well, two really), it was that I didn't know what it meant to have someone love me, and I didn't know how to be the amazing mother my kids would deserve.

Okay, this wasn't a hundred percent true. Nanna had taught me that I was worth loving. But she was the only one to instill that lesson in me, and it was often easily forgotten.

"I need another round," I told Josh.

Once it arrived, Josh and I toasted Nanna again, and I quickly forgot about my old life back home. Tequila was awesome that way.

After the shooters, I switched back to daiquiris. The four of us talked and laughed for the next hour.

"We're heading out now," Trent told us after Kelsey had yawned for the third time, which I loosely translated to mean, "I'm taking my beautiful girlfriend home and fucking her brains out."

Except I wasn't ready to leave yet. You could blame the daiquiris and tequila and Nanna's death for that. I wasn't ready to go back to my lonely apartment and face the truth—that I had lost the one person who had loved me unconditionally, other than my brothers.

"All right," Josh said, waving them off. To me he said, "Are you ready to leave, or do you want to hang out together a little longer?"

Hell yes to the latter.

4

JOSH

I waited for Holly to answer, hoping she wasn't ready to call it a night. Yes, when I had left Travis and the guys at the arena, I'd been more than interested in hooking up with some random girl. But for some reason, ever since meeting up with Holly, Trent, and Kelsey tonight, that need had burned away like the San Francisco fog. Now I was more interested in hanging out with Holly instead.

No, I wasn't falling for her, nor did I believe my life would be more complete with her in it. I didn't buy into that bullshit. The only true love I had room for in my life was hockey. Between the training, the practices, the games, and the road trips, there wasn't much time for anything else.

And let's not forget the complications that arose if you were traded. If you were married, your family now had to put their lives on hold to move to a different city and start all over again. Same deal if you were in a serious, committed relationship.

But what happened if you weren't?

What happened if she decided to move in with you and you weren't interested in the extra baggage—no matter how incredible she was in bed?

19

No, I wasn't talking from experience, but a few of my teammates had sworn off girlfriends because of it...like Travis.

But for a guy—like me—who wasn't interested in marriage or having a family, being a hockey player was the perfect career.

"I'm ready to go," Holly said, answering my question. "But I'm not ready to go home yet." Her mouth spread into a playful grin. "Let's go somewhere and really have some fun, mate." There were times when Holly's accent was stronger than normal. Apparently after having a few drinks was one of those times.

Did I mention my cock really appreciated her Aussie accent?

Before I could ask what she had in mind, she jumped up from her seat and held her hand out to me. "Let's go dancing."

A few minutes later, we were cabbing it to a new nightclub that had recently opened, which meant it was currently the hottest spot in town. Fortunately, the bouncer was a hockey fan. He waved us in with little more than a "Next year, man. Next year," and a fist bump.

Yes, being an NHL player had its advantages. And I for one wasn't against making the most of it—especially after our loss.

Inside, the club was as busy as expected, both on the dance floor and off. Pop music pulsated through the speakers, making it hard to have any sort of conversation. But I didn't come here to talk to Holly. And from the way she was swaying, talking was also the last thing she was interested in.

"Let's dance," I said, then without giving her a chance to reply, I grabbed her hand and led her through the crowd to the dance floor.

Didn't like dancing when the floor was packed? Then you'd obviously been dancing all wrong—and with the wrong partner. I slipped my fingers under the hem of her top and stroked the soft skin on her lower back. Her breasts pressed proudly against the fabric, beckoning me to tease them with my fingers, with my mouth.

She was wearing a tight gray skirt that hugged her sexy ass and revealed her toned, never-ending legs. Her toned and never-ending legs that I had fantasized about on more than one occasion wrapped around my hips.

The neckline of her cream-colored top, with the tiny buttons down the front, was designed to be professional, not to flaunt her cleavage. But that didn't stop me from imagining what her tits looked like under the soft fabric.

With her hands on my shoulders, she arched back and her breasts screamed, "Touch me!" But while they might've said that, I wasn't so sure if Holly would agree so readily. Just because a girl danced provocatively didn't mean shit. She was having fun, not giving me an open invitation to touch her the way I craved.

"I need a drink," Holly said after we'd been dancing for a while. I had to agree with her there.

We squeezed our way through the crowd to the bar and ordered our drinks. Beer for me and a strawberry daiquiri for Holly.

Curious glances were tossed our way. Some said the individuals recognized me. Other individuals couldn't care less about me but were more than interested in Holly—which came as no surprise.

"You wanna dance?" one guy asked her as we waited for our drinks.

The twinge of jealousy that shot through me? Yeah, I couldn't explain it either. Holly and I were dancing. We weren't involved. She had the right to dance with whomever she wanted.

And apparently, she agreed.

"Okay," she said to the guy. To me she added, "I'll be right back."

While I waited for our drinks, I watched her dance. But it had nothing to do with jealousy and everything to do with how she moved. Except unlike with me, she didn't dance close enough for the guy to touch her. Every time he tried, she maneuvered her body away from him. The move was subtle but there nonetheless—and it made me chuckle.

I continued to watch and appreciate her long, lean body. A dancer's body. With breasts. Though from the way she moved, I wouldn't be surprised if she had once been a dancer. From what Trent had told me, there wasn't much she couldn't do... other than laugh. Some women had laughs that caused all the dicks in a ten-mile radius to stand at attention. Not so with Holly.

But no one's perfect.

In contrast to her, the guy was your average male who didn't know shit about dancing. He mostly just swayed and stared at her. Or rather, stared at her tits. *That's not where her eyes are, dumbass.*

"Hi," a woman said next to me.

My gaze slid over to her and my puck-bunny alert system went into full effect—including the sirens and flashing lights. These girls were always easy to spot, once you had dealt with one or two of them.

"Hey," I replied.

"You were amazing tonight," she said, her voice a near purr. She was dressed the opposite of Holly, with a crop top that revealed her flat stomach and generous cleavage. She was pretty but had way more makeup on than I generally went for. She was the type of girl who spent an hour in the bathroom every morning before even her cat was allowed to see her.

On the other hand, she was the type of girl you never had to worry about when it came to spending the night. She was the fuck-and-bail type because of her fear of being caught without her makeup on.

"You saw the game?" Not all puck bunnies did. They couldn't tell you a thing about the sport. They just knew who the players were and had Spiderman-like senses, enabling them to detect a player within the vicinity.

"Of course," she replied. "Wouldn't have missed it for anything."

The bartender parked the beer and daiquiri in front of me and I handed him the money. The bunny's gaze dropped to Holly's drink, and she ran the tip of her tongue along her lower lip as if anticipating the taste of it herself.

"The drink's for a friend of mine." I nodded at Holly, who was now heading toward us, dancer boy no longer with her.

My gaze returned to the bunny. Something about her expression had me on edge. I'd seen it before when it came to her kind.

Now, we're all familiar with the concept of the proverbial caveman, and how men have a tendency to regress into one whenever their woman is approached by other men—even if the other man isn't a threat. We practically pound on our chests, grunting, "Mine."

Meet the female equivalent. Except instead of pounding on her cavewoman chest, she was more likely to go all saber-toothed tiger on the other woman—with claws and fangs out.

Care for a demonstration?

"Hey, sweetheart," I said to Holly.

Holly gave the bunny a fleeting glance, and understanding lit her face. I'd never called her sweetheart before, but she knew about puck bunnies. The topic had come up one day with Kelsey and Trent.

"Hi—" Holly began.

I pulled her to me and crashed my lips against hers. As if on instinct, her mouth opened and her tongue brushed against mine—and shit, if my cock didn't just get excited.

But before it could get any more excited, Holly pulled back

with a *Did-I-do-good?* smile on her face. I wasn't sure if she was asking about the kiss (which I definitely wouldn't complain about if she wished to do it again) or the stunt I'd just pulled.

I winked at her and she chuckled. Unlike her laugh, her chuckle was throaty and sensual. Like you imagined it would be if she were a jazz singer with a smoky voice.

The bunny smiled when we turned back to her, but it screeched to a halt before reaching her eyes. "And you'd be?" she asked Holly.

Holly held out her hand. "G'day, I'm Holly. I don't believe Josh has ever mentioned you. And you're...?"

"Autumn."

True or false? Whenever you hear Chris Hemsworth speak with his native accent, you get horny. No lying. You know it's true.

Well, it's no different for a man when he hears an Aussie accent coming from a gorgeous woman.

And the bunny knew this.

Which was why her tone was the opposite of Holly's friendly one.

Holly wrapped her arm around my waist, cozying up to me. My arm looped around her. I hadn't realized until now how perfectly she fit against me like we were destined to be together —if you bought into that crap.

"Thank you for keeping Josh company while I was dancing," Holly said, grinning sweetly at the bunny.

"You're welcome."

Did you see Autumn's fangs? She was about to sharpen them on Holly. No, I wasn't a psychic. I just recognized that look.

She smiled prettily at me. "Can I get your autograph? You're my favorite player."

"Sure."

Yes, I kicked myself for that rookie mistake the moment she

yanked down her low-cut top, revealing her lacy red bra and her humongous breasts—which I suspected had been greatly augmented. And while she hadn't revealed the entire nipple, she did flash enough to give me a good idea of what they looked like.

She held out a sharpie to me.

"What did you think of the goal he scored tonight?" Holly asked. "I swear my heart stood still when he shot the puck toward the net."

I tried not to laugh. I had two assists but hadn't come close to scoring, much to my chagrin.

"Same here," Autumn said. And what kind of goddamn name was Autumn? That was a season, not a name. Not that it was a bad name if she actually looked like an Autumn. But her blonde hair and pushed up tits reminded me of summer. Holly looked more like an Autumn, with her long auburn hair.

"She's kidding," I said, ignoring the sharpie.

Holly flashed her an oops-my-bad cringe, and I had to fight back yet another laugh.

"You're not a real fan, are you?" Holly asked, sounding scandalized at the possibility.

Autumn stuck out her chest in a way that reminded me of the puffer fish I had once seen on a nature show.

"That's not true," she said. "I'm a huge fan."

"If you were a real fan," Holly pointed out, "you'd want him to autograph a piece of paper and not a piece of your chest. Because if you were a real fan, you'd want to keep that autograph in a safe place. And something tells me your chest is not a safe place. I wouldn't be surprised if it's a highly frequented location."

I decided I'd better not introduce Holly to Travis. He'd likely fall in love with her. Never mind the hot accent, her smart mouth would have him hard in record time.

And of course, thinking that had my cock getting its own

ideas...especially when it came to what it craved for her smart mouth to do to it.

Inwardly I groaned and recited the National Anthem in my head. Backward.

That did the trick.

Autumn threw me a *How-could-you-let-her-talk-to-me-that-way?* hurt look that was as real as her breasts.

I shrugged a "whatever" and on impulse kissed Holly's temple.

That must have been the shiny new nail in the coffin that Autumn needed. She didn't even bother to ask for my auto-graph via the more traditional means. She flipped her blonde hair over her shoulders and stormed off.

"Wow, are they normally like that, the puck bunnies?" Holly asked.

"Yeah, pretty much. Some aren't bad. It's the more deter-mined ones that can be a pain at times. I swear sometimes they're more competitive than the actual players they're after." And that was saying a lot.

But this was probably why lately I had started to grow bored of them. Did that mean I didn't have sex these days? Hell, no. It just meant I tended to go after the girls who were only interested in a good time. They didn't care what the guy did for a living.

I grabbed the drinks from the bar and handed Holly her daiquiri. We then spent the next hour dancing and drinking another round. At that point, the club was on the verge of being overcrowded, and I spent more time signing autographs than I did dancing.

"You wanna get out of here?" Holly asked, and I could've kissed her.

All right. I did kiss her. I was all for positive reinforcement and rewarding brilliant suggestions—and you couldn't get more brilliant than that.

We left the club more buzzed than when we had entered it, and definitely sweatier. But best of all, neither of us cared that my team was out of the playoffs and Holly's grandmother had died. Tomorrow the ramifications would hit us, but for now we were appreciating the happy buzz.

At least we were until...

"Do you know what the worst part is about Nanna dying?" Holly said out of the blue as we walked along the waterfront after getting the cab to drop us off. Waves lapped against the concrete wall separating the ground from the ocean; otherwise, the world was quiet around us.

"No, what?"

"Having to go back home for the funeral." She shuddered—either due to the idea of returning to Australia or because the May air held a slight chill.

"How is that so bad?"

"One word. My mother." She giggled. Holly's drunk giggle was kind of cute. "Oops! Make that two words."

"I take it your mother isn't great?" If we were to compare mothers, mine would be as far from being Mother of the Year as Earth was from Uranus.

" 'Holly,' " she said in a snooty tone that spoke of high income and house staff. Maybe even a butler who looked down his nose at unworthy house guests. " 'How could you believe that a ninety-five percent on your math test was an acceptable mark? Holly, proper young ladies do not run around the house like heathens.' " Holly giggled again.

"Yeah, I'd say that's pretty bad. Though I'm sure my mom could top yours."

"Really? I didn't think anyone could be worse than my parents."

"My mom abandoned me when I was a kid."

What's the best way to shock someone? Do exactly as I just did. I usually didn't tell anyone the truth about my parents.

Blame it on the truth serum (AKA alcohol) this time. That, and because Holly had told me something about her parents. Tit for tat and all that crap.

With her green eyes round like the moon, Holly stared at me for a moment. "Oh, God. How could she do that?"

I shrugged. "She learned from the best—my father."

"Wait, are you telling me both of your parents just up and left you?"

"Pretty much. My father played in the NHL and married my mom when they were young. It didn't work out and he divorced her. It didn't help that he preferred screwing puck bunnies to being married. After a few years of raising me by herself, she decided one day she'd had enough and left. No forwarding address. No nothing."

Holly gasped. "What did you do?"

"The only thing I could do—I got up every day and went to school like I was supposed to, believing she was coming back. Eventually I realized she wasn't. That was about the same time the landlady began demanding past-due rent. Long story short, social services was brought in and I was sent to live with my grandparents." Nice story, huh? Don't worry, I'd say I turned out all right in the end. For the most part.

Although from the way Holly was looking at me like she longed to give me a blowjob to make me feel better—or maybe it was just wishful thinking on my part—I was toying with telling her what came next.

Once I turned sixteen years old, I stayed with billets. Think of them as foster care for junior hockey players who played for a team far from home. Some billets were great, while others were sadly lacking in the "great" department.

"Wow, and I thought it was bad enough when my parents abandoned my brothers and me to the care of our nannies. And Nanna," she said, instead of giving me the blowjob I could have gone for. *Too bad.* "My parents weren't around much, thanks to their careers. Dad was around even less than Mom, always traveling. Always at meetings. But they would never have let us fend for ourselves. I'm so sorry that happened to you, Josh."

She reached up and gave me a kiss. It wasn't a blowjob, but it was pretty goddamn hot. Hot enough to kiss away all my booboos.

"Is that why you don't want kids?" she asked once she had pulled away. She was clearly remembering the conversation we'd had when we first met. We were having dinner with Trent and Kelsey, and the topic of kids came up. Both of us had said that we didn't see kids in our future. "You figure that since your own parents failed you as a kid, you won't do much better?"

"Pretty much. I haven't exactly had the best role models, especially since my father used to play in the NHL and now *I* do. Not that it's a big deal. I've long since realized the whole marriage and family-making deal isn't for me. My hockey career is a bigger priority."

"Same here—except in my case, replace hockey with a financial career. And since I'm not even an American citizen and don't have my green card yet, I could easily be deported back to Australia tomorrow." She grinned at me. "Too bad we don't have anything to drink. We could've toasted to us not becoming parents and to avoiding marriage."

I laughed. "I would definitely toast to that." Then remembering how the conversation had started, I sobered up for a moment. "When's your grandmother's funeral?"

A soft sigh escaped her lips and she gazed at the ocean— and for the first time since I'd met her, the usually confident Holly looked lost. "Next Thursday."

"Well, in case you haven't heard, I'm now available. And I wouldn't mind checking out Australia for a few days."

Holly's head spun back to me, her eyes wide and hopeful. "Are you saying you'll go to the funeral with me?"

"Sure, why not? Unless you don't want me there. I mean, if

I'm cramping your style when it comes to all the horny men lining up for a chance to keep you there permanently." I winked at her.

Holly let out a delighted squeal and flung her arms round my neck, surprising me. Before I could respond, her mouth crashed against mine again. She still tasted like a mix of alcohol and strawberries, and it didn't take much prompting on my part for my tongue to invade her mouth.

She moaned, and I suddenly couldn't get enough of her. I tangled my fingers in her hair and pulled back on it, allowing myself to deepen the kiss.

By the time we stopped a moment later, we were panting like dogs in heat. My entire body was aching to explore the rest of her with my tongue, but this wasn't the place.

Hell, what was I thinking? Hooking up with friends was never a good idea.

Not that I spoke from personal experience, but I'd seen a few friends over the years cross the line and it never ended well.

If you didn't count Trent and Kelsey.

But there was always one exception to the rule.

That was what my head said. My body had other ideas—all which involved my cock buried deep inside Holly.

Get a grip, I told my body. It didn't listen, getting more excited over the word "grip." I mentally rolled my eyes at its reaction.

"How about we go back to my apartment?" Holly suggested against my lips. "Then we can toast to *not* becoming parents, and about you saving my arse by coming to Australia with me."

At the time it sounded like a great idea. I mean, seriously, what could go wrong?

Right. Famous last words.

5

HOLLY

Back at my apartment, Josh and I settled on the couch with a bottle of white wine and an episode of *Game of Thrones*.

Confession time. Believe it or not, we were the only two people on the planet who had never watched the show. My brother Chris had given me the season one DVD last Christmas. The gift had been a joke—if the way he and Simon had laughed when I opened it was any indication.

Josh and I were just past the part where the young boy—don't ask me his name, but I figured his family was important—was caught by his mom scaling down the castle wall. She told him off, but not too harshly, then made him promise never to do it again.

If she had been my mum, she would've grounded him for two days—at least. Had teenage me ever climbed out my bedroom window? There was a chance that I had. And there was also a chance I'd done it frequently. Had Mum ever caught me? Not on your life. The CIA would be jealous of my stealth when it came to sneaking out of the house.

My phone rang. Now, most people who phoned at two in the morning did so because there was an emergency. Or they were drunk and couldn't tell the time.

What was Simon's excuse? Math was never his best subject, and he kept forgetting that Sydney was seventeen hours ahead of San Francisco.

Normally I ignored him and called him back later, but given Mum's news from a few hours ago and my happy buzz…

"G'day," I said, answering the phone.

"G'day, long lost sister. I've got some good news."

Why did his tone make me think it was far from good news for me? As in, the kind of news that left him laughing hard for the next five minutes. "What's that?"

"Since you're coming home for the funeral, Mum is pushing forward with her plans for you and Wilfred to get hitched."

Inwardly, I groaned. "And how exactly is that good news?"

Simon laughed. *Jerk.* "Because I'll be highly entertained watching you squirm your way out of it."

"Well, there won't be any squirming happening. Not from me anyway. And Mum's crazy if she believes she can get me to marry Wilfred. I bet even *he* wouldn't go for it."

"Oh, don't underestimate good old Wilfred. He sounded pretty hot to the idea."

Really? I remembered him as the dorky kid Simon used to tease. I doubted he'd even want anything to do with any of us after that.

"Doesn't matter," I said, reaching for my wine on the coffee table. "Mum won't try to marry me off." I took a sip of my much-needed drink.

Simon snickered his *How-is-it-in-delusional-land?* laugh. "And what makes you so sure about that?"

I totally blamed his laugh and the alcohol buzzing through my system for what happened next. It really wasn't my fault—and I would swear it to my dying day.

"Because...because I'm engaged," I blurted. And then because that wasn't humiliating enough to say in front of Josh, I added, "And...and my fiancé is coming with me. For the funeral." *Face, meet palm.*

"You're engaged?" Simon asked. "As in, you agreed to marry some bloke?"

"That's right." *Couch, if you loved me as much as you pretended to, you'd swallow me whole now.*

When the couch didn't cooperate with my simple request, I said to my brother, "Well, now that you've told me about Mum and Wilfred, I'm going back to sleep. In case you haven't noticed, it's almost three in the freaking morning here." I didn't give him a chance to say anything. I ended the call.

I dropped the phone into my lap, then with a groan, covered my face with my hands. "I'm so fucked," I muttered.

"Is there something you're not telling me?" Josh asked.

With my hands still covering my face, I said, "Are you referring to anything specific?" Not the best stalling tactic, but it was all I could come up with on short notice.

"Oh, I don't know. How 'bout we begin with the part where your mom is trying to marry you off, and end with the part where you're going to Australia with your fiancé?"

"I'd rather not." *Oh, God, could this day get much worse?*

Josh peeled my hands from my face. Oddly enough, he looked more amused than anything. "Would more wine help?" he asked, the corner of his mouth quirked up on one side.

Yes. "No. That's what got me in trouble in the first place."

Josh ignored me and poured more wine into our glasses. "You might as well tell me, given I'm flying to Australia with you. Or is your fictitious fiancé going with you instead?"

I groaned again. But then realizing he wasn't letting this slide, I took a long sip of my wine. "My mum has been trying to hook me up with one of her friend's sons for over a year now.

Or at least she would have tried if Wilfred the Third had been around while I was there for Christmas last year."

"Wilfred the Third? The guy sounds like a major nerd."

"He is, but he's also a rich nerd and my mum thinks aligning our families would be a good thing."

Josh laughed and my girlie parts tingled. *Damn sexy laugh.* "What the hell does that even mean?"

"His grandfather started a very successful business that has been kept in the family since its inception, and my mum wouldn't mind being part of it, for strategic purposes. Much like how royalty used to marry off their sons and daughters centuries ago in order to align countries." I paused, letting him digest what I had said, hoping it made more sense to him than it currently did to me. "So, will you help me? Will you pretend to be my fiancé so she'll finally abandon this stupid idea of hers?" Yes, because my idea of pretending Josh was my fiancé was the work of a genius.

Josh laughed again. "You're kidding, right?"

Seduce him, my body cleverly suggested. My brain thought about it for a moment, seeing the merits of the crazy idea.

I shifted to straddle Josh's hips and lowered my head to his. I brushed my lips against his mouth. "Please," I murmured.

But then promptly forgot what I had asked him as I rubbed the achy part of me against the hardening length in his jeans. Instead of the voice of reason that normally hung out in my head, the horny one cheered me on. *Yes. Yes. Yes. Just this one time.*

I kissed Josh again. He eagerly returned my kisses and upped the ante. His hands roughly caressed my body.

Not in a bad way.

In an abso-freaking-lutely delicious way.

I moaned against his lips, and once again rubbed the aching part of me against the quickly hardening part of him.

The aching part that hadn't seen any action in an extremely long time, if you didn't count my fingers.

I wanted Josh—and I wanted him now.

Nothing else mattered beyond that.

My hands crept under his T-shirt and stroked across the ridges and valleys of his abs. Longing to see and not just touch them, I pushed up the soft fabric and was rewarded with the yummiest stomach muscles to ever exist.

Eager to see the rest of him, I slid the material up, revealing his chest as if it were a Christmas present. *Merry very early Christmas to me.* The chest, with a light smattering of blond hair, was as sexy and muscular as those muscles just south of it.

And his nipples? They just begged me to taste them.

So I did.

I licked the skin around the first one and was treated to the taste of man. Pure, hot, sensual man. Unable to resist, I popped a puckered nipple into my mouth and sucked it.

"Christ, Holly," Josh gasped and his fingers knotted in my hair. He tugged on the strands and a torrent of please-take-me-now heat surged to my core.

Nanna's death.

The fake engagement.

The funeral.

None of it was as important in this moment as sex with Josh.

Was it just me—or was it getting hotter in here?

Easily enough solved. While Josh removed his T-shirt, I started unbuttoning my cashmere cardigan. But the damn buttons didn't cooperate.

Oh, well. Who needed them anyway?

I yanked open my top, sending the tiny buttons flying every-where. Had whoever designed it thought about sex at the time? Clearly not. And they definitely hadn't given any consideration to the wearer having sex after a few glasses of wine.

Josh laughed. "Isn't it the guy who usually does that?"

"I'm an equal-opportunity shirt ripper," I said with a grin. And given that Josh was completely shirtless and I still had a bra on, I figured it was time I embraced the equal-opportunity-topless philosophy too.

Or something like that.

It was amazing how alcohol made a person more eloquent...and deep.

I giggled and reached behind me. A moment later my girls were free and happy.

But apparently not as happy as Josh (although the verdict was still out on that). The grin on his face at seeing my naked breasts was brighter than the summer sun—and just as hot.

With both hands, he palmed the pale globes and lightly pinched the nipples. Lightning shot to my core and I moaned. Loudly. I couldn't have prevented the sound if I had tried.

He leaned forward and popped a nipple into his mouth. His ultra-talented mouth.

And my nipple sang a round of hallelujahs.

My clit got jealous, craving a little of that action for itself. Couldn't say that I blamed it.

Speaking of wanting in on the action, my fingers traced their way to the button of Josh's jeans and presto—the button willingly slipped through the hole. Now if only the buttons on my top had been as obliging...

Josh released my nipple from his mouth. "Does this mean what I hope it means?"

"If you're hoping and meaning that we're going to have hot sex, then the answer is yes." At least I hoped it would be hot. Great looks didn't always equate to great in bed—a truth I had discovered a few times.

"I have condoms in my bedroom." Hopefully they hadn't expired yet. They might have been two years old by now. Good thing I hadn't bought the family-sized pack. The way I had been going, I hadn't made much of a dent in them.

"Sounds good." Josh helped me off his lap and I led him to my room.

By led, I meant we were attempting to tear off each other's clothes while stumbling to the room. Josh's jeans got caught around his ankles and he almost tripped. Clearly a drunk Josh wasn't as agile as a sober one on ice.

Laughing, we fell onto the bed, naked.

And then we weren't laughing.

Moaning and groaning were now the noises of choice as we kissed and nibbled and explored each other's bodies.

Josh's fingers found my happy place and it got a little happier. He thrust two fingers inside me and his thumb caressed my clit. "Oh, God, that feels sooo good," I said with a slight slur. I reached out and clumsily grabbed his hard length. And for the first time since he had removed his jeans, I paid attention to his cock.

His well-endowed cock.

Did you hear that sound? That was angels weeping at the beauty (and size) of it. Weeping because they wouldn't get to experience it. I would.

Their loss—my gain.

I caressed the head, red and leaking pre-cum, and smeared the liquid around with my thumb. "I need you inside me," I cleverly pointed out.

"Do you think you're wet enough for me?" he asked with a smirk. He knew I was.

"I'm soaking for you. I don't think I can get any wetter." I squirmed on the bed, getting even more turned on by the conversation. I spread my legs wide and slid my fingers between my lips, spreading the dampness around my super-sensitive clit. "See?"

Josh's eyes darkened and a small smirk slipped onto *my*

face. He was as turned on by this as I was. "I definitely agree with you there. Where are the condoms?"

"There's some in the nightstand drawer." I gestured in its general direction.

Josh leaned over and a moment later straightened with a string of condom wrappers in his hand. He ripped one open and fumbled the condom into place.

Guess we were both drunker than I'd first realized. But Josh wasn't drunk enough not to be able to get it up. His cock stood proud and eager and ready for action.

That made two of us.

He lifted my legs onto his shoulders, pressed his tip against my entrance, and slowly pushed inside me. My girlie part sat up and took notice, happy to once again have a visitor of the male variety.

Josh plunged deep inside me. You know how after you've been on a diet and finally get to have chocolate cake again, the cake tastes better than you remembered? No—I don't mean the crappy birthday cake they make for kids, with whatever Disney princess is big at the time. I mean the quality stuff.

Welcome to sex with Josh.

And the moan I just made? It had nothing to do with chocolate cake.

He pulled out of me—not far enough for his cock to leave my heat, but far enough to ignite every nerve ending in the most sensitive part of me—my throbbing core. The other most sensitive part? His talented, ever-so-thoughtful thumb kept it from feeling neglected. I writhed about, gripping the sheet.

As my body rushed headlong toward the edge of the abyss I had been waiting forever to revisit, it yelled, "Forget the fake engagement. You need to marry this guy so you can always have great sex."

I reminded myself that it only felt that way due to the wine. My brain whispered, "Liar. This is the best sex you've had in a while." And as I tumbled into the abyss while crying out in ecstasy, my brain conveniently ignored how this was the first time in forever since I'd had sex, period.

And it was the last time Josh and I would ever have sex together. Why? Because friends with benefits always got messy and complicated. I didn't want to deal with that.

So those angels who wept at how they would never get to have sex with Josh? I now knew their pain.

6

JOSH

What's the worst sound to hear when you wake up hungover? Make that the second worst sound after a sledgehammer outside the window—which pretty much sounded like the one in my head.

That's right—the chirping of a bird, happily pointing out you were an idiot last night for drinking so much. The one outside the window was also telling me if I hadn't gotten drunk, I wouldn't be feeling like crap.

No shit.

The memory of last night's loss came rushing in with a vengeance, and I groaned.

A moment later another memory joined it—and my eyes snapped open.

Huge mistake.

Sunlight glared through the open curtains. I shut my eyes again, not that it made a difference. The sledgehammer in my head wasn't vanishing anytime soon.

Reopening my eyes, I caught sight of the sleeping woman next to me. Her auburn hair glowed in the light like a halo, but angelic was the last word I would use to describe Holly. Not

40

unless angels were talented at given multiple orgasms to mere men. I might not have remembered everything, but something about what I did remember made me think that last night might have been the best sex I'd had in a while.

So, what was the problem—other than the headache? Because what guy didn't want to hook up with a woman who could make his cock sing hallelujah more than once in a night?

The problem was that most women I'd had sex with over the past few years were one-night stands. It was easier that way with my career. It was tough when you were on the road all the time. Girlfriends got clingy or suspicious that you were cheating. One-night stands didn't care.

But here was the thing with one-night stands—sleepovers tended not to happen, for good reason. Having sex and then escaping while the girl slept avoided all the awkwardness the next morning. The fact that Holly wasn't a one-night stand who I would never see again further compounded the awkwardness. She was the colleague of my best friend and his girlfriend's best friend. Avoiding Holly wouldn't be possible.

But did I want to avoid her? Not really.

Did I want to make what we'd shared last night a regular thing?

Don't get me wrong—I enjoyed a good fuck like the next man. But I didn't do the fuck-buddy arrangement. Too complicated. So as much as I enjoyed last night (well, what I remembered of it), it couldn't happen again.

Unfortunately, my cock chose to ignore the memo. It was more than willing to sink inside her once more, to help me remember details about last night. It didn't care that I was hungover. As far as it was concerned, I was still alive, which was good enough.

But while that might have been true in my dick's case, I didn't think Holly would share the sentiment.

I carefully shifted the bedding off me, making sure not to disturb her, and scooted to the edge of the bed.

I sat up—and Holly groaned.

Just not in the same way she had last night when she was getting all shades of turned on. This was more like a *Why-the-hell-did-I-drink-all-that-alcohol?* moan.

Either way, it was about to make my great escape more awkward.

"G'day," a sleepy, pained voice said with an Aussie accent that sounded a little rougher than normal. A little rougher but a whole lot sexier—if that was at all possible.

I turned to look over my shoulder at her. "Hey, how are you feeling?" My voice came out not much different than hers, minus the accent. Neither of us had survived last night unscathed, but after our day yesterday, no one could blame us for our actions.

And fortunately, no one had to know about them.

"Remind me next time I wish to mourn a loved one's death not to drink so much wine. And to skip on the daiquiris." She paused for a moment, thinking. "And the tequila shots."

In spite of myself, I chuckled. "I'll keep that in mind for next time."

Instinct told me to bail. For once I chose to ignore it. "I'll be right back."

Not bothering with my clothes, I left the bedroom, took a quick whiz in the bathroom, then after searching both there and in the kitchen, finally found some painkillers. After taking one myself, along with a good amount of water to rehydrate, I filled a glass for Holly and returned to her bedroom, picking up my trail of clothes along the way.

"Here," I said, handing the bottle of painkillers and water to her. "I thought you might need these."

She reached for them. "Thanks. Do you want some coffee? Or I can make us some food?" She didn't say it in a way that sounded like she was hoping I'd stay—for the long term, in a relationship. It was in a friendly, no-commitment tone. My favorite post-sex tone.

"Sure, that'd be great."

Twenty minutes later, we were sitting at the kitchen table, eating scrambled eggs and toast. While Holly had been cooking, I had showered, avoiding the awkward time until now. An uncomfortable tension sat between us—thoroughly enjoying how we had both been idiots last night when it came to getting off and the booze.

"So about last night," Holly said after a few minutes of us pretending to be engrossed with the food. "Trent and Kelsey don't need to know about it." She quickly shoved a fork full of eggs into her mouth.

I nodded. "Agree."

"I mean, it's better they don't know about it. There's no point of them thinking anything could happen between us." I bet runaway trains moved slower than the words spilling from her mouth.

"Agree."

"That would only make things more awkward for everyone," she said.

"True." Why did I have a strange feeling I was forgetting something—something monumental?

Her phone buzzed on the table. Looking like the cat who had eaten the entire cage of canaries, she answered it. "Hey, Kelsey....No, I'm fine. I had a few drinks then went home." The entire time that she was talking, Holly glanced everywhere but at me. "I can later. I need to book my plane tickets for the funeral."

At the last part, that strange feeling nudged me a little harder. I swatted it away like it was an annoying mosquito buzzing near my face.

Holly finally looked at me while listening to whatever

Kelsey was saying. She flashed me an apologetic smile. In the book on one-night stands, this would be where the author recommended bailing if you hadn't already. Great advice—but since Holly and I were friends, it seemed ridiculous to do that at this point.

A few minutes later Holly ended the call, then continued talking to me as if she hadn't answered the phone. "Anyway, about last night. We were drunk and not thinking clearly. So, how about we pretend it never happened?"

Laughter bubbled inside me at how flustered this conversation was leaving her. The regular Holly looked nothing like this. This version was adorable, with her hair adopting the I've-just-had-a-great-fuck messy look that turned men on. She was wearing black yoga pants and a white tank top with a comical koala on the front. Far from her usual fashionable self. Her face was makeup-free, and despite her hangover, she had a glow about her. A post-sex glow.

And I'd be lying if I said it didn't make me want to bang my fists against my chest, caveman style.

What? Don't judge me. There isn't a man alive who doesn't appreciate it when the woman he's given multiple orgasms to looks beyond merely satisfied. If he says otherwise, he's lying.

Holly's phone pinged. She glanced at the screen, and it was like a vampire had suddenly sucked all the blood from her face. "*Oh, God. Oh, God. Oh, God,*" she whispered before her hand covered her mouth as if to prevent any more "Oh, Gods" from escaping.

Now, I'd be the first to admit that usually when women were saying "Oh, God" that many times in a row, it was *not* because of a text. The strange feeling I was forgetting something? It was no longer a nudge. It was a full out push-you-over-the-cliff shove. "What's wrong?"

"Oh, God," was apparently the only answer Holly planned to give me, her gaze still locked on the phone.

I removed it from her hand and read the text—even though it wasn't mine to read.

> Chris: Why is it I have to hear from Simon that our baby sis is engaged? Thought I was your favorite brother!

While I was still holding the phone, another text came in.

> Simone: Can't wait to meet your fiancé.

Oh. Fucking. Christ. The conversation from last night bulldozed its way into my head.

She had asked me to pretend to be her fiancé. I hadn't given her an answer because we'd had sex instead—my one-track mind that easily distracted.

Holly dragged her gaze from the phone and settled her gorgeous green eyes on me. Warning alarms blared *"Code Red! Code Red!"* in my head.

"I swear, I'll never ask you for another favor..." she said, "and I'll do whatever you want just to make it up to you."

"Sweetheart, there's nothing you can give me that will make up for pretending to be your fiancé." Okay, that wasn't entirely true. A year's worth of blowjobs would be a good start.

"Sooo, that's a yes?"

I swear the woman could put puppies to shame with her puppy dog eyes. No one else pulled them off as convincingly as Holly.

"That would be a no." Did I mention I was immune to puppy dog eyes?

She slumped forward, elbows on the table, face in her hands. "Oh, God, I'm screwed. Now I'll have to spend the entire time there with my mum driving me insane. And I'll probably agree to marry Wilfred just to get her off my back."

"Maybe you can find someone else to be your fiancé."

She shook her head, her face still in her hands. "Not on this short notice. And especially not someone who can fly to Australia."

"Doesn't engaged usually mean you're expecting to get married at some point? Won't they wonder when the big day is?"

Holly dropped her hands from her face. "I was going to pretend to be engaged for a few months and then call it off. It's not like my parents expect me to get married next week."

"But won't your mom go back to pushing Wilfred on you again?"

"Not right away. So that will buy me time to come up with something else...like never returning to Australia again if it comes down to it."

"Are you sure there's no other way to get your mom off your back about this Wilfred guy?" Holly had never come off as the type of girl who let others tell her what to do.

Which meant her mother had to be a force to reckon with —much like a freaking hurricane.

She shook her head. "No, Mum's stubborn like that. She doesn't care that I don't love the guy. Love is irrelevant in her mind."

Sounded like she and my father would get on well. He didn't believe in love either. "Except I don't do relationships and I definitely don't meet the parents." I inwardly shuddered at the thought.

"Which is why you're perfect for this, Josh. And it's not like we'll have to hang out with my parents. I can show you around Sydney. That will give me an excuse for escaping. Plus, then I can introduce you to the nightlife there. Which will be another excuse for me to not be around so much. And...and I'll pay for your plane ticket, so really you have nothing to lose." She tilted her head to the side, the way girls did when they flirted—a look I wasn't familiar with on Holly when it came to her and me.

"Other than the funeral and meeting my mum for the first time, I promise you'll have fun."

I'd be lying if I said I never wanted to go to Australia. If a regular one-night stand asked me to be her fake fiancé, would I do it? Hell, no. But Holly wasn't a regular one-night stand. We had no expectations between us—other than to continue being the friends we were before last night.

"Okay, I'll do it, but with one additional condition."

Holly blinked, clearly unable to believe I had agreed to help her. "What's that?"

"The next time I need a fake girlfriend, you'll do it."

The smile that appeared on her face was enough to steal my breath. "Okay. Sounds fair."

"Even if it's five years down the road and you're married." You never knew when a fake girlfriend could come in handy. Not that I had needed one yet.

She held out her hand. "Deal."

A devious smirk curled onto my lips. "You don't need to give me a hand job. But if you want to..."

Her hand returned to her coffee mug. "We've already established last night was a mistake. So, there'll be no more sex or kissing. Or anything else along those lines."

My smirk hadn't gone anywhere yet. It just widened at the way she sounded flustered once again. "So you're telling me we won't be fuck buddies?" Yeah, not sure why I said that given it was the last thing I wished to do—but it also sounded like she wasn't interested in that either. *Perfect.*

"Exactly. We'll go back to being just friends—with no benefits. And fortunately, my mother is anti-PDA, so we won't have to worry about faking that. And since their house is almost a mansion, you'll have your own bedroom."

Rule #1 about one-night stands...they are exactly that. One. Night. Break that rule and you're asking for trouble of epic proportions. Most girls thought that if a guy wanted to have sex with them again, it meant they were now in a relationship. And that was never a good thing.

But while that might've been the rule, my cock was thinking, "*Fuck that!*"

I let out a mental sigh. This was going to be one very long trip.

7

HOLLY

Flying first class to Australia was expensive—as in, sell-your-kidneys-on-the-black-market freaking expensive. The bereavement fare? Sorry, that didn't apply to first class.

Which was why Josh and I had been crammed in coach for the past fifteen delightful hours. On the bright side...yes, I was still looking for that.

Josh shifted in his seat for the millionth time, his leg brushing mine. Again. And like every other time before it, the ache between my legs grew in intensity—to the point where I was ready to jump Josh if his leg or arm touched me once more.

It had been that way from the moment he had gotten into my car back in San Francisco when I'd picked him up on the way to the airport. My body got overly excited, remembering how it felt when his hands caressed my skin the other night.

I couldn't blame him though, when it came to his incessant squirming. The seats weren't designed for a six-foot-plus hockey player.

An hour later as I scanned the area in the airport where we were meeting my brother, my body was still fully aroused. And thanks to my no-sex rule, there was no relief in sight. At least not unless I planned to get intimate in the shower with my hand.

Why had I decided to torture myself with the no-sex rule? Because I had already done the friends-with-benefits thing.

Didn't know about that?

Long story super-short—it happened while I was working on my MBA. With a fellow classmate. I developed feelings for him after five months. Silly me. I moved on and focused on my schoolwork.

He moved on—with another classmate.

"Over there," I said, spotting my brothers strolling toward us.

Instead of my auburn hair and green eyes, they both had light brown hair and blue eyes. But that was where the similarities between them ended. Simon's hair was cut short. Chris's hair was wavy and hung an inch above his shoulders—a look Mum disliked on a man. Whereas Chris was long, lean, and muscular like a soccer player, bodybuilding was Simon's sport of choice.

Before I could even say G'day, Simon swooped me up in his arms and hugged me, squeezing the air from my lungs. As soon as he released me, Chris did the same. Well, that explained why both of them were still single. They'd probably hugged their last girlfriends to death.

Chris released me and I laughed. "Glad to see you missed me."

"It's not the same without my little sister underfoot." He ruffled my hair before I could bat his hand away.

"But what are you doing here? Mum only mentioned Simon would be picking me up. Not that I'm not happy to see you."

He winked at me. "Let's just say she has no idea I'm here."

I stepped back and turned to Josh. "Josh, these are my

brothers, Simon and Chris. Chris is the black sheep of the family."

Chris laughed. "Well, that might not be the case after your little announcement." He grinned at Josh like a crazed man. "So you're the Yank who stole my sister's heart. Good luck with that."

Should I tell my brothers the truth or keep them believing I was really engaged?

Or the real question was, should I tell *Simon* the truth?

When I was ten, I had been climbing a tree and fell. Was I injured? You'd better believe it. I sprained my ankle. My mum frowned against girls climbing trees so naturally, I couldn't tell her what really happened. If I had broken my leg, that would have been harder to explain—not so with a sprained ankle.

But before I had a chance to tell her my version of what happened, Simon blurted the truth. He hadn't planned to—it just happened.

When I was twelve, I kissed a boy. It wasn't a big deal—until Simon accidentally blurted it at the dinner table that night.

When I was fourteen, my first boyfriend broke my heart when I caught him kissing my classmate. This was the same boyfriend my parents hadn't known about until, well, you guessed it...Simon blurted out what had happened.

As much as I loved my brother, history was a bitch. And this bitch was warning me to lie to my brothers for the sake of my sanity.

Now, before you go all judgmental on me, I'm not normally a liar. I value honesty and do my best to uphold it. But there are times when twisting the truth is best for all concerned. I was just saving myself, my brothers, my parents, and Wilfred a lot of grief. And yes, it was easier stretching the truth than telling Mum that it would be an icy day in hell before I married someone I didn't love.

Not convinced that I was stretching the truth versus telling a flat out lie? I had slept with Josh, so when you thought about it, that wasn't much different from being married. And being married was only a step up from being engaged.

All right, it was a far stretch, but it still counted.

"That would be me," Josh replied, answering Simon's question about Josh being the one who had supposedly stolen my heart.

"Well, I've got great news for you two," Simon said, seeming a little too happy, given that Nanna's funeral was in two days.

"What's that?" I asked.

"You remember Mum's rule about no boyfriends or girlfriends allowed in our bedrooms?"

I nodded, not that the rule mattered anymore now that the three of us were no longer teens.

"Since they have a full house because of the funeral," he explained, "Josh will share your room. So you won't have to go sneaking around to have the naughty."

The corner of Josh's mouth jerked up. "Have the naughty?"

I rolled my eyes. "It's slang for having sex."

Josh laughed, and my girlie parts got excited again. "I figured that's what it meant. But thanks for the translation."

The panic rolling around in my stomach? It was absent from his face.

Which meant one thing—Josh wasn't experiencing the dilemma of being fully aroused like I was.

But I had my no-sex rule to uphold, which would be a lot harder to do now that we were sharing the same room.

Naturally, my tired brain made a beeline for the gutter when I thought about Josh and harder. My body fired up to a thousand degrees at the memory of his hard length inside me.

No. No. No. So not happening again.

I had no idea if the message got through. My body could be so goddamn stubborn at times.

But at least I didn't have to worry about Josh wanting to

have sex again. He and I had already agreed that what happened between us was nothing more than a one-night stand. As in only *one* night. Plus he was a hockey player who no doubt made one-night stands part of his career. Wasn't that what hockey players did? That's why they were players—so to speak.

The four of us walked to the parking lot where my brothers had left their vehicles.

"I'm guessing you won't be joining us?" I said to Chris.

"The welcome mat hasn't been extended if that's what you're asking. Plus I have a job later this afternoon that will take me out of the city until the funeral."

"Chris flies helicopters," I explained to Josh. "But that's not the career my parents had planned for him. He was supposed to take over Dad's position in the telecommunications company our grandfather created. And Mum thoroughly disapproves that he's a pilot. Apparently it's not a dignified enough career."

"And that's why you're the black sheep of the family?" Josh asked Chris.

Chris nodded.

"Never mind that he has saved lives when he assists with search and rescue missions," Simon pointed out. "Something our dear sweet parents can't claim for themselves."

"But that of course only makes him hotter to the girls," I said, grinning. Yes, Chris and Josh had that in common. And like Josh, I couldn't see Chris ever settling down.

Oh, who was I kidding? I couldn't see Simon settling down either. When you grew up in a family where your parents didn't love each other, they were just together for convenience, you didn't exactly yearn to replicate their mistakes.

So, you're probably wondering what Simon does for a living. He's a corporate lawyer...for my father's company. Which is why he's still welcome at my parents' home.

On the drive to my parents' house in Simon's Jeep Cherokee, Simon and I caught up on the past five months. But not in a way that excluded Josh—who was sitting up front with my brother.

"You should've seen Holly as a kid," Simon said to Josh. "She was nothing like the princess she is now." His laugh? Proof that one of us had been adopted. Why couldn't I have inherited the same laugh as him and Chris—just the feminine version?

"I'm not a princess," I said with a faked huff. "I can't help that I like looking good. It's not as if I'm delicate like one and need the staff to cater to my every need."

"That's because Nanna refused to let you be one." To Josh he said, "Our grandmother was convinced Holly was better off as a tomboy than dressed up like royalty and paraded in front of our parents' friends whenever our parents hosted a party."

"I bet if Mum had known that," I said, "we wouldn't have been allowed to stay with Nanna. Or at least I wouldn't have."

"That's right. Plus Mum would've married you off at a much younger age." Simon looked briefly at Josh. "Our parents don't believe in love. Just status."

By the time we pulled up to the security gate of my parents' mansion, Josh knew a lot more about me than I would've preferred—thanks to Simon. Like when I was a toddler, I had escaped our nanny and run naked into the party my parents were hosting. To say they were mortified was like saying the Sahara Desert was nothing more than a sandbox.

When I was eight, I broke my leg when I fell off my bike. Did I mention I'd been trying to fly off a ramp and land in the lake?

And then there was that unfortunate incident at my sixteenth birthday party involving my bikini top. Simon swore Wilfred had never been the same after that.

"That's not true," I said as the two men laughed. "I'm sure my boobs weren't the first ones he'd seen naked."

That just made Simon laugh harder as he attempted to

identify himself into the speaker so that security would open the gate.

Once we were permitted onto the property, he drove along the driveway, and I tried to imagine what Josh was thinking as we approached the house. The horseshoe-shaped, Mediterranean-style mansion, with the red terracotta tiled roof and balcony running along the entire length of the second floor, tended to impress visitors.

Me? I had always felt like a prisoner growing up here. You know how some teenage boyfriends climb the tree outside their girlfriend's window so he can sneak into her room? Let's just say that fantasy had never been a possibility for me.

Guard dogs would've been unleashed.

And guard dogs plus boyfriends didn't mix.

Not even a little.

"This is where you grew up?" Josh asked, his eyes in danger of popping out of his head.

I grimaced—feeling like kangaroo shit on the bottom of a shoe. His father had abandoned him when he was young, as had his mother. He'd never had the opportunities I did growing up.

And while I had viewed the house as a prison, Josh would have seen it as something else.

Simon parked his jeep in front of the house, next to a BMW I didn't recognize. As we exited the vehicle, Mum stepped from the house with a man wearing a white shirt and dark gray trousers. He looked vaguely familiar...and a lot hotter than I remembered. Where was my father? No doubt still at the office.

"Ohmigod, is that...?" I asked.

Simon grinned the mischievous grin I was more than familiar with. The one he usually wore right before he pushed me into the pool.

On instinct, I glanced behind me. Nope, a pool hadn't magically appeared there in the last thirty seconds.

"Yep, that's Wilfred," Simon replied.

"That's the geeky guy you were talking about?" Josh asked. "He's not quite what I was expecting."

That made two of us.

Wilfred's light brown hair hadn't changed. Much. It was short with a slight curl, and now he had a light beard. His thick glasses? Replaced by contacts—or he'd had laser surgery. And his body was definitely not what I remembered. His arms were well developed like Josh's, and even though he had trousers on, it was clear his lower body matched the top half.

"Holly," my mother said, "you remember Wilfred." It wasn't a question and the warmth in her tone was manufactured. Possibly in China.

"Yes, I do," I said, my tone the polar opposite of hers. And it had nothing to do with his looks. "It's nice to see you again, Wilfred."

"You too, Holly. But I now go by Drew."

"Drew?"

"It's short for my middle name, Andrew."

Drew was a much better fit. He looked neither like a Wilfred or a Fred.

Although from the way my mother was looking at him, I didn't think she agreed with me. To her, Drew didn't have the same impact as Wilfred the Third. Wilfred spoke of tradition—Drew, not so much.

"This is my fiancé, Josh." Because as good looking as Drew was, I still wasn't interested.

San Francisco was now my home.

Granted, I wasn't an American citizen yet, or even a permanent resident. The company I worked for had sponsored my green-card application—which I needed before I could be a U.S. citizen. Now I was just waiting for the U.S. government to approve it.

And waiting.

And waiting.

And waiting.

"Nice to meet you," Drew said, appearing slightly taken aback by the news of my engagement. Guess no one had filled him in on that part.

My mother? How was she taking it?

You know what they say about the eye of the hurricane? Meet the eye.

Drew and Josh shook hands. But other than the initial surprise at my news, Drew seemed genuinely happy to meet Josh.

"How come Holly hasn't mentioned you before?" dear old Mum asked Josh.

The best part about the fifteen-hour flight here was that it had given Josh and I plenty of time to come up with our story.

"Because I didn't think there was any point to it," I said. "Not until we knew for sure where things were going between us." Fortunately, the sky was cloud-free. No lightning bolts would be striking me for that lie. "And then one thing led to another, and Josh proposed to me on our first anniversary together. But I decided to wait until the right moment to announce it."

Right. If I had been a more skilled liar, I could've come up with something better. Something more creative. Something that didn't involve me being engaged to a friend turned one-night stand.

But when had I ever claimed that creativity was my strong suit?

Mum turned her gaze to Josh.

Remember those thirty nannies I mentioned? Remember how some of them could've been close cousins to Hitler? Even those nannies couldn't handle The Gaze. It was sharper than a steak knife dipped in lemon juice—and just as uncomfortable.

"And what is it you do?" she asked him.

"Christ, Mum," Simon said, "What's with the interrogation?"

I almost laughed out loud at that. Each of our boyfriends and girlfriends in the past had gone through the same interrogation—at least those we dared to introduce to our parents. It was as predictable as stores having Christmas decorations up right after Halloween. It was tradition.

"Language!" was her only response to Simon's question.

"I play defense for the San Francisco NHL team," Josh bravely said.

"That's all you do?" she asked as if he spent his days playing video games. I knew for a fact she had no idea what the NHL was.

I laced my fingers with Josh's and give them a light squeeze —only for the ache between my legs to get the wrong idea. I did my best to ignore it again. "The NHL is the North American professional hockey league. Only the best of the best play in it. And his team was in the playoffs this year." Could you tell I was proud of him? Well, I was.

Simon and Drew definitely looked more impressed than my mother.

"This is my cue to get back to work," Drew said, even though it was five p.m. I guess that was something he and I had in common. "I'll see you all at the funeral."

Once he and his BMW were headed toward the main gates, I turned to my betrothed. "How about I show you my room, so we can rest up before dinner?"

And then maybe I could Google suggestions on how to deal with the ache between my legs. The ache that was bound to get achier with Josh and I sharing the same room for the next six nights.

Oh, boy.

8

JOSH

"So...how are we doing this?" I asked, standing in Holly's bedroom. The size of it alone was bigger than my apartment living room...and that didn't count her walk-in closet.

The problem? There was only one bed—and not a big one at that. But at least it wasn't a twin.

"Well, we have three choices. You can sleep on the floor. Or there's the day bed." She pointed to a short, wrought iron sofa covered with a mound of pillows.

That's a bed? Maybe for a gnome.

"What's the third option?"

Chewing her lip, she glanced at the bed. "We're adults. I'm sure we can sleep in the same bed and keep our hands to ourselves." Her gaze swung back to me and her eyes narrowed. "You can keep your hands to yourself, right?"

"Sure I can, sweetheart. The question is, can you?" I winked at her and she rolled her eyes.

Yes, this was going to be a very interesting six days—especially when said hands craved to touch her soft skin, to tangle in her silky hair, and yank her head back while I kissed her deeply, to make her cry out my name.

Hell, my cock wanted in on the last part too.

Holly and I studied the bed as if expecting it to magically get bigger. When that didn't happen, Holly grabbed a pile of cushions from the sofa and created a barrier down the middle of the bed.

A smirk twitched at the corner of my mouth. "That doesn't exactly leave us much room. Is that your way of saying you don't trust yourself around me?"

"You wish!" she bit out.

Yes, I do.

She stalked to her suitcase and unzipped it. "I'm going to unpack and then have a shower. You can use the bathroom first if you want." She gestured at a different door from the one we had entered through.

"Teenage you had a bathroom in your bedroom?" It was a toss up on whether I should laugh or not be too surprised.

She shrugged her slim shoulders, a slight blush appearing on her cheeks. "I know, it's kind of excessive. Maybe that's why I love my apartment back home. It's normal."

"And you prefer normal?"

Smiling, she nodded. "Normal is great. Normal is what I missed out on growing up."

That, I could relate to, but for different reasons. Until my grandparents had taken me in, I had missed out on normal too. It was the reason I didn't see kids in my future. When your father played in the NHL, normal was not part of your life—far from it.

I know what you're thinking. Plenty of players in the NHL have had kids, and not all of them turned into mini car wrecks. But you know what they say about the apple and the tree....

Naturally, my cock got the apple and the tree analogy all

wrong. It threw in Adam and Eve into the mix—and somehow came up with me naked in the shower with Holly.

"So...about that shower," I said. "You planning on joining me?"

Holly flicked her teeth against her lower lip.

She was considering it.

Wait for it...

"Definitely not," she said. "Remember our rule?"

Ah, yes. The idiot no-sex rule I had sadly agreed to. But in my defense, I'd agreed to it while dealing with a hangover. That alone should've made it null and void.

My lips twitched up to one side. "So you're saying no shower sex?"

She looked as though she was about to answer, but not with the one I was hoping for. She didn't have a chance. She yawned instead. Twice.

"Why don't you have your shower first," I said. "I can wait till you're finished. You look ready to fall asleep on your feet."

Before she could argue otherwise, I turned her around by the shoulders and gave her mouth-watering ass a little pat to send her in the right direction.

Without another word, she entered the bathroom.

She re-emerged twenty minutes later, wearing nothing but a white bathrobe. Her face was free of makeup and her shiny red waves spilled down her back. She was like the angel and devil on my shoulder, all wrapped up into one erotic fantasy.

She peered at my open suitcase on the floor by the sofa, the contents a jumbled mess. "You didn't unpack?"

I shrugged. "Never do. I'm used to living out of my suitcase while on the road."

She gave a small nod and walked to hers. Then I watched with amusement as she awkwardly crouched next to her highly organized luggage, her hand clutching her robe shut.

I chuckled. "Are you done with the bathroom?"

"Yes, I can get dressed in the closet while you're showering."

Exhaustion suddenly steamrolled over me, and it was my turn to yawn. I grabbed a pair of briefs and my toiletries and headed for the bathroom.

All I had on when I returned to the bedroom following my shower were the briefs.

Was Holly impressed that I was practically naked?

It was hard to tell—given she was fast asleep.

Her arm and leg were slung across the cushions on the bed. Careful not to disturb her, I climbed under the covers and lay down in what little space had been left for me.

Before I knew it, I drifted off to sleep.

"OH, JESUS, BABY," I SAID TO THE GORGEOUS REDHEAD STRADDLING my hips and riding me like I was a prize-winning bronco. *Yahoo.*

"I take it you like having the naughty with me?" Holly said in the accent that had me hard in record time. Well, harder, given that I was already hard inside her.

A light rapping on wood intruded on the moment. We ignored it.

"I very much love having the naughty with you."

"Having the naughty" had become my new favorite phrase. Maybe I could record it for my voicemail message. "Hey, I can't come to the phone right now. I'm busy having the naughty."

I reached up to squeeze Holly's bouncing tits as the knocking sound interrupted us once more. Only this time the vision straddling me, who was an inch from making me see stars, vanished—and I groaned.

Mother fucking, cock blocking asshole.

Grunting my displeasure, I shifted...and fell off the bed with a thud. "Shit."

The insistent knocking came again. This time Holly—the real Holly, not my erotic dream Holly—stirred awake. Sunlight spilled through the window, much like when we had fallen asleep.

"Who is it?" she asked, her sleepy voice making me that much harder. God really hated me, didn't he?

"Simon," her brother said as I climbed back into bed. "Can I come in?"

Holly's gaze slid to me, her eyes wide. "Hold on a second." Before he could reply, she was snatching up the pillows between us and tossing them to the floor.

"Cuddle me," she whispered to me, her voice rough with panic.

I choked back a laugh. Whatever the lady wanted...

I pulled her against me so that her sweet ass pressed against my morning...well, afternoon wood. She gasped.

Yep, she hadn't failed to notice my dilemma either.

My thumb rasped against her nipple, hidden under her tank top. Her gasp became a moan. "Come in?"

The door opened and Simon strolled in. "Hope I wasn't interrupting anything." His expression and tone didn't mirror the apology in his words. Amusement was a better description. "Mum sent me to tell you dinner's ready."

"You couldn't have told us that through the door?" Holly grumbled.

"What? And miss out on seeing you two looking utterly in love? Not bloody likely."

And with that, he walked out of the room, chuckling.

Before Holly had time to react to his comment, I rubbed my cock against her ass, reminding her of my situation. "You sure about this no-sex rule of yours?" I murmured hotly against her ear.

For a second, her body melted against me. But then she

jerked away and scrambled out of bed. "Yes, Josh. I'm very sure. Us having sex again is a big mistake."

"Why's that?"

"Because one—I don't want to do the friends-with-benefits thing. With a few exceptions, they usually don't work. Someone ends up hoping for more emotionally than the other person can give. And two—we're in my parents' house. Them hearing us have sex is just plain icky."

A smirk formed on my face. "Because they've never had sex before?"

She shoved me on the shoulder. "Ohmigod, we're so not having this conversation!"

"So, how about we have sex where they can't overhear us?" Did I mention it was fun to watch Holly get flustered?

"Not happening." She turned around, grabbed her phone from the nightstand, and tapped away on it.

"What are you doing?" I asked.

"Checking my schedule for the next few days."

"Schedule?"

"You know, when you figure out what you're going to do that day, week, month, or year, and write it in your calendar. I don't have to explain what a calendar is, right?" Now it was *her* turn to smirk.

I snorted a laugh. "Other than your grandmother's funeral, you're pretty much on vacation. So unless you're scheduling in us having sex, what do you need a fucking schedule for?"

The horrified expression on her face was priceless—not to mention adorable and an utter turn on.

Right. Who was I kidding? Everything about her was an utter turn on.

"Do you even know how to survive a few days without a schedule?" I asked, but I might as well have asked if she knew how to blow fire out of her ass. "Have you ever done anything impulsive before?"

She sniffed at that. "I asked you to pretend to be my fiancé. I'd say that's pretty impulsive."

I shook my head. "That wasn't impulsive. That was you panicking when you found out your mother was planning to marry you off to Wilfred the friggin' Third."

"What about when I had sex with you?" she shot back.

"Doesn't count."

She frowned. "Why not?"

"You were drunk."

She couldn't argue against that. "Just because I'm not impulsive like you doesn't mean I'm not capable of being impulsive....I just prefer to know what I'm doing next. But anyway, it doesn't matter. Suffice to say we're complete opposites."

That wasn't completely true, but instead of pointing that out, I went with, "And we know what they say about opposites... they're explosive between the sheets."

"I guess we'll never find out," she fired back, either forgetting we already had found out, or ignoring the truth—that the one night between us had been more than explosive.

At least from what I remembered.

A thoughtful expression crossed her face. "All right, I'll recant the no-sex rule—but only while we're here. As soon as we return to San Francisco, we go back to just being friends."

Works for me.

9

HOLLY

There were so many things to love about Australia. The not-so-great thing about the country? It was nearly impossible to have outdoor sex.

And who wanted to have sex with the possibility of a tarantula looming close by?

So that was why on the day of Nanna's funeral, while everyone was in the living room celebrating her life, Josh and I were heading toward the staircase. Destination? My private bathroom.

"Holly," Aunt Sarah said, walking toward us across the polished tile floor in the foyer. And more importantly, blocking our escape route. "I'm sorry for your loss."

"And so am I," my cousin Lia added.

"Thank you," I said. "She'll be greatly missed." How I kept from sounding like a recorded message after hearing so many wishes of condolences was beyond me.

"And you must be Josh, Holly's fiancé," Aunt Sarah said to the poor man who'd heard this enough times today to last him more than a lifetime.

When I'd come up with the idea of pretending he was my fiancé, did I expect my mother to tell everyone?

Hardly.

And she hadn't.

It had been Dad who spilled the proverbial beans—much to Mum's chagrin.

Why wasn't she happy about that? Because she was still hoping for a union between Drew and me.

Ring-a-ding-ding.

What did my father think about all of this? I got the impression he couldn't care less if I got married or not—as long as I was happy.

And as long as it didn't interrupt any of his business meetings.

"Congratulations to you both. When's the big day?" Aunt Sarah asked.

"Not until next summer," I said. "All the good locations were booked until then, plus I'm so busy with work, I couldn't possibly begin planning the wedding sooner than that. And then Josh will be extremely busy once hockey season begins." Well, the latter parts weren't a lie, and I was pretty sure the first part was true too.

Or at least that was what a woman at the office had said a few weeks ago when she announced her engagement.

Lia grinned. It wasn't just a happy grin. It was a grin that warned me I was in big trouble. Like when we were fourteen and she convinced me I would look amazing with green streaks in my hair—and offered to color it.

Did I look amazing?

Sure—if you liked the seaweed-stuck-in-your-hair look.

So it wasn't a big surprise that I was bracing for something worse.

"I don't know if you've heard," Lia said, "but I started a company that organizes special events, and I specialize in weddings. So I can plan the wedding for you, and I happen to know of a great location available this August."

Of course she did.

With a smile plastered on my face, I wrapped my arms around Josh's arm. "Oh, that's so nice of you to offer," I said, tone sweeter than honey but far from real. "But Josh's eighty-year-old grandmother is looking forward to the wedding. Unfortunately, she's extremely afraid of flying. She would never survive such a long flight. Isn't that right, sweetheart?" I glanced at Josh.

He patted my hand, still wrapped around his arm. "That's right, babe."

"Excuse us for a few minutes," I said to the two women, "I have something in my eye and Josh was going to help me remove it."

Hey, I never claimed to be a good liar.

Before they could say anything, I tugged him away from the pair. "I need something to get me through this day," I told him, voice low. "And mind-blowing sex is on the agenda."

Josh laughed under his breath. Was this the first time we'd had sex in the shower since I agreed to his friends-with-bene-fits arrangement while we were here?

There might have been at least one other occasion.

But it was totally justified.

Sex with Josh was a great stress reliever.

We had barely entered my bathroom before I was unbuttoning Josh's white shirt, and he had the back of my sleeveless black dress unzipped. His gaze took in my green satin bra and matching thong, and his eyes darkened like I was the feast he'd been starving for.

He didn't kiss me right away. After I stepped out of my dress, he peeled the thong down my legs, then tossed it to the side to join his shirt on the floor.

Next off? My bra. While I might not have known much

about hockey, I did know he was extremely talented at removing bras.

"The caterer's food was good," he murmured in my ear, "but I've been craving the taste of something much better. Something much hotter." Before I had a chance to digest what he had said, he lifted me onto the bathroom counter. "Now open your legs and let me see you."

Wetness rushed to my core at his words and the deep, lusty sound of his voice. I did as he asked.

Did I feel vulnerable? Not at all. What had happened downstairs with my cousin—*that* had left me vulnerable.

This position and the hungry way Josh's gaze was eating me up made me feel safe, desirable. Alive.

"You might want to turn on the shower first," I warned. I wasn't exactly known for being quiet—which was why we were in the bathroom and not my bedroom. But thanks to the bathroom acoustics, there was still a risk of getting caught if we didn't take the proper precautions.

The smirk on Josh's face? Made me wetter and caused the ache between my legs to become demanding.

"Planning on being noisy, are you?" he asked. He didn't wait for my reply. He walked to the shower and turned it on.

He then returned and crouched between my open legs. With his hands on my hips, he moved my arse forward to give him better access. "As much as I love these on you," he said, unbuckling a stiletto, "they won't work for what I have planned."

"What exactly is that?"

He winked at me. "You'll see."

And I did. A moment later, he lifted my bare feet onto the counter, opening me up even more. "Now that's better," he said. "Then once we're back home, I'll have a great memory to jack off to in the shower."

I chuckled. "Hopefully the memory is as good as real life."

His smirk returned. "It won't be, but it will have to do."

As if he really needed to jack off in the shower to the memories of me. It wasn't like there was a shortage of women lusting for a piece of him. Nor was it likely he would go monk once we returned to the States.

"Okay enough talking," I said with a fake pout. "I need a little action."

And being the great listener that Josh was, he did exactly as I asked—his skilled tongue and fingers stroking my clit and finding all the right places to push me over the edge.

"Oh, God," I moaned, being as quiet as possible. Truth? I deserved a freaking gold medal for how quiet I managed to be.

All right, a participation ribbon.

The point was that I did *try*—and thanks to the running shower, no one would've heard me unless they were in my bedroom.

Josh retrieved a foil package from the drawer under the sink. Fortunately for us, despite my insistence that there would be no sex after our one-night stand, Josh had still brought a box of condoms with him.

A new box of condoms with an expiry date years beyond the end of this trip.

He removed his pants and briefs and slipped the condom onto his perfectly hard cock. Then his mouth was on mine. Tongues danced together as our hands explored each other's bodies.

With me still on the counter, he aligned himself with my entrance and pushed the head of his cock in partway. "How do you want this, Holly? Slow and easy—or hard and fast?"

No-brainer there. "Hard and fast."

With a quick thrust of his hips, he burrowed himself completely inside me—and we both groaned. It definitely wasn't going to take much before a second orgasm hit.

And I was right. A moment later we both came hard, the

softest part of me clenching tightly around Josh's thick length. The sound of the shower hitting the tiles drowned out his erotic, animalistic grunt.

And so thus continued the rest of our stay in Australia—with me enjoying a multitude of earth-shaking orgasms several times a day. And with me telling myself that I wasn't growing addicted to them. With Josh.

The flight home? No, there was no joining the mile-high club for us.

There was just me sticking to the rules—no matter how turned on my body was the entire flight home.

By the time we landed in San Francisco, one thing was certain—if I planned to stick with my rule of no more sex with Josh, I needed to keep my distance from him. At least until my body forgot what he could do to it.

That would be simple enough. Right?

10

HOLLY

Two months later, I entered the busy cafe and scanned the tables. Erin and Kelsey were already sitting at our favorite table in the corner. Twice a month we met up for lunch on the weekend—our girl bonding time.

Our time away from the men in our lives.

Which wasn't too hard for me to do since there was no man in my life.

What happened to Josh?

I'd been so busy with work lately, I hadn't had time to join him, Kelsey, and Trent for drinks since returning from Australia. And those few times I did manage to make it, Josh had been away. So other than texting each other like we had before and the occasional phone call, we hadn't seen each other since returning home.

Was I still hiding from him? You'd better believe it—thanks to his goddamn sex-on-a-stick pheromones.

Those same pheromones that my body reacted to whenever my thoughts drifted to Josh's and my time in Australia. Apparently, he didn't even need to be near me for it to happen—his pheromones were *that* powerful.

Our fake engagement? No, I hadn't gotten around to telling my family the sad truth: Josh and I had broken up. I figured I had plenty of time before I had to worry about it.

As I walked over to Kelsey and Erin, a good-looking man in shorts and a San Francisco Rock T-shirt approached me, a friendly smile on his face. And my mind instantly went back to Josh. *Ugh!*

"Hey, Holly. Haven't seen you in a while."

My mind quickly rifled through the Rolodex in my head for his name. He looked vaguely familiar.

And then it hit me.

"Oh, hi, Brad." He and I had dated a few times in university. I was working on my MBA and he was working on his master's degree in biomedical engineering. "What are you doing here?" I gave him a quick hug. We had ended on friendly terms when he moved away for a job offer.

"I heard they make the best coffee around." He winked at me.

I laughed. "I meant San Francisco. Are you visiting?"

"No—moved back last month. I accepted a great job offer I couldn't refuse." His gaze slid down to my left hand. "You know, if you're not seeing anyone, we should go out for dinner some-time and catch up on old times."

"I'd like that." I fished through my purse and handed him my business card, pretending the ache between my legs hadn't booed in frustration. It was unfairly comparing the one time I'd had sex with Brad against the incredible sex with Josh...and Josh was coming out the clear winner.

"Who was that?" Kelsey asked when I sat at our table a minute later. "He's hot," said the woman who was dating the hottest man on the planet—when you didn't count Josh.

I explained how I knew Brad.

"So you're going to go out with him?"

"I figured I might as well. It's just one date." I said, as a wave of nausea hit. Where was the waitress? I just needed something to eat and then I'd be fine. This wasn't the first time it had happened in the past few days.

Maybe I had some weird version of the stomach flu?

As if reading my mind, a girl in her early twenties approached our table. "Are you ready to order now?"

You definitely want the fries, the angel on my shoulder not-so-helpfully pointed out as I glanced over the menu. The devil on the other shoulder snickered knowingly.

After Erin and Kelsey ordered, I blurted, "I'll have the California rolls and a side order of fries."

Erin and Kelsey stared at me as if I had ordered steak fresh from a fire-breathing dragon. Unlike them, the waitress didn't even bat a mascara-coated eyelash.

"Since when do you eat fries?" Erin asked as the waitress walked away.

I shrugged. "I don't know. I guess I'm just craving them." In my mind, I glared at the angel, who was acting all innocent, while the devil cracked up laughing.

"You're. Craving. Fries?"

Wasn't that what I just said?

"Why?" I asked. "Is that a problem?" Maybe a sign of some sort of terminal disease I had contracted?

"Do you crave them often?" Erin asked.

"Not really. This is probably the first time." At least that was what I tried to say. And I would have succeeded if I hadn't yawned while saying it.

I really needed to get more sleep.

This wasn't the first time in the past few weeks that I'd wanted to crawl under the table (or desk) and steal a nap. Which was odd. I wasn't the napping type.

"Are you not getting enough sleep?" Erin asked.

I picked up my glass of water and sipped the cold liquid. "I thought I was, but apparently not."

"How are your breasts feeling?"

Now if only she hadn't asked me that while I was taking another sip of water. It went down the wrong way and I started coughing.

Kelsey laughed. "What kind of question is that?"

Erin ignored her. "Is there a chance you could be pregnant?"

Now it was my turn to laugh...until I was no longer laughing. I just stared at Erin, the blood in my head pooling somewhere near my feet.

I couldn't be pregnant, right? Josh and I had used condoms. Or at least I remembered using one the first time. And I was pretty sure we had used them the other times too that first night. We weren't *that* drunk. Plus we had definitely used them in Australia.

But what about the expiry date on the box in my bedroom? a pesky voice asked as I mentally counted the days since my last period. Turns out the condoms had been more than seven months older than the date marked on the box when Josh and I used them, which was why I had long since tossed them.

The problem was, I had no idea when it was. Normally I was super-organized, but writing down the first day of my period was never on my monthly to-do list. Apparently, it should have been.

My hesitation was all Erin needed. "Ohmigod, you really could be pregnant?"

"No...I can't be pregnant. I mean, I'm positive I'm not," I fumbled out, but the last thing I sounded was positive. "I've been stressed at work. That's all."

Relief rushed through my body. That must be it. Stress was known to wreck havoc on a woman's menstrual cycle. That was why I was late.

Why my boobs tingled.

And why the waistband of my clothes felt a little tighter than normal.

I wasn't late—I was getting my period.

The voice in my head cracked up—which was hardly very comforting.

"There's only one way to know for sure," Erin said. "As soon as we're finished lunch, we'll go to the drug store and pick up a pregnancy test."

"Sure. Okay." Might as well...for their reassurance that I wasn't pregnant. Which I wasn't. At. All.

Kelsey slid me a sympathetic glance.

In an attempt to distract me, they talked about an ad campaign Erin was working on for a very difficult client. "The jerk even insinuated that I wasn't allowed to take any maternity leave. I'm supposed to be there at his beck and call."

"What did you do?" Kelsey asked.

Erin snorted a laugh. "I pretty much told him where to shove his 'beck and call.'"

The baby at the next table began crying. And wow, for someone so small, the kid had quite the set of lungs.

"No! I want!" the toddler at a nearby table screamed.

Her mother attempted to placate her while the other mother tried to soothe the crying baby—and a sinking feeling lodged itself in my stomach.

God, please tell me I'm not pregnant.

But since I didn't believe in God, he chose to keep quiet.

Or possibility #2. He existed and was currently laughing so hard at my potential predicament that tears were rolling down his cheeks.

Our food arrived, and Erin and Kelsey did their best not to talk about babies. After we finished eating, we walked across the street to the drug store.

"Remind me next time to avoid being pregnant during the summer," Erin said, looking like she was ready to melt into a puddle. It wasn't as if San Francisco was even that hot during July. Nothing like L.A. or Santa Monica.

Don't worry, the voice in my head said, *if you're pregnant, it won't be a summer baby. If you're going to accidentally get pregnant, this is the best time to do it.*

That was the voice in my head for you—always the logical one.

Too bad it hadn't spoken up the first night Josh and I had sex. That would've been helpful—then the other times wouldn't have happened either.

And I wouldn't be left thinking about sex all the time. With him.

We located the family-planning aisle and on instinct, I grabbed a box of condoms. If I wasn't pregnant, then I'd be needing these. At some point. Going on the pill would be a good idea too. Just to be extra cautious.

Erin clearly was a pro when it came to pregnancy tests. Whereas I was as lost as a guy in the feminine hygiene aisle, she knew exactly what I needed. She grabbed a box from the shelf and handed it to me.

Or at least tried to.

If I didn't take it, I wouldn't be pregnant.

Yeah, I didn't think it worked that way either, but it was worth a try.

Erin wasn't so easily fooled. "Not taking the test isn't going to change anything."

I let out a slow breath and nodded. "You're right." But while I might have agreed with her, I still couldn't will myself to take the box.

It was Kelsey who finally did. "Don't worry, Holly. We're here for you. No matter what the test says and no matter what you decide, we're not going anywhere."

My lips moved into a smile. Not a very convincing one, but a smile no less. "Thanks."

I took the box from her and marched to the cashier. It was just a test. I'd taken tons of tests in university and during my MBA, and I had survived.

Not quite the same thing, the voice pointed out, laughing. *But keep telling yourself that if it makes you feel better.*

I inwardly glared at the stupid voice.

I paid for the pregnancy test and condoms and hightailed it from the store.

"So now what?" I asked Erin and Kelsey as we stood on the sidewalk. *Do I make a sacrifice to the goddess of pregnancy tests so that I fail this one...in a good way?*

I'd be perfectly willing to sacrifice Josh if it meant I wasn't pregnant.

And given he didn't want any children either, I was positive he'd be more than happy to sacrifice himself.

"You take the test," Erin said. "Don't worry. It's really easy to do."

Sure, easy for *her* to say.

"Do you want us to come with you?" Kelsey asked, her voice a blanket of sympathy. Now, if only I could pull it over my head like when I had been little and scared of the boogeyman. Nanna had given me a special blanket that she'd sworn kept all scary monsters away.

At my nod, they followed me back to my apartment building in Kelsey's car. While I didn't wish to find out the truth on my own, I was happy to have a few minutes to myself first to figure out what I would do if the test was positive.

I mean, other than cry.

Although right now, that sounded like a really good option.

By the time I parked my car behind my building, I didn't have an answer.

And I still didn't have an answer when Kelsey and Erin joined me a few minutes later on the front steps.

Have you ever visited a foreign country? When you first arrive, you're faced with the dilemma of understanding the language—even if it's the same one as your native tongue. If I asked you where I could find a flat, would you know I meant apartment? Between the different foreign customs, the different signs, the different way of life, the different money, and the differences in the language, it's easy to feel overwhelmed and a little bit lost.

That was exactly how I felt once inside my apartment. I had no idea what to do next. I turned to Erin. "What now?"

She smiled softly, her eyes sympathetic. "Unless things have changed since I conceived this one"—she rubbed her stomach like it was a genie in a lamp—"you pee on the stick."

Sounded like good advice. So why was my body refusing to walk toward the bathroom? *Hello, legs? You were working a few minutes ago.*

I let out a hard breath. "Okay, I can do this." I must have been convincing enough for my legs. They began moving, with my heart rate racing us to the bathroom.

Inside, I shut the door behind me but didn't bother to lock it. I opened the box and removed the instructions. My hands shook, making it tough to read the words. But what was there to read? I peed on the stick. It wasn't rocket science.

A minute later, I stood at the sink, the peed-on pregnancy test doing its thing on the counter. I washed my hands and bailed from the room faster than an emu being chased by a truck—the test abandoned next to the sink.

And, well, you know the rest. The three of us entered the bathroom. Kelsey picked up the test and gave me the news—sympathy and awe and happiness all shining back at me. "You're going to have a baby."

But pregnancy tests weren't a hundred percent accurate. It said so on the box. They were ninety-nine percent accurate. Which meant one out of a hundred times they were wrong.

So statistically speaking, this could be that one screwed up test—the test that gave the wrong answer.

"It's wrong," I said, sounding like a pouting toddler.

"I can get you another one," Kelsey offered.

"That's okay. I'm positive I'm not pregnant."

My life as I knew it wasn't over.

Funny how irony always got the last laugh.

11

HOLLY

What's the most frequently cited nightmare that people have? That's right. It's the one where you're speaking in front of a group, in your underwear and only your underwear. It doesn't matter who's in the audience, the implication is still there—nothing is more terrifying than this.

Except the nightmare had it all wrong.

Because I would've rather stood in my lacy black panties and bra in front of my peers than where I was currently sitting.

"You're pregnant," the woman in the white doctor's coat repeated after I didn't respond the first time.

Those two simple words were like lead cannonballs bouncing around in my stomach. I was going to be sick. As in, puking-out-my-guts sick. I eyed the trashcan, making sure it was within easy reach.

Dr. Sinclair studied me for a moment, possibly waiting for me to come out of my comatose state. After I'd decided five days ago the pregnancy test was indeed faulty, Erin had insisted I double-check with my physician. Better to be safe than sorry.

Of course, if I had done a better job being safe, I wouldn't be sitting on the examining table feeling like I was standing in front of an execution squad. But unlike in the nightmare, there were no black lacy bra and panties involved.

My gaze dropped to the file in her hand. "Is there a chance the results are wrong?"

"There's no doubt about it, Holly. You're pregnant." She wheeled the stool closer to me and sat on it. "I take it this wasn't a planned pregnancy?"

I snorted a laugh. "It wasn't even planned sex. It just kind of happened." At least that had been the case the first time. Not so much while Josh and I were in Australia. And ever since then, my body had been whining about how much it craved an encore with Josh. All right, make that five or six hundred encores.

That was why I had agreed to go out with Brad the other night. How did it go?

Not bad at first. He picked me up at my apartment and took me to a restaurant. Nothing fancy, but it was still a nice place. Things had gone well at first—until something suddenly hit me. No, I don't mean literally. Although a concussion might have gotten me out of the date sooner. It was just that Brad had been talking non-stop for the past fifteen minutes, and I had no idea what he was saying. I'd been smiling and nodding, but my mind had been somewhere else. Or more specifically, it had been thinking about how much fun I'd had with Josh in Australia—and I didn't just mean the sex.

Not once did Brad realize I wasn't even listening to him.

That was the first problem. The second one?

I was so aroused thinking about Josh, I had an even tougher time paying attention to Brad after that.

Okay, I know what you're thinking. I was on a date with a good-looking guy and was super-aroused (even if it was because my thoughts were focused on the wrong guy), so I must have had sex. You would think so, right?

Wrong. My body threatened retaliation if I even considered having sex with Brad. Or more specifically, it threatened no more orgasms ever again—which when I thought about it, that pretty much summed up the one time I'd had sex with Brad.

And since I loved orgasms, I took the threat *very* seriously. But did that really matter? No—because I'd already decided there would be no second date this time around with Brad.

Which was probably just as well. What guy wanted to go out with a pregnant woman when the baby wasn't his?

"You do have options," Dr. Sinclair said, tone non-judgmental.

I did have options—I knew that. Choices I had to make for myself even though it took two to make a baby.

Some people would say that Josh had as much right as I did when it came to deciding the baby's fate. Others would claim it was my body, my decision.

But given I knew Josh's view on *him* having kids, the final decision was mine. The question was, if I decided not to terminate the pregnancy, would I be able to hand the baby off to another woman to raise?

If I had been an unwed teen, the question would've been easier to answer. But I was twenty-eight years old with a great-paying job. And how would my colleagues react to me going through nine months of pregnancy only to give away the baby in the end?

Did it even matter what they thought?

An image flashed in my mind of a little girl, smiling as we played on the beach together, searching for shells. A little girl who loved me unconditionally, the same way I loved her.

And I knew in that instant, while I might not have wanted kids, there was only one option that was right for me.

My hand went protectively to my stomach. "I'm going to keep it."

It didn't matter if the baby was a girl or a boy, I wanted this baby—even if I had to go it alone.

Even if I had no clue what I was doing.

"All right then," Dr. Sinclair said. "Based on my calculations of your last menstrual cycle"—which I had roughly figured out at Erin's insistence—"that puts you in your eleventh, almost twelfth week."

Eleventh. Twelfth. Those were numbers. If there was one thing I understood, it was numbers. "What does that mean?"

"It means you're almost finished your first trimester. Second trimester begins at thirteen weeks." Her smile was warm and reassuring—like a teddy bear to a young child. "Do you want to hear the baby's heartbeat?"

"Really? You can hear that now?"

Her smile widened at the awe in my voice. "Yes, you can."

She helped me lie back on the exam table, adjusted my top to reveal my still-flat stomach, and squirted the cool gel onto my skin. She then moved a weird instrument around, searching...searching...searching.

"That's my baby?" I asked once she had stopped moving the device at what sounded like a small panting puppy.

"Yes, it is." Dr. Sinclair put the instrument away and wiped the gel from my stomach with a wad of tissues.

I really was having a baby. A pooping, crying, keep-you-up-all-night baby. A baby who would change my world.

The tears? Totally your imagination.

I blinked them away.

But for the first time since Erin suggested I might be pregnant, I no longer wanted to hide in an ocean of denial.

"I hope you don't take it the wrong way, Holly, but do you know who the father is?"

I nodded. *Shit.* What was I going to tell Josh?

Or maybe I didn't have to tell him anything.

Yes, because he'll never notice you're pregnant.

Although given we hadn't seen each other since returning from Australia, there was a good chance he would never know.

Unless Kelsey told Trent.

And Trent told Josh.

Maybe I could bribe them to not say anything to him. I could bake them cookies. Who didn't like cookies?

But he has the right to know, the know-it-all voice pointed out.

Sure, he had the right to know, but that didn't mean he wanted to know. By not telling him, I was doing him a favor.

The voice cackled. *Yeah, you keep telling yourself that if it helps you sleep at night.*

"It's not my place to tell you what to do, but I do recommend telling the father," Dr. Sinclair said as if privy to the debate in my head.

After giving me samples of prenatal vitamins, a bunch of instructions on being pregnant, and follow up appointments for a physical and an ultrasound, I was sent on my merry way.

As I entered the busy waiting room, a nurse called the next patient's name. A pregnant woman pushed herself up from her chair. The man with her smiled at her like she was his world. It was the same smile that she wore on her face.

My heart sighed a *Wouldn't-that-be-wonderful?* sigh, while my hand settled on my stomach as if to block the baby's view. He or she didn't need to see what they were missing out on.

Oh, wait, could babies even see yet? What about hear? Ask me how to calculate derivatives for a company and I could show you. But I couldn't tell you anything about having a baby.

Ignoring the pregnant couples in the room, I left to go on my first post-denial mission—to hit the bookstore. Once there, I wandered up and down the aisles, searching for what I needed.

At one point, I stumbled across the baby section, with

onesies, baby blankets, and stuffed animals. Not quite what I was looking for.

A small floppy bear on the shelf caught my attention. It wasn't a koala, but it was still adorable. It was the perfect present for the baby—to show him or her how much they were loved from the very beginning. I might've had no idea what I was doing when it came to being a mother, but I did know that much about this baby.

Taking the bear with me, I continued searching for the section I sorely needed. I eventually found it—and my eyes almost popped out of my head at the sheer number of books dealing with the topic of pregnancy and babies. *Oh, boy.*

Not knowing where to start or what was good, I randomly pulled out a book. *What To Expect When You Are Expecting.* Wasn't that a movie?

I mentally added it to my list of movies to watch. Maybe it would be helpful.

Or not.

I found a few more books that looked interesting. Books about being pregnant and books about raising a healthy baby. If I was going to do this, I would do it right.

Turning around, I walked into a solid wall of male muscle that hadn't been there before.

At the familiar deep and sinful male voice saying, "Hey," I let out a startled shriek as the books and bear fell from my arms.

12

JOSH

What's the last thing I expected to see when I entered the bookstore? That's right. Holly.

The same luscious redhead who had been starring in my fantasies ever since we'd returned from Sydney. The same luscious redhead I thought about every time I jacked off in the shower—more so than before we'd had sex together for the first time.

The other thing I hadn't expected? To find her in the parenting section. And while we were at it—having her shriek and drop a pile of books on my foot definitely hadn't made it onto my to-do list for today.

So I think we can agree I was surprised by the turn of events —even before what was about to happen.

Have you ever watched a horror movie? You know the part where you were certain something bad was about to happen? Hell, even the character who was about to die recognized something bad was about to happen. Her eyes were wide, her face pale, and if she found her voice, screaming would be her top priority. It was that moment just before the character decided running might be a good idea. Preferably away from the evil presence.

Now you know Holly's expression exactly.

Instead of picking up the books, she just continued staring at me. *O-kay.* I crouched down and gathered them up—along with the stuffed bear she had also dropped.

Pregnancy and baby books? *Huh?*

Maybe they were for Trent's sister, Erin. But while I could understand the baby books, the pregnancy books didn't make sense since the baby was due in a few weeks. Wasn't it a little late to begin reading up on the topic?

Or maybe it had nothing to do with Erin. Maybe Kelsey was pregnant. The corner of my mouth jerked up to one side. *Way to go, Trent, on knocking up your girlfriend.*

Although I was a bit surprised Holly knew and I didn't. But then Trent was a guy, and he probably didn't feel the need to tell me about it yet.

Remember the part about the character in the horror movie finally deciding that running might be a good idea? Well, when I stood back up, that was the look Holly was now sporting.

I handed the books back to her. "Hey, how's it going?" I asked, suddenly realizing how much I'd missed her. *Wow.* Where did that come from? I wasn't even talking about the sex —although it had been pretty spectacular.

No, I meant she was fun to hang out with.

Not all women could claim that.

"Hey, handsome," Maria said, sashaying up to us like a runway model. Which wasn't too surprising given she used to be one. "Did you find anything you like?" The Portuguese accent? Yes, it was hot, but not as hot as Holly's Aussie accent.

Maria glanced between Holly and me. "I'm not interrupting anything, am I?"

"Not at all," I said. "Holly, this is Maria, my teammate Adam

Bennett's fiancée." To Maria, I said, "Holly's a friend of mine." True—even if I hadn't seen her since Australia.

"It's Adam's birthday this weekend, and Josh is helping me with his present," Maria explained to Holly. "But because my favorite author's new book came out today, I asked Josh if we could come here first." She held the book up for Holly to see. On the cover was a picture of a man wearing only jeans and a cowboy hat, the woman's legs hiked around his waist.

And instantly my mind snapped to a memory of me holding Holly the same way, except we had both been naked at the time.

Don't go there, you idiot. Holly and I had been nothing more than a short-term fling. A short-term fling that had left my body thirsty for more. A more that my random hookups over the past two months hadn't been able to quench.

Not that there had been that many. For some reason, ever since returning home, they hadn't held the same appeal they used to. And because of that, their frequency had taken a nose dive.

Maria glanced at the books and bear cradled in Holly's arm. "Oooh, are you going to have a baby?"

I had expected Holly to say they were for a friend. My expectation was met by a panicked silence—and my belief that Trent and Kelsey were expecting a baby dove headfirst through the store window.

Holly was the one who was pregnant, which meant she was seeing someone.

Not that it mattered, I told myself.

"Congratulations." That sounded genuine, right? It didn't sound like I was surprised? Which I was. The last I'd heard, she didn't even want kids.

"Thank you," Holly said softly.

"I so love babies," Maria gushed. "When is yours due?"

"February twenty-third." Holly's gaze was focused on something over Maria's shoulder, and I was almost tempted to turn and see what it was.

Maria giggled. "Well, it's a good thing the father isn't a hockey player."

Holly's gaze shot back to Maria, the horror-movie expression having returned. "Why's that?"

"Because chances are good he won't be around when the baby is born," Maria said. "He'll be away on a road trip with his team. It's a hazard of the sport." Yet it hadn't stopped her from saying yes when Bennett proposed to her a few months ago.

Music played from Maria's purse. She reached in and answered her phone. "Hey, babe," she said, walking away from us.

"So..." I began to say. But what the heck did you say to the woman whose memory you jacked off to in the shower—only to discover she was carrying another man's child?

I paused, thinking of the right topic for this situation.

And drew a blank.

"Trent never mentioned you're seeing anyone," I said.

She clutched the books and bear against her chest. "I'm not."

Eyebrow raised, I gestured at her perfectly flat stomach. "So, it was an immaculate conception?"

"No, there was definitely a man there." She took a deep breath and let it out slowly. "It's your baby, Josh."

Of all the things she could have told me, that wasn't on my list of possibilities.

Not even close.

Holy. Shit.

13

HOLLY

Josh stared at me as if I'd announced I was going to give birth to a three-headed monster. *His* three-headed monster.

Alrighty.

Guess that answered my question.

"Are you sure it's mine?" he asked.

Guys, let me do you a favor right here and give you two hints for if you're ever caught in the same situation.

One—girls are a hormonal mess when pregnant. We're fragile. Our emotions are fragile.

But we can still kick major arse.

Two—never ask us if we're sure you're the father. I mean, if we have the reputation of enjoying sex with numerous partners during the time we had sex with you, then by all means question the child's paternity.

But other times...

"Given you're the only man I've slept with in ten months—yes, you're the father. Or maybe it really was an immaculate conception. If that's the case, Ryan Reynolds might be the father."

In case you were wondering, I was wearing stilettos. The perfect arse-kicking accessory.

Although at the moment, I was torn between kicking his arse or bailing—and introducing Junior to the joys of ice cream.

A big tub of ice cream.

With french fries.

"But you can't be pregnant," he said, frowning. "We used condoms."

Denial was a bitch. I should know.

Girls, let me take this opportunity to remind you, once again, to make sure your birth control hasn't expired. I still had no idea if the protection malfunction was due to human error or due to the expiry date being past due.

Either way, it was clear how this would all play out.

Junior and I would be going it alone.

But that was okay. I could do this. I was a smart and independent woman. *Go me!*

"Condoms aren't one hundred percent fail-safe. It says so on the box." My hand instinctively went to my stomach, maybe to keep Junior from hearing this conversation. No need for him or her to feel unloved from the get-go.

"Sorry about that," Maria's exotic accent said as she rejoined us, clearly failing to notice the tension that had sprung up between Josh and me. "Are you ready, Josh?" She held up a store bag, indicating she had already paid for her book.

Stepping away from the pair, I said, "It was nice meeting you, Maria." Were you impressed at how fast I could run in stilettos?

Josh didn't come after me. And no, that didn't surprise me. There was a better chance of Ryan Reynolds entering the store to declare his undying love for me than there was of Josh chasing me down.

As I passed the display of DVDs on the way to the cashier, one caught my attention. A pregnant woman in exercise gear was on the cover, glowing and looking relaxed and happy. Yoga for pregnancy. Yoga was supposed to reduce stress. If there was one thing I needed more than anything else right now, it was stress relief. Ice cream and fries only went so far.

I grabbed the DVD and continued to the cashier.

But before I got that far, a warm hand grab my arm. From the way my body responded to his touch, I didn't even have to look to know it was Josh.

"You can't tell me you're pregnant with my child, Holly, and then run off." His tone wasn't exactly pissed, but it wasn't happy either.

"I have a meeting I'll be late for if I don't get going." A very important meeting—involving a bowl full of comfort food. "We can talk later." Once the shock had worn off for both of us. Although I suspected Junior would be in college before that happened for Josh.

Fortunately for me, fate decided to throw me a bone, and Josh's cell phone indicated an incoming call.

He checked the screen. "Shit, I have to take this."

Sounded good to me. I hightailed it to the cashier and quickly paid for my purchases. Josh was still on his phone when I slipped out of the store.

A short time later, my purchases, Junior, and I returned to my two-bedroom apartment. I put the books, bear, and DVD on the coffee table and headed to the kitchen for a glass of milk.

My cell phone played Kelsey's song. For a second, I allowed my crazy hormonal thoughts to imagine Josh reacting to the pregnancy news the same way Trent would if Kelsey was pregnant. I had no doubts whatsoever that Trent would do cartwheels down the hallway.

And because my stupid hormonal thoughts weren't enough, stupid hormonal tears joined the pity party for two.

Needing to hear Kelsey's sweet and friendly voice, I accepted the call. "G'day."

"How did it go?" she asked, and I knew instantly what she was talking about.

"I'm one-hundred-percent-sperm-meets-egg-and-wham-your-life-is-forever-changed pregnant." I opened the fridge door and removed the container of skim milk.

"How are you feeling?"

"You mean in general or about the news?"

"Both."

"Well, my breasts are achy and swollen. I'm still dealing with nausea, but my doctor said that should go away soon. And I'm tired. But I did get to hear the baby's heartbeat."

"You did? And?"

I got a glass from the cupboard. "And...I'm definitely keeping Junior."

There might be have been a muffled shriek of excitement from Kelsey's end, but I couldn't be sure.

"You want some company?" she asked. "I could come over and we can watch a movie. Your choice?"

Did I wish to talk about what happened in the bookstore? Hell, no. Did I want to be alone to dwell on it? Double hell no —with an order of fries.

"That would be great," I said.

While I waited for Kelsey, I flipped through a pregnancy book. I was just reading about how I could expect my sex drive to rev up over the next few months (great news given that I was single) when the doorbell rang. I answered it and let Kelsey in.

"So what will it be?" she asked, holding up two containers of ice cream.

There was a reason I loved Kelsey. It was like she could read my mind.

Except for the part about the fries. But that was okay—no one was perfect.

After searching through Netflix, we settled on an animated movie that looked promising. First—it wouldn't have swearing in it, so it was Junior friendly. Second—there was absolutely no romance. Bigger bonus.

We settled down to watch it. Not once did Kelsey push me to talk about the unexpected pregnancy. Nor did she try to pry the father's name from me. She knew I would tell her when I was ready...*if* I was ever ready.

You see, here lay the dilemma. Josh was Trent's best friend. Kelsey was my best friend. Trent was the love of Kelsey's life. Done the math yet? Kelsey would be the one caught in the middle when it came to her loyalties—and I didn't want to put her in that position.

So, zipped lips it was.

Halfway through the movie, I had to pee. Badly. "You'd think for something so small," I said, referring to Junior, "I wouldn't need to go that often." We were both familiar with Erin's frequent trips to the loo.

Kelsey laughed. "You might as well get used to it."

While doing my business in the bathroom, I thought I heard the buzzer for the front entrance to the apartment building, but I wasn't positive. Since I wasn't expecting anyone, I refused to worry about it. Worrying wasn't good for Junior. Emptying my bladder was infinitely more important.

But once I stepped back into the living room, my resolve stumbled at the sight of the blond hockey player standing there. Josh.

"He said it's important," Kelsey said, looking between us.

Let's take a moment to recap what Kelsey didn't know. One—she didn't know that Josh had already been in my apartment previously. Two—she didn't know that Josh and I had had sex. And three—she and Trent didn't know that Josh had come to Australia with me. He and I had figured it was better that way.

No, this wasn't awkward at all.

Then a sudden understanding swept onto her face.

And the awkwardness factor tripled.

Fuck me dead!

"I should probably go," she said, "unless you want me to stay." The last part was directed at me.

"No, it's okay."

I walked her to the door and she hugged me. "Do you need me to get Trent to whip his ass?" she asked. "You know he would do it in a heartbeat."

Despite the nervousness wrapping around me like a Maypole dancer, I chuckled. "Arse whipping won't be necessary."

I closed the door after her and stood there for a moment, my back against it, eyes shut.

Was it really too much to hope for that when I reopened them, everything would be back to how it was three months ago? That I wasn't pregnant and wouldn't have to face Josh about our current dilemma?

With a hard breath, I pushed away from the door and joined Josh in the living room. He was skimming through the *What To Expect* book. Naturally, my heart took this the wrong way and squeezed hopefully. I blamed the pregnancy hormones for that. They really were annoying little buggers.

Josh glanced up. I knew I should say something, but I wasn't sure what else to say. If this situation was covered in *What To Expect*, I hadn't found that chapter yet. "Just so you know, I hadn't planned to get pregnant. I just wanted a good fuck to help me deal with Nanna's death." And to help me deal with my mum.

Wasn't irony just a bitch?

"I know it was an accident. And I'm pretty sure if I remember my biology class correctly, it takes two to make a baby. You didn't take advantage of me, Holly. I was as much a willing participant as you were."

Relief rushed through me that at least he didn't blame me.

"So what's the plan?" he asked.

"I'm keeping the baby." The words came out easier than expected.

"I kinda figured as much." His mouth slid into my favorite, teasing smirk. "The pregnancy and baby books gave it away."

I smiled, the movement small, but then the smile faded as I stared at the face of my new reality. And no, I didn't mean Josh. "I know you don't want children. Your hockey career comes first. So if you wish to walk away from this, I'm all right with that. I'm giving you the choice."

If my life were a romance novel, this was the part where Josh would sweep me off my feet and tell me he could never walk away. That he wanted his baby and me to be a major part of his life—and always would.

Of course, if my life were more like a Stephen King novel, a scary clown would crash through the door and drag Josh down a sewage pipe—leaving Junior without a father.

At least that would be easier to explain to our child. *It wasn't that your daddy didn't want to be your daddy. It was totally the clown's fault.*

If that didn't cause a fear of clowns, I didn't know what would.

Josh frowned. "News flash, Holly. I'm not my fucking father. Yes, neither of us planned this, but I'm not walking away. I plan to be there for you and the baby as much as you'll let me."

Okay, not quite the first option—but at least the scary clown kept away.

Did you notice what he didn't say?

That's right. There was no romantic gesture. Our goal was to keep our relationship uncomplicated. Well, as uncomplicated as you could get when you were having a baby.

He picked up the yoga DVD. "What's this?"

"Yoga for pregnancy. I thought it might be beneficial for the baby."

Josh glanced around the room. "How 'bout we start now?"

"Start what?"

"Yoga. The Rock goalies swear by it, and you've seen how fucking flexible they are. It wouldn't hurt me to do it with you." He moved the coffee table against the wall to give us some more space.

"But we don't have any yoga mats."

"I'm sure we can go without this time. I'll pick some up before tomorrow."

"Tomorrow?"

"If there's one thing training for hockey has taught me, it's important to schedule your workouts."

Now it was *my* turn to smirk. Josh wasn't known for scheduling anything. He was a spur-of-the-moment type guy.

The only exception? Hockey—naturally.

"All right," I said. "Yoga it is."

The ache between my legs sat up and rejoiced—having been on a hiatus for the past month. I blamed the morning sickness and exhaustion for that.

Not to be a party pooper, I reminded it, *but we're doing yoga, not having sex.* Clearly it had forgotten my no-sex rule when it came to Josh.

The ache rubbed its hands together and murmured, "We'll see about that."

Oh, boy.

14

HOLLY

Josh showed up the following evening with two yoga mats. Purple for me. Blue for him. I was wearing a pair of yoga pants, which weren't as loose at the waist as they used to be. My tank top was also starting to feel a little tight, especially across my chest.

What was Josh wearing? Basketball shorts and a team T-shirt. The soft navy fabric stretched across his chest and taut muscles—and the perma-ache between my legs let out a dreamy sigh.

Now, you were probably wondering how things went last night when it came to our first yoga session together. Don't worry, I was strong. The no-sex rule remained firm...much to the ache's dismay. Which was why I suspected it was about to play dirty.

It didn't help that I wanted to suddenly forget yoga and screw Josh instead. Maybe if we did it on the yoga mats, it counted as prenatal yoga.

No. No. No. Remember, we have the no-sex rule for a reason. We can't let the pregnancy hormones win.

Naturally, the ache between my legs didn't give a damn about that as it let out its war cry.

Which was another way of saying I moaned—even though Josh wasn't touching me.

We unrolled our mats in front of the big screen TV. I turned it on and hit play on the DVD player.

Those years of dance Mum had insisted on? They'd left me with a natural grace, flexibility, and balance that transferred to yoga. And judging from how well Josh was doing standing on one leg, his opposite foot pressed against his inner thigh, Junior would definitely be gifted with great balance.

"Now we're going to do the Downward-Facing Dog," the pregnant woman on the TV screen said. We had already been through several poses—my hormones being on their best behavior. Which was saying a lot when Josh's amazing man-scent and pheromones were doing all kinds of crazy things to my willpower.

I can be strong. I'm not going to lust over Josh...and his amazing body...and all those mouthwatering things said body can do to mine.

Inwardly, I glared at my noncooperative body, which had clearly taken over parts of my brain.

The woman explained what she was doing as she got into position.

I followed her lead, my feet and hands on the floor, elbows and knees straight, butt in the air.

"From where I'm standing," Josh said behind me, "that looks goddamn sexy."

I let out a huffed laugh. "Glad you approve." Still in position, I looked at him from between my legs, but only *his* legs and the part of him that had gotten us into this predicament were visible. It was hidden in his shorts but was definitely more noticeable than before.

The image of Josh taking me from behind flashed in my

head, and just like that, I was suddenly very wet for him. Very wet and very achy. *Dammit.*

I let out another small moan, which was easily passed off as a yoga-related noise. "Are you just planning to watch my arse?" I asked, "Or are you getting into position?" I almost groaned out loud at the image replaying in my head—of Josh getting into position...behind me, then inside me.

My legs trembled in anticipation. Hell, my whole body trembled.

"Isn't yoga supposed to be relaxing?" he asked, laughter in his voice.

"Yes."

"Well, watching your ass in the air like that is very relaxing." He stepped closer and settled his large, strong hands on my hips. Heat from his palms sank through the cotton of my yoga pants and made a beeline to the eager ache.

"You're not playing fair," I groaned and dropped to my knees, the pregnant woman on the TV long since forgotten.

"How am I not playing fair?" The laughter was still in his voice, mocking me with its deep, sinful sound. Every girlie part was now ripe with lust—and cheering me on to give into my horny hormonal needs.

I didn't bother to answer him. I clambered to my feet, wrapped my hand behind his neck, and pulled his head down to mine. Then my mouth was on his.

Yes, I was weak. After this, I would buy a T-shirt declaring it. But for now, the only thing that mattered was that I got laid.

Our tongues became reacquainted, sliding, tasting, teasing each other. Unconsciously, I ground my hips against his, rubbing my belly against his hardening length.

Now it was Josh's turn to groan, but not in a *What-the-hell-am-I-doing?* kind of way. He definitely wanted this as much as I did.

Unable to wait any longer, I scrunched the hem of his T-shirt up his abs and chest, craving his naked skin against mine.

Clearly hungry for the same thing as I, he yanked the offending fabric over his head and tossed it to the floor. A much more suitable spot for it anyway. My tank top joined it a second later—as did my sports bra.

"They're bigger than last time," he said with a goofy grin and palmed my breasts. "Yep, definitely bigger." He traced a nipple with his thumb, and I almost came at the heated sensation rocketing through me.

"Oh, God," I groaned.

Did the old man in the apartment beneath mine just hear that? *Crap*. Now I was providing free porn to seniors.

Josh took my nipple into his mouth. Because I didn't wish to be rated as better than pay per view, I bit my lip to keep from crying out again. I succeeded. Barely.

I ran my fingers through his hair and lightly tugged the soft, dark blond strands. He growled. The nipple in his mouth ached deliciously at the sensation, while everything below my waist begged for his attention.

My free hand slid between my legs and I cupped myself.

Josh smiled against my breast and popped the nipple from his mouth. It instantly missed his lavish attention. If it could scowl at him, it would have.

"Impatient, are we?" he asked.

I huffed a reply.

He smiled that sinfully wicked grin of his that always turned me on. Surprised that I could be even more turned on? That would make two of us.

"I guess I'll have to do something about that," he said. "Is it true what they say about pregnant women?"

"What's that?" My finger accidentally (or maybe not so accidentally) brushed against my clit, buried under my panties and yoga pants. I gasped.

"That pregnancy makes you hornier."

"I might have read that somewhere," I murmured against his lips.

"I have a feeling I'm going to like this part about you being pregnant." His voice was a warm brush against my mouth.

"I figured you'd say that. Now can you do something about my problem?"

"What problem is that?"

"The one where I'm incredibly horny and desperately need some relief." I placed my hand against his hard cock. He hissed under his breath. "And from the feel of you, I'm not the only one who needs relief."

He laughed, the sound deep and husky. "What about the yoga?"

"I'm sure I can survive one day without it." Heck, I could survive the entire pregnancy without it, as long as I had sex several times a day.

Good luck with that, a voice said, cracking up. Sure, if Josh and I were living together, I'd have sex pretty much whenever I craved it—as long as he was around.

Josh's fingers slipped under the waistband of my yoga pants, distracting me from my thoughts. I ground my ache against his hand. What? You figured I could wait for him to stroke me where I needed it? Not bloody likely.

Eager for more skin-on-skin contact, I slipped my hand under the waistband of Josh's shorts. Josh groaned—apparently I wasn't the only one planning to entertain the elderly man downstairs with free porn.

"Like that, huh?" I asked Josh.

"You can't even begin to imagine," he said with a chuckle.

Impatient to get to the good stuff, I peeled Josh's shorts and briefs down his legs. His length sprang free, proud and willing. I flung his clothes across the room, hitting the closed blinds with them. The white plastic crunched on impact. *Oops.*

"Fair is fair," he said, eyeing me like I was a ten-course meal created completely from chocolate. He stepped away from me and sat in the middle of the couch. "Now, strip!" His voice was smooth, deep, every inch a seducer.

"Ooh, I think I like you like this, Mr. Bossy." I winked, and with a sly smile, slowly shimmied out of my yoga pants. The only thing I had left on was my forest-green thong. My long auburn hair played peek-a-boo with my nipples.

I kicked the pants to the side and did a little dance, knees together, hips swaying side to side. Keeping my knees together, I sat back as if sitting on a chair made of air.

Did you see that? Josh practically drooling?

What guy didn't want his girl to pole dance?

Yeah, I know. I didn't have a pole in my living room (or anywhere else in my apartment), and I wasn't Josh's girl—but that didn't stop me from having fun.

I pushed myself up to stand. Who knew all those years of dance would be so useful? Although I was sure Mum would have a heart attack if she found out she had spent all that money so I could striptease for my fake fiancé.

Still in erotic dancer mode, I slowly traced my fingertips up my abs and palmed my breasts. Josh licked his lips, and a subtle thrill trembled through me at the power I had over him.

I lifted my arms in the air, moving to the slow jazz song in my head. I turned around, then stuck my arse out and wiggled it for Josh's entertainment.

He groaned.

I grinned.

But when you were pregnant and horny, there was only so much you could take before you went up in flames. I hooked my fingers under the waistband of the thong and peeled the material down my legs, still giving Josh a view of my backside.

I could practically hear him pant.

I swiveled back to him and sashayed my way over to where

he was sitting. He was still on the couch, lounging back, legs spread, his cock harder than when he had sat down. The man wouldn't be lasting much longer either.

I dropped a knee onto the couch and straddled him, settling my hands on his shoulders. I was so wet, I wouldn't have been too surprised if I was dripping on him.

Missing the feel of his lips against mine, I planted a teasing kiss on his mouth. But instead of teasing him, I was only torturing myself. Teasing wasn't enough. I needed him—all of him. I ran the tip of my tongue along the seam of his mouth. He parted his lips and welcomed me in.

While our tongues became reacquainted, his fingers had a mission of their own. His thumb found my happy place...and his slow, circular caresses brought me closer to the edge. One more millimeter—and I'd be hurling myself willingly over it.

The whimper? There might've been a small chance that was me.

His thumb brushed against my clit again.

Okay, *that* whimper was definitely mine.

Unable to wait a moment longer, I positioned myself against the head of his cock—then froze as I remembered something we were missing.

"Guess it's too late to worry about me getting pregnant. I'm clean if you...if you want to go without a condom." The condoms I'd bought at the same time as the pregnancy test were in my bedroom—which at this point might as well have been in the next state over and not on the other side of the wall. It certainly felt that way.

"I was recently tested and I'm clean too....So yeah, I'm all for going bare."

I practically groaned at his sensual one-sided grin. I was totally done for. "Bare it is."

I slowly lowered myself onto his length, releasing a soft moan as his width filled me. Once he was fully seated, I arched back, barely keeping myself from diving over the edge at the sensation of him naked inside me.

I groaned as his mouth found my neck and grazed his teeth against my sensitive skin. "That feels amazing."

He murmured his agreement, his hands moving to my hips. Getting the idea of what he wanted because I craved the same, I moved along his cock, slowly at first, then picking up the pace —faster, harder.

Then a flash fire to rival all others flared from my core, flooding my body.

I cried out Josh's name, my soft heat clenching hard around him, and dropped my head on his shoulder. Sweat dripped from our bodies, intermingling as one. While there were lots of things I wasn't too certain about when it came to pregnancy, there was one thing I was one-hundred-and-ten-percent certain of.

Pregnancy sex was hot.

"Wow," Josh said, once he was finally able to find his voice.

I giggled. "Wow, indeed."

"I was thinking we should make this a regular thing. The second trimester is when you'll be incredibly horny—"

"As we've just established."

"Yes, as we've just established. I don't want you to needlessly suffer."

I smirked. "How gallant of you."

He smirked back. "Isn't it? I mean unless you have someone else in mind. Because I'm not interested in sharing you, Holly."

Did I want to risk the messiness of another friends-with-benefit relationship? Normally I would have said no—after what happened in university. But the rules changed when pregnancy-hormone-induced lust was thrown into the mix.

Besides, I was a big girl. I knew what I was doing. This time I'd do a better job keeping my emotions out of it.

"I'm not interested in sharing you either," I said. "And no, there's definitely no one else. Just my fake fiancé." And thanks to my current situation, the lie my family thought was true was about to get more complicated.

Josh raised an eyebrow. "Your family still thinks you're engaged?"

"Engaged and childless. I haven't had a chance yet to tell them that we broke up."

"But you're going to?"

Let me give you some advice. Lying was stupid. There, I said it. If you were going to do it, make sure you had a strong shovel because you'd need it for the deep grave you would be digging.

And thanks to my so-called harmless lie, I'd be busy digging all the way to Australia.

Hopefully that was okay to do while I was pregnant.

Guess I could always check with my doctor first.

"Yes," I said, "I'll tell them we broke up. But I'm not telling them about the baby yet." One problem at a time.

"Are you telling them that I'm the father?"

I leveled my gaze at him. Maybe it would be a better idea to climb off him first—since his cock was still inside me.

I shifted off him and began retrieving my clothes. "What do you want me to tell them?"

"I want you to tell them the truth. All of it. The baby. The fake engagement. That I'm the baby's father."

I cringed—because telling my mum that I had never been engaged would be worse than if things just hadn't worked out between Josh and me.

But—what was she going to do? Go back to her original campaign of marrying me off to Drew?

That would go down well, given I was pregnant with another man's child.

"All right," I said, holding my clothes in front of me like a shield. "I'll tell them the truth."

Soon.

Eventually.

Once I'd pulled on my big-girl maternity panties.

Okay, back to the initial question at hand—did I want him to regularly service my horny hormonal needs while I was pregnant?

PROS

1. Sex with Josh was great.

2. I wouldn't have to worry about finding someone willing to have sex with me once I began showing.

3. Sex with Josh was great.

4. I wouldn't have to feel woefully unsatisfied because I had to rely on my fingers.

5. And I wouldn't have to resort to buying a vibrator. Were vibrators during pregnancy considered safe? Was the topic even covered in *What To Expect When You Are Expecting*?

6. Sex with Josh was great.

CONS

1. Josh didn't do relationships and he wasn't interested in complicated.

2. I could become addicted to sex with Josh, and then what would I do once he moved on to someone who wasn't the mother of his child?

3. Sex with Josh was great. After spending numerous months having great sex with him, how would I be able to go back to less than earth-shattering sex?

"So, is the offer still on the table to fulfill my sexual needs while I'm pregnant?" I'd worry about the consequences later. Right now the baby was more important. Sexual frustration led to stress, and that wasn't healthy for the baby. Earth-shattering sex was a great stress reliever, and that was a win for Junior.

And Junior's needs came first.

Josh nodded. "Yes, the offer's still on the table."

Awesome. Perfect. Great. "Then I accept your offer." I turned my back on the know-it-all voice in my head—the one pointing out that I was making a big mistake.

15

HOLLY

While I waited for her reply, I sent the same text to my brothers, then popped a french fry into my mouth. A plate of my favorite restaurant fries sat on the coffee table in front of me.

Crap. That wasn't good.

I was afraid to ask.

Me: How did you know the engagement was fake?

Never mind the part where I hadn't been "engaged" anywhere near five months. Neither of them had won the bet.

Chris: Really? You have to ask? You would never do something as impulsive as getting engaged to someone you barely know.

Me to Chris: How do you know I haven't known Josh for a while?

Chris: You looked ready to shag him not marry him.

God, had I been that obvious?

Mum: That doesn't surprise me. Hockey players aren't known to be faithful.

Me to Mum: I never said he cheated on me.

And how on earth did Mum know anything about hockey players? What did she do—Google them?

Right. Of course she did.

Although I was surprised she had found anything to indicate hockey players weren't faithful. Maybe Buzzfeed had a list for the Top Ten Sports Known to Produce Unfaithful Significant Others.

Mum: Then what happened?

"I want you to tell them the truth. All of it. The baby. The fake engagement. That I'm the baby's father."

Like that would happen.

So I went with a different kind of truth.

Me: Because my career comes first and
there's always a chance he could be traded. I
don't want to put my career on hold because
of it.

How was that for a brilliant excuse? Career trumped all in her books...including love.

What about Junior and the possibility of Josh being traded?

That was something I didn't want to worry about for now. Worrying solved nothing.

Simon: Tell Chris I don't owe him $50. You
weren't engaged for even 5 months.

Me to Simon: Neither of you won the bet,
mate. You were both wrong.

Chris: You know what this means, right?

Me to Chris: No, what?

Chris: Unless you sound really broken up
about the breakup, Mum will try to hook you
up with Drew again.

A moment later.

Chris: Who am I kidding? She'll jump right
back on that plan regardless if your heart is
broken or not.

That was what I was afraid of.

Me to Chris: There's more.

Chris: Like what?

Me: I'm pregnant.

Why was I telling my brother but not my mother? Because he would be supportive no matter what.

> Simon: You're really pregnant? I'm not sure if I should laugh or give you a lecture on safe sex. But I guess it's too late for that.

> Me to Chris: You told Simon? You know he can't keep his mouth shut. I don't care if you have to duct tape his mouth, you have to keep him from telling Mum and Dad.

> Me to Simon: You can't tell Mum or Dad. If you tell them, I'll...I'll. I was never good at revenge or threats. Just be forewarned that whatever I do to you won't be pleasant at all.

> Simon: Don't worry, your secret is safe.

I hoped he was right—given his track record with my secrets.

> Simon: Why don't you want them to know?

> Me: I'm not ready to deal with their reaction about me throwing away my career. Which I'm not. But that's not how Mum will see it.

> Simon: True enough.

> Chris: Don't suppose your fake ex-fiancé is the father?

When I didn't respond right away...

> Chris: Fuck. The wanker really is the father?

Mum: I agree. Your career comes first. He wasn't the right man for you.

Me to Mum: I know. But I still love him and it will take me a long time to get over what happened.

"So don't even think of trying anything when it comes to me and Drew," I said to my phone, even though she couldn't hear me.

Mum didn't text back. I could only hope that was a good sign.

Simon: You know at some point you will have to tell Mum and Dad. Or were you just planning to show up one day with the little ankle biter in tow?

Now that did sound like a brilliant option....

16

JOSH

It was that time of the year again—the middle of September and the beginning of hockey training camp. What did that mean? New hopes. New teammates. New head coach.

You heard me correctly. After we lost our series in the play-offs, the general manager and the higher powers decided to shake things up and sign a new coach.

And that wasn't the only thing to change. We lost a few of our old teammates when they became free agents. And one player retired. He was only thirty-three years old.

"Hey, man," I said to Mark Milone, one of our forwards. "You look exhausted."

"I am. Welcome to life with a six-month-old. I swear the kid thinks he's in college and life is nothing but an all-night party."

"I'd love to tell you it gets easier," Jyri Toivonen, our goalie, said. "But I'd be lying. Just be thankful you only have the one." He had two-year-old twin boys.

Oh, Christ. There wasn't a chance Holly was pregnant with twins, right? She only mentioned hearing one heartbeat at the doctor's appointment.

Sean, the third member of the daddies' club, smiled an evil grin at Mark, which was followed by an equally evil cackle.

"You okay, Josh?" Mark asked. "You look a little pale."

"He's right," Sean said. "You look ready to pass out. If I didn't know better, I would guess you'd knocked up your girlfriend." He slapped me on the back. "But we all know the great Josh Hoffer would never settle down with a woman. Why give up his off-ice player status when he doesn't have to?" He yanked his T-shirt over his head. "Which is a good thing too. If you did that, then who would we live vicariously through?"

"It's not like Hamilton will ever settle down," I said, side-stepping the discussion about me. *Thank you, Travis, for being the player I was—until my sperm went rogue.*

Except even before I'd known Holly was pregnant, the thrill of being a player off the ice had worn thin.

"Holy fuck," Mark said. "Are you telling us you have a girlfriend?"

I inwardly groaned. Was I really that transparent? "She's not exactly my girlfriend." In the seven weeks since finding out Holly was pregnant, we had been enjoying sex—*really* enjoying sex—and practicing prenatal yoga.

Our future as a family? It was something we both avoided talking about.

Avoidance—our new superpower.

Based on my teammates' expressions, you would've thought I had told them I was dating the Easter Bunny.

"So what is she?" Jyri asked.

She's my pregnant fuck buddy, who wouldn't be my fuck buddy if she weren't pregnant with my kid. But I couldn't tell them that.

"She's my friend who happens to be pregnant."

Well, that was one way to render those three speechless. At the same time.

"And who exactly is the father?" Sean asked, the first to

recover. The question was merely a formality. They already knew.

I let out a heavy breath. "Yes, it's mine."

"This is better than those fucked up reality shows Becca likes to watch," Mark said, a little too excitedly if you asked me. "So, are you guys involved, or are you just there for child support?"

I grabbed my jersey from my locker and pulled it over my head. "I'm not really boyfriend material. But I do plan to be there for my child in every way possible." I didn't want to be a reincarnate of my father. That much I did know.

But since your father wasn't much of a role model, the voice of reason asked, *how the fuck do you plan to be a good one?*

Sean exchanged looks with Mark and Jyri. "So, what do you think, guys? Should we induct him into the group?"

They both looked me over like I was a racehorse for sale. I rolled my eyes.

"Do you think he's ready?" Jyri asked, eyeing me with skeptical amusement. For some reason, his Finnish accent was always stronger when he found something particularly funny.

"Ready for what?" I asked.

"To join HDF," Sean said as if it were obvious.

"HDF?"

"Hockey Dads Forever."

I threw back my head, laughing. Let me guess—one of their wives came up with the name.

Three hours later, a weary team returned to the locker room. I stripped out of my sweaty uniform and headed for the showers.

"So when's the baby due?" Sean asked, standing under the shower head next to mine.

"February twenty-third."

He cringed—as did Mark, who was showering on the other side of him.

"What's so bad about that date?" I hadn't seen anything in *What To Expect When You're Expecting* to make me believe there was anything horrifying about it (or the month) when it came to pumping out babies.

"You could be out of town for a game," Mark explained. "That's what happened to me. Took Becca a month to get over it. Took my mother-in-law three months—and some days I think she still hasn't gotten over it."

Both Sean and Jyri cringed.

As it were, Holly still hadn't told her parents about the baby. Her brothers knew. And let's just say I wouldn't be traveling to Australia anytime soon to hang out with them.

The phone conversations with them had gone something like this:

"What the hell is your problem?" a rather pissed off Aussie accent said over the phone. It was three in the morning, and I had answered the phone without checking caller ID first, thinking it was Holly.

"You've got three seconds to tell me who this is before I hang up on you," I growled, the sleep in my voice making me sound even crankier. Did I mention it was three in the fucking morning?

It wouldn't be so bad if Holly's warm body was next to me. That would've helped me get back to sleep after I hung up on her dumbass brother.

And yes, I knew it was her brother—I just didn't know which one.

"It's Chris. Now will you tell me why you knocked up my sister? Especially since you two aren't really engaged?"

I choked back a laugh. It wasn't as if I had purposely impregnated her. It hadn't been part of some nefarious plan.

"You do realize this is between your sister and me, don't you?"

Should I be worried if I received a package from Chris in

the mail? Given the poisonous spiders and snakes over there, I was going with a yes.

"And you do realize if you do anything to hurt Holly, I will come over and hurt you?"

Note to self: no opening anything from Australia from now on.

Guess who then phoned me five minutes later? And yes, the conversation with Simon had been pretty much the same. Only a little more colorful.

Mark turned off his shower. "My advice is—do everything in your power to make her happy. Gain as many brownie points while you still can. You'll be cashing in a lot of them over the next year or so. Trust me on that."

Sean grabbed his towel from the hook. Drying himself, he asked, "So what's the vote, guys? Are we letting the rookie here join HDF?"

"I vote yes," Mark said.

Jyri nodded—with what was best described as an evil grin on his face. An evil grin mixed with hope. "Agree."

"That makes three of us." Sean threw me my towel as I turned off the water. I easily caught it with one hand. "But you have to agree to the initiation test first."

"Initiation test? What kind of initiation test?"

They shared a glance, devious smirks on their faces.

"You have to babysit Jyri's twins," Sean said. "Both Mark and I did it. It's become a tradition."

I thought about it for a second. "Can Holly help me?" No way was I doing this on my own, even if she knew as much about kids as I did.

They looked at each other, silently communicating their decision between themselves. "Does she know anything about looking after kids?" Sean asked, clearly the group's leader.

I shook my head. "We're both going into this parenting thing clueless."

Their grins were hardly comforting.

"Okay," Sean said. "Your friend can help you."

"And after I join the group, you'll share your parenting secrets?" I was going on the assumption they knew what the heck they were doing. But I could also be way off base on that.

All three nodded.

"All right, count me in."

"I'll talk to Kari and let you know when you can look after the kids for a few hours," Jyri told me.

Was it just me, or did he sound a lot happier than he had a few minutes ago?

"I'll give you a freebie piece of advice. Try to make it to every single medical appointment that you can. Those are easy brownie points. You don't want to waste them."

Oh. Shit.

A memory of last night's conversation with Holly flashed in my head. Well, not so much a conversation as her mentioning an ultrasound appointment today. In about twenty minutes.

And the clinic wasn't twenty minutes from here. Not even close.

"Dammit!" I rushed from the shower area, the guys' laughter escorting me. Yep, they had figured out I'd already fucked up my easy brownie points.

Now, I just had to hope it didn't cost me too much.

17

HOLLY

"You will let me know if the sperm donor steps out of line?" Simon said on the phone. I was parked outside the medical building where Josh and I would soon learn if our baby was healthy.

Was I nervous? Let me put it this way. Did seals swim?

I glanced around the parking lot, checking for Josh. "Would you and Chris quit calling him that? He has a name."

"That's right. It's Josh-the-fucking-sperm-donor. But you have to admit that's a mouthful. So Sperm Donor it is. Or I can call him SD. That works too."

I rolled my eyes. Yes, I loved my brothers, but they really could be kangaroo arses at times.

"Anyway," Simon continued, "Drew's been asking about you."

I laughed and peered down at my growing belly. "I bet he wouldn't find me quite so crush-worthy now." According to the pregnancy website I subscribed to, I was officially eighteen weeks today.

And there was no missing it.

Smiling affectionately at the bulge, I caressed it. I was still completely clueless about the whole mothering thing, but doing this felt right. Like somehow it let Junior know everything would be all right—I would love her no matter what.

And yes, I had decided Junior was a girl. Call it mother's intuition.

Simon cracked up. "Who knows? Maybe he has a thing for single pregnant women."

"Well, that's not creepy at all..." My comment only made Simon laugh harder. "Does he know I'm no longer engaged?" I asked. "Shit, you didn't tell Mum I'm pregnant, right?

"Yes, he knows you're no longer engaged. And no, Mum doesn't know yet. And neither does Drew."

"Oh, good."

"You should just tell her, then she'll get off your back when it comes to her plans for you and him."

I snorted an unladylike laugh. "Delusional much? That will just make her push things even more. But now she'll have ammunition—the baby."

Of course that was only if Drew didn't care if I was pregnant or not. If he did, end of problem...on that front.

"Good point. Well, good luck with that." A female voice on Simon's end said something, but it was too muffled for me to hear. "I have to go now, Hols. Talk to you later." And with that, he ended the call.

"What do you think?" I asked Junior. "Do I send Drew a copy of your ultrasound and write 'Wish you were here' on it? That's bound to scare him off."

Let's call that Plan B.

Plan A? No idea yet.

I still had time before the ultrasound appointment, so I walked to the nearby playground and sat on the bench. You couldn't get a better classroom than this for learning how to be a great mummy.

Several young kids were running around, giggling. A

toddler who was scooping up handfuls of gravel and dumping it on the sidewalk looked up from what he was doing. The woman with him said something and pointed at the approaching man. The kid squealed and toddled over to him. Laughing, the man swung him up and hugged him.

That sound? Ignore it. It was my ovaries sighing dreamily.

The toddler giggled and the mother gave them both a kiss on the cheek.

This time it was *me* who gave a dreamy sigh. Would Junior and I ever experience that?

Or would I spend my life balancing my career with being a single mother, with no chance of falling in love with a man? Right now I had Josh in my life and we were having sex practically daily. *Great sex*—in case you were wondering. Afterward? He went home and I spent the night alone.

That didn't exactly make for a happily ever after.

I returned to the medical building and headed upstairs to the ultrasound clinic. After I checked in, I located two empty seats, sat in one of them, and grabbed a magazine from the pile on the coffee table.

I should've been reading an annual report for a company I needed to analyze. So what trumped the all-important career-related task? The cute article about making bath time fun for little kids, with a picture of a happy, soapy toddler.

"Holly Whittaker," a woman in a lab coat called out after I'd been sitting in the waiting room for about ten minutes.

I guess that was it. Josh's practice must have gone longer than expected.

Or he didn't care enough to be here. That bitchy voice? Just ignore it—even if it might've been right.

The woman led me to a dimly lit exam room and asked me to lie on the exam table.

"I'm going to put some warm gel on your stomach first," she said. After doing that, she positioned the head of the ultrasound wand on my belly, then moved it around while watching the screen. Every few seconds, she tapped away on the keyboard.

What's the best way to make a patient nervous? One—don't speak to her. And two—study the screen with the same expression doctors wore when delivering bad news. You know the one.

Just as I was about to beg her to tell me what was wrong, a knock on the door jerked me from my near panic. The tech paused what she was doing and answered it. I couldn't see who it was or hear what they were saying, but a moment later, she opened the door wider and Josh strolled in, smiling.

Good thing I wasn't attached to a heart rate monitor, what with the way my heart did a happy dance at seeing him. The corners of my mouth slid up into a big relieved grin. "You made it!"

Those tears? They were nothing. Must have been dust in my eyes.

Josh reached for my hand. "Sorry I'm late. Practice went later than expected. Did I miss anything?"

I might have melted a little at the concern in his tone, and blinked back the new round of tears.

"Not at all," the tech explained. "I'm just taking measurements first and then I can show you your baby." She went back to doing her job.

Maybe sensing my fear, Josh kissed my temple. My heart paused a moment to let out a dreamy sigh, matching the one my ovaries had made at the playground.

There was no doubt about it—I was falling for him.

I know, bad idea. The sole reason Josh and I were "together" was because of the baby. If Junior hadn't existed, then things between Josh and me wouldn't be what they were now.

Right—even now there wasn't really an *us*. At least not in the sense I wished for. After what his father and mother did to him, he was too damaged to even consider it—too scared to try.

But could you blame him?

And let's not forget one important thing. I didn't know much about hockey, but I did know players got traded. Which meant Josh could end up moving away...and where did that leave Junior and me?

"I was talking to some guys on the team who have young kids and babies," Josh said, "and...well...they invited me to join their group, HDF."

"HDF?"

"Hockey Dads Forever."

I laughed. "You're kidding me, right? One of your teammates actually dreamed up that name?"

His shoulders raised in a *What-can-you-do?* shrug. "No, one of their wives. Anyway, they'll teach me everything I need to know about being a good father. It's like a support group."

"A daddy support group?" Was I the only one who thought that was utterly adorable?

My support group, who actually knew what they were talking about when it came to pregnancy and having a newborn, consisted of one member—Erin.

"Yes, but being hockey players, they came up with an initiation for you and me to do first before I can join them."

"What kind of initiation?"

"We just need to babysit my teammate's two-year-old twin boys for a few hours."

"That's it?" Oh, who was I kidding? What did I know about babysitting two-year-olds? The last time I'd hung out with one was never...if you didn't count when *I* had been that age.

"It shouldn't be too hard. I figured with the two of us, it'll be pretty easy."

Now if only I was as convinced about that as Josh. "Have you had a lot of experience looking after two-year-olds?"

His expression pretty much said it all.

Well, if it meant that much to him…"Okay."

"All right," the tech said. "I'm finished. Do you want to see your baby?"

And the winner of the dumbest question…

"Yes," Josh and I said at the same time.

She turned the screen around to face us. "There it is. Do you want to know the sex?"

Did we? I looked up at Josh, who was staring at the screen in awe. "Do you want to know?"

"I'm fine either way," he said. "Do you want to know?"

"I wouldn't mind knowing," I said, my gaze on the screen again

Could you believe it? That was a picture of my baby—Josh's and my baby.

I blinked back the new round of tears.

"Okay, let's find out," Josh said.

"You're having a boy," the tech told us.

So much for a mother's intuition. But given my own mum's lack of mothering intuition, clearly she and I had never inherited the gene for it.

Wow. I was having a boy—and nothing made me happier.

Judging from Josh's grin, I wasn't the only one who was happy. An image of him teaching our son to skate popped into my head. Along with the image of me skating alongside them, cheering them on.

And I mentally added "learn how to skate" to my to-do list.

18

JOSH

Kari handed Holly the large leather diaper bag, which looked ready to explode from everything stuffed inside. "Thank you for looking after the boys for a few hours," Kari said, grinning.

Instead of us babysitting Jyri and Kari's twins at their house, they had met us at the zoo—at Jyri's suggestion.

"Tomas. Mikko. Do you remember Josh and Holly?" he asked the boys.

Don't ask me which was which. They looked the same to me. Both had the same blond hair, blue eyes, and I'm-going-to-cause-all-kinds-of-trouble grins. "They're taking you to see the animals."

Holly and I had met the boys last night. And let me tell you now, there was a good reason both Jyri and Kari looked exhausted. The twins never stopped moving.

"Hi," Twin #1 said to me.

"No," the other one said. Ah, that must have been Mikko. "No" was his favorite word. Correction. It was the only word I'd heard him utter last night.

So that meant Mikko was in the red dinosaur T-shirt, and Tomas was in the matching blue one.

Got it.

"Mikko, you go with Holly so I can help Josh put your car seat in her car."

"No."

You might think "no" means no—and for the most part that's usually true. But with Mikko, it was all in the inflection of his voice. And in this case he wasn't screaming the word, so his "no" could be loosely translated to, "Okay, Daddy. That sounds like a great idea."

Jyri successfully handed Mikko off to Holly, then he and I walked over to his SUV.

"Kari and I really appreciate this," he said. "I can't remember the last time we had sex."

Huh? So that was why Holly and I had to meet them here? So he and Kari could go home and have sex?

Nice.

And in case you missed the sarcasm, there was more in that single word than there was animal shit at the zoo.

He fastened the car seats in Holly's Corolla. Why not my Nissan GT-R? Have you ever tried squeezing a car seat into a two seater?

And don't even say it. I was *not* giving up my baby. If you had ever ridden in one, you would understand why.

We returned to the women. Jyri and Kari said good-bye to the twins and told them to have fun. I could have sworn Jyri's words held a secret message—reminding the boys to be little hell-raisers and make their daddy proud.

Or maybe that was me being paranoid.

"Okay, guys," I said. "You ready to see the animals?"

"See bear." Tomas growled like one, then took off running toward the front gate. Not wanting to be left behind, Mikko ran after him.

"You corral them and I'll get the tickets," Holly said, before walking away and not giving me a chance to respond.

For little guys, those two sure could move. It took me a minute to capture them. With each holding on to my hands, we walked over to join Holly in line.

Thirty seconds—that was how long they lasted before they got bored of waiting. They released my hands and ran toward the gate again. Holly stepped up to the cashier window to buy the tickets, and I hurried after the boys a second time.

Once I caught up with them, I crouched in front of them. "Hold on you two. Holly's getting the tickets now."

"See lion." Tomas tried to duck past me, but I scooped him up before he got far. He giggled.

"Nice try, dude." Luckily Mikko decided not to run off, so to stall him, I asked, "What animals do you want to see?"

"No."

One corner of my mouth jerked up. "Is that a type of animal?"

"No."

"Ah, so it is a big animal?"

"No."

"A small one then?"

"No."

Meanwhile, during this enlightening conversation, Tomas discovered my nose and grabbed it.

"Do you know what that is, Tomas?"

"Lion."

I laughed. "Not quite. That's my nose. Can you say nose?"

"Lion," Tomas said.

"No," said Mikko.

A pair of never-ending legs wearing jeans and sneakers stepped in front of us. Their owner was pulling the plastic green wagon belonging to the boys—and I peered up at the sexiest mommy-to-be on the planet, now nineteen weeks pregnant. She was wearing a long navy and white striped T-shirt that hugged the form of my growing son.

I grinned at her. "You got the tickets?"

She flashed them at me. "You boys ready to see some animals?"

They didn't bother to answer. They just toddled off toward the gate again.

"I guess they're not ready for the wagon yet," Holly said as we followed after them.

Twenty minutes later, with us running after the twins the entire time, I was ready to call it a day. No wonder Jyri and Kari looked tired when they dropped the boys off. How the heck did they have energy for sex while we had the twins?

But then I glanced at Holly and my cock twitched. Who was I kidding? I would always have energy to fuck her.

The question was—would she want to have sex with me after our son was born? She was almost insatiably horny now while in her second trimester. But what about later?

And what about after our son was born? Yes, I'd still be in her life because of him, but what about her and me?

And did I want there to be an *us*?

Or would I be no better than my old man?

I pushed the thought away. My father had never tried to be one. I smiled at Mikko and Tomas. Unlike my old man, I was trying at least.

Would my father have babysat the twins to be part of HDF? Hell no.

"What's next, boys?" I asked them.

"Bear."

"No."

Taking Mikko's "no" to mean "Yes, Josh, I would love to see the bears," I asked them, "Grizzly bears or polar bears?"

"Bear."

"No."

"Okaaay," I said, and surveyed the map. "Both are in bear country, which is that way." I pointed to where we needed to go.

And the two Energizer bunnies in the form of two-year-old boys toddled off in that direction.

"Are all two-year-olds this energetic?" Holly asked. "Or are these two a rare genetic breed?"

I laughed. "Can you imagine what they're like on ice?"

"I'm afraid to." She flashed me a panicked look before glancing at her belly. "Why do I have a feeling our son won't be much better?"

"You might be right about that," I said, before jogging after our two charges.

Thanks to their short legs, they didn't get far. Holly easily caught up with us while pulling the wagon behind her.

We led the boys to the grizzly bear exhibit. Tomas got excited when he saw one and yelled, "Bear!"

"No."

Holly knelt in front of Mikko. "Do you want me to lift you up to see him?"

Mikko flung himself at her. "No."

Smiling, she scooped him up and straightened to stand. "Do you see the bear over there?" She pointed at the bear who was lying by the pond, checking out his reflection.

"No," Mikko yelled, pointing at the animal.

"What an adorable family," a woman next to us, with chin length gray hair, said. Her gaze dropped to Holly's belly. "Are you having twins again—or just one this time?"

A light blush hit Holly's cheeks. "We're not a family," she blurted. "We're just babysitting the boys."

The woman chuckled. "Well, you're certainly not babysitting the baby, are you?"

"No, he's definitely ours," Holly said.

"Then you're a family. Even if you two aren't married, you're still a family." To me she said, "I hope you realize how lucky you are, young man."

"I do." Okay, lucky wasn't exactly how I would describe our situation. None of this had been planned.

But since Holly had given me a chance to prove I wasn't a mess-up like my old man, I *was* lucky if that was what the woman meant.

I leaned down and lightly pressed my lips against Holly's to show her just how lucky I felt. It was just the brushing of lips, but it was enough to ignite a fire low in my belly.

Not the kind of fire that usually led to sex. This was different—I just had no idea what it meant.

Tomas spotted the nearby bench and hoisted himself onto it. I picked him up and pretended he was a plane. But the moment I stopped making the airplane noises, he squirmed to be put down.

I lowered him to the ground and threw Holly a *What-now?* look.

"Please tell me this gets easier once it's your own kid?" Holly said to no one in particular.

The woman chuckled again and patted Holly's stomach. "Don't worry, you get better at it with practice. I had four kids before I finally got it right."

She laughed at Holly's horrified expression—which no doubt matched my own. "I was kidding. I mean, not the part about four kids. I had five actually. But everyone starts off feeling like they have no idea what they're doing. That's probably why we give birth to helpless newborns instead of toddlers."

Two hours later, we dropped off two very sleepy twins.

"Congratulations," Jyri said, holding on to Mikko. The boy's eyes were closed, his head resting on his father's shoulder. "You're now officially a member of HDF."

Kari rolled her eyes. "Good luck with that," she said to

Holly. "You're going to be at the team barbecue next Saturday, right? It's a great chance for you to meet the wives and girl-friends."

Holly slid me a look that had so much meaning.

Oops. All right. That was the PG version of what I was really thinking. Along with me calculating if I had earned enough brownie points yet to make up for my royal fuck up.

"We'll be there," I told Kari with a confident smile.

Holly didn't look so confident.

19

HOLLY

"**I**nstead of your apartment," Josh said as we walked along the path to my car after dropping the twins off, "how about we go to mine?"

I almost stumbled at his question.

Guess how many times I've been to his apartment?

That's right. Never. He'd always come to my place. Every. Single. Time.

I mean, if you didn't count when I picked him up to go to the airport when we went to Australia, and then this morning when we went to the zoo. Both times he was waiting for me outside the building.

"So has the hazmat team deemed it livable? Is that why it took so long for you to invite me there?"

He rolled his eyes. "It just seemed more convenient to go to your apartment. It's closer to your job." He had a point. But it wasn't closer to where he trained during the off-season.

"I for one am excited to finally see your place. And I'm sure Junior is as well. Or he will be once he's born." I pressed the key fob to unlock the car doors.

"Now that we know the gender, maybe it's time we decide

on a name for him. Because no way in hell are we calling him Josh Junior."

I giggled. "How about Josh the Second?" I asked as I opened my door.

"And definitely not that!"

Had to agree with him there.

"I'm sorry I forgot to mention the barbecue," he said at one point as we drove to his building.

Had it hurt when I first heard about it? Damn right it had. It was one more pain-in-the-arse reminder that I was just the dumb friend who had accidentally conceived his baby.

Yes, cue the violin music...and throw in a cello for added effect.

"That's okay," I said, sounding anything but okay. It was a good thing I hadn't dreamed of one day making it big in Hollywood.

"I had meant to tell you, but then you reminded me about the ultrasound and the barbecue slipped my mind."

"You know what you should do? Program reminders into your phone. That's what I do." My phone was always buzzing to tell me what was next on my to-do list.

Much to Trent's amusement.

Now if only I had scheduled "Pick up new condoms."

Guilt kicked me in the butt for even thinking that. Along with...

"Ohmigod," I whispered, "I think the baby just kicked." I placed my fingers where I had felt the faint movement. Like bubbles.

"Hopefully that doesn't mean he's going to play soccer instead of hockey," Josh said with a laugh.

"Would that be a problem if he did?" I asked, hand back on the steering wheel. The kicking sensation had already vanished —much to my disappointment.

"Not at all. If he doesn't want to play sports and would

rather spend the day playing with a calculator, I'd be fine with that too."

"Ha ha. I don't spend my day playing with a calculator." I usually spent two-thirds of the day playing with it, but he didn't need to know that.

"I just want him to be happy with whatever he chooses to do. I don't want him feeling like he has to follow through on *my* dreams. He gets to have his own."

My ovaries melted at his words. Chalk it up as one more thing Josh and I had in common. We were both products of our own parents' expectations.

"Do you enjoy playing hockey?" I asked as we pulled up to his apartment building. It was newly constructed, modern, and the rents were probably astronomical.

"I do," he said. "I couldn't imagine doing anything else. It's my life. Turn right here." He pointed to the entrance of visitor parking. "In the end, my father got that part right."

I parked the car in a vacant spot, and Josh showed me around his building. And color me jealous. Hello, state-of-the-art fitness center. The building reminded me of Trent's condo—designed for professionals, especially those without kids.

Remember how I wasn't a spontaneous person—unless alcohol was added to the mix? I was a planner, and proud of it. But there was one thing I hadn't given much thought to. Care to venture a guess?

That's right. Josh and I had yet to discuss how things would work when it came to Josh, Junior, and me.

"So, this is it," Josh said as we stepped into the living room of his spacious one-bedroom apartment. The black granite counter was the only thing separating the living room from the kitchen.

"It's gorgeous." Gorgeous? Was that the right adjective for the chocolate brown walls and furniture that was modern, simple, and masculine—completely masculine?

Several dozen model cars were lined up on the glass book-shelves against one wall. Many of them were of classic cars from decades ago—cars that my brothers would've got hard-ons just thinking about.

"Are these the ones you made?" I asked, studying them. He nodded. "They're amazing, and the details are incredible." I examined what I recognized to be a classic model Bentley.

Like the model cars, the rest of the apartment was orga-nized and tidy.

Surprised? Don't be—check out his bedroom first.

"Wow, were there any survivors?" I snickered while doing my best not to cringe at the mess in his room. In contrast to the rest of the apartment, it was like stepping into Opposite Land. Anything that dared to be messy—clothes, bedding, car maga-zines—came here to die in peace.

"A woman comes in weekly and cleans the apartment," Josh said, scanning the messy room.

"But there's a major force field preventing her from entering your room?" I asked.

"What can I say? A guy likes his privacy."

What he really meant was that this was his man domain, and no woman had better disturb it. Although from what Trent had told me, none of Josh's one-night stands had been inside the apartment. I was the rare exception.

"Out of curiosity," I said, "how exactly do you see things working between us when it comes to the baby?"

"What do you mean?"

An image of a family flashed in my head. A family who all lived together. A family with a father who read a bedtime story to his son every night and who was there if the child woke from a nightmare.

What did I long for? A family in which both parents loved each other and lived in the same home. I wanted to return from work every day and spend the evening with the two most important people in my life—my husband and my son.

I wanted a family that was the opposite of the one I grew up with. A family where the kids were loved unconditionally and respected.

The part about my lack of a husband? A minor detail. One I'd worry about later on.

"It's just you don't exactly live next door to me," I explained. "During the off-season, you came over in the evenings for yoga and sex, and then you'd go home. But during hockey season, that won't be possible."

The cry of protest? That was the perma-ache between my legs. It had been busy appreciating the orgasms that had reset the earth's trajectory around the sun. It had been too preoccupied to consider the implications of hockey season—until now.

"And what about when the baby is here?" I asked. "You'll be away on the road. But when you're not, when will we see you?"

From the way he flinched, I got the impression he hadn't given this much thought. Josh wasn't a planner. His ideal world was where he winged things.

But that wasn't the world I lived in.

My world involved having a five-year plan.

My world involved planning for when I returned to work after my maternity leave.

My world involved researching how to be a good mother— because that was the kind of mother I wished to be.

"We'll figure it out," Josh said. "Until we get to that point, we won't know what works best for everyone. It's all speculation." He kissed my temple—and it was as if he had magical powers, capable of soothing me.

They were awesome powers.

Maybe I should include them in my birth plan.

Josh's magical powers or a freakishly large epidural needle stuck in my back? No-brainer right there.

He pulled me close. My body tingled with need, with desire, with love. Then his lips brushed against mine, melting away even more tension.

Wow, he was good.

"How about I make us dinner and then we can talk." His hand caressed my belly as he kissed me once more. "Maybe we can start thinking about baby names."

"Can I help with dinner?"

"Sure. Why don't I put on some music first? Don't suppose you like jazz?"

My mouth almost dropped open in the most unattractive way. "I love jazz. My grandmother used to play it all the time."

Josh turned on the music. "Do you like chicken fajitas?"

"I love them."

That got a grin out of him.

While Josh removed the ingredients from the fridge, he hummed. The humming then transformed into the same lyrics playing through the speakers.

Fuck. Me. Dead! The man had an amazing singing voice—as in, if the devil on my shoulder was giving the angel a hard time, he would be stunned into silence.

"I didn't know you can sing."

He frowned slightly. "I was singing?"

Smiling, I nodded. "You didn't know you can sing?"

My favorite sexy smirk slid onto his face—and the ache between my legs released a heartfelt, I-don't-suppose-we-can-have-sex-now sigh.

"Yes, I'm aware I can sing," he said. "But usually I just do it when I'm alone, cooking, and listening to music. I guess it's become a habit, and I don't notice anymore when I'm doing it."

"You should sing to the baby. He'd like that." I did—so why wouldn't Junior?

Smiling softly, Josh got down on his knee—and my heart

just about stopped beating. *He's not proposing, you idiot*, I reminded myself.

He began singing to my belly—the song currently playing. That sound? Don't worry about it. It was my ovaries exploding. *Bam.*

I wasn't the only one appreciating the song. The bubbling sensation in my lower belly from earlier returned. "He's kicking again. I told you he'd love it."

"Where?"

I placed Josh's fingers on the spot where I'd felt the movement.

He kept singing, his attention on my stomach.

"Do you feel it?" I asked, suspecting he didn't. It was too early in the pregnancy for anyone but me to notice.

He shook his head but kept singing, and my heart melted a little more. Would his dad have done this? To me this was proof that Josh was nothing like his father.

Not even close.

Tears misted my vision. Seriously, hormones? Couldn't a girl get a bloody break?

Once the song finished, Josh pushed himself up to stand. Before he could say anything, my arms were around his neck and I was kissing him.

It started out tender. For about ten seconds. Then my hormones see-sawed the other way and the kiss became heated. If I wasn't so busy kissing him, I would have scowled at the little buggers for the sudden case of whiplash.

But since I was preoccupied, I whimpered instead.

Dinner was quickly forgotten while my body hinted wildly in which direction it hoped the make-out session was headed. I pulled back, leaving a hair's width between us, my breath ragged. "I need you inside me. Now."

You remember in the fairy tale Hansel and Gretel when

they left a trail of crumbs to help them find their way home after they were abandoned in the forest?

Just replace the crumbs with clothes, and you get the gist of what the living room looked like between the kitchen and the bedroom.

By the time we got to his bed, not a single scrap of fabric remained on our bodies.

Not a single piece of clothing separated me from how I felt about him. Seeing him sing to his unborn son pushed me further along the continuum of falling-in-love to I've-fallen.

But falling in love while you were pregnant was dangerous.

Maybe that should be a warning somewhere.

Like those billboards warning about unprotected sex—or the ones warning about expired condoms.

Right. Well, maybe the last one should be a warning. Somewhere.

But the point was, I was falling in love with someone who hadn't planned to have kids or settle down—and my heart didn't have protection from that.

We fell onto the bed, Josh bracing himself above me, keeping his weight off me. His fingers found my aching part, and mine found his hard length. Neither of us was going to last long. We were rushing too hard, too fast toward our ultimate goal.

But just as I thought Josh would take me and finish the race to the end, he shifted direction. He pushed himself off me and started propping up pillows in the middle of the bed.

He then sat and crooked a finger at me to join him. The heated look in his eyes was almost my undoing. "How hungry are you?"

I chuckled. "I'm always hungry for you. You know that."

He grinned, the heat turning to amusement. "I do know that. But I meant how hungry are you for dinner? I want you to ride me, slowly. I want to feel everything."

His words surprised and confused me—we had been going sans condoms for several weeks now.

I straddled his hips, and lowered myself onto his hard length, inch by slow inch. He filled me in every possible way, and I took a moment to take it all in. The emotion—not just his cock.

Josh groaned—making me feel more powerful, more in control.

"Like that, do you?" I asked, barely keeping the building moan from my voice.

"Christ, I like everything about you." He cupped the back of my neck and brought my head to his. Then he kissed me long and hard.

The ache between my legs decided enough was enough—it wanted in on the action too. With my gaze locked on Josh's, I rocked my hips, slow and easy. We'd fucked lots of times since deciding my hyped-up libido warranted the friends-with-benefit arrangement. But this didn't feel like any of those times.

It felt different. New.

It felt like hope and love and happiness were holding on tight for the ride.

With each movement of my slick heat against his length, I spiraled higher and higher. And unlike when we usually had sex, this wasn't a quick rocket blast taking us to the heavens. It was a slow, sensual journey.

They say when you're in love, sex is better, hotter, more satisfying—and for the first time since losing my virginity, I could see how that was true. Every centimeter of my body yearned for Josh. Every millimeter couldn't imagine being without him.

Eventually, as we neared the peak, Josh placed his hands on my hips and helped me set a new pace. A faster one. One that would take us over the top. Together.

"Oh, God, I'm coming," I gasped, body damp with sweat.

"Don't hold back," he groaned. "I'm right with you."

The sound of his voice, thick with need and something else, was my undoing.

I came hard and fast, every part of me unraveling like the quick tug on a loose thread.

The sound I released wasn't a scream. It was the sound angels made when they came and the heavens rejoiced.

Didn't think angels had sex? Well, that was where you'd be wrong.

Still a little dazed, I lay next to Josh. He rested his hand on my belly and smiled at the baby bump—love, pride, and a touch of smugness on his face. "So, any ideas what you want to call him?"

"Maybe Aidan, Oliver, Nathan, or Lucas. And I like the name Theo."

"Do any of them have special significance, or are they just names you like?"

"If you're asking me if any of them belong to a male in my life, the answer is no." I shrugged. "I just like them. What about you? Do you have any suggestions?"

"I was thinking maybe Noah. After my grandfather. He was the one who helped me get where I am now."

"Noah," I said. "I like it. It's perfect. What about the middle name?"

"How about Trent?"

I pondered it for a second. Despite my feelings for Trent in the past, the name sounded perfect for Josh's and my son. "Noah Trent Whittaker. I like it."

A frown appeared on Josh's face. "Whittaker? Not Hoffer?"

"Since I'm single, doesn't the baby usually take the mother's last name?" Not that I was an expert on the topic.

"Hell if I know. This is all new to me. Maybe it's talked about in *What To Expect*."

Yes—our new bible. Now they just needed to write the

sequel—*What To Expect When Your Baby's Father is an NHL Player*.

It was bound to be another bestseller.

"Or I could ask HDF what they think," Josh said.

Good luck with that, Kari's words from earlier mocked me. Why did I have a feeling their opinion wouldn't be in my favor?

I tenderly kissed the corner of his mouth. "We don't have to decide yet. We still have four months. The main thing is we agree on Noah's name."

The more I said it—the more I loved it.

And so did our son. He leveled a well-aimed kick at where Josh's hand still rested on my belly.

"He just kicked you," I told Josh, smiling again. "Or gave you a high five."

Josh kissed me...and dinner was momentarily forgotten.

Eventually my stomach rumbled after another part of me was thoroughly satiated.

Josh laughed. "Guess it's time I feed you two."

We climbed out of bed and had a quick shower, with Josh taking special care with washing my belly. Afterward, he tenderly kissed it. I didn't know how much more I could take before I fell completely, irrefutably in love with him—something I couldn't afford to do.

Why? Because there was so much at stake when it came to Noah and when it came Josh's hockey career. Plus there was still a little thing called my U.S. immigration status.

Nothing was guaranteed.

By the time we'd finished eating dinner, I could barely keep my eyes open. I yawned. "I guess spending the day with two-year-old twins and all that sex afterward wore me out."

Josh brushed his thumb against my lower lip. "Why don't you stay the night?"

"You mean like a sleepover?" I asked, shock at what he was

asking sideswiping me. Shock and a good dose of hormone-induced happiness.

"Definitely like a sleepover."

We returned to his room, stripped, and climbed under the covers. Josh pulled me against him, my back against his chest and abs. His thumb stroked just below my belly button—as if saying goodnight to his son.

I should have let his sweet actions lull me to sleep, but there was one thing I needed to know first.

"What will happen once you're back on the road?" I asked softly.

"What do you mean?" He kissed my shoulder.

"I know you haven't been sleeping with anyone else since I got pregnant. It's not like you've had a chance based on my demanding hormones, and we agreed to be exclusive. But what about when you're on the road and you don't have me around to wear you out in bed? Does the exclusivity clause still apply?"

I turned my head in time to see his frown.

"I don't know about you, Holly, but I'm trying to make a go at what we have here."

I twisted around fully in his arms to face him. "But I thought you don't do commitments."

"I don't." His hand shifted back to my belly. "But I am committed to making what you and I have here work. You're my baby's mama, which puts you light years ahead of any other woman. Like I said before, I'm not going to sleep around on you—here or on the road. What about you?"

"I'm not going to either," I whispered. "Not that I'd be able to even if I wanted to. I'm not exactly considered desirable now that I have a baby onboard."

Josh ran his lips against my jaw, his day-old stubble delicious against my skin. If I wasn't so tired, I'd jump his bones. As it was, I barely had enough energy for this conversation.

"I can't speak on behalf of other men—and I'd prefer not to

think about them—but I find you extremely desirable like this. You can't even imagine how much of a turn-on this is." He caressed my belly.

"So you find pregnant women a turn on?"

He shook his head. "No, only you."

Somehow, I found the energy to kiss him—kiss him long and hard and with all my heart.

20

HOLLY

"You ready for this?" Josh asked as we walked along the sidewalk to his head coach's house. His sports car was parked on the street of the upscale neighborhood. In his arms was the container of baby quiches he and I had made last night.

In case you're wondering...ever since last Sunday when I spent the night at his place, he had made sleeping over at my apartment his new regular thing.

With the exception of last night—when I spent the night at his apartment.

What did I learn this week?

I loved spending the night with Josh. I loved falling asleep with him singing to Noah and waking up with his hand on my belly...and his morning wood pressed against my back.

I could spend the rest of my life sleeping with Josh and I would die a happy woman.

"I might be a little nervous," I said, trying to decide if the sensation in my belly was butterflies or Noah kicking, "but I'm looking forward to meeting your teammates."

Was I nervous about meeting a group of men who liked to

slam their bodies into their opponents while on ice? No—although that was kind of intimidating too.

I wasn't Josh's girlfriend or wife...yet I was having his baby. That was what was responsible for the butterflies playing Twister in my stomach.

But even though we hadn't given this thing between us a label, everything in the past week had shifted. There was now a perceptible change between us—the intimacy, the way we were around each other. It didn't feel like we were just friends.

It felt like something more.

Something incredible.

Something I didn't wish to end.

A sign on the door invited us to join the party out back. I was wearing a short-sleeved, black-knit maternity dress that skimmed my growing curves. The stilettos? They were locked away in my closet...for now.

I'd long since realized that stilettos and being pregnant didn't work well, at least not for me. Now, at twenty weeks, I was wearing black thigh-high suede boots.

What did Josh think of them? If the way he reacted when he saw them earlier was any indication, he was fantasizing about me wearing them while we had sex—the boots being the only thing I was wearing while he thrust inside me.

At the thought of screwing around with Josh, my horny hormones predictably perked up—ever ready to party.

I mentally rolled my eyes and did my best to corral the little buggers.

At the far end of the backyard, a dozen or so kids were running around and playing. Kari was with a tall blonde woman, watching the twins chase a ball around the lawn. She glanced in our direction and waved.

I waved back.

"Holly," Josh said, bringing my attention to the man in front of him. He was in his late forties, wearing a "BBQ Boss" apron and holding a spatula. "This is Coach Fusco. Coach, this is my girlfriend, Holly."

I slid a glance at Josh and my nervousness faded. The glow in his eyes wasn't warning me that he had said it for the coach's benefit. He really did see me as his girlfriend.

"You can call me Mike," the coach said. "And I see congratulations are in order. When's the baby due?"

Josh told him the date and Mike didn't so much as flinch—although it wasn't hard to know what he was thinking: *"Good luck with that!"*

A woman with blonde, chin-length hair approached us. "Sweetheart," she said, "the burgers are ready for the grill." She then smiled at us. "Hi y'all. I'm Molly, Mike's wife. It's so nice to meet ya." Her gaze dropped to my belly—like the magnet that it was. "So when are y'all due?"

"February twenty-third," I told her.

She didn't do as good a job of keeping what she was thinking off her face. "That's always a tough time of year. My advice is to make sure y'all have other people to help in case you go into labor while Josh is away."

Except I didn't have anyone who I could ask.

I didn't have a sister.

My brothers? Not on your life—and they would no doubt agree with me there.

Mum? Yeah, that would go down well. Noah might hear her telling me that I'd ruined my life by making the same mistake she had, and change his mind about being born.

Erin had given birth to her baby girl a few weeks ago, so she was definitely out.

That left Kelsey.

I made a mental note to ask her and prayed to the pregnancy gods that she would say yes. Then I prayed even harder that Josh wasn't away when I went into labor.

I would even throw in a sacrificial chocolate Easter bunny

—the extra-large kind—if it would help.

Josh did the rounds and introduced me to everyone. Unlike with the puck bunny from a few months ago, none of the women were disappointed to see me with Josh.

"How's it going?" Kari asked after Josh had introduced me to his teammates. Tomas was snoozing in her arms. It was hard to believe he was the same non-stop toddler from last weekend.

"Good. Just don't quiz me on everyone's names."

She laughed. "I know what you mean. It took me forever to get everyone straight. It doesn't help that it's always changing. Just as you get the girlfriend's name right, she's history. Or you finally remember the wife's name and her husband gets traded."

Did her girlfriend comment hurt? There was a good possibility, but I did my best to keep the pain at bay. It wasn't like NHL players held the monopoly on breaking up with girlfriends. Just because a guy referred to a girl as his girlfriend, it didn't mean they'd ride off into the sunset and have a happily ever after.

And just because she became pregnant with his child, it didn't mean they'd take the same carriage ride into the sunset either.

Two other women joined us: Bridget and Becca. And no, they didn't look anything alike. All three were slim and could easily be models, but that was where the similarity ended. Kari was tall and blonde like a gorgeous Scandinavian goddess. Except I didn't think most Scandinavian goddesses chased around two rambunctious two-year-old boys.

Bridget could've easily been my (slightly) younger sister. Only her red hair was practically down to her waist. Think Disney's version of *The Little Mermaid*...minus the tail.

Then there was Becca. With her black hair and fair skin, she was a shoo-in if Hollywood ever made a remake of Snow White (okay, make that a remake of two remakes of Snow

White). She was also the shortest and curviest of the trio and was rocking an adorable, sleeping six-month-old boy in her arms.

"Kari told us Josh is now a member of HDF," Bridget said, giving me a pitying smile.

Becca snickered. "I still can't believe they went with Hockey Dads Forever. I was only joking when I suggested it."

"Why? Is it bad that he joined?" I asked. So far, it didn't seem too awful, other than the initiation test he'd had to do. Correction. *We'd* had to do.

The three women cracked up. Was I the only one who didn't find that very reassuring?

"If your boyfriend's hoping to learn how to be a father, he's hanging out with the wrong group," Becca said.

"But they do try," Kari piped in. "So we have to give them credit for that."

The two other women nodded, fighting grins.

"It's not a bad thing," Bridget said. "At least they're making an effort. It's not easy for them when they're away a lot. They miss so much when it comes to the developmental milestones of their kids."

"That's why you have to do everything you can to make sure Josh doesn't miss too much while he's away," Becca said. "You'll get used to Skyping daily, plus videotaping your child practically all the time, just so you can share the videos with Josh."

"And definitely do that," Kari added. "There are a lot of temptations on the road. Some players are great at ignoring them, remembering what's waiting for them at home."

"But other players aren't so good at walking past the puck bunnies," Bridget said. The three women turned to look at her husband, Josh, and another player. Henrik Karlsson, if I remembered correctly.

"His wife—or rather ex-wife—discovered a selfie a bunny had taken with him and then posted on the internet. Both he and the bunny were obviously naked in bed at the time. It had gone viral, so there was no missing it."

That did sound familiar.

Was I nervous after everything they had told me? Not really. I trusted Josh. As long as I was his girlfriend, he wouldn't stray. I could thank his father for that.

"Hey, Josh," Becca said a little too brightly, looking over my shoulder.

I spun around. Josh, Jyri, Mark, and Sean, along with their teammate Travis Hamilton, approached us with beer bottles in hand.

Mark swooped down and kissed the forehead of his sleeping son.

Sean was carrying his giggling one-year-old daughter. He kissed Bridget's cheek, then asked her, "You four keeping out of trouble?"

"We could say the same to you," she said, grinning up at her husband as Josh pulled me back against him, his hand possessively on my belly.

I looked over my shoulder and was awarded with a tender kiss that melted every part of me. Chocolate left in the sun had nothing on me.

I was vaguely aware of Travis grunting a God-you-guys-are-so-pussy-whipped groan. Laughing to myself, I pulled away from Josh, winked at his teammate, and turned my attention to Sierra, Bridget's daughter.

"Who's that?" I asked her, pointing at the large yellow toy fish in her arms.

Sierra grinned, revealing a few baby teeth.

"Is this Flounder?" Sean asked her, and she giggled again.

"Why did you call it Flounder?" Josh asked. Maybe it was just my hormones, but was I the only person who thought he looked adorable when confused?

Okay, definitely my hormones.

Sean's eyes widened. "How can you not know who Flounder is? And you're going to be a father?" He sounded indignantly wounded but the mischief in his eyes said otherwise.

Josh glanced at me for help. Hell if I knew who Flounder was—but I was hardly admitting that. They'd probably burn me at the stake for committing such a parenting faux pas.

"Men, it looks like we'll have to stage an intervention," Sean said to his sidekicks. The smirk? Yeah, I'd be worried about it too.

"What kind of intervention?" Josh asked, looking between the guys.

"The Disney princess kind."

"But...we're having a son." Josh gently rubbed my belly, as if looking for further confirmation that Noah was indeed a boy. "Why would I have to know anything about Disney princesses?"

Travis cracked up.

Jyri waved it off. "That's irrelevant. It's essential you know who they all are. Like for example, who is the mermaid in *The Little Mermaid*?"

"You mean the hot one?" Josh glanced at me and I shrugged. The character's name was sitting on the tip of my tongue—or not.

"I guess if you're into animated characters," Mark replied, "yes, the hot one. Her name is Ariel. Does that ring a bell?"

Josh shrugged and I sympathetically patted his hand on my stomach.

"Again, you seriously expect me to care about the Disney princesses when I'm having a son?" Josh asked, the corner of his mouth curled up in a *What-the-fuck-happened-to-your-balls?* smirk. Pretty much the same one as Travis's.

Sean turned to the two other men. "Quick, name the princess who lives with seven short men."

"Christ, even I know that one," Josh said. "Snow White."

Judging from Travis's expression, this was news to him.

"Okay...name the princess who falls in love with the Beast, who incidentally looks a lot better than in his true prince form in the animated version of the movie."

Bridget, Kari, and Becca nodded in agreement. Josh rolled his eyes.

"That's easy," Mark said. "Belle."

"Correct." Sean threw Josh a look that said, "Even Mark—who has a son—knows the answer."

Josh rolled his eyes again, and Travis burst out laughing once more.

Ignoring them, Sean said, "Next question. Name the two sisters who lived in the Scandinavian-like kingdom?"

"Princess Anna and Queen Elsa," Jyri said, close to jumping on the spot like a kid who had to go to the loo, badly.

Sean beamed at him as if Jyri was his prized student. "Correct. And name Elsa's magic powers."

"She can turn things to ice with her hands."

I snickered at Josh's expression. The one that said he wanted to turn Sean to ice.

"And for the final question of the night, what is Sleeping Beauty's real name?" Sean asked.

"Aurora," both Mark and Jyri called out at the same time—a little too enthusiastically, waking Mark's sleeping prince.

The baby stirred at first, then let out a pissed-off cry. He didn't have a chance to protest for too long. Mark swept his son from Becca's arms and cooed to the infant, settling him down.

Like magic.

"Wow, you're good," Josh said to his teammate.

Mark puffed out his chest. Becca snorted a laugh.

"What?" he said to her. "I *am* good."

She went up on her tiptoes and kissed his cheek. "Of course you're good, dear. No one would ever suggest otherwise."

I smiled at the teasing between the men and their wives,

and the men and their teammates. They were like a family. The family Josh never really had.

The family I did have—for the most part.

When I was eight, we had this one nanny who smelled like an old sweater a group of hungry moths had turned into a tasty meal. And discipline? She made a grumpy old schoolmaster from the 1800s—complete with a wooden cane—seem pleasant.

One day, Chris and I had gone down to our favorite pond to catch frogs, even though this was strictly forbidden since proper young ladies didn't catch frogs.

Unfortunately for me, while trying to catch a particularly stubborn frog, I slipped on a rock, fell into the water, and sliced my leg open on a broken glass bottle. The good news? My parents were away for a few days. The bad news? Well, I think you can guess what it was.

Long story short...Chris and I deliberated for the next five minutes whether I should just bleed to death or tell Miss When I Was A Young Lady what had happened. It was a tight vote—and if Simon hadn't shown up and told me I would die a long and agonizingly painful death, I would have won. But because I sucked it up in the end and was taken to the doctor for stitches, I barely had a scar to show for it.

I checked the time on my phone and did the quick math. "Excuse me for a moment. I need to make a call." I turned around in Josh's arms and gave him a brief kiss. "I won't be long."

"You sure?"

That smile on my face? Directed entirely at Josh. "Absolutely."

I left him talking with his teammates and their wives and found a quiet spot in a nearby park. I sat on the empty bench and pulled up Mum's number. Part of me hoped she would answer—the other part hoped she wouldn't.

"Holly," Mum said. "Are you okay?" She sounded genuinely concerned. That was what I got for not calling her as often as I should. *Oops*.

"I'm fine. Better than fine." I took a deep breath and let it out slowly.

Quiz time—what's the best way to tell your mother you're pregnant when you aren't married?

I didn't know either, so I just blurted, "I'm pregnant."

Wait for it.

One.

Two.

Three.

Four.

Hmm. Maybe we were disconnected.

Five.

"Are you sure?" she finally said, in a tone that would send kittens scrambling in fear.

Not a single tear of joy was about to be shed from her eyes.

Shocked? Me neither.

Despite the immense disappointment in her tone, I smiled at my growing belly. "I'm twenty weeks now—so yes, I'm sure."

"Twenty weeks?" There might have been some unladylike cursing too—something I'd never heard from her before.

That couldn't be good.

"Is Jack the father?"

"Josh. Not Jack."

"I take it that's a yes?"

At least this time I didn't have to lie to her—completely. There was still the matter of how I had told her he and I were engaged...and then we weren't.

I know, this was what I got for lying in the beginning. If I had pulled up my big-girl panties, I wouldn't be in this situation.

I would've just been the daughter who got knocked up

while celebrating Nanna's life.

Nanna would be so proud of me.

No, really. She'd always wanted a great-grandchild.

"Yes, it's Josh's baby. I wanted to tell you because...well... you're going to be a grandmother—and I thought you might want to know."

"Of course I want to know." Marine drill sergeants sounded less harsh. "Does this mean the engagement is back on?"

Yeah...about that.

Let's take a moment here to remember why I had lied to her to begin with. She had wanted me to marry Drew. Drew had been interested in me, but at that time I wasn't pregnant.

Okay, I was—I just didn't know it yet.

So if the math added up correctly, marrying me off to Drew was no longer on the table.

"It isn't something we've discussed." Heck, until tonight, I hadn't realized Josh thought of me as his girlfriend.

But now wasn't the time to mention that.

"Right now we're seeing how things go. Getting used to the idea of being parents. Figuring this all out—the parenting thing, that is." Figuring out how to balance our careers, our relationship, and our son.

"So you're just going to be an unwed mother?" The way she said it, you'd have thought I had announced I was quitting my job, becoming a hippie, and starting a marijuana and pumpkin farm.

"I guess so. But given that the idea disgusts you, it looks like we have nothing more to say. Good-bye, Mum." I ended the call.

Well, I guess that's that.

Blinking back my darn hormonal tears, I spread my hand across my belly. "Don't worry, Noah," I said in the same sweet tone you used with young children, "I'll find you someone even better to be your grandmother."

Maybe I could rent one at Grannies-R-Us.

Too bad such a place didn't exist.

But I bet there were a few elderly women who hung out at a senior center who would love to apply for the job.

Me to Chris: It's now official. I'm a member of the black-sheep club. I told Mum about the baby.

Chris: Welcome to the group and an endless supply of chocolate milk and cookies.

I half sniffed, half laughed. Chris always knew how to make me laugh.

Me: Just what the OB ordered :)

Chris: Will you be okay?

I sniffed again.

Me: I think so.

A moment later my phone rang and I answered it.

No, it wasn't my mother apologizing for being a bitch. It was Chris.

We talked for a while. But not about Noah or Josh or my new black-sheep status. Instead he told me about his last flying job and about the crazy old man he and his co-pilot had to rescue in the outback.

"I swear to God it's true," Chris said as I giggled. "We show up and the guy is dancing around bare-arse naked, claiming he's getting in touch with mother earth and doesn't need rescuing."

I glanced up and spotted Josh striding toward me, his forehead a worried frown. "Josh is here now," I told Chris. Josh had texted while I was talking to my brother and I'd told him where I was.

Did he know about what happened with my mum?

No—I didn't wish to spoil his fun. I'd told him I needed to talk to Chris for a few minutes.

But one look at me and he realized something was wrong.

Chris and I ended our call as Josh sat next to me on the bench.

"What's going on?" he asked.

I was about to reassure him that everything was okay—but my hormones decided they were bored.

So instead of smiling reassuringly at him...I burst into tears.

Have you ever attempted a conversation while sobbing?

It was darn near impossible. All I could do was nod while my words sounded like a foreign language no one else knew.

In the end, Josh enveloped me in his arms and let me cry on his shoulder.

Before I managed to flood the place, the sobbing eventually slowed to a hiccup, and I told Josh about the phone call with my mum.

"I'm sorry," I said, pulling away. "I didn't mean to take you away from your teammates and then cry all over you."

"Hey, that's okay, Hot Stuff. And no matter what you might think, you're not alone. You've got me and your brothers. And you've got Trent, Kelsey, and Erin. You've got a lot of people who care about you."

I sniffed and nodded. "I know."

Besides, my parents hadn't been there for me for years. Why mess with tradition?

"You ready to go back to your apartment?" Josh asked.

"Definitely."

Before I terrified some poor little kid—because red hair, makeup, and heavy crying equaled one scary looking clown.

21

HOLLY

I was officially twenty-eight weeks pregnant—and in my third and final trimester.

Go me!

So far things were going great. My sex drive hadn't changed. I was still a sexed-up maniac. Josh just had to look at me and I was ready to jump his bones.

The man was a real trooper. Not once did he complain.

I exited my car in the mall parking lot as a text came through on my phone. I still had a few minutes before meeting up with Kelsey and Erin for lunch and shopping.

> Josh: How's the sexiest momma around doing?

Josh and his team were away on a road trip. A *very* long road trip—according to my libido. Apparently, no one in the NHL scheduling department cared that I was super-horny.

How considerate of them.

> Me: I take it you mean me?

Josh: Of course. Who else? So, what are you wearing?

I glanced at my forest-green maternity top, which hugged my body in the right places, and my maternity jeans.

Me: My black lacy bra and matching panties.

Hey, that was partly true. I *was* wearing them.

Josh: What else?

Me: A smile. Should I be wearing anything else? Where are you?

Josh: Just landed at Calgary airport. Waiting for the plane to arrive at the gate. But never mind that. Let's get back to what you're wearing…

Me: Guess this is your way of saying you aren't sitting on your hotel bed, alone, in nothing but your briefs.

Josh: Yep, that would be correct. But you can imagine it if it makes you feel better.

I ran my hand over my stomach and leaned back against my car.

Me: That would make me feel better.

That was a complete and utter lie. With that image now in my head, all it did was make me hornier than before…if that was at all possible.

> Me: I miss you. I miss taking you in my hand and stroking down your length…long and hard.

I giggled as I imagined him groaning at my words.

> Me: And as I do that, I'm thinking about putting my lips over the tip and sucking you until you can't hold back anymore.

I had meant to leave him all hot and bothered, but all I accomplished was to do that to myself. *Brilliant.*

Did I believe Josh hadn't been affected? Hell no. The man was as horny as they came. Which had been a huge positive for me.

> Josh: You're killing me, Hot Stuff. You do realize that, right?

I grinned.

> Me: You're welcome, Cool Stuff :)

> Josh: We have to disembark now. Will talk to you soon.

> Me: Okay. And good luck tonight. Noah and I will be watching the game.

Technically, it wasn't true. But at least Noah would hear me get excited whenever Josh was on the ice—or whenever the camera flashed to him sitting on the bench.

Before I had a chance to put my phone in my purse, it rang. *Dad?*

The last time I'd talked to him was a few weeks before I told Mum that I was pregnant.

I accepted the call. "G'day, Dad."

"Don't you mean Granddad?" Unlike Mum, he didn't seem upset about it. "Although personally, I don't think I look old enough to be a grandfather."

I laughed. Dad's hair had been gray for a number of years. It was Mum who looked too young to be a grandmother—thanks to her hair colorist.

"You're right, Dad. You look too young to be a grandfather.... So, I'm guessing Mum's still angry about my news."

"You might say that. But I'm sure she'll eventually come around."

"Sure, maybe when Noah is in college," I muttered.

"I wanted to make sure you're all right," he said, either not hearing me or choosing to ignore what I'd said, "and suggest that maybe you should consider moving back here."

"Why would I do that?"

"Because you're going to be a single mother. Wouldn't it be better to do that here, where we can help you out? I mean, your mum and I know all about being parents."

Good thing I hadn't been eating when he'd said that. I might have choked.

Any suggestions who we could nominate for the Most Delusional Parent Of The Year award?

"Thanks for the offer," I said, "but I like it here and I have a great job." Not to mention Noah's daddy lived here and not in Sydney.

"Just thought I'd suggest it. Well, I've got to get back to work. If you need anything, let me know, otherwise I'll talk to you soon." Before I could say anything, he ended the call.

Surprised at the short duration?

Don't be. Normally they were even shorter than that, usually due to a meeting he had to rush off to.

Kelsey and Erin were waiting to be seated when I arrived at the restaurant a few minutes later. Three-month-old Samantha was asleep in the infant seat next to Erin's feet.

"How's it going?" Kelsey asked as she and I hugged.

And yes—Kelsey had agreed to be my backup labor coach if Noah decided to come into the world while his daddy was away.

"We're still doing great." Minus the part where I needed to go to the loo every five minutes—especially when Noah found it particularly amusing to use my bladder as a hockey puck.

Speaking of which…

"I'll meet you at the table. I need to go to the bathroom." I didn't even wait for their reply. I hurried off in the direction I was well acquainted with.

Once finished there, I walked out of the washroom and collided with a tall, hard body coming toward the men's room.

"Sorry," I said, stumbling back while doing my best not to fall on my arse.

Which meant grabbing the closest thing to me—the man's arm.

"Holly?" a surprised Aussie accent said.

My head jerked up and I blinked—while trying to recall if *What To Expect* warned of possible delusions during pregnancy. Possible delusions that looked especially hot in a dark gray suit. "Drew? What are you doing here?"

"The company sent me. We're examining expansion opportunities in the U.S." His gaze dropped to my belly, but if he was surprised that I was pregnant, he didn't show it.

But maybe he wasn't surprised. My pregnancy was hardly a national state secret—especially where Simon's loose lips were concerned.

"Why didn't you tell me you were coming?" I asked, smiling.

Was I happy to see him? Yes—now that Mum had given up trying to marry us off to each other.

Thank you, Noah, for putting a wrench in that plan.

Whatever you want once you're born, it's yours.

"I was planning to contact you once I arrived," Drew said. "I just haven't had a chance yet."

"Well consider me contacted. How long are you here for?"

"Just until tomorrow night this time. But I'll be back next month and will be staying till the end of January. The company rented an apartment for me."

"Nice. Are you here with someone?" I indicated to the restaurant.

"Just a business associate. Who I guess I should get back to. But I would love to get together with you for dinner next month."

"That would be great. I'm sure Josh would like to see you again." All right, maybe that was a bit of a stretch. More like amused.

Thanks to Mum, Drew had my number—which she must have given him prior to my little announcement. I entered his into my phone.

"Holy smoking hot male," Erin said as I rejoined the girls at our table. She and Kelsey had had a bird's eye view of my run-in with Drew. "Who was he, and why were you exchanging numbers with him?"

"That's Drew."

That was all I needed to say. They knew all about him. Did they also know about what had happened between my mum and me?

Yes. Erin had decided her parents would adopt me like they had unofficially adopted Kelsey and her brother when their parents died.

She was kidding of course—about all of it.

But it was the thought that counted.

"Is there something wrong with him?" Erin asked, eyes wide, as if she was expecting me to announce he was an ax murderer—of chocolate bunnies.

I laughed. The women at the next table winced. "There's

nothing wrong with him. Not as far as I know. I was just never interested. That's all." Of course, back then he hadn't looked like he belonged on the cover of GQ.

"So you're planning to get together with him to reminisce?" Erin asked.

I chuckled. "You make me sound old. And sure, why not? It's not like we're going out on a date. I'm currently with Josh."

As you might have guessed from the sexts, we were still boyfriend-slash-girlfriend. Other than when the team was away on a road trip, he and I slept together. Every. Single. Night. Surprised? Don't be. I'd given him a key to my apartment last month so he could join me in my bed after his home games. Usually I was asleep by then, but I was always happy for him to cuddle me awake.

What's the best way to deal with an adrenaline overload?

Hot. Steamy. Sex. Lots of it.

And I had to say the sacrifice on my part was well worth it.

But that was as far as things had progressed between us. There had been no discussion of moving in together once Noah was born. I had even tried bringing it up once—but when he began acting like someone who had sat naked on a red ants' nest, I'd dropped it.

So why couldn't I go out with Drew—as a friend?

It wasn't like I was cheating on Josh—which I would never do.

"When did you and Josh want to do the prenatal photos?" Kelsey asked after the waiter had taken our order. The pictures she had taken of a pregnant Erin and Erin's husband were gorgeous.

I removed my phone from my purse to check the Rock's schedule and came up with three possible dates next month that worked for Kelsey. I sent Josh a text.

He responded a minute later.

Josh: What are prenatal photos? Is that where you're naked?

I smirked. Josh had a thing about seeing me naked.

Me: Not necessarily. I was thinking something we wouldn't scar Noah for life with.

Josh: So with clothes on?

Me: Yes, the clothes stay on.

Josh: Can they come off afterward?

Me: Once we're alone—yes.

Josh: Can't wait!

He told me which dates worked best for him, then a moment later sent another text.

Josh: And you know what else I can't wait for?

Me: Watching me eat crackers and ice cream?

Don't ask—I had abandoned fries and ice cream months ago. It took forever for Josh to quit laughing at me every time I scooped the crackers into the ice cream. Which, I might add, required talent to do without breaking them in half.

Josh: Seeing you naked. Making you come. Being inside you.

The ache between my legs seconded that, temporarily forgetting none of this would happen for three more days.

Me: Make that two of us :)

"What are you up to?" Erin asked, laughter in her tone. "Sending sexts to Josh?"

My face played traitor and both Erin and Kelsey laughed. "Are you telling me you two don't send sexts to Darren and Trent?"

Erin scowled at Kelsey. "Don't even answer that question."

Kelsey laughed. Trent—the love of Kelsey's life—was Erin's brother.

But Kelsey didn't have to answer. Her eyes and light blush gave it away.

Then a moment later, the blush deepened when her phone chimed and she read the text.

And while she typed her reply, I counted down the minutes until Josh was home again, doing to me exactly as he had promised.

Anyone know how to speed up time?

22

JOSH

"Can you explain again why I agreed to this?" Trent said, grunting under the weight of the desk.

Confused?

Let me rewind for a moment. A few weeks ago, I came home from my road trip to a surprise. No, not the one where Holly was in nothing but my favorite black lacy bra and matching panties—although she had been wearing them at the time.

This surprise was six-foot tall, one hundred ninety pounds of muscle, with an Aussie accent. That's correct. Wilfred the fucking Third had shown up in San Francisco, and Holly had agreed to get together with him for dinner while I was in Vancouver next week.

Before you think I was an idiot, let me first clarify something about men. Even when we aren't jealous—we're jealous. It's part of the caveman gene you can thank our ancestors for. So even though I knew nothing was going on between Holly and Drew, that didn't stop the jealous streak from body-checking me.

What did this all have to do with Trent and the desk? Well,

I'm getting to that.

A few weekends ago, Holly and I had gone baby-furniture shopping. We didn't buy anything in the end because she wanted to paint the room first.

So while the girls were enjoying a relaxing weekend of spa treatments (all arranged by me...and maybe Trent helped a little), Trent, Travis, and I were moving the furniture from the spare room, cramming it into Holly's storage locker, and painting the room.

And not just painting the room a solid color.

This was where Travis came in. While flipping through the baby magazines Erin had lent her, Holly had come across a design perfect for Noah's room. The walls had been painted gray with two small eucalyptus trees on either side of the crib, leaning toward each other. Near the top of each tree was a cute koala bear. Neither Trent nor I could paint the design—but Travis could.

Now, some guys might go all caveman when they believe another man's encroaching on their woman—even if he isn't. Remember what I said about the jealousy gene? And maybe another time I would have done that too, but I also knew that wouldn't impress Holly.

If anything, it would piss her off.

So instead of being an asshole caveman, I'd decided to surprise her with the early Christmas present of the spa weekend and her dream baby room. The white furniture was sitting in the living room, still in its boxes, waiting for it to be assembled. Which was exactly what Trent and I would be doing while Travis painted the trees and koalas.

Impressed? I thought so.

"You agreed to help me because you're a great guy that way —and you know I'm right. Kelsey will think you're the best boyfriend ever for giving her this weekend, and you'll get the best sex of your life tomorrow night."

Here's some free advice, ladies. Men will do anything for great sex. Want me to repeat that in case you missed it the first time? Nothing motived a guy more than the promise of sex so awe-fucking-inspiring, he would be seeing stars for a week.

"Hey," Travis said, "I don't get any sex out of this deal."

I raised an eyebrow, partly because of his comment—and partly because while Trent and I were carrying the heavy desk, he was carrying a box containing the contents of said desk. "It's not like you have any issues getting laid," I huffed.

He smiled an evil grin. "Are you saying you two men, who have girlfriends, have issues getting action between the sheets?"

"I don't have issues getting laid," Trent grumbled as we squeezed the desk through the doorway. "And sex with Kelsey is already great."

"Then you're doing this because Holly is your friend, and you want to make your friend happy," I pointed out—swooping in for the overtime win.

Several hours later, the furniture in the spare room had been relocated, and the two coats of paint had been applied.

I surveyed the result, making sure there was nothing that needed fixing or redoing. The three of us were standing in the room, beer in hand. Pizza was on the way. Even though Holly wasn't here, I planned to spend the night in her apartment, to get an early start on the decorating.

"So, what exactly is the deal between you and Holly anyway?" Travis asked.

"She's the mother of my unborn child and my girlfriend." No new revelation there.

"I get that. But you two will be parents soon, and you're still living on the other side of the city, with no interest in giving up your apartment."

As Holly had mentioned a few weeks ago—although a lot more subtly than Travis. He was more like the bull in the china shop. The bull who'd had his nuts kicked.

"I happen to like my apartment." Even if I didn't spend much of my time there these days.

Truth? Knowing I still had my apartment was a safety net. A way to keep my heart safe. I'd already been let down by two people who were supposed to love and protect me, and they had walked away. At least this way I had a place to go if that ever happened again—just replace my parents with Holly.

"I agree. It's a great apartment. But that's not my point."

"What is your point?"

He exchanged looks with Trent as if to say, "Hey man, you're the one with the girlfriend. You explain the problem."

"What are your plans for the future?" Trent asked. "Your contract ends in July and then you're a free agent. What does that mean for you and Holly and Noah?"

And there you had it. Trent stating the piece of reality I'd been trying to ignore for the past few months. I wish I had a crystal ball to know what would happen come summer. Hell, I wish I had a crystal ball to tell me what would happen come trade deadlines at the end of February...the same time Noah was due.

Did players get traded near the end of their contracts? Definitely. Especially if the team's star players' contracts were also up for renewal. Especially if the team's organization no longer saw a place for the player on the team.

I'd already been there once before, prior to signing with the Rock.

All a player could do was suck it up. Be a man. And move to the team that did want him—at least for the time being.

Which meant I had no idea what the future held for me when it came to my hockey career, Holly, and Noah. I had no idea where I could end up if I was traded. Would Holly even want to join me if it happened? She had a career here that she loved.

These were all questions the two of us had avoided discussing, always focused on the here and now.

"You do know she's not a permanent U.S. resident, right?" Trent said. "She can only work here because of her job with Bristol Mathews. If she leaves it, then her work visa will be revoked, as will her green-card application. And if either of those things happens, she can't work or stay in the country."

The first night Holly and I had fucked, she mentioned she didn't have a green card and could be deported at any time. But as far as I knew, only criminals got kicked out of the country, and Holly wasn't a criminal.

"And if she can't stay in the country..." Trent left that hanging, but I knew what he meant. If she couldn't stay in the country, it meant losing my son.

It meant losing her.

Just the thought of that was like being the bull who'd had his balls kicked in the china shop.

"You know what that means, don't you?" Travis said. "You have to marry her."

I stared at him, unblinking. I cared a lot for Holly, but I wasn't the marrying kind. Hell, I wasn't even the commitment kind of man.

What if I fucked it all up like my old man?

And what if she goes back to Australia and marries Wilfred the Third?

A part of me, the selfish part, figured it was a great idea. I didn't need a kid. I'd never wanted to be a father to begin with.

But another part of me, the larger part, didn't want to lose my son.

"Shit," was all I could say.

"I think it's time you and Holly talk about what you plan to do," Trent said. "You're both my friends and I don't want to see either of you hurt. But if you continue living in denial, someone *will* get hurt."

And when it came down to it, he would whip *my* ass if I ended up hurting her.

Christ, if that happened, I'd whip my own ass.

"You're right," I said on a sigh.

"Right about which part?" Travis asked. "That I get to be your ring bearer—or you two need to talk?"

The corner of my mouth quirked up to one side. "I was thinking you'd do a better job as a flower girl."

"Well as long as I'm the flower girl and not the groom. Not that there's anything wrong with Holly, mind you. She's gorgeous as sin, even with your love child in her belly."

"You better believe she's gorgeous as sin. And my son only makes her that much more gorgeous. My seed is *that* powerful."

Trent snorted. "You better not let that secret out. Or else you'll have lines of women outside your door, begging for some of that powerful seed. And Holly might not appreciate it."

He was right about that.

Trent and I tidied up the paint cans while Travis sketched the mural on the wall.

"At least once your hockey career is over," I said, grinning at the defenseman, "you've got a new career painting murals in kids' rooms." Which was a shitload more than I could say about my own post-hockey career options.

Here's the thing about pro athletes. Most of our childhood was spent dreaming of one day going pro—like the players we idolized. Some of us went to college to get a degree, but even then, we weren't thinking about a future beyond hockey. Even in college, I had been more focused on playing and impressing the scouts than thinking about what my degree would mean for my future.

What was my degree? History—with a specialty in European history and a minor in marketing.

Not exactly a degree high in demand, but I'd always loved history.

What did I plan to do once I eventually retired?

Not a single fucking clue.

My phone pinged and I checked the text.

Holly: Miss me? :)

I did—but that was nothing new. I'd gotten used to sleeping with her when I wasn't away on road trips. But this was different. I missed just being with her and talking to her and touching her.

Only I didn't mean in the I-want-to-have-sex-with-you-now kind of way.

I meant in the I-can't-believe-you're-having-my-baby kind of way. The miracle-of-life kind of way.

But this wasn't what I told her.

Me: Definitely. Hanging out with Trent isn't the same thing as hanging out with you. For one, he doesn't look as hot in a black lacy bra and panties.

Me: And in case you're wondering, he doesn't look hot in the red ones either.

Me: But don't tell Kelsey or else she'll want to dump his sorry ass.

Holly: Ha! I'm positive Kelsey already knows he isn't hot in anything but his underwear.

Holly: I mean other than when he's out of them ;)

Did her saying that bother me—in that jealous caveman way? A little. But don't blame me. Blame our caveman ancestors. On the other hand, I knew nothing had ever happened between Holly and Trent. Trent would never have crossed that professional line.

> Me: How is girls' weekend going?

> Holly: I now have pretty toenails. And every single part of me is in happy heaven. I think I'm in love

My breath stalled in my chest at the last part. Did she mean with me?

And more importantly, if she meant me...how did I feel about it?

Before I could further examine this unsettling—yet not completely unsettling—thought, another text came through.

> Holly: Sorry, dropped my phone. I think I'm in love with my massage therapist. In the most platonic sense, mind you.

> Me: Remind me to give you massages ;)

> Holly: I will! Thank you so much for this! XOX

> Me: You're welcome. Enjoy! See you tomorrow.

"How does this look?" Travis said, standing next to the stepladder. On the wall was an outline, drawn in pencil, of the design that looked like the one from the magazine.

"It's perfect." And it was.

An excited thrill skated through me at how much Holly would love it.

Maybe more than she loved the massage therapist.

Two points for me.

And zero points for Wilfred the Third.

23

HOLLY

How many of you believe spending a weekend being pampered at a spa resort is relaxing? I mean, how could it not be—between the massages, the manis and pedis, the yoga, the facials?

But by the time Kelsey and I finally left the Wine Valley Resort early Sunday evening, I was ready to crawl into bed and sleep for the next month. Every time we had been about to leave, Kelsey checked her phone, then came up with something else for us to do.

But I couldn't complain—it had been a lot of fun.

And I knew exactly how to thank Josh for the weekend— once I'd recovered from my exhaustion.

As Kelsey drove us back to San Francisco, I held the envelope with the prenatal photos she had taken last week.

Did you want to see them? You might want to grab a box of tissues first—or maybe that was just me. Those out-of-control hormones still loved playing the game *Let's Make Holly Cry*.

Fifty points if I cried in public.

The first photo was black and white with me sitting on the

park bench. My butt was near the front of the seat, a slight curve to my lower back, which accentuated the baby bump. My favorite part? Josh had been standing behind the bench and was kissing me on the lips. There was something sweet yet possessive about the photo.

And hello...hotness factor.

The second photo? Josh and I were both standing, with Josh behind me again. Our hands cradled my baby bump from above and below. It was both tender and sweet...and made my heart ache at how much we looked like a family. Even if Noah hadn't been born yet.

"So," Kelsey began, her focus on the road as she drove, "have you and Josh decided yet what will happen once Noah is born? Will Josh live with you two?"

I shook my head, even though she couldn't see me, and flipped on my happy, optimistic voice. "He's not giving up his apartment, but that's probably a good thing." Yeah, I know. I hadn't exactly answered her question. Did you think she noticed?

Okay, she might not have noticed if I hadn't followed that with, "There are so many unknowns about our future—there's no point in me getting too attached to him."

Brilliant. Really smooth going, Hols.

"What do you mean?"

Well, since the kangaroo was out of the knapsack...

"For starters, what happens if he's traded? I can't go with him. I'd lose my job."

"But you'd get a new one."

I let out a small laugh. *Oops.* Apparently, I forgot to turn on my casual, happy-go-lucky mode. "It's not that easy. For one, I don't have my green card yet. If I lose my job or leave it, it's back to Australia I go."

"Does Josh know this?"

I might have mentioned it once—before I got pregnant. I

vaguely remembered that conversation from the night we got drunk—but I wasn't one hundred percent certain it happened. "We haven't discussed it, so I have no idea."

But given his team wasn't purely American born, he must've known I needed a work visa to stay in the country—even if he didn't know the specifics when it came to the immigration laws.

Kelsey shot me a side-glance. "Why haven't you discussed it? Maybe he can do something about it."

"Like what? Marry me? It's either that or I find a new job that will sponsor my green-card application. But it's not that simple."

"So Josh just has to marry you and you'd get to stay? That doesn't sound too bad."

"Sure, except for two problems. First, this is all assuming he'd want to marry me. He's always made it clear he's not the marrying type."

"What's the second problem?"

I looked down at my belly. "When and if I get married, it will be because the man loves me. It's not so I can stay in the country." If I had wished to marry for convenience, I would've married Drew like Mum wanted.

"But then Josh won't get to see his son," Kelsey said.

Now if only *What To Expect When You're Expecting* covered this....Heck, if only any of the pregnancy and parenting books I'd bought covered it. Wanted to know what a birth plan was or the pros and cons of an epidural? The books had you covered. Wanted to know how to make your life sound less like a reality show? Then you were royally screwed.

"I know—but so far none of this is an issue. I love my job and it will still be there when I return from maternity leave. And going on mat leave doesn't cancel my work visa. So for now, I can stay in the country."

Kelsey was quiet for a few minutes, so I figured the conversation was over. I checked my phone to see if Josh had texted me.

Josh: Drive safe!

"You love him, don't you?" she asked softly as I replied to his text.

"Unfortunately. Yes."

"Unfortunately?"

"Unrequited love always sucks the big one."

She chewed her lip for a second, still watching the road. "That's true. But I don't think in this case it is unrequited. He loves you too. He just doesn't realize it yet."

"Even better. Now I just have to hope he figures out he's *possibly* in love with me before it's too late."

Did Kelsey miss the sarcasm? Yeah, I didn't think so either.

By the time we arrived in San Francisco, I could barely keep my eyes open. I hadn't heard from Josh since we left the resort, so I figured I wouldn't get to see him tonight.

Or for the next four days—while he was away on another road trip.

Kelsey pulled up in front of my Victorian-style building.

And I blinked.

Josh was sitting on the steps. Waiting for me.

Even though he had a key to my apartment.

"He didn't want you to have to carry your bag upstairs," Kelsey explained.

My eyes must have grown as large as the full moon. "You knew he was here?"

She nodded. "I called him during your last bathroom break and gave him our ETA."

After I thanked Kelsey for the ride and the fun weekend away, Josh helped me from the car and grabbed my bag from the trunk. The man was buzzing with an energy that was hard to figure out. It was like he was both excited and nervous at the same time—not your typical Josh.

He threaded his fingers with mine and led me upstairs to my apartment. Once inside, he nodded at the spare room. Noah's room—once I got around to setting it up. Another thing on my to-do list for while he was away.

Curious as to what was going on, I walked into Noah's room and flipped on the light switch.

My breath? Completely stalled in my chest.

The room looked exactly like the one I had recently seen in a maternity magazine—including the adorable koala mural on the wall behind the crib. The crib, changing table, and drawers were white as was the thick rug on the hardwood floor. There was even a stuffed koala, sitting in the corner of the crib.

Speechless, I glanced at Josh.

He rubbed the back of his neck, and for the first time since I'd known him, he appeared uncertain. Vulnerable. "Do you like it?"

"You did this?" I asked, my voice soft, as I blinked back the tears that had nothing to do with my hormones.

"With Trent and Travis's help. Travis painted the mural."

"He paints?"

"Apparently. Do you like it?"

I turned around and flung my arms around his neck. "I love it! It's perfect!" There might have also been kissing involved. The deep kind. The kind that woke up all my girlie parts from their nap.

I don't know how long we'd been kissing—a few minutes, a few hours—before I finally pulled away. "And I know Noah will love it too."

As if agreeing with me, the baby in question kicked me in the side. I grabbed Josh's hand and positioned it on the spot. Noah did it again. That brought a big smile to Josh's face. He never got tired of feeling his son kick.

"I know you worry that you'll be like your father," I told Josh, "but you'll never be like him. He would never have done something so sweet and wonderful."

The smile spreading on Josh's face? It was enough to power the entire San Francisco Bay area and Sausalito during a power outage.

I reached up and kissed him, a brief brushing of lips. "And thank you for the weekend. I'm guessing that was so you could do this?"

My gaze fell on the single bookshelf—and two classic model cars on the middle shelf.

Josh had decorated the room to reflect Noah's parents. Except one thing was missing...

"Why isn't there anything to do with hockey in here?" I asked.

"Because it didn't feel right. My father practically shoved hockey down my throat to the point where I resented the sport. It didn't feel right to do the same to Noah. If he wants hockey stuff in his room, then great. But that will be his choice."

Did you feel it? The ground trembling? That was me falling completely and utterly and irreversibly in love with him.

I bit my lip, to keep the words from tumbling out. I didn't want to scare him away, and I was positive the L-word would do exactly that.

"How can he not love the sport?" I asked. "He and I will be at all your games, cheering you on, showing you how proud we are of you."

Noah kicked in agreement and I smiled.

For a second, I thought I saw love in Josh's eyes and my pulse picked up, pounding in my ears. But then the love disappeared as quickly as it had come.

My hormones and I really needed to have a heart-to-heart. The last thing my poor fragile heart asked for was to imagine things that weren't true.

Josh bent closer, his breath a kiss against my ear. "So, about my favorite black bra and panties..."

And suddenly I forgot how tired I had been.

Sex when your boyfriend is the sweetest man alive?

Best sex.

Ever.

24

HOLLY

Josh smiled at me, the Christmas tree lights glowing softly on his face. Did I mention he was shirtless?

And wearing only his briefs?

Then he got down on one knee.

Beep. Beep. Beep. Beep.

Mentally cursing the bloody clock, my eyes still closed, I slammed my hand around my nightstand...until I murdered the noise.

And since it had prematurely ended the dream, I considered murdering the clock too.

I pushed myself out of bed—not that my body agreed with that thanks to my cold that had begun the other day. But it didn't matter what my body wanted. I had to go into work for a few hours before I was officially off for the next three days.

Why wasn't I spending Christmas with my family in Australia? I mean, ignoring the part about my mum being mad at me. Flying that far when you were thirty-three weeks pregnant was never a good idea. Instead, I would be spending Christmas dinner with Trent and Erin's family. And yes, Kelsey would be there too, which was an added bonus.

Where was Josh going to be? He was flying to Connecticut in a few hours to spend Christmas with his grandparents.

I swear by the time I was finished showering, there was barely any hot water left. On the bright side, I was temporarily able to breathe again because of the steam. Always an added bonus.

I changed into my clothes and groaned as I caught sight of myself in the mirror. My skin was pale, but my nose still looked like it could've guided Santa's sleigh tonight—if Rudolf hadn't already signed up for the job.

The worst part? I wasn't allowed to take anything to make me feel better. All medications were off limits. So I did the only thing I could—I put on my makeup and hoped I didn't look as bad as I felt.

But it didn't take long to realize that plan had been a big pregnant bust.

"Why on earth are you working today?" Gladys asked as I walked into the Bristol Mathews reception area. She was our five-years-past-retirement-age receptionist who we couldn't live without.

"I didn't take the day off." It sounded like a good answer to me.

"But, hun, you're sick, and you need to rest up for the baby." Did I mention Gladys had six kids—and a hockey team's worth of grandchildren?

"It's only a half day, so I'm sure I'll be fine." At least that was what I said in my head. It didn't quite come out that way thanks to my merry-crap-tastic congestion.

"Well make sure you drink plenty of fluids."

Right. Because on top of my agenda for the day was to spend most of the morning peeing in the loo. "I'll be sure to do that," I said with as much of a smile as I could muster.

Thirty minutes later, Trent strolled into my office—interrupting my delightful morning of attempting to read a business report between the frequent rounds of nose blowing.

"Shit, Holly. You look awful."

"It's a goddamn miracle you have a girlfriend, mate—what with the way you sweep a girl off her feet."

His mouth jerked up to one side. "Has anyone ever told you you're cranky when you're sick? Because if they haven't, let me be the first...." Risking his life, he sat down on the other side of the desk. "Besides, the last I heard, I wasn't the one who swept you off your feet. And while we're at it, I do plenty of feet sweeping when it comes to Kelsey."

That I didn't doubt.

"But you shouldn't be here," he continued. "You should be at home, resting."

I snorted. "Now you sound like Gladys."

"That's because Gladys and I are brilliant—and you know it."

I rolled my eyes, mostly because it was true but I didn't want to admit it. "I'll be fine. It's only a half day, and then I'll go home and rest up for tomorrow....But maybe I shouldn't go to your parents' tomorrow. I don't want to risk Samantha getting sick." And I was sure Erin and Samantha would appreciate it too.

"But it's Christmas. You can't spend tomorrow on your own. That's just not right."

"I won't be alone," I said.

A puzzled frown creased his forehead. "You won't be? I thought Josh was flying to Boston today."

"He is. But Julie Andrews is available anytime I need her. And what better way to spend Christmas than with a Julie Andrews movie marathon?"

"Sounds like fun," he said with a smirk.

"It will be—and you're just jealous you're missing out on it."

He threw back his head in laughter. "Okay, you keep telling

yourself that. But remember, the offer is still open for tomorrow. We'll just make sure Sammy is in a hazmat suit."

"And I'm sure she'll look adorable in it." Was the sarcasm noticeable even with my stuffy nose?

Soon after Trent left my office, my phone pinged with a text.

Josh: How's the sexy momma doing today?

Me: Ha! Not looking too sexy right now. You're definitely not missing out on anything. Have a good flight!

Josh: You shouldn't be at work. You should be at home, looking after yourself.

How did he know I was at work? Oh, yeah, where else would I be?

Me: I'll be home soon enough. Then Julie Andrews and I have a hot date planned for tonight and tomorrow. It's going to be epic.

Josh: Sounds it.

Me: I know. Aren't you sorry you'll be missing out? lol

A knock at my open door jerked my attention away from my phone. I returned it to my desk as I said, "Come in," to Gladys.

She entered carrying a mug. "I made you a warm drink with lemon juice and honey. It's safe for the baby, and it will help with the cough and congestion."

"Thank you," I said, glad for anything that made me feel even the tiniest bit better.

I took the mug from her and sipped the heated drink.

She handed me a piece of paper. "This is the recipe. You

should drink it throughout the day. It will also help to keep you hydrated. Very important for fighting a cold."

"Thanks." And a trip to the grocery store after work was now on the agenda.

She left me with my drink, my report, and my thoughts. My pesky thoughts about how much I missed Josh. I hadn't seen him since Sunday, four days ago. The team had been away on a pre-Christmas road trip.

The good news? They weren't scheduled for any more until the new year.

The not-so-good news? Josh would be in Boston until December twenty-seventh.

But if I was lucky, by the time he returned my cold would have vanished and I could give him his Christmas present.

In the new black lacy slip that was practically see through.

Even Santa's elf couldn't top that.

"Okay," Trent said, barging into my office a few minutes past noon. "You've been here long enough. Time to go home. And if you don't leave now, I'll drag you home kicking and screaming if I have to."

Noah kicked in agreement. *Traitor.*

I released a long breath—which when you were thirty-three weeks pregnant wasn't as long as you would like. "All right. You win. Just give me a few minutes and I'll go willingly. No kicking or screaming required. And you won't need to drag me home either. I'll drive myself."

"Five minutes. That's all I'm giving you."

I didn't need that much time in the end.

By the way—what's the worst time of the year to hit the grocery store?

Based on how crazy things were at the one I stopped at, you'd think everyone was getting ready for a zombie apocalypse.

I spent forty minutes in the store just to buy lemon juice and a container of honey. Oh, and there might have been a package of brownies and a new can of whipping cream in the basket too—for those three-o'clock-in-the-morning, emergency brownie cravings.

The latest food that I couldn't survive without.

As I stepped onto my floor in my apartment building, a faint yet delicious smell greeted me. The same smell, only a little stronger, also greeted me when I opened my apartment door.

People didn't break into apartments and take the time to cook the victim a meal before offing them, right?

Because someone was definitely in my kitchen.

Cooking.

"G'day?" I called out, still standing in the doorway. "Is someone here?"

A rapid heartbeat later, Josh stepped from the kitchen. Which did nothing for my heartbeat—except now it was beating fast for a different reason.

"Aren't you supposed to be on the plane to Boston?" I whispered as he walked toward me. He had to be a mirage. A cold-induced mirage.

"I changed my mind." He took my hand and led me to the living room.

"But why? I thought you were looking forward to seeing your grandparents."

He indicated for me to sit on the couch. "Do you really think I could go anywhere when you're so sick?"

"It's a cold, Josh—not the bubonic plague."

"Doesn't matter. You're supposed to be taking it easy for both yours and Noah's sake."

"I am taking it easy," I said through my stuffy nose. Then coughed a really sexy, phlegm-laden noise. "Not that I'm not happy to see you or anything"—because I was. More than he could ever imagine—"but aren't you worried about getting sick?"

"If I get sick, I'll deal with it. Anyway, I told my grandmother why I couldn't make it for Christmas. She was more concerned about you and her great-grandchild. So she emailed her chicken noodle soup recipe, which is bound to help you feel 'right as rain' in no time. Her words, not mine."

I laughed, which probably sounded worse than it normally did, then covered my mouth. Sparing him from the agony of listening to it. "Sorry."

"For what?"

"For laughing. I know it's kind of a turnoff." Which was why I couldn't believe he was still around. But if it weren't for the baby, he wouldn't be. He'd be busy with puck bunnies and whatever.

He didn't laugh or smirk. He smiled as though I was being funny. "I don't know what you're talking about. I think your laugh is cute."

I made a funny noise—which under any other circumstance that didn't involve a cold would be a snorted laugh. "If I wasn't already highly acquainted with your singing voice, I'd say you're tone-deaf."

"Anyway," he said, ignoring me, "she emailed me the recipe for her famous chicken noodle soup, and I made you some. Stay here." He left me on the couch and returned a minute later carrying a tray with a bowl of the world's most delicious smelling soup. Even with my stuffy nose I could smell it.

He lowered the tray onto the coffee table and handed me the bowl and spoon. Careful not to burn myself, I sampled some. Did it taste as great as it smelled? No. It tasted to the nth power better.

"You're the best boyfriend ever."

"No, I'm the best boyfriend ever because I'm planning to stay and watch the Julie Andrews movie marathon with you."

He winked at me and left me on the couch, to return a short time later with his own bowl of soup, French bread, and an assortment of my favorite cheeses. He set them on the coffee table.

And that wasn't all.

He handed me a mug of something that looked suspiciously like the honey and lemon drink Gladys had made me. "Trent emailed me the recipe. He said the receptionist insisted I make it for you while you're sick."

"You braved the grocery store Christmas Eve day just for me?" I asked in my God-you're-so-sweet tone.

"Of course. So which movie are we watching first?"

"Have you ever seen *The Princess Diaries*?"

"Can't say I've had the pleasure," he said with a smirk, and I chuckled.

"Since it's already Christmas in Australia," I said, "I should call my family first."

Chris wasn't staying in Sydney over the holidays—being the family black sheep that he was. He and his single mates had gone to Brisbane.

I called him first.

"Merry Christmas, sis," he said. "And how's my favorite nephew doing?" His *only* nephew.

"He's doing great so far and kicking lots."

"Sounds like you have yourself a future football star, not a hockey player," he said.

Were he and Simon still calling Josh the Sperm Donor?

Not at all. That ended right after I joined Chris in the land of black sheep. If anything, my brothers tended to call him just to check up on me, and the three of them had become friends.

Would my brothers whip Josh's arse if he did anything to hurt me?

You'd better believe it. That much hadn't changed.

We chatted for a few minutes—until my congestion kicked

in and I could no longer talk. I handed Josh the phone, at Chris's request, and left to hit the loo.

Josh had finished talking to him by the time I returned. He didn't say anything about the call—just kissed me on the forehead and waited while I called Simon.

"Mum showed me Noah's ultrasound picture," Simon told me after we had been chatting for a few minutes. "As far as I can tell, he's gonna be quite the handsome little ankle biter. Definitely takes after his favorite uncle."

"She did?" I said, not really hearing what he had told me after the first part. Even though I knew what she thought about my pregnancy, I had sent her and Dad a copy of the ultrasound picture. On the back I had written, Noah wishes you a Merry Christmas!

I had included it with a Christmas card from me and Josh but figured she had probably ripped it up and tossed it in the trash.

"Yes," Simon said. "And I think she's coming around. About the baby, I mean."

That was hard to believe.

"One of my colleagues is having a baby," he went on to say. "Or at least his wife is. And he said babies can hear voices from outside the mum's stomach."

"That's true."

"So can I talk to Noah?"

My eyebrows shot up my forehead. "You mean right now?"

"Yes, right now."

I hiked up my top, revealing my belly, increased the volume on the phone, and placed it near my belly button. "Okay, you can talk to Noah now."

"Hey, little mate," Simon said. "I'm your super-cool Uncle Simon. I know you'll probably think Chris is cooler because he can fly helicopters—and I guess that *is* pretty cool, if heights don't scare you." Simon wasn't a fan of heights. "But I can teach you all kinds of things that Uncle Chris can't. Like surfing."

After he finished speaking to Noah, we talked for a short while longer, then ended the call.

Next up? Calling my parents.

But because talking to my brothers had taken so much out of me, Josh and I watched *The Princess Diaries* first.

Afterward, I did the one thing I'd been dreading the most for the past couple of days. I pulled Mum up from my contact list and tapped on Call.

Why Mum and not Dad?

Maybe because if I didn't phone her first, I'd chicken out.

"Holly?" Mum's voice sounded uncertain as she answered.

"I wanted to wish you and Dad a Merry Christmas." Hopefully she understood what I'd said. Thanks to my cold, even my brothers hadn't understood everything I'd told them.

Naturally, they thought it was funny.

"Merry Christmas to you." She still sounded uncertain. "How are you and Noah doing?"

Noah? Not the baby?

Did I know what to make of it? Had the Titanic been hit by an ice cube?

"We're doing fine. He's kicking a lot. I think he's just excited to see his bedroom, which Josh decorated for him." I smiled at my sweet and wonderful boyfriend next to me on the couch.

"So you're still with him—the football player?" Her tone was derision free. Another surprise.

"Hockey, Mum. Josh plays ice hockey."

"Right. Is that a yes?"

"Yes, that's a yes."

"Are you two getting married?" Again her tone was neutral.

Since I knew his opinion on the topic of marriage, I simply said, "No."

Truth? I would've had a better answer if my head wasn't about to explode from congestion.

Never a pleasant way to go.

Mom was silent for a moment before saying, "You know, if things don't work out between you two, you can always move back here. Then you'll have someone around to help you. Lots of someones. Me. Your brothers. Your father."

The surprising part? She actually sounded like she meant it.

"Thanks, but I really do love it here and I have a great job." And somehow, I would make everything work.

Feeling a sneeze steamrolling toward me, I grabbed a tissue just in time. "*Achoo!*"

And for a millisecond, my brain didn't feel so clogged.

Too bad the joyful sensation didn't last long.

"I've got to go now, Mum," I said, although I was positive I didn't have to tell her I was dying and wished to do so sooner rather than later. Preferably while watching *The Sound of Music*.

We said our good-byes, and I promised to keep her updated about Noah and me.

Disappointed? Were you expecting some grand gesture from my mum to mend the fractured bridges between us?

Fortunately, I knew her better than that. For her, everything she had said and the fact she had shown Simon the ultrasound was a grand gesture.

While I went to the loo again, Josh made dinner for us. What was on the menu?

More chicken noodle soup (because that was all I wanted to eat) and spaghetti and meatballs (mostly for Josh).

And for dessert?

You guessed it—brownies and whipped cream.

But not just any brownies. These came from Maggie's Bakery, which was well-known for their super-chocolaty brownies. They were easily the best brownies in the entire universe.

Boyfriend brownie points earned so far? Well, the dessert alone was worth at least two thousand. Between that, the soup, the Julie Andrews movie marathon, Josh staying in San Francisco instead of flying out east for Christmas, and what he did for Noah's room, he had enough points to last him a few years short of an eternity.

Not that I was about to tell him.

We ate dinner while watching *Mary Poppins*—because there was no better movie around to teach you about hiring a nanny.

By the time we were finished, I was surprised Josh hadn't left the apartment screaming from OD'ing on Miss Andrews. To make it up to him, I let him pick whatever he wanted to watch on Netflix.

At some point I fell asleep, my head on his shoulder—positive life couldn't get much better than this.

Eventually, my super-comfy pillow moved and I stirred awake.

"Hey, Merry Christmas," Josh said softly.

I peered through tired eyes at the DVD clock. Midnight.

Using Josh's arm as leverage, I pushed myself up to sit. "I'm sorry. I didn't mean to fall asleep. How long have I been sleeping for?"

"An hour and a half."

"You didn't watch any more Julie Andrews movies while I was sleeping, did you?" I said, with barely enough energy to give him a half smirk.

"No, I figured you'd kill me if I did."

"Damn straight I would."

Josh kissed my forehead. "All right, sleepyhead. Let's get you to bed." He started to move off the couch.

"Not yet. I want you to open your present from me."

Like a young kid on Christmas morning, his face brightened. "Well, considering it's Christmas in Australia, I can go for that."

Several presents sat under the tree, but there was one gift that hadn't been there before. A gift that was slightly larger than a ring box.

Josh removed the present and handed it to me. "Merry Christmas."

I shuffled over to the tree and picked up my present to Josh, my hand shaking slightly.

You know how some people love finding the perfect gift? That wasn't me.

Don't get me wrong. I loved giving presents. But the idea of trying to find the perfect gift left me longing to hibernate until Christmas was over.

Josh looked at me expectantly, and I carefully unwrapped the gift. Once the paper had been removed, I was left holding a velvet covered box.

Even though the box was slightly too big to be a ring, that didn't stop my heart from hammering Jingle Bells against my ribs—but at a much faster tempo.

I opened the box and gasped at the gorgeous silver butterfly necklace resting against the black velvet. The delicate wings were created with various swirls and scrolls.

"It's beautiful," I whispered. If I wasn't so sick, I would have shown him how much I loved it. "Thank you."

Was I disappointed it wasn't an engagement ring?

Maybe a little. The romantic side of me, which would've preferred to be married than be a single mom, had been hoping he would get down on his knee and propose. My practical side rolled its eyes at that.

I was in love with him, but I wasn't sure if he was in the same place. I didn't want to get married just because he believed it was the right thing to do for Noah.

"Your turn," I said, indicating at the gift in his hand.

He ripped off the wrapping and tossed it aside. Then his eyes went wide at the picture on the box.

A 1958 Chevy Impala model kit.

"The man in the store said it was challenging." It was Josh's preferred style of model—both challenging and a classic car.

"I love it. It's perfect. Everything's perfect...." He hugged me. "Now how about I get you to bed?" He kissed my cheek, his lips lingering there for a heartbeat.

Once we were in bed, he snuggled up to me. I was in that state between here and there, when you weren't sure if you were awake or already asleep. Where come morning, none of what happened during those few blissful moments would be remembered—or if it was, you were convinced it had been nothing more than a dream.

As exhaustion pulled me deeper, Josh murmured what might have possibly been, "I love you, Holly."

25

JOSH

Christmas Day was great—and not because Holly had moved from Julie Andrews to catching up on *Game of Thrones*.

Although let me point out that watching naked women on TV is a lesson in torture when the woman you're dying to have sex with is sick.

The kind of torture where you have to excuse yourself so you can jack off in the shower or else die from an excruciating case of blue balls. The guys on the show who were being slaughtered? They had it easier. Their deaths were at least quick.

New Year's Eve was the best too—especially since Holly had no longer felt as though she was dying from the plague.

So, let's flash-forward to the beginning of February...

Oh, you were wondering what happened the next morning after I'd blurted out "I love you" to Holly on Christmas Eve?

Nothing.

Abso-fucking-lutely nothing.

She never mentioned it the next day, so I wasn't sure if she had heard me when I said it. Or if she'd heard me but didn't feel the same way so was avoiding the topic.

I never said it again—possibly because a part of me feared she would tell me she loved me back, but once Noah was born, she'd feel differently about me. Right now her hormones were all over the place—so who knew what she was really feeling?

Okay, truthfully? I was a coward. Too many uncertainties existed when it came to our future together, and that scared the shit out of me.

And yes, I had meant it when I told her I loved her. Except it hadn't dawned on me until I'd blurted out the three simple words that I really did love her. I had just been too much of an idiot to realize I'd been falling in love with her for the past few months.

Anyway, back to the here and now—in the dressing room, getting ready for our game against the Penguins.

"Where's Jyri?" I asked Travis. Jyri was usually the first one here, stretching. The guy near the entrance to the shower area? The one doing the splits? That was our backup goalie, Matti.

Travis shrugged at my question. "No idea. I saw him not long ago, talking to coach Fusco."

"He's not injured, is he?" That was the only reason I could come up with for why he wasn't here yet.

"Not that I know of. He seemed fine during practice this morning."

The door opened and Fusco entered with a player who looked vaguely familiar and was in full goalie gear.

Oh, this wasn't good.

Not good at all.

My gaze slid to the other two members of HDF. They were thinking the same.

"All right," Fusco said. "There's been a change in the goalie lineup. As of an hour ago, Jyri has been traded to Detroit. Matti will be starting goalie and Jordan has been called up to join us.

All right, let's get out there." And that was all the time we got to grieve the departure of our teammate.

To grieve the loss of our most experienced member of HDF.

I mean, who was more experienced at being a daddy than the father of twin two-year-old boys?

The game was tough like we had expected. By the end of the third period, we were tied at 2-2. Which meant overtime.

Then this time tomorrow I'd get to see Holly—who was now thirty-eight weeks pregnant.

That's right—for those of you doing the math, she was due in two weeks...give or take a day or two.

How was I feeling?

Excited—and nervous as hell. Despite all the daddy-to-be coaching I'd received from HDF during the past twenty weeks, I was still terrified I would fire-truck it up.

Hey, don't laugh at my baby-approved swear word. I was now on a cussing restriction.

And forget the typical fine of twenty-five cents per swear word. Holly had decided I needed a stiffer penalty because a quarter was nothing compared to my annual income.

Now, each swear word garnered Noah a nice hefty ten-dollar fine toward his college fund.

So fire truck it was.

Overtime went well—as in we won. The Rock players rushed onto the ice to celebrate.

"Fucking great job," I told Mark, who had scored the overtime goal. I gave him an enthusiastic one-armed hug.

He laughed. "So when Holly's not around, you're allowed to swear?"

"Damn straight."

Did Becca know about the ten-dollar-a-cuss-word fine leveled on me? No, which was why Mark would never tattle-tale to Holly. The consequence was too great when it came to me "accidentally" mentioning it to *his* wife.

Back in the locker room, I was getting ready to strip off my hockey gear and head for the shower when the assistant coach nabbed me. "Media's asking for you."

"Of course they are," I grumbled. "It's not like they're standing around, dripping with sweat."

But maybe I could stand in front of them and shake my body like a wet dog after a swim in the ocean. Think that would impress them?

He slapped me on the back in a sympathetic gesture. "You only have to go out for a few minutes."

At least no one would be asking about my impending fatherhood. Other than within the team, I hadn't gone public with the news. As far as I was concerned, it wasn't anyone's business.

I returned to the dressing room, where the reporters were waiting. "Good game tonight," one said to me. Then after I answered a question about Jyri's trade, he said, "You'll be a free agent in July. Any ideas on what you can expect?" In other words, did I think I would get traded before then.

That was the billion-dollar question.

A question I'd asked myself at least a thousand times. I got paid well, but I wasn't a star player and would never be. I'd already been traded once before. And to be honest, as much as I loved the game, the constant uncertainty about my future in the league was tiring.

But what else would I do?

I guess when it came down to it—*that* was the real billion-dollar question.

I BS'd my way through the answer, reminding them it was the GM's call and he would do what was best for the team. After a few more questions, the assistant coach signaled the interview was over.

I could have almost kissed him.

Once I'd finished showering and had changed into my suit

for our flight back to San Francisco, I entered the secured room where the team had kept our cell phones.

How did people get ahold of us prior to game-time and during games? They had to contact the team and in turn, the news was passed on to us. This way the team could determine what was an emergency or what wasn't. Like when Travis's grandmother once phoned, wondering where he had put the jar of pickles last time he was at her house.

The woman loved her pickles.

Why was I telling you this? Because now you'll see why when I checked my texts, I was surprised to see one from Trent—telling me Holly had gone into labor...several hours ago.

Shit.

26

HOLLY

uck. Me. Dead! That was the last thought to go through my head as the contraction hit. I stopped walking and braced my hands on my bed—breathing through the pain.

Whoo whoo.

Hee hee.

Until the contraction had returned a moment ago, I'd been "enjoying" the private labor and delivery room. Josh's hockey game had been on TV (yes, I had a TV), but now the game was over and the TV was off. There was nothing I wanted to watch.

So I had been walking around the room. It was part of my birthing plan. And high on the agenda was natural childbirth. So no epidural for me.

But could you blame me?

I shuddered at the mental image of the scary epidural needle as the contraction faded.

Phew!

"How are you doing?" the perky cheerleader of an OB resident asked, entering the room.

Abso-fucking-lutely fantastic.

That's right—I was allowed to swear all I wanted, in my head, without the repercussions of the swear-word jar.

What Josh didn't know...

"I'm fine." Yes, it was a lie. I *wasn't* fine. I was in labor and it hurt like hell and I was alone.

Well, not completely alone. Kelsey was with me...and Trent when he was brave enough to be in the room.

I wasn't sure if it was the concept of labor and childbirth in general that freaked him out—or if it was because I was the one going through it. I wasn't his girlfriend. I was his colleague.

Speaking of Trent, he picked that moment to pop into the room.

"Have you heard from him yet?" I asked, straightening and ignoring the super-caffeinated resident for a moment.

"Yes, he just called. The team's flight is delayed due to the storm that hit out east. So far there's no ETA for him getting here."

Good thing he hadn't announced that while I was having a contraction. I might have kneed him in the nuts—not that the news was Trent's fault.

I completely blamed Mother Nature.

Note to self: no Mother's Day card for her this year.

Did Josh ever say "I love you" again after I thought I'd imagined him *possibly* saying it on Christmas Eve? The answer was no—so I just wrote it off as a wonderful dream.

Had I said those three little words yet? No—I didn't want to put him on the spot if he wasn't there. Why did falling in love have to be so complicated? There really should be a book on how to let a guy know you're in love with him without freaking him out. Or at least a chapter in *What To Expect*.

"Alrighty," the resident said, suddenly sounding a little impatient. Guess it was time for her coffee break, so she could fill up on her annoying perkiness. "I need to check your cervix again."

Truth? Trent should have been a sprinter instead of a mutual fund portfolio manager. I'd never seen a man vacate a room that fast before.

Chuckling at his hasty retreat, I removed my maternity yoga pants and underwear and climbed onto the bed. Kelsey studied the wall behind my head while the resident stuck her fingers up my woo ha ha.

"You're four centimeters."

Seriously? I'd always been quick at everything—especially academics. So why did this have to be the first time a snail progressed faster than me?

Maybe this is for the best, so Josh can be here for the birth of his son, the annoying voice in my head said at the same time another contraction hit. Hard.

I bitch slapped the voice. Was it not experiencing the same contractions I was? Did it really believe I wanted to wait until after Josh arrived before I gave birth to Noah?

Hell, that could be in twelve hours!

FIVE HOURS LATER, I WAS READY TO RIP MY BELLY OPEN AND remove Noah myself. It was official. I was never having sex again.

Ever.

"Remember to breathe, Holly," Kelsey said, wiping a damp cloth across my forehead.

"I am breathing," I whimpered.

Looking for Trent? He was in the waiting room. Kelsey had tried sending him home hours ago, but he had refused to budge. But it had more to do with his girlfriend being here than it had to do with me being in labor.

Kelsey's phone dinged from her purse. She removed it and read the screen. "Josh wants to know if he can talk to you."

"He texted you?"

"No, he texted Trent, and Trent relayed the question to me."

I slid a glance at the nurse who had come into the room to see how I was doing. At the last check, I was seven centimeters...and extremely cranky at that.

I was beginning to think the NHL season would be over before Noah came out.

"He's going nuts not being here for you."

"Okay," I whispered, too tired to speak louder than that.

"Where's your phone?"

"In my bag. Side pocket."

She retrieved my phone and handed it to me, then sent a text on her phone. Less than a minute later my phone rang.

I accepted the call. "G'day," I said, willing the next contraction to stay away long enough for me to talk to Josh.

"How are you holding up?" he asked—and his deep, sinful voice soothed me to my bones. I missed that voice.

I missed him.

You know what I didn't miss? The contractions.

Another one slammed through my belly, and I did my best to breathe through it while Kelsey removed the phone from my hand. Possibly to prevent me from crushing it single-handedly.

Hee hee.

Whoo whoo.

Hee hee.

Whoo whoo.

Once the contraction had passed, I released a slow cleansing breath and took the phone back from Kelsey.

"Sorry," I said. "I had a contraction."

"You don't need to apologize. I'm the one who's sorry. I should be there with you instead of stuck at the airport in Pittsburgh."

"That's not your fault. We both knew the odds of you being away when I went into labor were high." It just would have been lower if Noah had been a little more patient and waited until closer to his due date.

But it was too late to tell him that now.

"Our flight's been approved to leave in the next hour."

And then he had a five-hour flight. The airport was at least an hour away—which meant roughly seven more hours before I would see him.

But I couldn't focus on that. I needed to focus on the here and now. "Remember how you were going to sing to me while I was in labor?" I asked, sounding more like a little girl than a grown woman.

"Yes."

"Can you still do that, at least until you have to board your flight?"

Instead of answering, he sang a soothing jazz song, and I relaxed a little more. His singing had that effect on me.

At least it did until another contraction hit.

Hee hee.

Whoo whoo.

Kelsey took the phone from me again, but turned up the volume so I could focus on Josh's singing.

Hee hee.

Whoo whoo.

Eventually Josh had to leave to catch his flight. "I'll be there soon, babe. I—" He said something else, but I missed it as another contraction ripped through me.

Bloody. Hell.

"Okay, Holly," Dr. Perky said, having refilled on caffeine an hour ago. "I need you to give me another big push."

Drenched with sweat, I flopped back onto the bed. Giving

birth was definitely not a glamorous activity. I was positive Josh was less sweaty after a hockey game.

"I can't," I whispered. That was the extent of my energy.

"C'mon, sweetheart," the grandmotherly nurse said from somewhere near where the resident was sitting, "you're almost there."

"You can do it," Kelsey said, the only person who had been able to keep me relatively sane during the past few hours. After what she had witnessed, I wouldn't be surprised if she changed her mind about having babies.

Maybe she and Trent would adopt a puppy instead.

Another contraction hit. With all the strength I had left— and some I had borrowed from who knows where—I pushed hard. People in the parking lot several floors down no doubt heard my inhuman scream. *Lucky them.*

Ever heard of "the ring of fire"? No, it wasn't from *Lord of The Rings*—although it might as well have been. It was the burning sensation you experienced when the baby's head pushed through an opening much *much* smaller than it. Except the term ring of fire didn't even begin to describe the insurmountable pain.

It was misleading—false advertising.

And if you hadn't already done so by now, this was the defining moment when you decided to never, *ever*, have sex again.

I didn't even have a chance to recover from the contraction. Another one hit with the same intensity as before. The cheer-leaders in the room didn't even have to tell me to push. I couldn't have *not* pushed even if I had tried.

"Okay, Holly, you can do it," someone said. The resident? My eyes were squeezed shut. "One more big push and he's out."

I did as I was told—with another round of noises that might've caused Noah to have second thoughts about being born.

"And here he is," the resident said.

Then a moment later.

"Or rather, here *she* is."

Huh?

I opened my eyes. "She? What do you mean 'she'?"

The resident held up what was definitely a girl.

"But the ultrasound technician said I was having a boy." But really, what did I expect the resident to do? Wave her magic wand and turn the baby into a boy?

"Ultrasound isn't a hundred percent accurate," she explained.

Oh, sure. Now they tell me that.

The nurse placed my crying baby on me so we were chest-to-chest. And just like magic, my beautiful newborn daughter instantly quieted.

"She's gorgeous," Kelsey exclaimed and kissed my sweaty forehead. "If you're okay for a moment, I'll go tell Trent."

"Trent's still here?" I said weakly.

She nodded and smiled. "Of course he is."

Despite feeling like roadkill that had been driven over several times, I smiled at her. "Thanks for being here for me, Kelsey. I don't know what I would have done without you. But why don't you take Trent home before the poor man collapses from exhaustion?"

She chuckled. "Right—because he's been working hard for the past few hours, pushing out a baby. But you're right. I should probably get the big baby home. You good if we come back later today to visit?"

"Absolutely."

Baby girl and I were eventually wheeled into a private room. She was bundled in a blue receiving blanket covered with puppies, wearing a little pink hat Kelsey had picked up in the gift shop before leaving the hospital. The excitement of being born must have been too much. My daughter was fast asleep in the clear bassinet.

As I studied her perfect little face, I fell in love with her more than I ever believed possible.

"It will be okay, little one," I said. "No matter what happens with your daddy, I'll always be there for you. I'll be the best mummy any girl could hope for."

I'd be the mother I never really had—until recently.

Even if in the end I had to do it alone.

27

JOSH

"You may now use your cellular phones," the stewardess announced as we taxied toward the terminal shortly after our flight had touched down in San Francisco.

"Any word yet?" Travis asked as I checked my texts.

Trent had sent one three hours ago.

> Trent: Congratulations, Daddy! Mother and daughter are doing fine.

I shut my eyes, positive I'd misread the message. I was tired. Clearly my brain wasn't working at full capacity.

"Everyone," Travis called out. "Josh's girlfriend had a girl!"

Cheers and congratulations broke out from my teammates, coaching staff, and everyone else involved with the team.

Guess that made it official—I had a daughter.

The unexpected pride? If I hadn't been sitting, it would've knocked me on my ass. Holly and I had been so focused on a son that didn't exist, I hadn't even considered how I would feel if we had a daughter.

"And because of that," Travis added, "drinks tonight are on him...even if he won't be there."

That got snickers from my teammates.

"What were you thinking, man?" Mark asked, from across the aisle—the only HDF member with a boy. "Now we'll have to watch more girlie kiddy shows."

"Are you saying you're not comfortable enough with your masculinity to survive?" I laughed and he flipped me the bird.

I had a billion questions I wanted to ask Trent, but given the text had been sent during the night, it meant he was probably at home, sleeping. So I held back on my Q&A and caught a cab to the hospital.

Where was my car?

Safe in my apartment garage. Travis had picked me up on the way to the arena when we flew out. Since it had been a long night for the team after being stuck for so long in Pittsburgh, I told him I'd just grab a cab.

"Don't you play hockey for the Rock?" the cabbie asked as we sped toward the hospital.

"Yep." I was too tired and too excited to deal with a fan, so I stared out the window, hoping he'd get the hint.

He didn't.

"Great game last night."

"Thanks."

"My son isn't going to believe that I'm driving Josh Hoffer. He's a huge fan. He's ten years old and hopes to play for the NHL one day."

Him and thousands of other boys.

He went on and on about his son and asked tons of questions about playing for the NHL. Were you surprised I listened to him? Don't be. Why? Because this was the kind of man I would've loved to have as my father when I'd been his kid's age.

His son wasn't just fulfilling the cabbie's life-long dream of playing in the NHL. The dream was completely his son's.

You had to respect a man like that.

At the hospital, I stepped off the elevator on the maternity floor—not bothering to wait until the door was fully open—and walked toward the nurse's desk. A few people in the waiting room gave me a double glance—possibly wondering why I was wearing a suit. I ignored them and asked at the desk for Holly's room.

Did you see that? The nurse's expression? The wide eyes? The "O" shaped mouth?

Once she'd recovered enough to make a coherent sentence, she replied, "Are you a friend?"

"I'm her boyfriend."

Rule #1 when it comes to social media and being an NHL player? Always be the first to post the information—that way you have a little more control over the situation.

The team's publicist had mentioned that to me but I had brushed it off.

Now who felt like the dumbass?

The nurse told me which room Holly and my daughter were in, and I quietly slipped inside, doing my best not to wake them. Holly looked so peaceful, it was hard to believe she had given birth a few hours ago.

Without me.

I'd be lying if I said it didn't bother me that I hadn't been here for her. She didn't blame me, but I still couldn't shake the feeling I had failed her and our daughter.

After placing my luggage by the wall, I peered into the clear plastic bassinet by Holly's bed. And smiled.

Looked like all the studying I had done on the Disney princesses would come in handy after all.

Go ahead and quiz me—I took my studies very seriously.

And gained the reputation in HDF of being unbeatable.

The prize?

Beer and chicken wings at Sean's favorite sports bar. The sauce was the best freaking hot sauce on the planet.

The little princess in the bassinet stirred. I gently scooped her up, supporting her neck, and cradled her against me. Then I walked to the wooden rocking chair and sat.

She peered up at me and gave a little yawn...and my heart melted right there.

"Hi, I'm your daddy," I said softly. "I'm the one who was singing to you while you were in Mommy's belly. I'm so happy to finally meet you, little one. I'm the man who's going to protect you and your mommy. And I'll teach you how to keep all the dumbasses in line." I cringed. "Oops. I wasn't supposed to say that word. How 'bout we don't tell Mommy?" I smiled down at the little bundle.

"How about Mummy forgets she heard you say it—just this once?" my favorite Aussie said and I looked up.

28

HOLLY

Nothing is sexier and more breathtaking than the sight of a baby in the arms of a big, rugged hockey player.

Don't believe me? Take a look.

Josh was sitting on the wooden rocking chair, cradling our daughter—and I knew without a doubt that he had already fallen unequivocally in love with her.

But how could he not?

"I see you've already met your daughter," I said softly.

He smiled at me in the way that always turned me heated. Even after twelve hours of labor and pushing out a seven-pound baby, he still had that power over me.

"I have. She's beautiful, just like her mother."

And apparently south of the equator wasn't the only place to heat up. My face got pretty hot too. "Thanks."

"Any idea what we're going to call her?" he asked. "I'm guessing Noah is no longer on the table."

Definitely not—even though I really did love the name.

"I thought maybe we could name her after my grandmother. Lily."

He studied his daughter for a moment. "She looks like a Lily. All right, Lily it is. If it's okay with you, I'd like her middle name to be Grace—after *my* grandmother."

Lily Grace. "It's perfect."

"I was thinking," he said, smiling at Lily in a way that clearly suggested she already had him wrapped around her finger, "of maybe taking a picture of her and me together. Then the team can release it. People are going to find out I'm now a father"—he nodded at the door—"and it's not like I'm trying to hide that I have a child."

"That's a great idea." Plus, then I'd have a copy to look at whenever Josh wasn't around.

"I was also thinking"—he glanced back up at me—"that maybe we could move in together. Probably your apartment since she already has her room there."

Did you hear that? No? That was because I'd stopped breathing. I wasn't too surprised that he wanted to go public about the birth of his daughter. But had I even for a second thought he would suggest we live together as a family?

Was Australia's national animal the polar bear?

"I still have my apartment, but I can sublet it until my lease ends," he said. "Or I can stay where I am now if you'd prefer."

I think I might have blinked. I couldn't be sure. My mind was still trying to digest what he had just said.

And then it hit me. Well, more like what he had meant by the second part hit me. Did he really think that I didn't want him to live with me and Lily?

I grinned. "I would love it if you moved in with us."

Like a family.

Which we now were.

He smiled at me, clearly relieved. Then he returned to smiling broadly at Lily. "And your Daddy is going to sell his Nissan GT-R and buy a nice car-seat friendly vehicle. Then I can take you and your mommy for rides."

His words warmed me up inside. "You're really going to sell it? But you love that car."

He looked up at me. "I do, but what's the point of it if I can't take Lily for rides?" He went back to smiling at his daughter.

I grabbed my cell phone from the nightstand and shuffled over to join them. The picture I took of father and daughter was nothing like what Kelsey would have taken—but I thought it looked utterly adorable.

Since I hadn't told my parents yet, I fired off a text with the photo. Next, I sent one to Erin and Kelsey. Erin immediately responded.

> Erin: Congratulations! She's adorable.
> Samantha and I can't wait to meet her.

Mum texted right back, congratulating both Josh and me, and telling me she couldn't wait to meet her granddaughter.

A moment later I received a text from Drew.

> Drew: Congratulations, Holly. She's beautiful
> like her mother. Look forward to meeting the
> newest Whittaker someday real soon.

I leaned down and kissed Lily's forehead, then kissed my boyfriend's scruff-covered cheek.

"How're you feeling?" he asked.

"Sore. Like my body doesn't belong to me." The second part wasn't anything new. I'd been feeling that way since getting pregnant. But at least then I had a baby inside of me.

The best thing about being pregnant? Having a tiny life growing inside you.

The worst thing right after giving birth? Hello, stretch marks and postpartum flabby stomach.

But I would be going home with a healthy baby—and a sweet and caring boyfriend.

What more could I wish for?

Right—for Josh to love me like I loved him.
And for my green-card application to be approved.

29

JOSH

Valentine's Day—the sappy, stress-out-any-man-in-a-relationship day that the creators of chocolate and greeting cards had dreamed up.

Or so I once thought.

I smiled at the two most important girls in my life sitting next to me on the couch. Lily was busy sucking away at Holly's breast. The butterfly necklace I had given Holly for Christmas sparkled in the sunlight streaming through the window.

"I'm going to pretend I'm not jealous," I said.

Holly's head jerked up from watching the hungry baby eat. "What are you talking about?"

"I had staked claim to those gorgeous breasts. They're mine and no one else's." The smile on my face? One hundred percent smirk—even if the breasts weren't one hundred percent mine. At least not for now. They were currently on loan like fine artwork in a museum.

"Lily might have something to say about that." Holly yawned, which didn't surprise me. She hadn't slept much since Lily's birth three days ago. When Lily wasn't sleeping, she was eating.

And for something so small, she sure liked to eat frequently.

"Why don't you have a nap once she's finished lunch?" I said. "I'll make dinner." Which had been my plan all along.

"Are you sure?" Holly yawned again. "It's not like you got much sleep last night either."

"I got more than you did." At least on the road, I'd get to catch up on my sleep. I was one of those lucky bastards who slept pretty much anywhere. Good thing too, with all the traveling the team did.

Lily pulled away from the breast, a drowsy, satisfied expression on her face. It wouldn't be much longer before she was napping too.

"I'll change her and put her down for her nap while you go and rest up." I pushed myself off the couch, removed Lily from Holly's arms, and carried her to her bedroom. "Hey, beautiful. What do you say Daddy changes you, then you sleep while I make dinner? Does that sound like a plan?"

I would have discussed the rest of my plan with her, to get her female opinion on it, but I didn't want to risk Holly overhearing.

Holly and Lily had been home for a day now. And what was the number one thought parading through my head? No, not the one where I craved to make love to Holly—although it was certainly up there.

I was already wondering how I'd be able to go back on the road with the team. I couldn't get enough of seeing my two girls.

I couldn't get enough of waking up with Holly next to me.

Now, I know what you're thinking—that all those times she and I had slept together during the past few months must have counted for something.

But they didn't.

Sleeping together and living together weren't the same thing.

Living with her was so much better.

Even if I had to learn not to be quite the slob I was before.

Okay, I'll admit it, it was a work in progress.

Lily started fussing as I changed her wet diaper, so I did what had become a habit even before she was born—I sang "Unforgettable" to her. By the time I got to the second line, "Unforgettable though near or far," she settled down and watched me as I continued singing.

Once she was changed into a clean diaper and sleeper, I wrapped her up in a pink receiving blanket and settled her in her crib.

How did I do? With the blanket, I mean. HDF Lesson #15 had been on the fine art of swaddling the baby in a receiving blanket.

Except wrapping a teddy bear was *not* the same as swaddling a squirming baby. Not even close.

Next, I did what all new fathers do...I watched as she fell asleep, then retrieved my phone and shot some more photos of her—for when I was on the road.

Did I have any pictures of Holly and Lily together? You'd better believe it.

After I stopped staring at Lily, I began making dinner. I'd already given Holly red roses that morning. I know, clichéd. But I was a man. What did you expect?

Since the meal didn't need to go into the oven yet, I put it in the fridge for later and checked my social media sites.

Normally I didn't read the comments. I doubted most players did. Or when they did read them, they skimmed to the ones from people they knew.

The last time I'd posted anything was from the day Lily was born. It was the photo Holly had taken. There were the expected comments about how cute she was. Naturally a given.

There were numerous comments about ovaries exploding because of how hot I looked holding a baby.

Did anyone else think that sounded painful?

And there were several comments questioning why no one had heard until now that I had a girlfriend...and questioning if Holly had trapped me into a relationship. If I ventured a guess, I'd say those comments came from puck bunnies.

The rest congratulated Holly and me on the birth of our daughter.

As I parked my phone next to Holly's on the coffee table, hers vibrated and lit up with a text.

> Drew: Call me. Heard of a great job opportunity here. I think you'd be perfect for it.

"She's got a great job *here*," I muttered, even though he couldn't hear me.

"Who has a great job?" Holly asked, startling me. When had she become a ninja?

"You do." I pointed to her phone. "Are you looking for a new job?" *In Australia?*

She picked up her phone and sat next to me, then read the text and shrugged. "As far as I know I'm not. As far as I know, I still have one once I return from mat leave."

"What happens if you don't have a job?"

She placed her phone back on the coffee table. "I will, so let's not talk about hypotheticals. Especially not when our daughter is sleeping." She shifted her leg over mine and straddled me. "Especially when I just want to do this..."

She planted a kiss on my neck, then nipped the skin there. Instantly my cock grew interested, forgetting how Holly's soft heat was off limits for a few weeks while her body recuperated.

I grabbed her hips, itching to rock her body against mine.

And the award for Best Restraint While Incredibly Horny went to...

All right—I didn't exactly win it. I might have accidentally rocked against her the tiniest bit.

Honestly, that was just a tiny bit.

Her mouth continued its journey up my neck to my jaw. She nibbled the skin there too. A groan escaped my lips—a groan that was part lust, part exasperation at her teasing. Teasing when she knew that was as far as we could go.

As if guided by my groan, her mouth found my mouth, and her teeth gently tugged at my lower lip.

Eager to welcome her in, my lips parted.

Imagine you were stranded in the desert—and all you could do was fantasize about the tall glass of water you would finally drink once you were found. *If* you were found.

Kissing Holly was nothing like that. It was like being found, having the tall, cool glass of delicious tasting water...then falling into a lagoon—complete with waterfall—and drowning.

Drowning in the best possible way.

Our tongues slid against one another, reacquainting themselves...as if Holly and I hadn't kissed for several days instead of several hours.

By the time our lips finally parted, our breaths were ragged. I shifted my head, my breath brushing the shell of her ear. Every part of me was alive with awareness. Every part of me—including the depths of my soul.

"I love you," I murmured. Even though I had no idea of her feelings toward me, saying it felt right.

She jerked back, as if she had been stung, and stared at me through wide green eyes. "What did you say?" Her accent was thicker than normal. Thicker and sexier.

The corner of my mouth tugged into a smirk—instant defense mode. "You heard me."

"I did. But I wanted to double-check, in case I misunderstood."

"Fair enough." I cupped my hand against her cheek. "Holly,

I love you. Have for a while now. I was just too much of an idiot to tell you."

She still stared at me, stunned.

Who here was expecting that reaction from her? For now, how about we pretend it didn't bother me—that it didn't feel like I had just laid myself bare? "The real question is, how do you feel about me?"

That was as far as I got. Holly's mouth was on mine again, kissing me, telling me through actions, not words, how she felt about me. The kiss was everything. Tender. Demanding. Sweet. Hungry.

Now if only Lily hadn't picked that moment to decide nap time was over. Through the baby monitor on the coffee table, she let out a little whimper. Before we could respond, it was followed by a full-out, her-lungs-were-one-hundred-percent-into-this wail.

With a sigh, Holly gave me a quick kiss and pushed herself off my lap. "Don't go anywhere."

I didn't have a chance to tell her I'd get the little kiss-blocker. She danced out of my reach and headed for Lily's room.

She returned to the couch a few minutes later with Lily in her arms and snuggled up against me. The little bundle with a light covering of red hair on her head peered up at us.

"So before you demanded to be part of this conversation," Holly said to our daughter in a sweet, cooing voice, "your daddy was telling me he loves me." She turned her beautiful emerald eyes on me. "And I was about to tell him I love him too. Have for a while now. But why wouldn't I? He's the sweetest, kindest man alive...who happens to look incredibly sexy in a hockey uniform." She glanced back down at Lily. "But pretend you didn't hear the last part. Okay?"

I laughed. "Good idea, or else you might have just scarred her for life." I kissed Holly's temple—which then became a slightly less tender kiss when she turned her head back to me and I captured her mouth with my own.

Lily made a small noise that sounded more encouraging than "Ewww my parents are kissing."

We both glanced down at her, content.

Knowing that at this moment, life couldn't get better.

Too bad the feeling wouldn't last forever...

30

JOSH

When I was eight years old, Billie, my best friend at the time, and I had gone to his house after school to play video games. Just like we did every day after school. And like any other eight-year-old who lived for his favorite game, I lost track of time.

Okay, truth be told—I was kicking Billie's ass at the game and was about to break our all-time record.

The part about breaking curfew? A minor inconvenience. Nothing a simple "I love you" to my mother wouldn't cure.

Did I break the record? You'd better believe it.

I felt like a champion. Invincible. Ready to take on the world.

Maybe that was why I hadn't realized something was off the moment I stepped into my apartment—the night my mother had decided she was tired of being my mother and up and left.

Apparently, some things never changed.

"Josh," one of the assistant coaches said as I approached the dressing room. Since we were playing Colorado on their turf, I was still wearing my gray suit and white dress shirt. The tie had been removed the moment the team and I stepped into the arena building.

I paused to see what he wanted while my teammates filed past us.

"You're needed in conference room A. Just down the hallway." He pointed in the direction I needed to go.

I headed down the corridor, my thoughts on the upcoming game instead of wondering why I was needed in the conference room. Maybe if I had been thinking about that instead of the game, I would have been better prepared for what came next.

I entered the room to find Don McDonald, the team's general manager, at the head of the oval table. And that was when the alarms in my head finally went off.

Fuck.

"Have a seat," McDonald said, gesturing to the chair across from him. In front of him was a closed file folder. My closed filed folder, no doubt.

I would've rather stood but did as I was asked—my mind going through what I would tell Holly.

Double fuck—with a fuckedy-fire-truck thrown in for good luck.

"You've been traded to Montreal. Tony Crisp, their GM, will call you shortly. You'll be flying there tonight." He got up and left.

And there you had it...

From experience, this was pretty much how it went down for everyone. There wasn't even a chance to say good-bye to my teammates.

And there were no words to convey how I felt, even if the trade didn't come as a huge surprise.

I sat there for a moment, all kinds of thoughts stomping through my head. The most common ones centered on the theme of how my father had failed me and Holly's father had put his career ahead of his kids.

And now I was about to be no different.

After a few seconds or minutes or hours, I dialed Holly's cell. Several rings later her phone clicked to voicemail.

"Hey, Holly." Fuck, how was I supposed to do this? "I've been traded to Montreal. I'm flying out tonight. I'll call you as soon as I can. I love you. Give Lily a kiss for me. Bye." I ended the call.

The numbness and foreboding setting up camp in my gut? That was real.

31

HOLLY

"Who's my pretty girl?" I cooed as I changed Lily's diaper in Samantha's bedroom. Josh was away on a road trip, so Lily and I were spending the evening with my friends. "Do you miss Daddy? I miss Daddy."

Lily replied with a yawn.

Didn't she look adorable when she yawned? I was positive no other baby in the world looked as adorable while yawning.

Once I'd finished changing her, we headed downstairs.

"Does she know yet?" Trent asked, his voice coming from the living room. He and Kelsey must have arrived while I was upstairs.

I entered the living room. You know the saying about hearing a pin drop? Well, if I'd used safety pins on Lily's diaper, we could've tested that theory.

"What's wrong?" I asked, my heart rate racing faster than a Ferrari on an open race track. And the sympathy on their faces wasn't doing much to help slow it down as it hit a sharp turn.

"We heard the news on the way over…" Trent said.

"What news?"

He and Kelsey exchanged looks. "Josh hasn't told you?"

"Told me what?" Did you sense the impatience in my voice? Blame it on the boulder that had found its way to my stomach.

"He's been traded."

It will be okay, I told myself. Maybe he got traded to San Jose or L.A. or Anaheim. We could make that work. It wouldn't be ideal, but somehow we could make it work.

Now, if only my heart was as convinced as my brain. "To where?"

"Montreal."

"Oh." Montreal? Wasn't that in Canada? It would've been bad enough if he had been traded to another U.S. team—but to another country? That was a whole new level of bad.

And why was I only hearing about it now from Trent? Why hadn't Josh told me?

Deep down I had always suspected Josh would be traded. Why? Because what was dear old Murphy's favorite hobby? That's correct. He liked to screw you around when it came to that damn law of his.

I had also suspected, deep down, Josh would be traded because he was going to be a free agent soon. But had I at any point thought he would be traded to a Canadian team—traded to the land of snow, polar bears, and freezing winters? Nope. Never.

"I guess that's it then," I said more to myself than to anyone else. Josh and I had finally admitted that we were in love, so fate decided to have a good laugh at our expense.

Yes, sometimes life really did suck.

But what did this all mean for Lily?

It meant that Josh would still be a part of her life, but he wouldn't be there for her—not in the way that he wanted.

"What do you mean 'that's it'?" Kelsey asked.

"Josh is moving away," I said, "starting a new life. Without us."

"But can't you move with him? I've seen him when he's with you. He loves you."

"I know he does." I didn't doubt it. "But I'm not a U.S. citizen and I don't have a green card, so even if he just moved across the country, I can't go with him. And sure, I could marry him if he had been traded to another U.S. team"—I added because I could tell that was where Kelsey's thoughts were headed—"but Canada is something else. It doesn't matter if he and I are married, I can guarantee I won't be allowed to work there. Then all my years of hard work will be for nothing."

And I'd never be completely happy. I would always have that one regret in life—the one where I gave up the career I loved.

But I guess when it came to my happiness, I would lose either way. Heads, I gave up the job I loved. Tails, I gave up Josh.

There were no winners in this game. No opportunity for a do-over.

"So what are you going to do?" Kelsey asked.

"Don't worry. Lily and I will be fine. From the moment I discovered I was pregnant, I was prepared to be a single mother." True—I wouldn't be your typical single mum. But for all intents and purposes, this was close enough.

No one looked too thrilled with that option, but there was nothing we could do. Playing in the NHL had been Josh's dream. Most people didn't get to live out their dreams, especially with something like that. So I couldn't expect Josh to give up his. Not when this mess wasn't his fault.

How about I just blame the condom that had failed us?

Except then I wouldn't have Lily.

Right—so no blaming the condom either.

There had to be a better answer—one that worked for all of us.

"Hey, I didn't come over to depress everyone," I said. "Let's talk about something else. How was your photo shoot yester-day?" I asked Kelsey.

While she shared a hilarious story about a noncooperative sheep and a model who wasn't a fan of farm animals—especially ones who decided the model's leg made a great spot to take a pee break on—my thoughts slipped back to the all-important question. *Where the heck did I put my cell phone?*

Welcome to Mommy Brain. They should have *that* as a warning on the condom box. "Improper use of condoms can lead to pregnancy and your brain's inability to function properly, especially during the most inopportune moments."

Still sitting on the couch, I leaned down and looked through my diaper bag. Usually I kept my phone in the side pocket but for some reason, I had dropped it into the main one before leaving the apartment, and it had ended up wrapped in Lily's ducky blanket.

Erin returned from the kitchen where she had disappeared a few minutes ago. "Dinner's ready."

Everyone stood up—everyone but me.

"I'll be right there," I said. As they headed to the kitchen, I checked my voicemail messages.

"Hey, Holly. I've been traded to Montreal. I'm flying out tonight. I'll call you as soon as I can. I love you. Give Lily a kiss for me. Bye."

And that was it. Josh didn't sound either sad or happy at the news—just blown-over shocked.

But not as shocked as I was. It felt like a kangaroo hadn't paid attention to where he was going and knocked me onto my arse.

Josh wasn't even coming home first. He was flying straight to Montreal—and I had no idea when I would see him again.

I kissed Lily's forehead. "Well, Lily-Flower. It's just you and me now."

Just as I had always imagined it would be.

My phone vibrated in my hand. For a second I thought it was Josh. Disappointment sidled up to me as I read the name. Drew.

That wasn't to say I was disappointed it was him. I wasn't. Just disappointed it wasn't Josh.

> Drew: Please tell me you're considering that job you are perfect for.

> Me: I have a job I love.

With a company who was sponsoring my green-card application so I could stay in San Francisco.

> Me: And I love it here. It's my home.

But was it?

You know the saying about home is where the heart is?

My heart was with Josh, who was moving to Canada, at least for now. But it was also here in my arms—and I could love Lily anywhere.

> Drew: Just consider it.

32

JOSH

If you've never been to Canada, there are several things you should know. It snows. A lot.

They have the best maple syrup ever known to man.

The beaver is their national animal, but I had yet to see one wandering down the street.

They don't have dollar bills. They have weird coins called the loonie and the toonie.

It snows. A lot.

They also accept American credit cards—which was a good thing. Because of the Canadiens' tight schedule, I hadn't been able to return to San Francisco to get my stuff.

So until recently, all I'd had with me was the three days worth of clothes that I had packed for the Rocks' road trip. And then just when I thought I was finally flying home for a few days, Montreal and the Eastern States were hammered with a snow storm. Flights were canceled. And once again I was stuck in my hotel room with no place to go.

Fortunately, there was this great invention called Skype.

"How's my gorgeous little girl doing?" I said to my phone,

the image of my three-week-old daughter peering back at me from the crook of Holly's arm. She smiled—and I pretended her beautiful smile was for me and not due to gas.

"Daddy misses you and can't wait to hold you again." To hold her for the short amount of time I would be home.

And when I say short time, I meant two days—as in less than forty-eight hours. That was as much time as the Canadiens could afford to lose me for.

Lily made a little sound I interpreted to mean that she couldn't wait for me to hold her.

The camera shifted, and both Holly and Lily came into view on the screen.

"She misses you too," Holly said. "We both do. Any news yet if you're coming home soon?"

"The team rebooked the tickets. I'll be home Thursday." In six days. "But I'll only be there for two days."

"That's okay. We'll be happy to get even that much."

Holly's smile? No, it didn't fool me either.

"Trent got tickets for your game at the end of the month." When the Canadiens were scheduled to play in San Francisco. "And it won't be much longer before you're back for the summer," she added.

"That's right," I said. "But then who knows what will happen after that..."

"What do you mean?"

"I'm going to be a free agent soon." Holly and I had already discussed this.

What did my becoming a free agent mean? It meant one of several things could happen.

The Canadiens or another NHL team might offer me a contract. If that didn't happen, a European team might want me to play for them, which allowed me to keep playing hockey. The downside? I would have to move to Europe for a few years

—which was worse than my current situation with the Canadiens.

And then there was door number three…

No one would want me.

I'd have to start a new life—a life that no longer involved hockey.

Yes, it wasn't like I would be playing hockey for the rest of my life. At some point, all hockey players retired. Their bodies weren't what they used to be. Their performance suffered. Or they decided other priorities in their lives were more important.

But if I retired, what would I do for a career? Hockey was all I knew.

Well, hockey and European history—but there weren't a lot of opportunities involving the latter.

"But maybe San Jose, L.A, Anaheim, or Vegas will offer you a contract," Holly suggested. "They're closer at least."

True—but it was a long shot that any of them were interested in me. And let's not forget that there were seven NHL teams in Canada. Even if the Canadiens didn't offer me a new contract, there was still a chance one of the other six teams would—and would be the only NHL team to do so.

Which put me in the same situation as now.

But I didn't want to get into it on Skype.

Instead, I got Holly to tell me about her day and about everything Lily had been up to. And then I sang to my daughter like I always did.

By the time we were finished, Lily had fallen asleep in Holly's arms—and all I wanted to do was kiss both of my girls.

All I wanted to do was make love to my beautifully hot girlfriend.

At some point.

Soon hopefully.

She still needed the okay from her physician.

"I'll talk to you soon," I told Holly after she had struggled to hold back another yawn.

"Okay." Then a smile grew on her face. It was the same smile I'd frequently seen during her most horniest of months—when she was about to seduce me out of my underwear.

"And just so you know," she said, "I have an appointment with my physician on Wednesday, and I wouldn't be surprised if she gives me the okay to have sex." She ran the tip of her tongue along her lower lip—and my cock grew hard at the memory of her soft lips around it.

Six days? Six freaking long days? I wasn't sure I could survive one day—never mind six—before I was inside her again.

And then just like that, she ended the call—leaving me groaning.

"Goddamn tease," I said, smirking at the blank screen.

She might have ended the call, but that wasn't enough to wipe away the image of her smile and her lips from my mind.

I stalked to the bathroom, stripped off my clothes, and climbed into the shower. Hot water rained on me, filling the space with steam. I wrapped my fingers around my cock and gave it one long, firm stroke.

What was I thinking about as I jacked myself off? Holly, of course. Hot, naked-in-the-shower Holly.

It didn't take long before the tingling in my lower back spread throughout the region. My balls tightened hard and my seed shot from me, accompanied by the primal grunt from between my lips.

It took me a moment to recover my wits and finish showering.

Was I satisfied? Not really, but it was enough to take the edge off until Thursday night.

And in the meantime? I would be sending the good doctor subliminal messages. Because come Thursday—if all things went well—I wanted to finally sink inside Holly again and enjoy her sweet heat.

I wanted to make a new memory that would help me get through the next few months.

And I wanted to talk to Holly about our future.

Together.

33

HOLLY

What were the first words out of my mouth the moment my physician stepped into the exam room?

"Can I have sex now?"

She hadn't even had a chance to ask me how I was doing.

That didn't sound too desperate, right?

But could you blame me? I wasn't your typical new mother who saw her lover every day. Tonight was my one shot at making love to Josh—or else I'd have to wait a few more weeks.

And I'd rather have a Tasmanian devil chew on my leg than have to wait that long.

Anyhow, the appointment had been yesterday. Did I get the approval? I mean, after I clarified I wanted to have sex with my boyfriend once he returned from Montreal. Yes, I had realized after blurting out the question that it could've been taken the wrong way—that I wanted to have sex at the exact moment my doctor walked into the exam room.

Well, let me put it this way when it came to the approval—I might have done a few mental cartwheels down the hallway at the news.

"Can you believe we get to see your daddy soon?" I asked Lily as we drove to the airport. Josh had told me he'd catch a cab home, but why should some random cab driver get to spend time with my boyfriend instead of me? Was the cabbie counting down the seconds to finally hold Josh and kiss him and make love to him?

I seriously doubted it—even if this was San Francisco.

Lily didn't say anything, asleep in her infant car seat.

By the time we arrived at the airport terminal, my body was begging me to jump his bones the moment I saw him. My heart was pounding, agreeing with the idea but at the same time as nervous as a cow at a community barbecue.

Lily's car seat was attached to the stroller and she was busy cooing and gurgling at me as I pushed her through the airport. In her hand was her favorite toy—a plastic set of keys made for babies.

Guess which super-hot, super-sweet daddy sent it to her from Montreal?

I knew she wouldn't last long in her stroller. She never did. She preferred to be strapped to my chest in her baby carrier. Why wasn't she?

Because as soon as I saw Josh, I would be hugging and kissing him. But it wouldn't be a little hug and a peck on the lips.

We were talking about a full-blown, fireworks-lighting-up-the-night-sky kiss.

And I didn't think Lily wanted to be the filling in our sandwich, so to speak.

We waited outside the exit for arriving passengers. My eyes instantly teared up at the sight of Josh walking through the door. It took only a few quick strides before he was in front of me, pulling me close. My arms went around his neck.

Was this how I had fantasized it would be?

Truth? My fantasy was dirtier. Sexier. Naughtier.

But I could hardly fulfill that fantasy at the airport with so many people around.

His free hand cradled the back of my head and his mouth was on mine. It felt like a lifetime since we'd last kissed but at the same time, everything about it was familiar.

"Get a room," a guy said and cackled.

We separated, my face a little more heated than before.

Josh turned his attention to his daughter. "I can't believe how much she's grown in two weeks," he said, unbuckling her safety harness.

He scooped her out of the car seat and kissed her forehead. Lily cooed and gurgled some more. She knew exactly who her daddy was.

I won't bore you with the next part—because I know you want to get to the good stuff. Suffice it to say we went home, Josh spent time with Lily and me while he packed his things to take to Montreal, we had dinner, and then we put Lily to bed.

Not wanting to waste what little time we had left together, we returned to our bedroom. Or if you were looking for a more accurate description—we stumbled to our bedroom, our lips fused together.

Somehow we made it there with little damage to the hall-way. There might have been a slight incident involving the doorway—but when it came to the new bruise on my hip, it was nothing a little time wouldn't heal.

Once inside our room, I slipped my fingers under the hem of his long-sleeved T-shirt and ran them up the smooth skin of his abs. His muscles flexed then relaxed at my touch.

That moan? One hundred percent me.

But touching him with my hands wasn't enough. I craved to feel all of him against me. I shoved the fabric up his torso.

"I'd give you a hard time about being impatient," he said with a chuckle, "but you make a very valid point." He reached back to grab the collar of his top and yanked the material over his head.

In the time it had taken him to do that, I had removed my nursing top.

I know...the bra wasn't what you were expecting, was it? From the way Josh was staring at it, I would say he felt the same way. It wasn't boring and practical looking like my regular nursing bras. It was made completely of black lace and left nothing to the imagination—not that Josh needed to use his imagination.

He palmed my larger-than-normal breasts, feeling the weight of them in his hands, then brushed a thumb across one highly sensitive nipple. Even though I'd breastfed Lily not long ago, the tingling sensation in my breasts warned me it didn't matter. I was about to have milk letdown, which happened whenever Lily wanted to eat. Great for feeding a hungry baby—not so great if you wanted to get down and dirty with your lover.

"Unfortunately, the bra will have to remain," I told him.

He pouted.

"Trust me. Right now these breasts"—I pointed to them—"are fully loaded, and ready to fire at any unsuspecting boyfriend."

Josh had already witnessed firsthand how far my boobs could shoot milk when Lily was nursing. If a noise distracted her and she turned her head to check it out—you had better duck for cover.

Naturally, he had been impressed.

He laughed. "Duly noted." His hands shifted from my breasts and traveled to the button of my jeans.

Yes, *my* jeans. Not my maternity jeans, which I'd worn until a week ago. And not Josh's jeans. Hey, don't judge me. They were comfortable and looked better than my maternity ones—not to mention they reminded me of Josh.

Anyway, back to my jeans: they finally fit. Cue the fanfare.

Now, let's for a moment consider your mega-income-celebrity mummy. If I handed you her pre-pregnancy photo and one taken four weeks post-birth, could you tell which was which?

Not bloody likely.

But hey, if I had a full-time nanny and a full-time personal trainer and spent several hours a day training...

My point?

I placed my hand on Josh's, the one getting ready to undo my jeans. "I'll warn you now, I don't look the same as I did before." And I certainly looked nothing like a puck bunny, who clearly had never given birth.

"Holly, that doesn't matter to me," he said, his voice low and rough and turn-me-on husky. "No matter what you might believe, I still think you're gorgeous and sexy. And the fact that you gave me a beautiful and extremely smart daughter makes you even more gorgeous and sexy."

"Okay," I said, my sex-starved tone hinting that I hungered to make love to him at least two or three times tonight. A tone that demanded less talk, more action.

Would I be sore come tomorrow? Probably—but it would be worth it.

Josh slowly unzipped my jeans and equally slowly peeled them down my legs. Like with my bra, my panties were black and lacy and new.

"I like them," he said, "but I think I'll like them better off you." He slipped them down my legs. I stepped out of them and he tossed them to the side. "That's much better."

Still crouching, he traced his fingers up the inside of my legs and planted a gentle kiss on my stomach, the same way he used to when I'd been pregnant. Once he got to my aching core, he gently cupped me.

"Are you still sore here?" he asked.

"If you had asked me that four weeks ago, I would have said yes. But I'm fully healed now. I'm good to go." *Very good to go.*

"You wouldn't lie to me about this, would you?"

I crooked my finger at him, telling him to stand. Which he did. I cupped my hand against his face. "I promise you. Now, let's get back to the part where you're going to be naughty with me. *Very* naughty." I winked at him.

"Well, as long as you're sure." And then his lips were on mine and we were kissing again.

His clothing? While our mouths were busy, I got to work making sure we were on equal ground. With a quick flick of my fingers, I unhooked his jeans button. Then I unzipped them and slipped my hand in through the opening.

Well, someone was extremely happy to greet me.

A smile grew on my face and I pulled away from Josh's lips. "Did you miss me?"

"Very much," he said in what almost sounded like a moan.

"I guess I need to give you something to remember me by, for while you're away."

Now it was his turn to smile, his face a breath away from mine. "That would be greatly appreciated."

I chuckled and pushed his jeans past his hips and down his legs. He stepped out of them—then in a swift move, he had me on the bed, my legs over the side, Josh lying next to me, kissing me.

His hand returned to my aching core and he traced his fingers between my folds. "Someone's hot, wet, and ready."

Think my neighbors heard my moan?

Who needed pay per view when you had Josh and me to liven up the building?

"If you're referring to me," I said, "then you've got that right. I'm more than ready for you."

"Did you miss me?" he asked, echoing my earlier question. Only in this case, he circled my clit with his finger.

I moaned—louder than before. "Very much."

"Good."

And that was the end of the conversation.

It didn't take long before we got back into the old rhythm—in the same way you never forgot how to ride a bike. We explored each other's bodies, knowing what the other person liked. Knowing how to get the desired reaction, to the point where neither of us would last much longer.

Josh looked down at me, and I nodded at the burning question in his eyes. I was more than ready for him. I wanted him inside me. *Now*.

He positioned himself at my entrance and slowly entered me. "Christ, I missed being inside you," he moaned, then gave me a deep and thorough kiss. Oh God, I wouldn't last much longer.

"I missed that too," I said.

He flexed his hips, burrowing himself deeper.

Yep, definitely missed him being inside me.

"Oh, God," I groaned as an intense climax crashed through me, pulling me under—causing me to gasp for air.

Wow. Just. Wow.

Josh collapsed beside me, and once the euphoria had subsided for us both—and awareness had returned—he knotted his limbs with mine.

"That memory will definitely keep me going for the next few weeks." He kissed the tip of my nose. "Unless..."

"Unless, what?"

"Since you're on mat leave anyway, why don't you and Lily stay in Montreal with me until the season's over?" Possibility glowed in his eyes.

In case you didn't get it, he meant the hockey season, not winter.

One was doable—there were only ten days left until Spring.

The other?

"It's not that easy," I said, always the planner, never the spontaneous one. But have you tried being spontaneous when you had a baby? "And it might affect my immigration status, which means I might be sent back to Australia because of that. Plus all my friends are here." I stroked my fingers against his jaw and his one-day scruff. "If I go to Montreal, Lily and I will be on our own while you're away. I won't have the same support system I have here."

I gave him a sad smile. "So as much as I would love to be there with you, it won't work. I'm sorry." Plus I needed to begin searching for a nanny soon. D-day—also known as my first day back to work—was two months and counting.

A small part of me shuddered at the idea of returning to work. It wasn't the job I was dreading. Remember? I *loved* my job. It was the idea of being away from Lily during the day, along with balancing motherhood and my career that made me feel unsettled.

Seriously—how had my mum managed to go back to work when my brothers and I were little? Or had we driven her crazy enough that she couldn't wait to get back to her career?

That was always a possibility. A *very* good possibility.

Josh pressed his lips together, and let out a heavy breath. "What's going to happen, Holly, if I'm offered a contract with another team? Yes, maybe it will be with L.A. or San Jose or Anaheim, but the odds of that aren't great. And even then we still won't see much of each other, other than on Skype."

"What do you expect me to do? Give up my job and marry you?"

He pushed himself up to sit. "Why not? You're smart, have a great degree and work experience. You'll find another job."

Did you notice what he didn't say?

Once upon a time, a young maiden lived in the kingdom of kangaroos and koalas. Like her mother before her, she was expected to marry for convenience—not for love. And we all knew how that story went, didn't we?

Yes, I got that he loved me and was trying to come up with a way for Lily and me to be in his life, but it all felt off-kilter. He never said he longed to marry me because he loved me and he couldn't imagine spending another moment without me in his life.

Wasn't that what most girls dreamed of hearing from the man they love?

Because what girl wanted her happily ever after to sound like a business proposal?

I sat up, the sheet held against my chest. "Never mind that I don't want another job," I said a little harsher than I had intended. "Never mind that I don't want to get married just so Lily and I can be with you. What happens if the only contract you're offered is in Canada? Then what?"

He didn't argue I was wrong. He couldn't. Like me, he knew it was a strong possibility the only team who would offer him a contract once he became a free agent was a Canadian team.

And then I was expected to give up everything just to be with him, and so his daughter could be with him.

You want to know the truth? Being an adult sucked the big one.

There, I'd said it. Disney needed to turn my life into a princess movie.

I was positive it would be the next blockbuster.

Except in real life, there were no bibbity-bobbity-freaking-boos.

Josh's jaw jerked. "Look, I didn't come here for us to argue. I just thought it was a viable option so we can be together." He looked toward the rain-splattered window and let out a long breath. "This is our last night together for a few weeks, and I'd much rather spend what little time we have left with me making love to you."

The frustration in his face eased, to be replaced by my favorite panty-dropping smirk—if I had been wearing panties. "Now, can we have some hot and dirty make-up sex?"

Despite everything, I laughed. Besides, he was right. Why waste time being angry when we didn't have much time before he had to leave again?

"So, you don't even want dinner?" I asked, laughter in my voice.

He grinned, everything being good for now—as long as we avoided the elephant in the room. "Dinner might be good."

I lay back and tugged him down to join me. "What do you want first? Dinner? Or..." I trailed my fingertips down his chest, under the sheet covering his hips, and along his hardening length.

He didn't answer with words...instead he showed me exactly what he hungered for—with his mouth and tongue, with his fingers, with his cock.

Dinner? Totally overrated anyway.

34

HOLLY

It was that time of the year again. The time that hockey fans lived for—well, maybe not if your favorite team didn't make it in.

That's right. Playoffs had begun two weeks ago.

Did the Montreal Canadiens make it into the first round?

I entered the team box where the wives and girlfriends were gathered, waiting for the game to begin. What was Lily wearing? Her Canadiens red jersey of course—like me and everyone else.

Was I nervous being here when I didn't know anyone?

Were flamingos pink?

"Hi," a woman, who I hadn't even noticed approach, said next to me. In her arms was a baby a few months older than Lily. "You must be Holly." Then to Lily she said, "Aren't ya just adorable?" Lily gurgled and waved her arms as if to say hi.

Or to agree that she was indeed adorable.

"I'm Emily, Sam Grainger's wife," the woman said. "And this is Ethan. He's six months old. I'm guessing Lily is about three months?"

"Three months next week."

Emily introduced me to the other wives and girlfriends—who of course all gushed over Lily. Their friendly smiles and hellos instantly put me at ease.

"How come you didn't move here with Josh?"

Was Emily's tone judgmental? Not at all. Like the other women with her, she was just curious—which made me relax even more.

I explained my reasons—the job and green card part. I didn't mention the part about Josh suggesting we get married but not for the right reasons.

Even Kelsey and Erin didn't know about what could've easily made it to the list for The Top Ten Ways How *Not* To Propose To The Woman You Love.

"I don't blame you for feeling that way," Emily said. "I was lucky when Sam got traded here. It wasn't like I was giving up a great job. And I was able to make my experience work for me. I created my own online business that can be done anywhere." Emily was a social media consultant.

Could I do something like that? I wasn't so sure—especially with my career goals. They weren't exactly easy to convert into something I could do online.

I know. I know. What happened to thinking outside the box?

Fortunately, I didn't have to figure it out, at least not for now. The game was starting. The Canadiens were currently tied in the series, so tonight's game—the final game in the series—could go either way.

Unfortunately *for me*, they won in overtime. Lily had long since fallen asleep in my arms but stirred at the cheering from the team's box.

I smiled softly at her. "Hey, sweetie. Looks like Daddy won't be coming home to us next week after all."

Was I disappointed? Of course.

But I was also happy for Josh and his team. Because, hello?

We were talking about the chance to win the most coveted trophy in the NHL.

But like anything of value—winning it came at a cost.

Eventually the women met up with their men. Careful not to disturb his sleeping daughter in my arms, Josh kissed me in the way that I loved. The way he always did whenever we hadn't been together for so long—hard and possessive.

Once he was finished showing me how much he missed me, he glanced at Lily with the same adoring expression he always had whenever he looked at her. There was no doubt just how precious she was to him—the one girl he'd kill for.

Did you pity her future boyfriends? Yeah, me too.

"Can I hold her?"

I carefully handed her to him, doing my best not to wake her. Are you surprised she was still sleeping with how noisy the room was? It was true—babies really could sleep through almost anything.

Unless you wanted them to sleep.

Then just the tiniest of sounds woke them up.

"Did you want to go out with the team to celebrate?" I'd overheard his teammates discussing where they were going after this.

Did you see that? The hesitation?

That was because there was no hesitation when he shook his head. "The only person I want to celebrate with tonight is you." He kissed my jaw, his new beard riling me up.

Yes, he was sporting a playoff beard—in all its sexy glory.

And in case you didn't know, oral sex when the guy has a beard is pretty damn amazing.

"You sure?" I asked.

"Very sure."

Sam slapped him on the back. "Man, she really has you pussy whipped."

"Hey, I haven't seen my girls in a month," Josh said. "But I promise when we win the next series, I'll be chugging beer alongside you guys."

Emily rolled her eyes at her husband, then to me said, "Any man who puts you ahead of everything else is a real keeper. And don't let my dum..."—her gaze dropped to the sleeping six-month-old in her arms—"my wonderful husband tell you otherwise."

We returned to Josh's hotel suite soon after, where I got Lily settled in the playpen in the living room, then joined Josh in the bedroom. Normally he was restless after a game. After a series win? Well, I was surprised he wasn't bouncing on the bed.

But instead of joining him on the king-sized bed, I stood at the end of it and swayed my hips side-to-side, erotic dancer style. Jazz music played in my head.

My hips still moving, I slowly unbuttoned the waistband of my jeans, and equally slowly inched the zipper down. Josh ran the tip of his tongue against his lower lip—and I immediately relived in my mind a few choice moments when he had used that talented tongue on my girlie parts.

I almost moaned at the memory.

I shimmied my jeans down my legs, leaving Josh practically panting. I stepped out of them, so all I had left on were my underwear and Canadiens jersey.

I winked at him and could've sworn his eyes grew darker.

Seduction is power, ladies—never forget it.

With the music still playing in my head, I inched the hem of my jersey up my body. I'd lost a bunch of weight since Josh had last seen me. Turned out, breastfeeding was the best diet ever. But unlike with most diet plans, my breasts weren't the first to go.

They were still impressive.

And based on the way Josh licked his lower lip when I gave

him a peek at them, I'd say he had no complaints with what he saw.

I tugged the jersey over my head and dropped it to the floor. Then I crawled over to Josh on the bed. "One of us is a little overdressed here," I said, unfastening the hook on his trousers. "Let me help you out."

I unzipped them and pulled them down his legs. His cock strained against the fabric of his briefs. Yes—someone was very eager for what was coming next.

After neatly folding his trousers, I placed them on the end of the bed. I then straddled his hips, and began slipping the buttons of his dress shirt through the holes. Now, if I were a guy, this is where my patience would've been sorely tested. And an alpha hero? He would've ripped those buttons off in one easy move.

Don't doubt it for a second.

But while Josh wasn't going all-romance-hero on me, his level of patience was wearing thin. He lifted his hips and grounded his hard length against my clit. *Oh. God.* My panties grew wetter, my body betraying its impeding impatience.

I quickly finished unbuttoning his shirt. He removed it and tossed it to the floor. I leaned down and took his nipple into my mouth. Josh groaned—and girl power saluted me.

I sucked and teased the hardening nub with my tongue, relishing each erotic sound Josh made, each demanding movement of his body. After I'd had my fun with the first nipple, I moved over to the other one and treated it to the same level of attention.

Josh continued squirming under me, his hands moving all over my body. In my hair. Down my back. Cupping my breasts. Grabbing hold of my arse.

Once I was finished teasing him, I sat back, pressing my clit against him. It whispered for me to rub it along his hard length

—to make my core happy. To give it a chance to sing an impressive round of hallelujahs that left angels weeping with envy.

Ignoring my clit's pleas, I shifted off Josh and removed his underwear. The moment his cock was freed, it sprung up, enticing me, a drop of desire on its tip.

I licked it off, then took the head into my mouth, and flicked my tongue across the sensitive part. Josh hissed.

I sank my head lower, taking more of him into my mouth. I cupped his balls in my hand and gave them a light squeeze as I sucked his cock. Josh groaned and I continued cupping him while bobbing my head up and down.

"I'm going to blow my load any second," Josh said, voice strained.

Remember what I said about seduction was power? Well, so was this.

I released him from my mouth and grinned at him. "Blow away." I returned to what I was doing, and a moment later he did exactly as promised.

I greedily swallowed, then lay on the bed next to him as he recovered.

"Christ, now I'm *really* glad I didn't go with the guys," he murmured, and I laughed softly.

Then he proceeded to show me what I could expect a lot more of once he returned to San Francisco for the summer.

THE ROOM WAS STILL DARK WHEN I WOKE UP TO LILY'S WHIMPER through the open door. Josh was still asleep next to me. Was it just me who thought he looked sinfully hot while he slept?

If it weren't for Lily, I could've seen if he was ready for sexy times #4 for the night.

That's right for those of you doing the math. The fourth time.

Jealous?

I grabbed my phone from the nightstand and went to join Lily.

"Hey, sweetie, you hungry?" I scooped her up and carried her over to the couch. I had just switched her to the other breast when my phone rang. *What the hell?* Who would be calling me in the middle of the night?

Oh. Right. Simon.

I picked up my phone and my heart almost tripped over itself at the number. Mum?

35

JOSH

The worst thing about waking up with three a.m. wood?

When you realize the only one in bed with you who can relieve it is your hand.

Holly's hushed voice came from the other room, too quiet for me to hear what she was saying. A soft glow leaked past the door, which had been left open a crack.

"No," Holly said as I entered the room. She was sitting on the couch, her back to me, talking on her phone. "It does sound like an amazing opportunity. But what about my life here? This is Lily's home."

I know it was three a.m., when most sane people were still asleep, but thanks to my morning wood, I was fully awake.

Why am I telling you that?

Because I hadn't missed the one important word in what Holly had said.

Here—that was what she had told the other person. But her life wasn't here in Montreal. It was back in San Francisco.

Which meant she was talking to her mother.

Yeah, yeah, I knew Simon was the only one who had trouble getting the time zones straight. But since Christmas, her mom had suddenly wanted to play the role of grandmother—which was a helluva lot easier to do if Holly and Lily lived in Australia.

So the *here*? Holly was referring to North America.

That, or her mother didn't realize Holly and Lily were visiting me in Montreal.

Holly was quiet for a beat before saying, "Really? Drew doesn't mind the fact that Lily belongs to someone else?" The snorted skepticism in her tone helped lessen the shock from the kick to my gut.

Another pause. "No. No, he hasn't. But it's not as simple as that....No, I'm not interested in marrying him like that....Until we know what's going to happen, there's no point worrying about it."

Her voice then softened, almost as if she had given up the battle within herself. The battle I wasn't privy to. "Okay, if that happens, I'll give the job offer some serious consideration....All right. Good-bye, Mum." She was silent for another beat, then ended the call.

Did her words sting? Like hell they did.

"I take it your mother's still trying to get you to move back to Australia," I said, causing Holly to startle.

And no, it wasn't a question.

Was it the first time her mom had tried to do that? Nope.

Was it the first time Holly sounded like she was seriously considering it—that everything she and I had together meant nothing?

Abso-fucking-lutely.

She smiled softly—but everything about her held an edge of weariness. A night of hot and dirty sex, and then waking up a few hours later to feed a baby would do that to you.

"I didn't hear you come in." She glanced at the sleeping

bundle in her arms. "Let me put her down then I'll join you in bed."

I nodded and returned to our room.

She entered it a few minutes later, yawning, and cuddled up beside me on the bed. I gathered her in my arms, prepared to talk about what she and her mom had been discussing.

I never had the chance.

The tension in Holly's muscles drained away and her breathing evened out.

Did I fall asleep right away? Nope—I couldn't stop dwelling on the phone call.

She and I had already discussed us getting married. She shot me down faster than a body plummeting from the Golden Gate Bridge.

Why? Because she wasn't interested in marrying me—but did that mean she wasn't interested in marrying Drew?

Since I wasn't sleeping, how about we do the math?

First—he wasn't an American, which meant if she married him she still couldn't stay in the country like she could if she married me.

Second—she didn't need to marry him to stay in Australia.

Third—she was an independent, resourceful woman who could easily be a single mother. She didn't need a man to look after her and Lily.

Fourth—she had never considered herself the marrying type, especially growing up in a family where her parents lived together but didn't love each other.

And finally—she didn't love him. At least I didn't think she did.

When you added it all up, it didn't make sense. What was Drew offering that Holly needed to consider?

By the time I finally fell asleep, the early signs of dawn were peeking in through the slit between the curtains.

I woke up several hours later, feeling like I hadn't slept at all. The midmorning sunlight streamed into the room through the gap in the curtains. I glanced at the alarm clock.

Shit, it was already nine minutes after ten.

Not surprisingly, Holly wasn't next to me in bed. Nor were she and Lily in the other room. But there was a note on the kitchen counter:

> Lily and I have gone for a walk to explore this fine city. Be back soon.
> Love Holly.

I sent her a text.

> Me: Where are you?

She replied a minute later.

> Holly: Teaching Lily the fine art of shopping in a foreign country :)

> Me: Tell me where you are and I'll join you.

She texted me and we agreed to meet at a cafe near her location. I arrived a few minutes before they did and was already seated when they entered. Holly spotted me and walked over to my table, Lily happy in her front carrier.

I stood up and kissed Holly briefly, then kissed Lily's head. "How's my baby girl doing?"

Lily gurgled and cooed and drooled her answer.

I helped Holly remove her from the carrier, then sat back in my seat with my daughter in my arms.

"What can I get for you to drink?" the college-age waitress asked as Holly and I were studying our menus. Then she looked at me and her eyes went wide. "Don't you play for the

Canadiens? My boyfriend and I are huge fans. We go to all the games. Well, we did until you made the playoffs. The tickets are too expensive."

I'd never heard anyone talk that fast before. If there was a world record for it, she probably held it.

Or was in training for it.

Lily cooed at the waitress and giggled.

The girl smiled at her. "Ooh, aren't you just the cutest little thing. Is this your daughter?" She looked between Holly and me.

"Yes, she is," I told her, and smiled at Holly, proud at what she and I had accomplished together—even if Lily had been unexpected.

"You guys look adorable together."

We thanked her, and she took our order and left.

"See—*she* thinks we're great together," I pointed out to Holly.

Holly chuckled. "She said we *look* great together, not that we are great together."

"So you don't think we're great together?" I said it in a playful tone, but that wasn't the emotion churning in the pit of my gut.

"Sure I do."

"But not enough for you *not* to consider Drew's offer?" My tone wasn't so playful this time.

"How did you…? Right, the phone call from my mum."

"So it's true?"

What do professional hockey players do before they play against their opponent? They watch the team analysis video. They study the goalie's and the players' weaknesses and strengths. They never hit the ice without some sort of team strategy in mind.

They never hit the ice blind.

Yet here I was, asking if something was true when I had no

idea what Drew was offering her.

"Look, I'm not sure this is the place to discuss this." She glanced around the busy cafe.

"So, does Drew still want to marry you?"

Okay—that was *not* what I had in mind. But since we were here...

I waited patiently for her to answer.

All right, not so patiently. I drummed my heel against the floor.

Wait for it.

One corner of her mouth twitched up. Then the other side did the same.

And if that wasn't puzzling enough—she threw her head back in laughter.

Which gained her a few odd glances.

Mostly from me. My girlfriend was seriously losing it.

"Why would you think he's interested in marrying me? For one, that man can have any woman he wants. He doesn't want one with a baby in tow."

"Hey, there's nothing wrong with Lily." I smiled at my daughter. "Is there, sweetheart?"

Lily grinned at me and cooed.

Right—never mind that. We were talking about Drew and Holly. "I heard you ask your mother if Drew doesn't mind that Lily belongs to someone else?"

"It's not what you think. Yes—my mum is hoping I'll move back to Australia. And yes—she and her friend are hoping he and I will get together because as far as her friend is concerned, that's the only way she's going to get grandchildren. Drew hasn't exactly been working hard in that department as far as she's concerned. But like I said, Drew isn't interested in me that way."

"Then what was the offer you and your mom were talking about on the phone?"

"There's an opportunity with the company Drew had dealt with before. But the position is in New York City."

"And you're considering it?" Frustration stomped through my tone.

Lily squirmed in my arms, whimpered, then let out a lung-filled protest.

"She's hungry," Holly said, taking Lily from me. She adjusted her clothing and effortlessly got Lily into position on her breast.

Now guys, if there's ever a time not to argue with your girlfriend or wife it's while she's breastfeeding your child. It won't score you any points if you do—and you'll be too distracted, knowing the baby's getting to suck on the breasts that you used to enjoy.

And who will end up winning the argument? That's right, she will.

But that's easy to say when you aren't the one itching to continue the argument through to the next round. When you know she isn't going anywhere until she has finished feeding your child.

When you know you have a captive audience, no matter what.

"Why don't you want to marry me?" I asked.

I know—that was *not* what you were expecting me to say. But now that we had cleared the air about Drew not being interested in Holly that way, I wanted to know why she wasn't interested in marrying *me*.

Fair enough question?

She let out a long sigh—the type of sigh where you braced yourself against any piece of furniture fastened to the floor or wall. "Why do *you* want to marry me, Josh?"

"Because one—I love you. Two—we made an amazing little girl together. And three—because it just makes sense."

"Why does it make sense?"

"Because no matter what happens with my career come July, I won't have to worry about you being sent back to Australia if something happens to your job before you get your green card." We had already gone through this before.

Except my answer didn't seem to change anything. She still looked resigned.

"Are you still saying you don't want to marry me?" I asked.

She gave me a sad smile—and I grabbed the edge of the table...even though it wasn't fastened to the floor.

"No, I'm saying I don't want to marry you because it's the convenient thing to do. Otherwise I might as well have married Drew when he was interested." She glanced at the blanket covering her and Lily. "Anyway, it doesn't matter why I don't want to marry you. Unless something happens between now and the end of May"—when she was supposed to return to work—"none of this matters. I'm not going anywhere. I mean, other than back to San Francisco the day after tomorrow."

She repositioned Lily on the other breast, then smiled at me again. Except this time, her eyes held the usual sparkle I loved so much. "I love you, Josh. Just because I'm not agreeing to what you're proposing doesn't mean I don't love you. That's not going to change. But right now, the only thing I'm interested in is spending as much time with you as possible. For the three of us to spend time together."

Like a family, I said in my head.

Like the family I'd never really had growing up.

Like the family I'd never wanted...until now.

As much as I hated it, she was right. We didn't have much time left before Holly and Lily had to return to San Francisco. I didn't want to waste a second of it arguing.

Besides, she wasn't saying "no" to marrying me because she didn't love me.

That meant I had a chance to change her mind.

I just had to figure out how.

JOSH

A week later, I was sitting on the hotel bed. No, not the one in Montreal. This one was in New York City. I checked my phone to see if Trent had texted me yet. He and Kelsey were flying in to spend a few days in the city and to see tonight's game against the Rangers.

At least that was the plan. But their flight had been delayed several hours. Why? We could thank Murphy for that and his dumbass law. If I didn't need to talk to Kelsey about Holly, there would've been no delays.

You're right—the plan was for me to *try* to talk to Kelsey about Holly. Who knew if she was going to be as forthcoming as I would like—or if what I wanted to ask her would violate some secret friendship pact that guys were oblivious to?

Trent: We've landed. See you after the game?

Me: Absolutely.

Holly: Good luck on tonight's game. Lily and I will be cheering for you. XOX

The next text was a picture of Lily smiling at the camera with her Canadiens jersey on. Never thought I would miss anyone as much as I missed my daughter. My daughter and her smart and gorgeous mother.

Which was why I needed Kelsey's help.

> Me to Holly: Thanks. Miss you! Give Lily a kiss from me.

Then...

> Me: What do I get if the Canadiens win tonight?

Holly: Phone sex :)

Oh, don't act all surprised. How do you think I survived the month she and I were apart? Phone sex was a great way to get close when you couldn't *be* close.

Don't believe me? Give it a try some time.

> Me: I like that incentive. I'll be sure to keep it in mind during the game.

I returned my phone to the night table, and unrolled my yoga mat on the floor, taking care not to block the TV.

"I told Emily you do yoga," Sam said, watching whatever sitcom he had found—even though he had a TV in his own room.

"And?"

"And she's signed herself and me up for yoga classes this summer."

I laughed. "And you're not happy about that?"

He shrugged. "I'm not exactly a yoga guy."

"And you know this because you've done yoga before?" Yes, I might have still been laughing.

He grunted and I laughed harder.

"So why don't you just tell her you don't want to do it?"

"Because I figured if *you* did it then maybe there was something to it. And because that's what you do when you love someone."

"What—take yoga classes with her?" Because if that was the case, with the six months of prenatal yoga classes I took with Holly, she had more than enough proof of how much I loved her.

You didn't know about that? After the first month of doing yoga to the same two DVDs, it got boring. All right, boring was an understatement. Anyway, I hired a yoga instructor to come to Holly's apartment twice a week to work with us.

Why? Because six more months of the same two DVDs would have driven me serial-killer insane.

"Well, not necessarily yoga," Sam said, "But sometimes you just have to man it up and do something you might not necessarily like, but you do it anyway to make her happy. You have a girlfriend. You know how it is."

"Sure." Did I? Because from where I was standing, it didn't look like I had made Holly happy enough to want to marry me —or be with me wherever my career led me next.

Which was part of the problem.

I wasn't ready to give up my career and she wasn't prepared to give up hers—even for the sake of our daughter.

Which probably made us the worst parents ever—and not much better than our own parents had been.

This was the same thought that plagued me until I stepped onto the ice two hours later for our game.

IN THE DRESSING ROOM AFTER GETTING MY PHONE BACK, I READ Holly's text.

Holly: Sorry about the game.

In case you hadn't guessed—we lost. Badly.

Me: Is phone sex still on the table?

Holly: On the table. On the floor. On the bed.
Wherever you want it.

I smirked at that.

Me: Meeting up with Trent and Kelsey first. Will
take a rain check on it if you're offering one.

Holly: Of course. And this rain check doesn't
have an expiry date—and it can be used any
time tonight.

Trent and I had already planned where to meet up once I'd returned to the hotel and changed. I sent him a text, telling him I was on my way, and headed to the quiet bar he had suggested.

The best thing about Trent and Kelsey? They didn't talk hockey after a game—especially if my team had lost. They knew nothing they said would change the outcome, so what was the point of discussing it?

Which meant we could go straight to the topic I had in mind: Holly.

"How's Holly and Lily doing?" I asked Kelsey.

She frowned, clearly confused at my question. "Don't you talk to Holly?"

"Yes, but you see her a lot more than I do, so I was just curious."

"Well, unless there's something she's not telling me, she seems fine." She exchanged glances with Trent.

"What?" I asked.

"She's been talking about a job offer in Australia she's starting to consider."

"But she already has a job in San Francisco." That she was returning to soon. She'd even hired the nanny last week.

Kelsey bit her lip. I was definitely missing something here.

"Tell me," I said, a little more forcibly than I should have, if the don't-shoot-the-messenger look Trent threw me was anything to go by. "Look, I don't want to see her leave. I love her and I love our daughter."

"I know, but you're not around anymore and things won't get better if you land a contract back in Canada or with another team. Doesn't Holly at least deserve to fall in love with a man who will be there for her and Lily? Doesn't she deserve a man who wants to spend the rest of his life with her because he can't imagine being with anyone else? He can't imagine a life without her." She reached for Trent's hand and threaded her fingers with his.

"So I'm supposed to give up my hockey career for her?"

"No, but why do you want to marry her?"

"She told you that?"

Kelsey's confused frown returned. "You didn't suggest you two should get married?"

"Yes, but she shot me down."

Kelsey rolled her eyes as if I was a complete and utter moron—and maybe I was. "How did you propose to her?"

"Well..." The conversations Holly and I'd had leaked into my dumbass brain. Not once had I actually proposed to Holly. Even though I had told her I loved her, I had still made it sound like a business arrangement between us. I had made it sound like the only reason I wanted to marry her was to keep her from being deported if she ever lost her job and to keep from losing my daughter.

And so she could join me if I was offered a contract elsewhere.

"You didn't, did you?" Kelsey's tone was sympathetic more than anything else—and further confirmed that I was an idiot.

I sank back in my chair and shook my head. "No, I didn't."

Not once had I considered telling Holly exactly how much I loved her and that I wanted to spend the rest of my life with her. Not once had I let her know what was really in my heart. So in the end, no matter how much I'd try to do otherwise, I had been like my old man.

Shit.

"If it counts for anything," Kelsey said, "she really does love you, and I don't think she wants to go back to Australia. She just wants to do what's best for Lily."

Kelsey said something else but I didn't hear her. I was too busy figuring out how to show Holly how much I loved her and wanted to marry her because of that.

I was too busy figuring out how to propose to her.

37

HOLLY

There's an age-old debate as to whether God is a man or a woman. Now, if I actually believed in God, I would completely go with the man theory.

Why?

Because a woman—or at least one who had attempted juggling a diaper bag, baby, stroller with infant car seat attached, suitcase, and everything else she needed while traveling—would have ensured woman-kind sprouted an extra arm or two whenever she gave birth or adopted.

Although an extra friend or two also worked well in a pinch.

As I pushed Lily's stroller toward the luggage carousel at LaGuardia Airport, Kelsey rushed over and hugged me. She then peered down at Lily, who had fallen asleep the moment I put her in her infant car seat after walking off the plane.

"I can't believe how much she's grown since I last saw her," Kelsey said.

Which was four days ago.

"She's a regular little bean sprout," I said, grinning at my sleeping daughter.

My phone pinged an incoming text. I glanced at the screen.

Drew: Interview all set. They're looking forward
to meeting with you this afternoon.

What was that all about?

Drew had convinced me to at least meet with the company who had been interested in me joining their investment team. I figured it wouldn't hurt to at least see what they had to say since I was in New York City.

The home of Wall Street.

The place I had originally longed to work—until I landed the job offer in San Francisco. This job was a step up from my current one, with the potential for other great opportunities.

The job offer in Australia? I had told them the other day that I wasn't interested.

I hugged Trent and glanced around the crowded area. "Is Josh here?"

And in case you were wondering—Josh didn't know about the interview.

Not yet anyway. I decided to see how it went first.

"No, we'll meet up with him later," Trent said. "The team's practicing and then they've got a meeting."

Oh. Later was when I had my interview.

While we waited for my luggage, I caught up on everything they had done in the short time they'd been here. Trent had gone to Columbia University and had been dying to show Kelsey the city.

Eventually my luggage arrived on the carousel and Trent removed it, then we headed to the parkade and their rental car.

For those of you who are familiar with Manhattan, you are no doubt on the floor now, having laughed so hard you fell off your chair.

The rest of you are scratching your heads, wondering what was so funny. There's a reason the majority of cars on the streets of Manhattan are cabs. And there's a reason most New Yorkers ride the subway or hop in a cab to get around. From what Trent had told me, parking in New York City is expensive.

Not to mention New York City drivers are certifiably nuts.

Don't believe me? Then you have obviously never been here. Sit on the beach in San Francisco and what do you hear? The swoosh of the wind, the crashing waves against the shore, the squawking of seagulls.

What do you hear when you stand on the corner of Broadway and 42nd Street?

Constant honking—the 24-7 honking that doesn't involve a goose.

As Trent drove us from the airport, the tall Manhattan skyscrapers beckoned to me—told me this was where I belonged.

"What do you think?" I asked Lily, who was still asleep and probably didn't have an opinion either way. At least not yet—at least not for a few more years.

But instead of driving to Manhattan like I'd expected, we drove past the city toward Long Island.

"Where are we going?" I asked.

"You'll see," Kelsey said, smiling, although I got the idea she was fighting to keep from grinning.

Just as I was beginning to wonder if Trent was driving us to Canada, he pulled into the parking lot of a small indoor skating rink. Only one other car was parked in it.

"Why are we here?" I asked.

"You'll see," Kelsey said as Trent pulled out his phone and typed something. "We'll wait here with Lily and call you if we need you."

"Why do you need to wait? Where am I gonna be?"

She pointed to the building. "In there."

"And why exactly do I need to go in there?"

"You'll see," Trent said with a wink, echoing what Kelsey had already told me.

I glanced back at the building. "Are you sure? It looks closed."

"I'm positive."

Alrighty then. I opened the car door and walked to the entrance. According to the hours of operation listed on the door, the building was currently closed, but since Kelsey and Trent were so adamant I go inside, I pulled on the door handle.

The door opened without protest, and I entered the building. The first thing I noticed was the lingering smell of arena, sweat, and floor cleaner.

The second?

Have you ever watched a zombie apocalypse movie? This building reminded me of one, with that eery quiet that always came before zombies popped out of nowhere.

No one was manning the front desk, but on the floor was a sign that said FOLLOW ME, with a trail of red rose petals leading toward a closed door.

Since I hadn't heard of any zombie infestations hitting the New York area, I figured it was safe to follow the petals. No zombies would be lumbering toward me from a dark corner.

Given the building housed a skating rink, I probably didn't have to tell you where I ended up. On the bench near the opening to the rink was a sign proclaiming PUT US ON, a pair of figure skates, and a hoodie.

I slipped on the hoodie, which had been designed for a tall, muscular man. The warm, fleecy fabric flooded my body. I slipped my phone into a pocket, then picked up the skates and sat on the bench.

"Okay, I've got the skates on," I called out after I had put them on. I surveyed my surroundings, but as far as I could tell I was the only person here. "Now what?"

No sooner than I had said those two words, jazz music began playing through the speakers.

"Ready for your first skating lesson?" Josh said from behind me. His deep voice almost melted me on the spot, despite the cool arena temperature.

I twisted around to find him standing there with his hockey skates on and his favorite hoodie—and the world's sexiest smile. If there was ever a smile to swoon over, *this* would be the one.

"I think so," I said, grinning at him. "Just be prepared to witness me fall on my arse."

"Don't worry. I'll massage all your aches away tonight."

I laughed. "In that case, you might be very busy." I turned back to the ice and took a tentative step forward. "All right. Let's do this."

"Are you forgetting something?"

I checked the bench to see what else I could have missed. "What?"

"Well, considering I haven't seen you in a week…"

I turned back to him in time for his lips to capture mine in a kiss—a kiss capable of melting all the ice in the rink.

And I could've kept kissing him for another few hours, but he stepped away—much to my lips' dismay.

"Better now?" I asked, smiling.

"Much better. Ready for this?" He gestured at the ice.

Did you see it? The sliver of vulnerability on his face?

I had no idea why he would feel vulnerable. It wasn't *his* dignity and pride at stake.

He knew how to skate.

And he knew how not to land on his butt.

"Okay, Cool Stuff. Show me how it's done."

My years of dance did *not* prepare me for walking in figure skates. That thin blade under the boots? Designed purely to make the unskilled look far from graceful. It also made for a wobbly walk.

But that was nothing compared to stepping down from the rubber mat onto the slippery ice. My legs instantly tensed and I held up my arms for balance...or at least to attempt to balance.

"You're doing great," Josh said from the rink entrance. I was still blocking the way, keeping him from joining me on the ice.

Purely accidental—in case you were wondering. I just didn't know how to move forward.

I grabbed the low wall and pulled myself away from the entrance. Josh effortlessly stepped onto the ice, then skated forward a few meters to demonstrate what I was supposed to do...if my legs chose to cooperate.

"Okay, I think I got it." *Or not.*

Taking great care not to fall on my arse, I slowly let go of the wall.

So far so good.

Josh reached for my hand, which I gladly gave him. If I was going down, so was he.

With my muscles tense like an overly wound elastic band, I pushed my foot against the ice like he had shown me. Surprisingly, not only did I *not* fall on my backside, I actually moved forward. Could you believe it?

I attempted it again—and was rewarded with the same result.

"I'm skating!"

Josh grinned at me. "Yes, you are."

He kept hold of my hand while I continued skating, my legs shaky. I was positive if anyone else witnessed this, they'd be laughing their arses off.

But I didn't care.

I. Was. Freaking. Skating.

We skated around the rink, our progress super-slow. But by

the time we had completed a lap, my legs weren't quite as shaky and my muscles were no longer as stiff as before.

"You enjoying this?" Josh asked.

"Yes." I flashed him a quick smile. "This was the best surprise ever." Other than the one that ended up being Lily.

The music ended and "The Way You Look Tonight" began to play. Josh sang the lyrics as we continued skating around the ice, with him still holding my hand.

When he got to the line "Keep that breathless charm," he stopped skating and turned to face me. "Holly, I never expected to ever fall in love but I did—with you. And even though together we made a beautiful little girl, I would still feel the same way about you even if she hadn't been conceived. I would have still fallen in love with you. I would have still wanted to spend my life with you—and only you."

My eyes misted at his words. The words I had longed for him to say all this time. But...

"Did Kelsey tell you to say that?" I asked, voice hushed and strained with emotion.

"No. She made me figure it out myself. But I should have told you all of that from the beginning. While I might not have said those words back then, it was certainly how I felt. I was just too much of a dumbass to realize you didn't know that was how I felt. I'm sorry it's taken me so long to figure that out."

He put his hand in his hoodie pocket and got down on one knee. No, I didn't start sobbing like most girls would have. I had my big-girl panties on. My incredibly sexy, black lace, big-girl panties.

"Holly Whittaker, will you spend the rest of your life growing old with me? Will you marry me?" He removed his hand from the pocket along with a small black box.

The tears? Yes, I'll admit it. Now they were running down my face.

But before I could answer him, there was one thing I had to do—while I still could.

I removed my phone from the hoodie pocket and speed dialed the number.

Drew answered on the second ring. "G'day, mate. You must have ESP. I was about to call you with the address."

"I won't be needing it," I said.

"Why not?"

"Because Josh just asked me to marry him, and I said yes—or at least I will once I get off the phone." I spluttered a laugh at Josh's relieved expression. Relieved but definitely confused. "I was hoping you can tell them that while I thank them for the opportunity, I'm going to pass."

"Are you sure about this?" Drew asked—his voice neither pissed nor worried. If anything, he was as confused as Josh was.

Was I sure about this—any of this?

As sure as the earth was round. I had never truly felt committed to the interview—and now I understood why.

"One hundred and fifty percent sure," I said and ended the call. Then to Josh I said, my gaze never leaving his for a second, "Yes, Joshua Hoffer, I would love to marry you and grow old together."

"And maybe at some point, we can give Lily a brother or sister?"

The smile on my face was so big, my cheeks ached. "I think that can be arranged."

Still kneeling, Josh opened the box, removed the platinum ring, then slipped it onto my finger.

"Oh God. It's beautiful." On the part where the diamonds sat, the metal was loosely twisted. A large square diamond sat in the center, with three small diamonds on either side. It was the most gorgeous ring I'd ever seen.

Josh stood up, then his mouth was on mine. My arms went

around his neck, and I returned his kiss. Our tongues glided together in a slow, sweet dance.

Admit it—that was *the* best proposal ever asked. And I wasn't saying that because I was biased.

All right, ten percent was due to me being biased.

Twenty percent, tops.

We continued kissing for one more slow song before the music abruptly stopped.

"I guess that's our cue that public skating is starting soon," Josh said. "But first, you want to explain that call?" He pointed at the pocket with my phone in it.

"That was me being spontaneous—for you and only you."

There was still the issue of what I would do if he was offered a contract with another team. It was like that game where you were given a scenario and you had to say what you would do if it happened to you.

But in real life, it was impossible to predict that until it actually happened. So until we knew what team he was offered a contract with, I refused to speculate.

All I knew was whatever choice I made, it would be the right one for Lily and Josh and me.

As we skated back to our stuff, I asked, "How did you arrange all of this?" I gestured to the rink.

He winked at me. "I happen to know people in high places." And a few hundreds slipped to the right person probably didn't hurt either.

"Well, tell them thank you from me. It was perfect."

Josh stopped skating and wrapped his arms around my waist. "No, it's you, Holly, who's perfect. Perfect for me."

Then he kissed me once more, deeply—and what could be more perfect than that?

38

HOLLY

What's five-month-old Lily's favorite game? Watch this.

I placed Snuggle Bear on the cream-colored rug in Lily's bedroom and covered the floppy bear with the pink baby blanket. "Where did Snuggle Bear go?" I asked Lily in a sing-song voice. Since she wasn't quite able to sit on her own yet, a pile of cushions propped her up.

The little girl blew a raspberry—her favorite new sound, which she loved to practice whenever she could.

Smiling at her, I whipped the blanket off the toy. "There she is."

Lily giggled. Didn't she have the cutest giggle ever?

The apartment door clicked open then shut.

"Daddy's home," I said, loud enough so Josh would know where to find us. A moment later he entered the room, wearing shorts and a white T-shirt that clung deliciously to his sweaty body. "How was your run?"

From the look of him, he had pushed himself to hell and back, pausing only long enough to down his favorite sports drink. But could you blame him?

Yesterday, he was officially a Montreal Canadien.

Today he was a free agent—with no idea where his future would take him for the next year or so.

When would he find out if a team offered him a contract? Anytime between nine a.m. today and the beginning of the NHL season—in October.

So anytime in the next three months—which made it really hard to plan things.

What was I doing home on a Friday morning when I had returned to work last month?

I loved my job, but I also loved being with Lily—and I needed the flexibility so we could fly out and visit Josh whenever possible, depending on where he ended up. We had already decided I would stay in San Francisco no matter what, and Josh would live with us during the off-season until he eventually retired from hockey. It wasn't the greatest solution, but we would make it work.

But I did have a long talk with my boss and then his boss. In the end, they offered me the opportunity to job share with the woman who had been covering for me while I was on maternity leave. She wanted to get her Masters degree in International Business. Job-sharing allowed her to do both that and work.

It was a win-win for us both.

And the best part? The switch in hours didn't jeopardize my work visa status. Not that it would matter once Josh and I were married.

Josh knelt on the hardwood floor—to avoid getting sweat on Lily's rug. "The run was good." He picked up the pink blanket and covered my head with it. "Where did Mommy go?" he asked Lily.

She, of course, blew another raspberry.

The blanket was yanked off my head. "There she is."

Lily giggled—and Josh leaned in to give me a brief kiss. "Guess I should have a shower now."

"That might be a good idea." I gave his shoulder a little shove. Not enough to move him, but that didn't matter. He pretended to fall over anyway.

Lily giggled once more. One of her other favorite toys was the kind that you pushed over and it wobbled up again.

"Uh, oh," I said, "Daddy fell down."

Not overly concerned about this, she went back to practicing her air raspberries.

Joshed pushed himself back onto his knees, pulled Lily's koala T-shirt up (one of a million gifts my parents had sent her), and blew a raspberry on her belly.

What's her second favorite thing to blowing raspberries? Daddy blowing them on her stomach. She giggled and reached up to him.

She really was Daddy's little girl.

Just as her T-shirt proclaimed.

He kissed her forehead. "I'm all yucky, but as soon as I finish my shower I'll pick you up. Deal?"

Lily cooed in reply.

She and I played while he showered, my heart suddenly pounding in my chest—like the countdown clock on New Year's Eve.

Ten. Nine. Eight...

Only in this case, it taunted me with the reminder that nine a.m. was rapidly approaching.

There would be no spectacular firework show once the clock struck midnight.

But on the bright side, Lily's crib wouldn't be turned into a pumpkin either.

For the past few weeks, rumors had been circulating about which teams were showing an interest in him, but while Josh chose not to talk about them, Trent had pointed out they were exactly that—rumors.

And because I didn't want to stress out about where Josh could be moving to next, I avoided anything where I might glimpse a knock-me-on-my-arse rumor.

And that included telling my colleagues that under no circumstances, whatsoever, were they allowed to mention hockey in my presence.

To do so would not be pretty.

Naturally, I saved this announcement while holding one of Lily's dirty diapers, so that might've had something to do with their total cooperation.

"If we're lucky, San Jose will sign Daddy," I told Lily.

But luck had nothing to do with it.

Nor did wishing on a shooting star.

But in case it did, I might have tried it. Once or twice.

Okay, thrice.

But you know what they say about three times the charm…

"And I've heard Vancouver's really nice," I told her—in case he signed with another Canadian team.

Please, please, please, if he has to join a Canadian team, make it Vancouver. Not only was it closer to San Francisco, it was the one Canadian city that didn't suffer from brutal winters.

Maybe I should've also wished for that when it came to the shooting stars—as Plan B.

As Josh stepped from the bathroom, his phone rang from the kitchen table. He briefly glanced in my direction and I could've sworn I stopped breathing.

I could hear him talking to whoever was on the other end but was unable to hear what he was saying. I couldn't even tell if it was good news or not.

After what felt like a hundred and twenty years, the phone call ended. Josh walked toward Lily's room—his expression giving nothing away.

"Was that your agent?" I asked. *Seven. Six. Five...*

He shook his head and I released a shaky breath. "It was the Rock. They were calling me to tell me I got the internship."

"Internship?"

"I didn't say anything to you in case it didn't pan out, but I've decided to retire from hockey."

"You have? But I thought you weren't ready to give it up yet." I couldn't believe I was actually trying to talk him out of it —*what was I thinking*?

I was thinking that I didn't want him to give up on his dream, his goal, because of Lily and me. I didn't want him to one day regret this.

He sat on the rug. "I know, but I've been talking to a few players who recently retired. I decided this is the right time to do it. For me. For us." He brushed his lips against mine. "And I was talking about it to someone I know in the marketing department. They have an internship position, and because of my experience with the team and my marketing minor in college, they offered it to me. I don't know if it will result in a permanent position, but the experience will be worth it."

"But you're sure this is what you want?"

"Yes, this is what I want. Of course, my agent wasn't thrilled with the idea."

"I bet." Not when Josh had been making four million dollars a year.

"But since my agent isn't the one I'm marrying and my agent isn't the one I plan to spend the rest of my life growing old with, he doesn't have a lot of say in my decision."

Josh lowered his head to mine, this time giving me a deeper, longer lasting kiss than the last one.

And those fireworks? The ones that lit up the night sky at the end of the New Year's countdown?

They had nothing on the ones going off in my body.

After a few minutes, Josh ended the kiss, resting his forehead against mine. "That was definitely worth ending my hockey career for. You're worth ending it for."

And for the first time since Josh proposed to me, I could finally fully breathe—knowing the man I loved would always be there, by my side.

Knowing that each night I went to sleep and each morning when I woke up, he would be there. Always.

Knowing Josh wouldn't be sacrificing what he loved to make Lily and me happy.

He was doing what was right for him and what was right for us.

As a family.

EPILOGUE
JOSH

Five and a Half Months Later

Whoever said Christmas was for kids was wrong. Because when you were a ten-month-old baby, Christmas was totally for the parents.

That's right, Lily was almost a year old. And today she would be experiencing Santa for the first time. She had already seen him at the mall a few times but had no idea of his significance. She had been more excited with the pretty, shiny Christmas tree decorations.

Had she already joined the throngs of kids waiting to see Santa at the mall? Nope—we wanted her first experience with the guy to be less traumatic.

Don't believe me that Santa could cause PTSD? The next time you see him at the mall, grab some popcorn and watch. Mothers love to get photos of their kids sitting on the big guy's lap. But babies and young kids don't always share the sentiment. The instant the baby realizes he's on a stranger's lap, he starts bawling. And that is the wonderful photo now gracing the family's Christmas cards.

Plus we didn't want to risk Lily ending up with an overheated guy in a red suit who couldn't stand kids. He was only doing it to earn some "easy" cash during the holidays. We wanted someone who was excited to play the role, and we wanted to avoid the stressed-out craziness.

But most of all—we wanted Lily's first Christmas to be special.

So that brought us to why we were here at Trent's sister's house. Erin and her husband were having a Christmas party for their fourteen-month-old daughter and her toddler friends. Their house looked like Christmas had exploded all over the place, in the most awesome way.

I placed Lily on the floor. As soon as her knees touched the carpet, she was crawling toward the tree—and to one glittery decoration in particular. Good luck to her future fiancé. If this was any indication, she'd be wanting a large sparkly engagement ring.

Speaking of engagement rings—I made my way over to Trent, who was by the wingback chair near the window. He didn't see me approach. He was too busy staring at his girlfriend, who was talking to Holly.

Kelsey glanced in our direction, and from the way she suddenly blushed, she too hadn't missed the heat in his eyes. She quickly looked away and answered whatever Holly had just asked her. Did I care what Holly had said? No—I was preoccupied with fantasizing about what I wanted to do to her tonight, once our daughter was asleep.

"Did you get *it*?" I asked Trent, keeping my voice low.

He nodded, knowing exactly what *it* I was referring to.

Trent had decided that he didn't need to date Kelsey for several years to know he wanted to spend the rest of his life with her. The "it"? An engagement ring.

"Have you seen Travis yet?" I asked, still keeping my voice low so the kids didn't overhear me.

"He's getting changed now."

Who was playing Santa's helper? The image of Holly in a sexy red-and-white dress and thigh-high boots popped into my head. Yep, this was my new sexual fantasy for the next two weeks.

Hey, what did you expect? When it came to Holly, I was horny 24-7. Only now I didn't have to suffer while on road trips. I got to come home to my living fantasy every night.

Yes—life was great.

Except for one thing.

Holly hadn't settled on a date yet for our wedding, even though we'd been engaged for seven months. That wasn't to say her mother and my grandmother hadn't hinted loudly that we should decide on one soon.

Holly scooped up our daughter, and the two of them and Kelsey joined Trent and me.

Kelsey wrapped her arms around Trent's neck and gave him a kid-friendly kiss. "Having fun yet?"

He leaned down, his mouth close to her ear, presumably to tell her something. Whatever it might've been was *not* kid-friendly, if Kelsey's new round of blushing was any indication.

"Da da da da," Lily said and gave me a toothless grin.

Don't get too excited. She also liked to call me "ma ma."

"Can you keep an eye on her while I help Santa?" Holly asked me, then handed the little princess off and kissed my cheek.

"Da da," Lily said to Holly.

"I'm hoping Santa's helper will do a lot more to me later than just kiss me on the cheek," I told Holly, not worrying about scarring Lily for life with that comment.

"Don't worry, I've got a lot more planned for later." She kissed the top of Lily's head. "Once we get this one to bed."

"I'm holding you to that."

Lily giggled. "Ma ma ma."

"Okay, sweetie," Holly said to her. "I'll be back in a few minutes with Santa." She looked between us. "You think you two can keep out of trouble while I'm gone?"

"Define keeping out of trouble," I said with a smirk.

She rolled her eyes and disappeared into the hallway with Kelsey.

Kelsey returned a few minutes later with her camera. "Okay, boys and girls," she said to the five toddlers dancing in the center of the living room to the kids' Christmas music. "Are you ready to see Santa?"

The toddlers stopped moving, mostly because Erin had turned off the music. They looked at Kelsey with their adorably clueless expressions. None of them knew who Santa was.

The best thing about that age? It didn't take much to get them excited. Their parents cheered as if this was the best news they'd ever heard, and the kids jumped up and down in excitement.

So. Fucking. Cute.

Holly walked in with Travis close behind. And no—she wasn't wearing a sexy Santa's helper outfit. She had on her navy wraparound dress and a bright red elf hat with white trim. But either way, she still looked hot as hell.

On the other hand, I had to choke back a laugh when it came to Travis. Clearly his Santa's outfit had been designed for someone who wasn't six-three. And the beard didn't look too comfy, especially for a guy who never even bothered growing a playoff beard. The extra stuffing around his middle was pretty amusing too, given his muscular build.

But if his size intimidated the toddlers, they didn't show it. They just stared at him, unsure what to do next. If anything, Travis was the one who seemed a little nervous. Amazing how a rowdy bunch of toddlers could have that effect on a man.

Travis sat on the wingback chair, and one by one the toddlers visited with him.

Finally it was Lily's turn. Holly placed our daughter on Santa's lap.

Lily reached up and managed to tangle her small fingers in his beard, then yanked the white strands. "Da da da."

"I think she's saying her daddy needs to grow a beard," Travis said and threw in a few "Ho ho hos" for added effect.

Holly laughed. "That's okay. I'm perfectly happy with him the way he is."

I pulled her against me and murmured in her ear. "Perfectly happy with me enough to finally pick a wedding date? Because I want to spend every day of my life with you, and I'm more than ready to make it official." My voice turned husky for the next part. "And I'm ready to spend our honeymoon with me fucking you so much, you won't have the energy or desire to leave our room. That, Hot Stuff, is a promise."

The tremor of her body? Yep—I was definitely getting to her.

"Oh, you are, are you?" she murmured back, a smile in her voice. "You make a very interesting proposition. I'll take your promise under advisement."

What did I crave? To put my hand on her sweet ass and pull her to me, then tell her in excruciating detail what I planned to do to her during our honeymoon.

But there were two reasons as to why I couldn't do exactly that. One—this was a kids' party...so having my hands on her ass was not permitted. Two—Lily's attention span when it came to Santa would only go so far.

Santa handed Lily a present and I removed her from his lap. With her clutching the small gift, we returned to Holly.

"What do you say, sweetheart?" I said to our daughter. "You ready to convince Mummy to pick a date for our wedding?"

"Ma ma ma. Da da da."

I chuckled. "See? Even Lily is ready for us to get married."

Was I worried that Holly didn't really want to marry me, and that was why she hadn't set a date yet? No—not at all.

So why the delay? It was the idea of organizing it that had her putting it off. It wasn't like we were just dealing with friends and family who lived in the U.S. We were dealing with two continents on the opposite side of the world from each other. Which meant it would be a nightmare to plan.

And guess where her mother was pushing for us to have the ceremony and reception.

"You know, we don't have to have a big ceremony," I suggested. "We can have a small one in San Francisco for our close friends and immediate family. Then we can have one reception here and one in Australia."

Her eyes lit up. "You would be okay with that?"

"I would be okay if it was just the three of us at the justice of the peace, with Trent and Kelsey witnessing it. I just want to marry you, Holly. The rest of it isn't important."

She pressed her lips lightly against mine. "I love you, you know that?"

I smiled. "So I've heard."

"So in that case, are you doing anything Saturday, May sixth? Because if you're available, I would love to make it official, and let the world know how much I love you. And I definitely appreciate your way of thinking as to how we'll spend our honeymoon." She winked at me.

All of that got a huge grin out of me. "May sixth works for me. I can't wait."

Then she gave me a not-so-kid-friendly kiss.

And life? It couldn't have been any better. Why? Because while our start as a couple hadn't been typical, what we had between us was damn great...and it was about to get a whole lot better and keep getting better.

And that was a promise.

PART II

DECIDEDLY WITH TINSEL

A BY THE BAY BONUS SHORT STORY

BLURB

After my partner for the Tinsel and Tatas Winter Festival competition breaks her leg while swishing down the resort's ski hill, I have no choice but to pair up with Drew Chapman—my colleague, childhood crush, and part-time nemesis.

1

JULIETTE

The last place I'd expected to be when I woke up in the Lake Tahoe resort this morning?

That's right. The hospital.

But that was precisely where I was, in a private room, waiting for the doctor to give me the verdict.

Or rather, waiting for the cute ER attending to give my best friend the verdict.

The room was a stark contrast to the hotel lobby. Not a single rope of tinsel or shiny red bauble could be found here. No festive tunes played through the speakers. No one was dressed like an elf.

The Grinch would've been proud.

I hummed "'Tis the Season" but didn't even make it past the second round of *fa la la la las* when the door swung open.

Dr. McHottie strolled in, X-rays in hand. "So, Miss Morrison—"

"You can call me April." My bestie fluttered her long dark eyelashes at him.

"Right, well, April, you have an incomplete break of your left tibia."

Her face paled. "Is that fatal?"

I patted her sympathetically on the shoulder. "He's talking about the bone in your lower leg."

Which was definitely not good news.

For either her or me.

April was supposed to be my partner for the Tinsel and Tatas Winter Festival competition. But instead of being in her hotel room, doing some last-minute work like someone else here, she'd decided to go swishing down the ski slope.

Did I mention she'd never skied a day in her life until this morning?

Dr. McHottie smiled at her. "The good news is it's not fatal. But we will need to cast it."

Her eyes went round like two sparkly-blue tree ornaments. "But I can still participate in the Tinsel and Tatas competition, right?"

He shook his head. "Sorry, but no. Not unless you want to risk further damage, which I don't recommend."

My heart sagged, all hope squeezed from it. Without a partner, I was now ineligible to compete.

Unless I could find someone to fill in for her.

But the chances of finding a colleague available to partner with me was as likely to happen as spotting black bears singing Christmas carols.

"I'm so sorry, Juliette."

I flashed her a commiserative smile. "Hey, it's not your fault the tree didn't get out of the way."

"I shouldn't have gone skiing. I know how important this competition is to you."

The competition itself didn't mean anything to me...beyond how it was raising money to help young women who were battling breast cancer.

But winning it? That meant everything.

My mom had recently gone into remission after a tough battle with breast cancer.

Actually, let's reverse things up a little further....

The owner of the ad agency where April and I worked wanted to whip the owner's ass of another company.

Why?

Because they used to be married.

To say it didn't end well was like saying Beyoncé was just a singer. The result was a rivalry between Kathleen and her ex that was more bitter than a lemon soaked in battery acid.

To motivate her employees to win the coveted Tinsel and Tatas Winter Festival trophy, she'd offered the winning duo a week's paid vacation and a $350 bonus for each partner.

Why did I want this so badly? It meant I could take my mother to a spa resort for a restorative, week-long vacation.

It was the least I could do. She'd been through enough twenty years ago after learning of my father's infidelity. We were living in Australia at the time due to his job transfer.

Mom dumped his sorry ass, and she and I moved back to the U.S.

She had been there for me on my good days and my bad. She had been there for me when my best friend in Australia had broken something important to me. She had been the one to pick up my shattered pieces.

"It'll be fine," I told April. "I'll figure something out."

I dropped April off at the resort's main entrance and waited while she crutched her way into the warm building. Then I parked my car in the visitors' parking lot and hurried to the hotel, hoping the dime-sized snowflakes wouldn't turn my hair into a wet mess.

I entered the lushly decorated lobby and smoothed my hand over my hair. If the Christmas lights on the pine trees at the main entrance hadn't given it away, once you stepped through the sliding doors, you couldn't miss that it was now the holiday season. Pine boughs hung in waves along the reception counters, the fireplace mantel, and the rustic wooden staircase railing.

In the far corner, the Christmas tree, which almost brushed the high ceiling with the golden star perched on top, had captured the attention of a group of little kids. The decorations had a rustic woodland-critter theme that made me smile. They reminded me of the ones Mom and I bought after her divorce was finalized.

April was next to the couch, watching the magician entertain another group of kids. She spotted me and crutched to where I was standing.

"Isn't that Drew over there?" She nodded at the tall, dark-haired man in question, and my heart tripped over itself.

Stupid, *stupid*, heart.

"Yep, that's him." I took in a long, fortifying breath, inhaling the crisp pine scent from the Christmas tree.

Drew was talking to a man I recognized as Josh Hoffer, a former forward with the San Francisco NHL team. He'd retired about five years ago. A tall, pretty redhead stood with them—his wife, if the adoring looks he kept flashing her were any indication.

She was also a vaguely familiar-looking redhead, but I couldn't figure out why.

"Why don't you ask him to be your partner?" my best friend not-so-helpfully suggested, referring to Drew.

Oh, let me list the billion reasons.

But I couldn't tell her any of them. To do so meant admitting to her that Drew and I knew each other from when we were teens. Back when he'd been known as Wilfred the third.

It also meant revealing why our favorite pastime included

glaring icicles at each other and practically snarling like rabid chipmunks.

Fun times.

All right, maybe I was exaggerating a little. Drew had been my best friend, the boy I'd crushed on when my family lived in Australia. Keeping my distance from him was the perfect solution to prevent my heart from forgetting itself and traveling down that road again.

"He's got a partner," I said instead. "Remember her? Tall. Gorgeous. Resembles a Victoria's Secret model, complete with pouty lips. Does that ring a bell?"

Drew and Bridget had been dating for the past year. Rumor had it they were practically engaged.

"Where've you been for the past four months?" April asked.

"What do you mean?"

Speaking of Bridget, where was she? Shouldn't she have been clinging to Drew's arm, baring her perfect, white fangs at any female who came within ten feet of him?

Or maybe it was just me who got to enjoy the privilege.

"They broke up," April said. Cheers broke out from the group of kids watching the magician. Or at least I assumed that's what they were cheering about. "It was probably the most exciting office gossip we've had in a while. Where were you?"

After the rumor had started that they were practically engaged, I skipped anything to do with Drew. Even if it meant taking a longer route just to avoid walking past his office.

But I preferred to think of it as not so much avoidance as being healthy and getting in some extra exercise.

"I guess I was busy working," I replied.

"It's obvious you have a thing for him. Not that I blame you. He is hot." April's glance flicked to him, and she fanned herself with her hand. "Plus, he has that sexy Aussie accent going for him."

"I don't have a thing for him." I shifted the purse strap on my shoulder and unzipped my ski jacket. I'd bought the pretty, light pink coat specifically for this trip. To impress my boss.

"I notice you didn't argue the hot part."

I snorted a laugh. "That's a given. Besides, what do his looks have to do with anything? The Tinsel and Tatas competition is an athletic event. It's not a beauty contest."

April's eyebrows shot up. "Since when does building a snowman count as being athletic?"

"You know what I mean."

"Why can't you just admit you have a thing for Drew? I happen to think you guys would be great together."

"You mean when we're not trying to kill each other."

Metaphorically speaking.

"I swear it's like foreplay between you two. All I know is when you guys finally get horizontal together, things will be explosive." She mimed *kaboom* with her hands.

I frowned. "You want he and I to have sex? Together?"

I was beginning to believe her leg wasn't the only thing that hit the tree. Her head got intimate with it, too.

"No, I was thinking more along the lines of you two dating... and having sex."

Remind me never to give April a can of gasoline. She would probably pour it onto a fire—because that was exactly what it would be like if Drew and I were to date.

Not.

A.

Good.

Idea.

"You know I'm not interested in dating anyone or being in a relationship. I don't need that distraction. My career comes first." And second. And possibly even third. "And look what happened when I was distracted with someone I thought was a wonderful boyfriend. Turns out he was married."

April grimaced, fully aware of how badly that relationship

had gone. "Not all men are cheaters, Juliette. Sure you had bad luck with that one jerk, but not all men are untrustworthy."

Right—I was positive Mom would feel differently.

My father had been married to her while he was having an affair—with Drew's mother.

2

DREW

The moment Juliette approached me in the hotel lobby, my Spidey senses went on high alert. Her subtle floral scent always had that effect on me.

Up until then, I'd been talking to Holly and Josh, happily oblivious to her presence.

How did I know the couple?

Holly and I had grown up together in Sydney, Australia. At one point, our parents decided arranged marriages should be brought back in fashion.

I had to admit it, though, if you had to be stuck in an arranged marriage, you couldn't go wrong with Holly. The woman was smart, sassy, and bloody hot.

And her husband thoroughly agreed with that assessment.

"What happened to you?" I eyed April's newly casted leg. I'd seen her four hours ago, and she'd been in one piece.

"A tree and I had a difference in opinion on the ski hill this morning. It came out the winner. This means Juliette needs a partner for the competition. I don't suppose you know anyone who could partner with her, do you?" She grinned at me like an overly eager puppy.

Juliette rolled her eyes.

That odd sensation in my chest at the sight of my archenemy?

Ignore it. It was probably heartburn.

"Kathleen wants one of her employees to win the trophy, which won't happen if Drew and I are paired together." Juliette snorted as if the idea was preposterous.

"She's right, mate. The only way I'll win is if I'm paired with a human-bein', not a she-devil." I jerked my chin at Juliette.

Her light brown eyes flared, but no lasers shot at me. Always a plus. "And it's not like I can win while partnered with the rump of a horse."

A smirk pulled at the corner of my mouth. "Nice come back, Juliette. I take it Romeo still has your tongue."

She grunted. She'd always hated the *Romeo and Juliet* reference, especially when she learned of their tragic demise.

Holly laughed. "I see nothing has changed between you two. It's great to see you again, Juliette. It's been forever."

Juliette stared at Holly for a second before recognition flickered on her face. "Ohmigod! Holly! I didn't know you were living in the U.S."

"San Francisco, actually."

The two women hugged, and Holly introduced Juliette to Josh.

Juliette's and my battle—as well as Juliette and Holly's reunion—came to a temporary standstill as Kathleen stalked toward us, appearing none too happy.

Or rather, foaming at the mouth would be a more apt description. As always, not a strand of her wavy brown hair was out of place, and she wore a charcoal gray suit I could guarantee was by some fancy-ass designer who my mother no doubt worshipped.

Bridget was with her, gliding across the carpeted floor as though it were a catwalk. Her looks gained her more than a fair share of male attention, but my ex-girlfriend didn't seem to notice their heads turn in her direction.

Her gaze was locked on me.

I tried not to sigh.

By sigh, I didn't mean in the same way those horny frat boys were sighing.

It was more along the line of a we're-not-going-on-that-Ferris-wheel-ride-again sound.

"We'll talk to you two later," Holly said. She and Josh rounded up their two ankle biters and hightailed it toward the magician.

Kathleen's razor-sharp gaze homed in on April's casted leg, and her frown deepened. "You two"—she pointed at Juliette and me—"You're partnering up. Jamieson and Kincaid are out of commission due to food poisoning."

I inwardly groaned. I'd told those two guys the sushi looked a little funky.

And now I didn't have a choice about being Juliette's partner. When the queen commanded something, her worker bees had little say in the matter. Although, usually, Kathleen trusted us to know what we were doing.

On the other hand, what better way to piss Juliette off than being paired with her? Score one for me.

Kathleen lifted her chin, a commander readying her troops for the charge. "And I don't have much hope when it comes to the remaining two partners. They're brilliant at their jobs, but they lack the do-or-die mentality you two possess."

I think that was supposed to be a compliment.

Possibly.

Bridget's lips pushed out in a pout. Her gaze shifted to Juliette, and a glower pinched her eyebrows together.

"Remember," Kathleen said, not paying attention to her assistant, "if you win the trophy, there's an extra week paid vacation and three hundred and fifty dollars for each of you.

And I'll throw in an additional hundred dollars each if you humiliate my douchebag ex-husband."

Juliette's eyes lit up at the mention of the new incentive, emphasizing the flecks of gold and amber in the warm brown. For the first time in who knew how long, she actually smiled in my presence.

And bloody hell, I'd forgotten how incredible her smile was. She glowed like a Christmas angel.

Kathleen gestured for the rest of the team to join our small group.

Loud cheers rose from the other side of the room. "Go, Ashford Bright! Grind their sorry tushies in the snow! Gooooo, Ashford Bright!"

Clearly, Kathleen's ex-husband's employees had quite the holiday spirit.

Kathleen scowled in their direction.

Oh, this wasn't good.

Unlike our group, his employees looked like a team. All were wearing matching black ski suits with the company logo on the back. They meant business. We were dressed like normal people, in whatever warm clothes we could find, since most of us didn't typically hang out on ski slopes.

Kathleen thrust her hand into the middle of our now larger group, indicating that we do the same. "Who's the best?"

At her louder than necessary voice, the kids who were watching the magician cast us alarmed glances.

"We are," most of us replied, although not at the same time. For one duo, it came out more like a question.

***

WHILE JULIETTE RACED UPSTAIRS TO GRAB SOMETHING FROM HER room, I headed outside. Holly and Josh and their two cute ankle biters, bundled in snowsuits, walked with me.

Two-year-old James was in his daddy's arms. Five-year-old Lily leaped along the path, stopping every few feet to kick at the snow piled alongside it.

The falling snow had tapered off, and the sun shone through a break in the clouds. The faint buzz of a snowblower followed behind us, while the pine-scented wind ruffled the American and California state flags on the nearby poles.

"Why is it you and Juliette haven't hooked up? God, the chemistry between you two is explosive." Holly fanned herself.

"What the hell are you talkin' about, Hols? You remember Juliette, right? We went to school together? Her parents and my parents hated each others' guts and were always trying to outdo each other. Does any of that sound familiar? And let's not forget how Juliette started the rumor I had a shrine in my bedroom to some pork goddess she invented."

Every time I walked past my classmates after that, I had to put up with oinking noises.

Holly snickered. "You have to admit, she was creative. But for a private school, the kids sure were dumb if they actually believed her. Besides, didn't you start that bloody awful name everyone ended up calling her? What was it again?"

Moustache face.

I shrugged.

"What I don't get is why you two were best friends, and then suddenly you turned on each other."

I shrugged once more. "I don't remember the details of how it began. I just remember our families used to be friends, then everythin' turned to kangaroo shit." As for what happened between Juliette and me, I knew as much about it as Holly did. One day Juliette and I were friends, the next, she was ignoring me and spreading the pig-goddess rumor.

"Do you want my opinion?" Holly asked.

"Not really, but I'm sure you're goin' to give it to me anyway." I smirked, and Josh laughed.

"You two doth protest too much. It's obvious you have a thing for each other. Maybe it's time you forget the past—other than the part where you used to be best friends—and see where all that chemistry takes you."

"You mean have"—I caught myself as Lily paused her jumping to look back at me—"S-E-X?"

"I was thinking more along the lines of having a relationship with her. You know, date, spend time together."

I groaned and inwardly rolled my eyes. "Why is it when someone falls in love, they believe everyone else should fall in love, too?"

Holly grinned at me, mischief in her green eyes. "That's not true. But you're my friend, Drew, and I want to see you happy like Josh and me. You deserve that."

<hr>

"HAVE YOU EVER BUILT A SNOWMAN?" JULIETTE SURVEYED THE snowy open area where the first event was taking place: the snowman building contest. Her shoulder-length blonde hair peeked from under her off-white, cable-knit hat.

Between the hat, the black ski pants, and the light pink winter jacket, I had to admit that she looked sexy as all hell.

But damn if I was admitting that to her.

"Yes, because there's lots of snow in Sydney during the winter," I said dryly.

Instead of tossing back a sarcastic retort like I'd expected, she grinned, and something stirred inside me. Against all better judgment, my gaze dipped to her mouth, and not for the first time, I wondered what it would feel like to have her lips on mine.

"But you've lived in the U.S. for several years now."

"Are you tellin' me you're an award-winning builder of snowmen?" That would certainly be helpful. It's not like my job as a market research manager prepared me for something like this.

"Not exactly." Her grin widened. "All right, not at all. But how hard can it be? I've watched *Frozen*."

I returned her grin. "And you're plannin' to create a talkin' snowman?"

"We would definitely win the contest if that were the case. But alas, I might be blonde but that's where the similarities between Elsa and me end."

The contest official announced we had an hour to complete our creations. And for the next while, Juliette and I built a snowman that looked nothing like Olaf or the snow monster.

Yup, I'd seen the movie, too.

Once we were finished, Juliette surveyed our snowman. "It's not half bad."

"It looks like three giant snowballs on top of each other."

"But they're nice-looking snowballs. All right, what's next? Arms?" She scanned the area.

"What are you lookin' for?"

"Sticks. Isn't that what you use for snowman arms?"

"Sure, if you want it to look like everyone else's snowman. We have to up our game."

She studied our tower of giant snowballs, her lips pressed in a contemplative line. "In that case, how about we switch things around, so he's doing a headstand?"

"That's not a bad idea."

Juliette had always been the more creative one of us. She'd even entered an art contest when we were thirteen years old. The winners won a scholarship to a local art program that Juliette had wanted to attend.

Did she win?

No clue. One day we'd been best friends, and the next, she was spreading the rumor about me around the school.

And things rapidly deteriorated between us after that.

Three months later, she and her family had moved back to the U.S.

We restacked the giant snowballs, so the base was now on top. Stubby snow arms were positioned on either side of the head, and a pair of legs were added, sticking straight up in the air.

The finishing touches included feet, a carrot nose, eyes, and buttons. The Tinsel and Tatas organizers supplied the last three items.

"Time!" the volunteer judge announced through the megaphone.

Juliette beamed at our creation, her hat and hair glowing in the sunlight like a halo. "That's much better than our first prototype."

She was right. Despite our lack of snowman-building competency, our snowperson looked good.

We waited while the judges wandered around, inspecting the different snowmen. I swear Juliette was holding her breath as they checked out our snowgymnast.

"The third-place winners for the snowperson building contest are Robert Philips and Rebecca Dunwich."

Applause broke out among the spectators.

Kathleen was busy pacing on the sideline, muttering to herself.

"The second-place winners are Crystal Hayes and Gwen Ottaway."

Kathleen's pacing picked up speed. Crystal and Gwen were employees of her ex-husband's company.

"And the first place winners are...."

3

JULIETTE

"**A**nd the first place winners are...."

I was vaguely aware of grabbing Drew's arm, my heart pounding like a jackhammer set on high speed. Any louder, and it would've set off an avalanche on a nearby snowy peak.

"Drew Chapman and Juliette Rogers."

For a second, I stood still, positive I'd misheard her.

Then I let out a shriek and threw my arms around Drew's neck. His arms went around my waist, keeping us from toppling over.

"Oh, God, we did it, Drew. We won the first contest."

While I might have been celebrating the win, my body had different ideas. Electricity crackled and popped through me, starting where his body touched mine. My ski pants and jacket were a buffer against the wind and the cold, but they failed to insulate me against the impact he had on my traitorous body.

Truth?

I was surprised the surrounding snow hadn't evaporated from the electrical storm we were generating.

My gaze dropped to his lips, and my breath came out short and ragged.

God, what would it feel like to have his lips on mine? To taste him? To explore his mouth?

Driven by an unexplainable craving, I reached up on my toes as Drew also shortened the distance between our mouths.

Four inches separated them.

Three inches.

"Congratulations, you two."

Kathleen's voice clanged in my head, an annoying snooze alarm determined to drag you from a good dream.

I'm not sure which of us leaped away first—Drew or me—but we both turned to where her voice had come from.

Kathleen stood there glowing as if she had personally won the contest.

Her assistant, Bridget, nodded at me with a polite, plastic smile that held the warmth of an icicle in Antarctica. Her gaze shifted to her ex-boyfriend, and the ice melted away into a genuine, blinding smile.

Oh. Boy.

"Contestants," the Tinsel and Tatas volunteer announced through the megaphone. "Five minutes until the snowshoe relay race."

If I was hoping for a few minutes alone with Drew, I could forget it. Kathleen walked with us to the next event, while giving us advice as if she were the coach for the Olympic snowshoeing team.

Bridget sashayed along on the other side of Drew, looking like a sexy model getting ready for her ski-wear fashion shoot.

Without thinking through why I was doing it, I adjusted my knit hat, sliding it back slightly, and unzipped my jacket to reveal my cleavage—if I'd been wearing only my bra underneath and not a sweater, that is.

At the starting line, Drew and I strapped on the snowshoes.

"Have you done this before," I asked, straightening. Kathleen and Bridget were in the spectators' zone, giving us a reprieve from Kathleen's coaching advice and Bridget's pouty lips.

"No, but how hard can it be?"

The volunteer for the event explained the rules.

Drew stretched his arms across his body, first one and then the other. "You want to go first?"

I nodded and got into position.

"On your marks," the volunteer called out. "Get set." The foghorn wailed, and I took off running.

When I said running, I meant it in the loosest possible sense of the word.

From the corner of my eye, I caught the contestant next to me stumble and go down for the count.

Focus on the finish line. You've got this. For Mom.

Above the muffled *clomp-clomp-clomp* of my snowshoes landing on the snow, loud cheers pushed me to keep moving. I increased my pace, working hard to avoid tripping over my feet.

I made it to our pole at the other end without incident and tore the flag off it. Then I shuffle-clomped-ran to the starting line.

"C'mon, Juliette!" Drew yelled. "You can do this!"

I flashed back to gym class when he'd cheered me on during a relay race.

Drew had been a skinny thirteen-year-old and a helluva lot shorter than he was now. Neither of us had been athletic.

That hadn't stopped him from cheering me on, though, positive I was going to beat my classmates.

And you know what?

He'd been right.

Channeling that girl, I pushed harder.

Just six more yards to the finish line.

Five more.

But fate wasn't smiling on me.

I placed my foot down wrong, stepping on the edge of my other snowshoe.

And...

Landed in a heap.

I awkwardly scrambled to my feet and resumed my record-breaking speed. *Clomp-clomp-clomp.*

Several contestants were ahead of me. Adrenaline pumped through my body, encouraging me on. My lungs were on fire, and my legs would be cursing me to hell for the next week.

I can do this. I can do this. I can do this.

The cheering and chanting increased in the fresh mountain air as we all approached the finish line, but Drew's voice was what gave me the extra speed I needed. "C'mon, Juliette! You've got this, babe."

I crossed the finish line and passed the ribbon to Drew.

And he was off.

I jumped up and down, scream-cheering him on, even though my lungs hadn't forgiven me yet.

He ran to the end without any catastrophes, replaced the ribbon on the pole, and shuffle-ran toward the finish line.

"You're almost there, Drew! Run! Run! Run!"

He'd made up good time after my mishap, but the two duos who worked for Kathleen's ex-husband were ahead of him.

"C'mon, Drew!" I yelled.

But it didn't matter how much I screamed, it wasn't enough.

He came in third place.

Drew bent over, hands on his thighs, breathing hard.

Unlike last time, Kathleen didn't join us. She was too busy glaring at her ex-husband to spare us a second glance. Bridget looked as though she wanted to give Drew a consolatory hug, but she couldn't exactly leave Kathleen's side to do that.

"Sorry about that," Drew said once he'd finally regained his breath.

"That's okay. It was my fault."

I had to do better next time.

For my mother.

Since there were a few more heats to go with the first and second place winners advancing to the final round, we had an hour to kill before the next competition.

"You want to get a hot chocolate?" Drew asked.

"Sure. Why not?"

"Juliette," a winded Bridget called out, approaching us at a slow jog. "Kathleen needs you for a few minutes. Something about you walking Biscotti."

"She wants me to walk her Teacup Yorkie?" That would be a first.

"Absolutely. You'd better hurry. You know Kathleen doesn't like to be kept waiting."

I glanced helplessly at Drew. I loved dogs, but Biscotti didn't exactly fall into the category of dogs that loved me.

Or any other human.

"I'll come with you." Drew flashed me an uncertain smile that bordered on sympathetic.

"No." The word shot out of Bridget's mouth, slicing through the cold air. "She only wants Juliette to walk Biscotti."

"She does realize the next event is in less than an hour, right?" The event we couldn't afford to forfeit.

Bridget nodded.

Alrighty then.

I jogged along the path to where Kathleen was now talking to Tony, one of Drew's colleagues. "Hi? Bridget said you want me to walk Biscotti."

Kathleen shook her head, a puzzled frown wrinkling her brow. "Biscotti is at his doggie daycare while I'm here. He hates snow."

Tony rolled his lips together, laughter crinkling the corners of his eyes. I had no idea what was so funny, and I didn't have time to ask.

I jogged back to where I'd left Drew, expecting him to already be gone by the time I returned. He was talking to Bridget and shaking his head when I approached the pair.

He smiled at me, looking relieved. "That was fast."

"False alarm. Did you still want the hot chocolate?" I was warm after all the running around for nothing, but I could still go for some chocolaty yumminess.

Bridget's phone pinged, and she checked the screen. A disappointed sigh whooshed out from between pouty lips. Without saying anything to us, she walked in the direction I'd just come from.

Drew and I made our way to the nearby concession stands. He removed his wallet from his coat pocket. "Peppermint hot chocolate with extra whipped cream?"

"You remembered?"

His smile caused my insides to jiggle like a bowl full of raspberry Jell-O. "Of course I remember."

He ordered the two beverages and handed one to me. Then we walked around the area, checking out the different winter festival activities and crafts.

Festive holiday music played through the speakers, reminding me of the Christmases Mom and I spent together, just the two of us. The days leading up to December were spent making crafts and treats—a different tradition to the one I'd grown up with before she divorced Dad.

Did we still embrace that tradition?

Absolutely. After I almost lost her to cancer, the tradition became even more important to us. We usually sold some of our creations and donated the money to the charity that had helped Mom when she needed it the most.

I licked the side of my whipped cream and moaned, "God, this is soooo good."

Drew didn't say anything; he was too busy staring at my lips.

My eyes suddenly became preoccupied with *his* mouth, while fantasies of kissing him waltzed through my head.

No, no, no. I was so not going there again. The thirteen-year-old who had once crushed on him had long since left the building.

This is Drew. Remember? The crusher of dreams? Does any of this sound familiar?

Drew's mouth curved into another smile. He reached up and wiped the end of my nose. An electrical current spiraled through my body at his touch, sending a rush of adrenaline into overdrive. My heart rate quickened, my body tingled, and the ache between my legs came out of hibernation.

"You had cream there."

Oh, he wasn't staring at my lips after all.

"Thanks," I said. "Not the professional look I was aiming for."

He chuckled. "We're buildin' snowmen, runnin' around in snowshoes, and doin' whatever else the organizers have planned. Lookin' professional is hardly on the agenda."

He leaned in closer, his warm breath brushing the shell of my ear. "And I happen to think you look good."

At the way his rough Aussie accent wrapped around each syllable, my insides ignited, and I sucked in a sharp breath.

"So, what have you been up to since my family moved from Australia?"

For the next forty minutes, he caught me up on the highlights of his life, and I caught him up on mine.

Not once did we mention our parents.

Not once did we mention the feud that had torn our families apart.

I laughed at his story about how he'd had enough of being a dork and decided to work out and rethink how he dressed. It was also the same time he switched to using the abbreviated version of his middle name: Andrew.

"I don't know what you're talking about. I never thought you were a dork. I thought you were cute." Heat flared in my cheeks at how that sounded. "I mean, if anyone was a dork, it was me with my braces and the way my hair always looked like I'd stuck my finger in an electric socket."

Drew stopped walking. "I never thought you looked like a dork. And your hair certainly didn't look like that. I thought you looked pretty."

His soft gray eyes searched mine. I missed those eyes. Whenever I'd had a bad day, the understanding and kindness gazing back at me had been a Paddle Pop ice cream to the soul.

"Where did you get the ridiculous idea your hair looked like that?" he asked.

"Your mother. I overheard her mentioning it to someone." My father—who hadn't even bothered to defend me.

"Well, that would explain it. Compassion has never been my mother's strong suit."

I couldn't argue with him there.

4

DREW

What was I thinking about while Juliette and I trudged through the snow to the next event?

I was wondering what the hell happened all those years ago that ended our friendship. All I remembered was our parents constantly trying to outdo each other.

If one couple bought a new car, the other duo had to purchase a better one.

If one couple hosted a much-talked-about party, the other duo had to throw a bigger, more celebrated event.

But none of that had been Juliette and me. We'd been the down-to-earth pair. The friends who climbed trees together, passed coded messages in class, biked to our favorite hangouts together, and made fun of our parents behind their backs.

Then everything soured, and we transformed into them overnight.

The next competition was the toboggan race. We found our assigned sled and climbed on. Juliette's sweet ass settled against my cock, and that was pretty much the end of me. It didn't care if there were several layers of clothes between us. It wanted to enjoy her soft heat. Now.

318

Sorry, mate, not happenin'.

"Sledders, on your marks," the volunteer announced in the megaphone.

"We can do this. We can do this," Juliette muttered to herself. "We have to win."

"Get set. Go!"

In unison, we thrust our bodyweight forward as I pushed back on the packed snow.

And we were off—thanks to Newton's laws of motion.

I wrapped my arms around Juliette's waist. She clutched the rope attached to the front of the sled tighter.

Her giggled shrieks followed us down the slope as we picked up speed, the cold wind nipping my face. I tightened my hold on Juliette, fighting back the urge to cop a feel. Crikey, who knew I had that much restraint?

Kathleen's ex-husband's employees were on either side of us. And fuck, we were neck to neck. It was anyone's competition.

The finish line lay a few meters ahead of us. I leaned farther forward in case that gave us an extra edge and inhaled Juliette's subtle floral scent.

Her hair was tucked behind her ears, revealing a strip of bare skin. And for a heartbeat, I wanted to press my lips against it.

To explore it with the tip of my tongue and my teeth.

To see if she tasted as good as she smelled.

But I didn't have the chance.

Our sled slid over the finish line.

I'd been so busy fantasizing about tasting her skin, I hadn't paid attention to whether we had won or not.

And Juliette wasn't acting the way I'd expect if we had won. Her gaze was directed at the official with the megaphone.

The volunteer judges conferred.

"And the winners of the toboggan race are..." the official

announced a moment later. "Drew Chapman and Juliette Rogers."

Juliette scrambled off the sled and performed a comical happy dance. I think it was supposed to be The Floss, but I couldn't be sure.

Laughing, I pushed myself to my feet. Juliette barely gave me enough time to straighten before she flung her arms around my neck.

Shit, did she ever feel good there—like she belonged.

AFTER THE FINAL COMPETITION OF THE DAY, WE HEADED TO OUR hotel rooms to get ready for the company dinner Kathleen had organized. After that, we'd have the rest of the night free to do whatever we wanted.

I showered—and possibly jacked off to images of Juliette in my head.

Completely by accident.

I swear.

Juliette was standing with April and several of their colleagues when I entered the private dining room. Her hair was tied in a low bun, blonde curls framing her face, and her short, sleeveless black dress revealed an endless stretch of bare skin. Christ, she looked gorgeous.

She always looked good at work, professional. But this was a new level of sexiness I hadn't seen on her until now.

I grabbed a cold one at the bar and joined her. She smiled at me the same way she once had back when we were best friends. And I swore it was game over.

Several crisp dings rang through the noisy room. Everyone stopped talking and turned to Kathleen, who was standing at the front, a glass of white wine in her hand.

"Thank you, everyone, for joining me this weekend. There's

a reason I wanted our annual Christmas party to be part of the Tinsel and Tatas Winter Festival weekend. Over ten years ago, I was diagnosed with breast cancer and have been in remission for almost nine years."

I glanced at Juliette to see if she knew about this. She looked as surprised as I felt, her skin slightly paler than before, eyes wide.

"Because of this," Kathleen continued, "I understand how important the charity is that will benefit from the money raised this weekend. It helps young women diagnosed with the disease cope with the challenges they now face.

"I just wanted to say thank you. Your donations, and those of your colleagues who couldn't make it this weekend, amount to over fifteen thousand dollars. And as promised, I'll be matching it." The room broke out in a loud chorus of cheering and clapping.

"We've had a busy day," she said once the noise quietened again, "and we still have tomorrow. So let's enjoy dinner and relax. The fun will continue in the morning and will hopefully include bringing home the trophy." She raised her wine glass. "Cheers!"

"Cheers!" we echoed.

Everyone took a seat at the long table. Unfortunately, I wasn't fast enough to sit next to Juliette. I had to settle with sitting across from her.

Later, as dinner was winding down, Juliette pushed herself up from her chair. She grabbed her shawl from the back of the seat, opened the French doors near her, and slipped soundlessly onto the balcony.

5

JULIETTE

A cold wind swept across the balcony from the snowy mountain peaks as I walked toward the railing. I wrapped the shawl around my shoulders. Ahead of me, the forest stretched out like welcoming arms, the pine trees resembling giant shadows in the low angle of the full moon.

Why was I out here freezing my butt off?

After feeling Drew's eyes on me through dinner, I was hot enough to melt a glacier. I needed to cool down prior to heading inside.

There was also one other thing I wanted to do first.

Glancing up, I searched the inky black sky for a shooting star, but other than the millions of twinkling lights above my head, I couldn't find the one thing I needed.

"Aren't you cold?"

I didn't have to turn around to know it was Drew. Even before he spoke, I'd sensed him.

"Not really." Not yet anyway.

He walked over to stand next to me. "What are you doin' out here?"

"Looking for a lucky star to wish on."

"To wish on?"

I grinned at the skepticism in his tone. Even as a kid, he hadn't believed in the powers of wishing on a shooting star.

"What are you wishin' for?"

"To win the competition. For my mother." The last part was said at a near whisper.

"For your mother?"

I didn't have to look at him to know he was frowning. I could hear it in his voice.

"She was diagnosed with stage three breast cancer over two years ago and has been in remission for the past year. I want to take her to a spa resort in Napa Valley in the spring. The prize money and the week's paid vacation will go a long way with that plan."

Drew placed his warm, strong hands on my shoulders and turned me around to face him. "I'm so sorry, Juliette. I had no idea."

A small smile tugged at my lips. "She was pretty private about it."

I searched his eyes for signs of his parents, the callous individuals they'd been.

But the only emotion staring back at me was sadness for what my mom had gone through...and lust.

The same lust that burned in my veins from his touch.

For a long moment, our gazes remained locked as I replayed in my head all those times we'd come close to kissing during the day's competitions.

"I really want to kiss you, Drew. I know I shouldn't—"

That was as far as I got, then his lips were on mine.

I'd always figured he was a good kisser.

I'd been wrong.

He had a gift for stealing your breath away and leaving you senseless.

The kiss deepened.

And my knees forgot their function.

Oh well, who needed them anyway?

Drew wrapped one arm around my waist, pressing me to him. It was the only thing keeping me vertical.

What the heck was I doing?

I wasn't supposed to want Drew. Not anymore. Not after he made my life miserable during those final months in Australia. Not after I had doused the crush I'd had on him.

Except, that didn't explain why I wanted him so badly.

I needed to get him out of my system. It was as simple as that. All I had to do was have sex with him, then I could go back to avoiding him. Could go back to focusing on my career so not to make the mistake of falling for the wrong man again.

"I want you," I murmured against his lips. "I want you so badly." The only reason I wasn't ripping off his shirt was due to our colleagues being on the other side of the glass doors. We'd already given them enough of a show—if they happened to glance outside.

I stepped away from him.

Drew stared at me as if he'd imagined that I'd said I wanted him. But my face must have confirmed I was serious because he nodded. "I want you, too. But do you think that's a good idea?"

"It's a perfect idea. Then we can resume avoiding each other once I've got you out of my system. And vice versa."

The corners of his mouth twitched. "You really believe that?"

"Absolutely."

"All right. Your room or mine?"

"Do you have condoms in your room?" Getting laid on the trip hadn't exactly been on the agenda, so I hadn't packed any.

He nodded.

"Your room it is."

We re-entered the private dining room. Our colleagues were

no longer sitting at the table. Some had disappeared, including April. Others were chatting.

No one seemed to notice our return.

We slipped out of the room, this time through the main doors, and headed for the elevator. The door dinged open as we approached. Only one other couple entered with us.

Drew and I kept a professional distance between us.

The other couple?

Not so much.

The woman leaned into the man, their lips moving against each other. Moans worthy of being in porn filled the small space.

I jumped my gaze to the ceiling. It really was a nice ceiling, with the isosceles triangles forming interesting square patterns. The triangles made from a bumpy reflective material that gave us a slightly distorted view of the amorous couple.

The moaning grew louder. If the darn elevator took any longer, I was positive we'd learn the pair's names while they were in the throes of passion. I bit my lower lip, willing the elevator to move faster. Trying to not squirm and let the occupants know just how turned on I was getting.

Thankfully, the door pinged open five seconds later. Drew grabbed my hand, and we hurried down the hallway.

If I hadn't been wearing stilettos, I might have sprinted to his room.

Have you ever seen the movie *Jurassic World*?

Claire, the heroine, had a gift I didn't possess...the ability to run in heels while a T-rex chased her.

Fortunately for me, no women-eating dinosaurs were in the hallway.

And if there had been?

I would've hit it in the face with my heel if it had planned to keep me from fucking Drew out of my system.

Drew stopped at a door and opened it with his key card. No sooner had the door clicked shut behind us, our lips reunited.

My fingers hungrily shoved his shirt buttons through their holes. His were busy unzipping my dress and unhooking my bra. His fingertips brushed my heated skin, and it was a miracle I didn't rip his shirt off, buttons be damned.

I kicked off my shoes and wiggled out of my dress, letting the fabric fall to the floor.

Drew made quick work of his remaining shirt buttons. Translation: He yanked the shirt over his head and tossed it to the side.

The only light came from the full moon reflecting off the snow outside the windows, the soft glow highlighting the ridges and valleys of Drew's abs and chest.

The skinny teen from my youth?

He had definitely vacated the premises.

I pressed a light kiss on his chest, the skin hot to the touch. Drew's hand slowly traced along my rib cage and up to my breast. He cupped the aching mound desperate for the warmth of his mouth. His other hand caressed the skin on my lower back.

As if sensing what my nipples craved, Drew popped one into his mouth and teased it with his tongue prior to lavishing the other one.

Our mouths then found each other again and resumed their heated explorations.

I fumbled for the button on Drew's trousers and clumsily slipped it through the hole. Soon after, Drew's pants were unzipped, and my fingers were searching for treasure.

Had I ever given any thought to Drew's cock? The answer was no.

If you didn't count the one or two brief incidents when the question had accidentally crossed my mind.

Okay, more like ten times. But three of those were during

work-related parties, and I may or may not have had two glasses of wine at the time.

So they didn't count.

My fingers brushed his hard length. Drew groaned into my mouth, and before I knew it, we were naked on the bed, exploring each other's bodies.

Drew found my clit, his thumb brushing it in small circles. With each pass, I moved closer and closer to the edge.

My last sexual encounter had been a long time ago.

A very.

Very.

Very.

Long time ago.

Maybe that was why his touch and the way my body responded were nothing like I'd ever experienced before. I writhed on the bed, a wanton creature begging for more.

I eagerly wrapped my fingers around his rigid length. The spicy scent that was all Drew enveloped me, further awakening my senses, and I relished the satin sensation of heated flesh against my palm.

Drew jerked his hips forward with a groan. "You might want to be careful. I won't last much longer if you keep that up."

I smiled. "That's fine by me. I'm more than ready to have you inside me."

"Are you sure about this?"

Now he asks? "Absolutely."

"I probably should've grabbed the condom before we got this far."

I giggled at his perturbed expression as he glanced at where his clothes were strewn across the floor near the door.

"I'm not going anywhere." I released my hold on him as he moved off the bed.

He stalked over to his trousers, removing his wallet from the pocket. The crinkle of a foil wrapper being opened followed.

Drew returned to the bed fully sheathed.

I opened my legs wider and welcomed the press of his tip against my entrance. I hooked my legs around his hips, and he slowly pushed his way in, giving my body a chance to adjust to his width.

Once he was fully seated, he circled his hips, hitting a part of me that had eluded my ex-boyfriend and the few other men I'd had sex with. I moaned and was rewarded by the satisfied smirk on Drew's face.

I had expected our foray into "colleagues who fucked" to be quick. A mindless tumble between the sheets that was over before I had a chance to acknowledge what was happening.

I couldn't have been more wrong.

Drew took his time, taking me higher and higher and higher with each move of his hips. At first, his gaze was directed at where we joined, watching as he moved in and out of me.

But then his eyes shifted to mine.

At the heat in them, an emotion I couldn't get a firm grasp on overwhelmed me, and I finally let myself go, tumbling down, down, down into the sweet abyss.

I cried out his name. I might have also thanked God while I was at it. I couldn't be sure.

With several more thrusts of his pelvis, Drew groaned out his release and practically collapsed on top of me.

Once he'd recovered enough, he climbed out of bed to dispose of the condom. But before I could slide from under the covers to return to my hotel room, he was beside me again.

He tenderly kissed me once more. I had always wondered what it would feel like to be a bird flying in the sky while fireworks were going off around me, the brilliant colors shimmering in the night air. This—his kiss—was all that and more.

He lay on the bed and pulled me to him. I rested my head on his chest, the fast beat of his heart matching mine perfectly.

Like we belonged together.

A sinking sensation cozied up to me.

No, no, no, no....

When I suggested that Drew and I have sex, I thought it would be enough to get the lust I felt for him out of my system.

I was wrong.

So very wrong.

Because as I listened to his heart's rhythmic pounding, memories of the past few years swirled through my head. The sweet gestures he thought I hadn't noticed. The teasing comments that quickened my pulse. The way he looked at me —like the Drew I'd known prior to everything shipping to hell in an ice bucket.

I hadn't gotten Drew out of my system.

Just the opposite.

It was as if the key had been turned on Pandora's box, but instead of trouble being released to cause havoc, my heart was the thing set free.

For the past few years, the fear of my teenage crush on Drew being rekindled had weighed me down. But I had gotten it all wrong. My fear was nothing more than a child's security blanket, the thing that kept imaginary monsters at bay. The truth was, I'd been falling in love with Drew all this time.

And now I had no idea what to do.

Telling him, right after having sex with him, that I was falling in love with him probably wasn't the smartest thing to do.

Especially if he didn't feel the same way.

6

JULIETTE

I pried my eyes open, and the faint early morning light greeted me.

Memories of last night slowly formed in my head.

Of Drew and me outside.

Kissing.

Going to his room.

And....

I glanced down, confirming what I'd already suspected.

I was naked and in Drew's bed. I must have fallen asleep while listening to his heartbeat. That was the last thing I remembered.

I didn't have to turn around to know he was still asleep next to me. I could hear his slow, rhythmic breathing; feel the heat of his body inches from mine.

Part of me longed to stay here until he woke up, take a chance and tell him how I felt about him.

And if he felt the same way?

We could spend the morning making love until we had to meet up with everyone.

If he didn't share the sentiment?

I would leave, and we'd never have to mention it again. In time, I was positive my heart would get over him. Eventually.

But while part of me craved to stay snuggled under the covers with him, the other part didn't exactly want my colleagues to catch me sneaking out of his room. Because no matter how things turned out in the end, I wasn't eager for them to learn what Drew and I did last night—even more so if Drew wanted it to be nothing more than a one-night stand.

Careful not to wake him since I wasn't ready to have the conversation with him yet, I inched my way from under the covers and scanned the floor for my clothes.

After quickly dressing and running my finger under my eyes to remove any traces of makeup, I slipped out of his room and shut the door.

I turned around, ready to escape back to my room via the fire exit.

Except my plans to go undetected fell like a soufflé taken out of the oven prematurely.

Bridget was standing there, looking as though someone had used the heel of her Jimmy Choo as a fire poker. Not angry, but utterly heartbroken.

Then pity filled her eyes. "Oh, God. I'm so sorry, Juliette. I never thought Drew would stoop to that level."

"What are you talking about?"

"Drew used you to make me jealous." She heaved out a breath that held more pity than her eyes.

"Why would Drew use me to make you jealous? You guys broke up a few months ago."

A tiny voice in my head pondered the wisdom of that question.

"He and I are still dating. We're just keeping it private this time. You know how annoying office gossip can be. But don't worry," she continued with a smile that under any other circumstance would've been sweeter than honey and just as sticky. "I won't tell anyone I saw you sneaking out of his room. The last thing I'd want is to damage your reputation." She gave a dramatic shudder.

Restraint worthy of an Olympic medal was required to not roll my eyes.

Her comment, though, woke a nest of angry bats in my stomach.

Drew was no better than his mother.

No better than my own father and my ex-boyfriend.

Not bothering to spare Bridget another word beyond a mumbled, "Thanks," I retreated to my room, grabbed clean clothes, and jumped into the shower.

Bridget's words joined me, and I rolled them around in my head, examining them from every angle.

By the time I was finished, I knew I needed to hear it from Drew. If he still wanted Bridget, I would lock my heart away, only this time use a sturdier padlock so no one could hurt me again. I wouldn't tell Drew how I felt about him.

Although, I had to admit if our places were reversed, I wouldn't be as understanding as Bridget if my boyfriend was having sex with someone else. Not unless I was hoping to turn it into a threesome.

Not wanting to mentally go there, I hurriedly got changed.

April texted me, asking if I was ready to meet her for breakfast. I replied I was heading down and would meet her in the lobby.

I stepped from the elevator, confidence twirling inside me like the Sugarplum Fairy.

Until I spotted Drew. In the lobby. Near the Christmas tree.

With his lips pressed against Bridget's.

Well, I guess that answered that. He and Bridget were still together.

God, I really was a magnet for losers.

7

DREW

When I'd woken up this morning, it was to an empty bed and the sound of the hotel room door clicking shut.

The woman I'd made love to last night was gone, leaving only the hint of her perfume on the sheets as proof that she'd been there.

For the past several years, Juliette and I had been at war with each other.

Or so I had thought.

But last night, while her head rested on my chest and I was stroking the smooth skin of her lower back, I realized I'd been wrong all this time.

I'd fallen in love with her.

Maybe not right away. But in time, once she'd shared a glimpse of the old Juliette, I'd given her my heart.

So when I stepped off the elevator a moment ago, I'd felt confident. Not only would Juliette and I win the trophy, but I would also lay my heart on the line.

I scanned the lobby for Juliette. Bridget was with some of our colleagues and smiled as soon as she spotted me.

She walked toward me. "Hi, Drew."

"G'day, mate. I don't suppose you've seen Juliette, have you?"

Her smile widened. "Can't say that I have. Are you looking for her?" Her gaze shifted to something over my shoulder.

Before I could turn to see what she was looking at, her lips were on mine.

It took a second for my brain to register what was going on. I stepped away from her. "What the bloody hell was that for?" I said under my breath. "I already told you we're not goin' there again."

She shrugged, but there was nothing remorseful about her expression. Just the opposite. "I thought maybe you had changed your mind."

"Well, I haven't."

I walked away from her, making a mental note that from now on to not let her within a meter of me.

"Hey, Drew," Tony said as I approached the small group. "We're going for breakfast. You want to join us?"

"Yeah, sure."

The resort had several restaurants. If Juliette was already having breakfast, it wasn't in the one we went to. We ordered our food, and a short time later went outside for day two of the competition.

Juliette was already waiting at the first event when I arrived. Her cheeks were adorably flushed from the freezing temperature. The wind blew fine strands of hair in her face, even with her woolly hat on.

April was with her, so now wasn't a good time to bring up last night.

"G'day, ladies." I smiled as if I'd been given the moon and all the stars in the universe.

April responded with a cheery greeting. Juliette mumbled something, her gaze darting everywhere but to me.

By the time April crutched away to find a spot to watch the first event, there wasn't enough time for Juliette and me to discuss last night. The next competition began.

Which Juliette and I won.

Had I expected her to throw her arms around my neck like she had done yesterday?

Absolutely.

I'd even thought she would kiss me—because damn, I wanted to kiss her.

But even though she had been laughing during the ice sculpture contest (right, don't ask me how we ended up winning that), she was now frosty.

The playfulness and intimacy of yesterday had left the wallaby farm.

"What's goin' on with you?" I inquired at one point.

Which, in retrospect, was a dumbass question.

Juliette's eyes widened, and I was surprised steam didn't hiss from her ears. "What do you mean what's going on with me?"

"I just thought after last—"

"Nothing happened last night." And the sweet Juliette from the evening before was gone, replaced with the one I was more familiar with.

"Funny, I remember things differently."

A hard breath escaped her. "Last night shouldn't have happened—for the sake of our jobs." This time her voice was slightly less snappy. "Office flings are never a good idea, especially if you're a female. People get the wrong idea. And since you *are* involved with Bridget, it doesn't look good for me. People will view me as another of your office flings. A member of your harem."

I frowned. "Excuse me?"

"I'm sure you don't need me to repeat any of that. You're a smart man, Drew. Figure it out for yourself." She stormed off.

What the fuck had I done wrong?

It was like we were thirteen years old all over again.

And hell if I needed that.

The rest of the day continued much like the morning.

We won all the competitions—yes, pissed-off Juliette was unstoppable.

But each time we won, we practically ignored each other, choosing to celebrate with our colleagues instead.

No one seemed to notice our sudden cold attitude toward each other.

Or maybe they were so used to it, it was just business as usual. Yesterday's warmth between us had been nothing more than a blip. Easily ignored.

How did my heart feel about all of this?

It was confused. Frustrated. Ready to demand a big romantic gesture to show her how much I loved her.

How much I'd always loved her.

My brain chose to sabotage what my heart tried to tell me and played a delightful montage of my childhood, pointing out how much Juliette was like my mother.

Closed off. Always trying to outdo the other person.

Although the difference between them was that my mother had never shown a tender side to her. She had always been a block of ice.

At least Kathleen was ecstatic about Juliette and I winning the Tinsel and Tatas trophy. She enthusiastically hugged us several times.

"Thank you, you two, for making my dream a reality." Her grin was wider than when she'd told us last night that she had been in remission for nine years. "My ex-husband bet me ten thousand dollars that one of his teams would win the trophy. So thanks to you, not only am I *not* ten thousand dollars poorer, the charity will be ten thousand dollars richer."

For a breath, Juliette's and my renewed animosity vanished,

and we exchanged thank-god-we-didn't-know-about-that-beforehand glances.

Juliette recovered first. "You're welcome. We're just glad we could help. My mother was diagnosed with stage three breast cancer and has been in remission for the past year. I understand how important the charity is."

Kathleen's smile faded. "I'm sure you already know you're at a higher risk of developing breast cancer because of that. So make sure you keep ahead of it. The worst thing you can do is let it go undiagnosed."

Juliette nodded. "I know."

Hearing Kathleen tell her that was a kangaroo kick to the stomach. When Juliette had told me last night about her mother, I'd forgotten it put her at a higher risk of also developing the cancer.

A sudden need to protect her barreled through me, almost knocking me on my arse.

Not that it made a difference to her.

What the hell happened last night?

The question kept echoing in my head. Things had been going so well during the competition yesterday and last night after dinner. Had Juliette really gone from hot to cold in such a short time?

I searched my mind for what could've happened but nothing came to me.

Juliette excused herself to get ready for the gala and walked past Bridget without giving her a second glance.

The same couldn't be said for Bridget.

A cold smile slithered onto her lips that made even the venomous inland taipan seem friendly.

That same smile vanished the moment she noticed me stride toward her, frowning. "What did you say to Juliette?" I asked.

Bridget's eyes widened and her mouth formed a perfect

"O."

"I have no idea what you're talking about, Drew. I haven't spoken to her all day."

My eyes narrowed, all the better to see the evil bubbling deep in her soul. If she had a soul. "Don't waste your coy act on me. You know damn well what I'm talkin' about."

"No. I. Don't."

"Look, I know you think you and I are goin' to get back together, but we're not. So stop this bloody charade and tell me what you did to her."

That cold smile?

It returned in full viperous glory. Christ, just how blind had I been while dating her?

"Maybe I didn't do anything. Maybe it was all you, Drew. Or maybe Juliette doesn't trust you and saw what she wanted to see. Now, if you don't mind, Kathleen needs me."

She strolled off, and I could've sworn I heard her cackle like the evil witch she was.

God help the next poor bloke who fell for her manipulative lies.

Her answer, though, still didn't explain Juliette's hot to cold attitude.

The same attitude I'd witnessed several times when she lived in Australia and we were friends.

The same attitude she'd had whenever someone hurt her.

"Maybe Juliette doesn't trust you and saw what she wanted to see."

If Bridget wasn't going to give me a straight answer, I would go directly to the source.

I strode toward the elevators, but a bus must have recently returned from the nearby ski hill. The area in front of the elevators was packed with resort guests waiting to go to their rooms.

Not wanting to wait another second to talk to Juliette, I scanned the lobby for the nearest stairwell and hightailed it up to her floor. I didn't know which room she was in, so I knocked on each door.

And was met with the same answer each time: I had the wrong room.

Unfortunately, none of the guests who opened their doors knew who Juliette was or had any idea which room she was in.

I got lucky with the seventh door I knocked on. Tony answered. "Hey, mate. You don't by any chance know Juliette's room number, do you?"

"She's in the room across from me." He pointed to the one he was referring to, and I heaved out a thank-God sigh.

"Thank you." I walked the short distance and knocked on the door. No one answered, and I couldn't hear any sounds coming from inside.

I tried again. "Juliette? It's me, Drew. I need to talk to you." Again, no answer.

"What's going on with you and Bridget?" Tony asked behind me, and I glanced over my shoulder at him. "Are you two back together again?" His eyebrows rose in a you-can-do-a-helluva-lot-better-than-her gesture.

"Christ, no. Where did you get the idea that we were?"

"I saw you kissing her in the lobby this morning."

"I wasn't...." I turned to Juliette's room. *Oh. Shit.*

8

***

JULIETTE

The best part about having a best friend who worked for the same company as you?

That's right, you had somewhere to hang out when you were at the same company event, and you didn't feel like being alone in your hotel room.

More so when you were dealing with a broken heart.

"Are you planning to kiss Drew under the mistletoe at the gala?" April asked.

We were in her bathroom, getting ready for the Tinsel and Tatas Gala...and having a glass of wine. The sweet scent of strawberry vanilla shower gel still lingered in the air. April's favorite product. She'd insisted on bringing it with her to Lake Tahoe, and I'd gotten to appreciate it after the final competition. Instead of showering in my room, I'd carted my stuff up to hers.

April released a long dramatic sigh from her perch on the toilet seat, her broken leg propped up on the cushions from the couch in her room. "You kissing him under the mistletoe would be the perfect end to the perfect weekend."

I glanced at the bottle of wine on the bathroom counter,

340

checking how much was left. Maybe she had finished it while I was retrieving something from her bedroom.

Nope. It was still half full from when I'd filled our glasses.

"I'm not sure how you breaking your leg amounts to a perfect weekend."

"Okay, that wasn't exactly the high point of it. But you and Drew finally realizing you're in love with each other will make up for it." She glanced down at her leg. "All right, it will partially make up for that."

I checked the light on my curling iron to see if the barrel was hot enough yet. "I have no idea what you're talking about."

"Oh, please. Everyone knows you two are in love. There's an office bet whether you two will finally realize it this weekend. But you might not want to mention it to Kathleen."

"You actually bet on my love life?"

April laughed. "Who do ya think set it up?"

"So let me see if I got this straight. You broke your leg yesterday so Drew and I would be forced to partner for the Tinsel and Tatas event?" I smirked.

April might've been a card-carrying romantic, but even she wouldn't go this far when it came to an elaborate scheme to get two people together.

"No, but you must admit I couldn't have planned it better. My broken leg was just destiny when it came to getting you two together. Like my nanna used to say, things happen for a reason."

"Well, your nanna got things wrong when it comes to your broken leg. And you've also got things wrong. Drew doesn't love me. He's still into Bridget."

"Where did ya get that dumb idea from?"

I grabbed a thick strand of my hair and wrapped it around the curling iron. "It's not a dumb idea. I saw them kissing this morning when I got off the elevator."

Of all the things April had expected me to say, this wasn't one of them if her expression was any indication.

"Are you sure they were kissing?"

"I'm pretty sure I remember what kissing is. So that would be a yes. They were kissing."

"On the lips?"

"What are we, back in middle school? Yes, on the lips."

April made a face as if she was working out a complex calculus problem on the bathroom ceiling. "Hmm. That doesn't seem right."

"Doesn't matter. That's just the way it is. I should have known better. I had sex with him last night, and the next thing I know, he's making out with another woman. Like mother, like son and vice versa."

April stared at me for several heartbeats. "I'm not even sure where to start with any of that. How about we begin with the part where you had sex with Drew last night?"

I pretended not to notice her smug smile. "It's no big deal. And we won't be doing that again. It was to get each other out of our systems. And now we move on."

"What do you mean, like mother, like son and vice versa?"

"While my family was living in Australia, his mother had an affair with my father. So clearly, Drew doesn't care about other people's feelings. Just like his mother. Bridget told me he was using me to get her back."

"Oh, please. He's not interested in Bridget. Everyone knows that but Bridget. And you, apparently. Whatever Bridget told you was a lie."

"What about their kissing?"

"Have you talked to Drew about it?"

I set the curling iron on the counter and grabbed my eyeshadow from my makeup bag. "Why would I talk to Drew about him kissing Bridget?"

If there was one conversation I didn't want to have with him, that would be it.

"I love you, Juliette. You know I do. But you really are dense sometimes. You should talk to him. Tell him how you feel. And don't try denying you love him. I know you do."

"But what about his mother?"

"What about her? She cheated on Drew's father. Your father cheated on your mother, but that doesn't mean you're going to follow in his footsteps. No more than it means Drew will do the same."

She had a valid point. Just because our parents were messed up, it didn't mean we couldn't learn from their mistakes.

Sure, Drew broke the statue I'd made for the contest, but that was when we were thirteen years old. It wasn't the end of the world, even if it had felt like it was at the time.

Last night, I'd thought I was falling in love with Drew.

I was wrong.

I'd stopped falling a long time ago.

I had been in love with him all this time but had been too stupid to realize it.

"I've got to tell him," I whispered, more to myself than to April. "I've got to tell him I love him."

"Yes! Finally! And I'm going to play fairy godmother and help you get ready for the gala so you can sweep your man off his feet." She yanked my eyeshadow from my hand.

By the time she was finished with my hair and makeup (quite the accomplishment, I might add, given she was in a cast), I barely recognized myself.

I removed my short black dress from the closet.

"You're not wearing that." April crutched her way to where I was standing.

"Sure I am. It's the only dress I brought with me that's dressy enough for the gala."

"Sorry, but it just won't cut it." She nudged me aside, pulled out a garment bag, and handed it to me. "You're going to wear this."

"I can't wear your dress."

"Yes, you can. It'll be perfect. We're the same size, so you know it will fit. And it's not like I can wear it with a cast and crutches. You'll wear my dress, and I'll wear yours."

"Are you sure?"

"Absolutely. Now put it on."

I slowly unzipped the bag, taking care not to catch the teeth on the dress, and peeled the bag away. "Oh, it's gorgeous," I breathed. This was the first time I'd seen the gown. April had bought it when I wasn't with her and had been super secretive about it.

"Put it on."

I disappeared into the bathroom and did as commanded, then returned to inspect my reflection in the full-length mirror.

April really was my fairy godmother.

The sleeveless, floor-length gown was pastel blue and covered in tulle embroidered with a floral design. The bodice was strapless, other than a band of butterflies resting on one shoulder.

"God, if Drew isn't already in love with you, he will be after seeing you in that gown. You look gorgeous, Juliette." She glanced at the alarm clock. "Now hurry and go find your prince."

We rode down the elevator and entered the ballroom. The space had been transformed into a magical wonderland, with sparkling decorations and leafless trees covered in artificial snow. Snowflakes the size of me shone from the ceiling onto the dance floor and swirled to the classical music from the string quartet.

I wandered through the forest of partiers, searching for Drew. Bridget was with Kathleen. One glance at me, and her pretty face turned into a vicious scowl. Ouch.

But I didn't have time to worry about that. I had more important things to do.

"Jason," I said to one of Drew's colleagues. "Have you seen Drew?"

"Sure, I saw him a few minutes ago. He was leaving the hotel."

Oh, damn. "Thanks!"

I hoisted the hem of my gown, revealing silver stilettos, and ran toward the main entrance.

I stepped from the warm lobby into a strong, whistling wind and heavily falling snow. At some point in the past hour, the beautiful crisp blue sky had turned dark and wintery.

Without a second thought, I dashed through the vicious wind, its frigid fingers eager to ruin my hair and makeup. Snow slid down the front of the bodice and between my breasts.

For the record?

That wasn't too pleasant, and I was positive my skin was turning a shade of blue to match the dress.

I ran along the icy sidewalk to where Drew's truck had been parked, but it wasn't there.

He'd already left.

I released a disappointed sigh, my warm breath transforming into a white cloud, and turned back to the hotel.

"Juliette!"

I barely heard the word over the wind and spun around to see if I had imagined it.

Drew was jogging toward me, his hair covered in melting snow, and my breath froze in my lungs.

"Christ, what are you doin' out here? It's freezin'." He removed his tux jacket and slipped it around my shoulders.

"Do you love her?" I whispered, almost afraid to ask—in case April had been wrong—and I was about to hand my heart over, ready for it to be slain. "Do you love Bridget?"

He shook his head.

"I'm so sorry how I acted today." The words flew from my mouth, yanked out by the wind. "But I saw you kiss Bridget this morning after she told me that you'd used me last night to get her back, and I thought you were no better than your mother—and, well, my father—but you're nothing like they were. And, sure, I held onto my anger all these years after you broke the statue I made for the Rosewood Art Contest. But, well, I love you, Drew."

I felt like I had run two marathons in a row, my mind spinning with everything I had just told him.

Drew stroked his thumb along my cheek, probably to remove the snow that was clinging to my skin. "We're goin' to be circlin' back to most of those in a minute. But is it true? You love me?"

I nodded. "I've been in love with you for years, since we began working together. But I hadn't let myself believe it until this weekend."

Drew didn't say anything. He scooped me up in his arms and carried me to the hotel.

My feet, which were protesting the cold, cheered his gallant move.

He stepped inside the hotel, and the warm air greeted me. I expected Drew to lower me to my feet, but instead, he kept walking.

His destination?

The elevators.

Like magic, one opened as we approached. Drew carried me onto it and pressed his floor.

"You can put me down now." My mind and my body were slowly defrosting. And the first thought I had was that I told Drew I loved him but he hadn't reciprocated.

On the bright side, he didn't love Bridget either.

"Don't worry, I'll put you down soon enough."

An elderly couple joined us. If their elegant outfits were

anything to go by, they too had been at the gala.

The woman grinned at me. The man winked.

And I smiled.

The couple got off the floor beneath ours.

"Have a great night." Amusement sat square in the man's tone.

We wished them both the same.

Drew finally lowered my feet to the floor once we reached his room. I had declared I loved him, and he clearly wanted to have sex.

Oh well. If it warmed me up, then I was all for it. Plus, I really wanted out of the wet dress.

Tomorrow, I'd worry about the consequences of us having sex now.

We entered his room and removed our shoes. Drew led me to the bathroom and turned on the water for the large bathtub. Then he placed his hands on my shoulders and turned me around.

The sound of a zipper slowly cut through the air, and the bodice of my dress loosened. Drew's lips pressed lightly against my shoulder, igniting a tingling warmth that seeped through my body. I sucked in a soft breath.

With dizzying care, he peeled the gown off me, his fingertips burning a trail along my flesh. I stepped out of the dress, wearing nothing more than my black lace panties, and swiveled to face him.

Never had I felt more naked and exposed than in this moment. But it wasn't because I was wearing next to nothing. It was the way Drew was gazing into my eyes—like he was seeing me down to my soul—the love I felt for him glowing from within.

He kissed me once more, but this time his mouth tenderly brushed my lips.

Any residual cold I might have felt went up in a puff of

steam.

Drew turned off the water, stripped out of his clothes in record time, and climbed into the tub. I removed my panties and joined him.

We eased into the water. Drew leaned against the slant of the tub and pulled me to him. His hard length happily reminded me it was still willing and very able.

Drew wrapped his arms around me, warming me up even more. "All right. Let's begin from the top. What are you talkin' about with the statue?"

"The one I sculpted for the art competition. The dove holding a twig with a heart-shaped leaf in its beak."

His hand lightly rubbed up and down my arm. "I remember the statue. I didn't see you for a week while you were working on it. I was beginning to believe I'd never see you again. Why do you think I broke it?"

For a second, his question didn't register. Shock snuggled up to me that he remembered the statue. I could guarantee my father didn't.

"My mother told me you were the guilty party." Instead of sounding confident like they had outside, the words were hesitant, almost questioning.

"That wasn't me. I knew how important it was to you. You practically had it under house arrest."

I glanced over my shoulder. "I believe you." And I did. Something about his voice told me he was telling the truth.

"Now, what's this about my mother and your father?"

I spent the next few minutes recapping what I'd witnessed the day I stumbled across them having sex. "I came close to bleaching my eyes after that."

"Christ," Drew groaned. "I don't blame you. That's an image I don't appreciate thinking about either. Is that why your family moved back to the U.S. so quickly? One minute you were in school, the next you were an ocean away."

"Mom and I returned to San Francisco after she discovered the truth. She didn't learn it from me, though. My father had convinced me to stay silent. But Mom grew suspicious and soon after discovered the truth. Dad stayed in an apartment in Sydney until his contract was up. I have no idea if your mother and my father were still hooking up while he was there."

It wasn't something I liked to contemplate.

Drew pressed another kiss on my wet shoulder. "I'm so sorry you had to go through that on your own. I wish I'd been there for you. But what happened between our parents was all about them. It has nothing to do with us. We aren't our parents." He kissed my neck; his hot breath fanned my ear. "I love you, Juliette. I've been in love with you for a while but didn't know how to tell you. And given that you always seemed ready to slice my dick off with a machete, well...."

I laughed softly and shifted to straddle him. "I don't think your cock or any other body part was ever at risk. I was crushing on you when we were teens, and I was afraid the same thing would happen again when we ended up working for the same company. I only acted that way to protect my heart from you. It didn't work."

He smiled. "I didn't realize that. I had a massive crush on you back then, too. That's probably why I acted like a little shit when our friendship deteriorated."

"You did? You really had a crush on me?"

Drew nodded.

I lowered my mouth to his and languidly kissed him. His hands explored my soapy body. Mine traced over every inch of him.

We continued relishing the feel of each other, stroking, teasing, craving, until the water began to cool.

Then we dried off, and the remainder of the evening was spent making love.

And there was no place I would have rather been.

EPILOGUE
DREW

four months later

Ileaned back against Juliette's car, which was sitting in the driveway of her mum's house, and kissed my beautiful girlfriend. They hadn't even left yet for their week at the spa, and Juliette already glowed in the midmorning sunlight.

So you were probably wondering who had actually broken Juliette's statue.

"One would think that you two aren't going to see each other for two years." I didn't have to look at Juliette's mother to know she was grinning.

While my parents might not have been on her list of favorite people—I couldn't blame her for that—the sentiment hadn't been extended to me.

She'd always liked me, even though my parents had acted like little shits.

Anyway, back to the real criminal who broke Juliette's statue.

350

It had been none other than her own mum.

She had accidentally broken it, but when Juliette had been devastated about what happened, her mum blurted it was me.

She'd felt bad about it, but after things disintegrated between Juliette and me, she was too afraid to admit the truth to her. She'd already suspected her husband was cheating on her. She didn't want to lose her daughter, too.

She had apologized profusely to us both since the truth came out.

"Drew and I have a lot of time to make up for," Juliette said, smiling against my lips.

"All right then. I'll wait for you in the car." The front passenger door clicked open and banged shut.

My mouth brushed Juliette's. "She sounds pretty excited about the trip."

"She is. And so is her very grateful daughter. Thank you, Drew, for giving me this week with her."

Juliette wasn't talking about how I'd helped her win the trophy during the Tinsel and Tatas Winter Festival. Although that was part of it.

I had surprised them both by booking them into a five-star resort with spa facilities to match. And because Juliette meant the world to me—and I wanted to make up for what my mother had done to Juliette's mum—I had booked mother and daughter all the spa treatments they could wish for.

"You're welcome." I kissed her again. Now that I got to kiss her whenever I wanted, I planned to make the most of it.

For now.

And for always.

READ ON FOR AN EXCERPT FROM
DECIDEDLY WITH LOVE

1

EMMA

Dear Dr. Lovejoy,

I'm a huge fan of the Harry Potter series. My bedroom is even decorated in a Harry Potter theme. But my new boyfriend told me that the books are for kids, and I should get rid of it all. What should I do?

"As if there's any question. Dump him," I said under my breath as the bell above the door jingled. A moment later, Kate entered Aphrodite's Boutique. Glowing.

I slipped the independent newspaper under the counter. Did I have a Harry-Potter-themed bedroom? No…although that would be cool, especially since the series had been my favorite as a kid. Why? Because I could relate to Harry. No, I didn't have any magical powers—which was too bad.

Like Harry, I had no parents or family. But unlike Harry's

mother, mine didn't fling herself in front of evil himself because she loved me more than anything.

Not even close.

Kate strolled past the display of sensual bath products, massage oils, and scented candles near the front of the store. Her gaze paused briefly on the section farther back with the sexy lingerie.

As she walked to the counter, I pretended to straighten the heart-shaped cookies in the basket near the till.

Correction—as she practically *floated* to the counter. Her expression held the look of love. I hadn't personally experienced it. I thought I had in college....I was wrong. *Silly me.*

How did I know it was the look of love? Hazard of my job—love all around me—in case you missed it from the store's name.

Aphrodite was the ancient Greek goddess of love, beauty, procreation, and pleasure. Just not the self-induced pleasure I was more familiar with.

Still glowing, Kate placed a large paper coffee cup on the counter and held her left hand out in front of me. Unlike the last time I'd seen it, her ring finger now sported a diamond capable of making all other gemstones jealous.

I squealed. "Ohmigod, Jamie proposed?" I rushed from behind the counter and hugged her. "I'm so happy for you both."

The tears in my eyes? Dust. Must have entered the store at the same time as Kate.

Right—it was raining. My point? The tears had nothing to do with Kate finding the most amazing guy in the world. And it had nothing to do with how at seventeen minutes past six that morning, I had officially become a twenty-eight-year-old spinster.

A spinster who didn't even have a cat.

Maybe I needed to get a cat.

"Thank you," Kate said, hugging me back. "You were so right in your Dr. Lovejoy column. He would never have settled down if he thought I'd be around for him no matter what. When I moved out of our apartment last week, he finally realized he couldn't live without me."

"I figured he'd come around sooner or later."

Dr. Lovejoy? Yeah, there might be a slight chance that I wrote the weekly column in The SF Metro, one of the city's independent papers. Was I a doctor? Not exactly. Lovejoy was my last name...but I didn't have a PhD or anything like that. I had a business degree with a minor in psychology. I did take a human sexuality course in my undergrad years, but the professor who taught it had been as exciting as a wet towel left in the rain.

Kate hugged me again. Was I jealous that she was now engaged? Not at all. Everyone deserved to find love.

"But remember," I said, "no one is supposed to know I'm Dr. Lovejoy." It was a fluke that Kate had figured it out. My bio didn't proclaim I was also the owner of what most people referred to as the "love store." And very few people had figured out that I was the same Lovejoy who wrote the column. Heck, very few people were aware that my last name was Lovejoy.

"Don't worry, I haven't told anyone. Like I promised. Anyway, I need to get back to work." Kate owned the coffee shop next door. "I just had to tell you the good news and drop off a little thank-you present." She indicated at the paper coffee cup. "It's your favorite. Skinny butterscotch latte."

"Oh, God, I love you!" I said, a step away from squealing.

"I know you do," she said over her shoulder, chuckling, and left the store.

"Come to Mama," I said to the coffee and took a deep, satisfying whiff of the butterscotch richness. My coffee mug with,

"You're my sunshine on a rainy day" on it sat empty and alone by the cash register.

"Sorry," I said to my mug, "I'm not risking any of this amazing coffee by pouring it into you. I was up late last night baking cookies for the store. I need this happy dose of caffeine."

Yes, it was official. I was losing it. I was reasoning with a mug. Next up? I'd be asking it advice on my lack of a love life.

And no, the irony wasn't lost on me. I wrote an advice column and owned a store that specialized in love and romance, but when it came to myself, I had yet to find Mr. Right.

Or even Mr. Close Enough.

As I sipped my precious beverage, the bell above the door jingled, and three women in their late seventies entered. They took in the store—the fountain, lingerie, bath and massage supplies, books, housewares—with eager grins on their faces. It didn't matter if you were looking for a touch of romance or the whimsical or full-out sexiness, you could find it here. Although if you were looking for something featured in *Fifty Shades of Grey*, you'd be sorely disappointed. Leather and whips were not on the agenda.

I drank another quick sip of my coffee and placed it on the counter behind me. The three women shuffled farther into the store until they came to the fountain.

That's right. I have a fountain in the store. And yes, the goddess of love is perched in the middle. Nice touch, huh?

"Wow," the woman in the light blue trench coat said, examining the fountain. Her expression was one of awe...and mischief. "It reminds me of the *Fontana di Trevi* in Rome." She turned to me as I approached. "Are you familiar with the Trevi Fountain?"

Was I ever. "Legend claims that if you throw a coin into the Trevi Fountain, it guarantees your return to Rome. The second coin will ensure a new romance. A third coin guarantees marriage."

Do I believe in the legend? Well, I've already thrown in about fifty dollars' worth of coins over the past two years, and I'm as single as the day I was born.

I know. I know. The legend only applies to the fountain in Rome. And heck, mine isn't even a replica of it. But it's always nice to dream. Besides, the fountain is there for another reason....

"That's right," the woman said.

"And just like with that fountain," I explained, "all the coins thrown into this one go to charity."

The woman in a trench coat covered with large, bright pink flowers glanced at me and smiled. "What charity?"

"The James Bell Youth Center. I've been donating the money to them for the past few years. I'm currently saving to have a mural painted on their wall. You know, to brighten the place and to give the kids hope."

And I was almost there. At least I was there when it came to the supplies. I wasn't close to the amount needed when I factored in the cost of the artist.

The women fished through their purses and removed some coins. The woman in the blue trench coat, who had asked me about the Trevi Fountain, turned around so her back was facing it. "You need to throw the coins over your left shoulder with your right hand."

The other two women followed suit and turned around.

"Are we supposed to make a wish first or just throw in the coins?" the shorter woman asked. Her white trench coat hung below her knees.

"If this was the real Trevi Fountain, no wishing would be necessary," the woman in blue said. "But it wouldn't hurt to clarify things, just in case."

The woman in white nodded as if this made sense.

The woman in blue threw in her coins. *Plop. Plop.*

Guess she wasn't interested in returning to Rome.

The woman in white threw her coins next. *Plop. Plop. Plop.*

The first woman peered over at her, eyebrow raised. "You want to get married?"

"Why wouldn't I wish to get married? I loved being married to Frank. Best years of my life."

"Is there anyone you have in mind?" The woman in the flowery trench coat asked.

"Possibly."

"Would it *possibly* have to do with the handsome gentleman in apartment thirty-four?" The woman in flowers then said to me, "He's been a widow for five years now. There isn't a senior in our building who hasn't been lusting over him."

The woman in white giggled. "Including poor Mathew in apartment forty-eight. But I'm pretty sure he's barking up the wrong redwood tree. He's gay," she added, in case I hadn't figured that out myself, I guess.

"So is that a yes?" the woman in flowers asked.

"Possibly."

"I'll take that as a yes," the woman in blue said, grinning. "Okay, Fanny, your turn."

The woman in the flowery trench coat got into position and threw the coins over her shoulder. *Plop. Plop.*

Ah, she was looking for a new romance.

She switched the coins from her left hand to her right and tossed them over her shoulder. *Plop. Plop. Plop.*

"Wait!" The woman in blue said. "You're hoping to get married *and* have an affair?"

Fanny laughed. "I'm almost eighty. How much energy do you think I have?"

"Then why did you throw in five coins?" I asked. Maybe she knew something I didn't when it came to the fountain's love-making abilities.

And no, I don't mean its abilities to fuck. I mean its abilities to help me find love.

Maybe I had been doing it all wrong.

"The first two were for me. It's been twenty years since my dear Robert passed away, and I'm finally ready to climb back on that horse again."

"Except now you're too old to ride the horse—if you get what I mean." The woman in white snickered.

Ohmigod, was I seriously listening to eighty-year-old women talking about sex?

"What about the other three coins?" I asked, almost afraid to hear the answer.

"Those are for my grandson. He's twenty-eight years old and still single. I want him to hurry up and get married and give me some great-grandkids *before* I end up next to my poor Robert in the ground."

Okaaay. "I'm not sure the fountain works quite that way." Oh, who was I kidding? The only magical powers the fountain had were to add to my energy bill and provide money to the youth center.

"Well, I'll take whatever it's willing to give me. A person who never made a mistake never tried anything new. Albert Einstein said that."

I had no idea what it had to do with the fountain or her grandson—and figured I was better off not knowing.

A musical tune played from her purse. She removed her phone and answered it. "No, I didn't forget my appointment, dear....I'm at Aphrodite's Boutique....You know, the love shop." She gave whoever was on the other end the address. "Alrighty. I'll see you soon."

Fanny ended the call and dropped the phone back into her purse. "Speak of the handsome devil himself. That would be my grandson. Apparently I forgot about my doctor's appointment." She flashed an *oops-what-can-you-do?* grimace.

The woman in blue laughed. "What did I tell you about setting up reminders on your phone?"

Fanny shrugged. "I keep forgetting to do it. What can I say? I'm still an old-fashioned-paper-calendar type girl."

"So why didn't you write it on your calendar?" the woman in white asked.

Fanny shrugged again. "I forgot to."

"Or more like you don't want to go to the doctor, so you intentionally didn't write it down."

Fanny winked at me. "It might have been something like that."

Her friends laughed.

"I guess we'd better get cracking before my dear grandson arrives to drive me to the appointment I'd rather not go to. Anyone interested in checking out the vibrators?" Fanny asked with a chuckle. "You do have vibrators, don't you, dear?" she asked me.

The woman in blue threw her head back, laughing. "It's not vibrators we need."

"True," Fanny said, then to me asked, "I don't suppose you have any magic potions to help my grandson fall in love with a woman?"

"Is that your way of saying you don't believe in the fountain's magic?" the woman in white asked.

"No, it's my way of saying my grandson is too goddamn stubborn for his own good and needs all the help he can get in that department."

Fighting back a grin, I shook my head. "Sorry, the only magic in this store belongs to the fountain."

"Darn. That's too bad."

While Fanny waited for her grandson to show up, the three of them wandered around the store.

Five minutes later the bell above the door jingled again. I

glanced up from the display of romantic cards I was organizing near the front counter.

Holy. Shit. What was he doing here?

Who was *he*? Travis Hamilton. The guy I'd had a thing for during our junior year of high school.

The guy who broke my heart.

ACKNOWLEDGMENTS

First, I want to say a big thanks to everyone who fell in love with Trent and Kelsey from *Decidedly Off Limits* and were excited to read *Decidedly With Baby*. Your enthusiasm for this book is heartwarming. This was especially true when it came to the members of my Facebook reader group (Stina's Sweethearts). You guys are the best!

I also want to thank my editor Bev, as well as Hope and Jessica from Flat Earth Editing for the copyediting and proofreading. All three individuals helped make this book sparkle. Naturally, I can't forget Brenda St. John Brown who shared her own brilliant suggestions and wisdom when it came to this book and beyond. And hugs and kisses to all the bloggers and reviewers who have fallen in love with the By the Bay series.

And finally, I would like to thank my cheerleaders who have been there for me while writing this book. Christina Lee, my husband Ralph, my kids, and even the cat. Well, I'm assuming that was why she was meowing at me all those times the kids were at school and it was just her and me at home.

ABOUT THE AUTHOR

Born in Brighton England, Stina Lindenblatt has lived in a number of countries, including England, the U.S., Finland, and Canada. This would explain her mixed up accent. She has a kinesiology degree and a MSc in sports biological sciences.

In addition to writing fiction, she loves photography, and currently lives in Calgary, Canada, with her husband and three kids.

For news about her books and to sign up for her newsletter, check out her website at stinalindenblattauthor.com.

www.ingramcontent.com/pod-product-compliance
Lightning Source LLC
Chambersburg PA
CBHW011315310726
48973CB00011B/2939